What people are saying . . .

"After my son died, I could not get of⸍
Mary was unable to leave her pallet, J
knew. Mary, the mother of Jesus knev
through." —Nancy Krahenbuhl; a mother

"A story meant to touch the innermost depths of your soul. A mother's deep love for her son is surpassed by his exceeding love for humanity. A story so convincing that it will lift the human spirit." —Chaitram Prashad, ELCA Pastor, Good Shepherd Lutheran Church, Des Moines, Iowa

"Authors Barbara Swant and Ruth Anderson present in this book the 'greatest story ever told,' from a perspective unique to Biblical literature. This is Mary (called Myriam, her proper Hebrew name), the mother of Jesus, directly addressing the reader. Mary narrates the familiar stories from the Gospels, but as her intimate remembrances, in her own voice. Swant and Anderson have taken the meager personal details of the Gospel stories and fleshed them out in so direct a way that you feel as if you are right there with Mary as a loving mother, experiencing all her emotions, all her joys, her fears, her exhilarations and ultimately her pains, from before the birth of Jesus through her witnessing his horrifying crucifixion at the foot of the cross. This is truly Mary's Story in a way that you have never heard it before." —Steve Barnett: multiple Grammy™-award winning record producer, composer and arranger

Mary's Story

**After 2000 years of silence,
Mary tells her story.**

Barbara Swant

Ruth Anderson

Quill House Publishers
Huff Publishing Associates, LLC
Minneapolis

HPA

Publisher:
Huff Publishing Associates, LLC
www.huffpublishing.com

QUILL HOUSE
PUBLISHERS

Quill House Publishers
www.quill-house.com

Barbara Swant and Ruth Anderson, www.marysstory.com

Publishing consultant: William Huff, Huff Publishing Associates, LLC
Cover image: istockphoto.com, ©Tina Lorien
Book design: Dorie McClelland, Spring Book Design

Library of Congress Control Number: 2011920430
ISBN: 978-1-933794-39-6

Contents

Acknowledgments

We gratefully acknowledge Bill Huff, Scott Tunseth, Dorie McClelland, and Helena Brantley for their excellent work and for making this book possible.

We thank everyone who has shared a personal experience of love and loss with us. Your honesty, faith, and courage have been an inspiration. In so many ways, your stories make up the words and music of *Mary's Story.*

We thank our church, our friends, and all of the many, many people who have given so generously of their time and talent on the dramatic productions of *Mary's Story,* the recording of the music, and the discussions and first readings of this book.

Most of all, we thank our families for their love, encouragement, and hard work since the time *Mary's Story* began.

Preface

Mary's Story is a fresh new look at one of the world's oldest stories. It is the story of Jesus of Nazareth told by his mother. The glory and hope of his birth. The joy of his childhood. The despair and horror of his death, and the work of his followers that resulted in a new world religion.

We have written the story as we believe Mary would have told it. How she raised her son to believe in love and peace and complete obedience to God so that he could assume his leadership of the Isra-elites. How everything went terribly wrong when the political forces of volatile first century Palestine combined to demand his death, and how she could not save him. And finally, how she struggles to make sense of her son's death and survive her grief.

Mary's Story takes you back to a world that was hard and unforgiving, where Roman rule was total and oppressive. It takes you to Mary's side and makes you want to share her fight to save Jesus. It makes you feel her pain as she watches her son sacrifice his life for his beliefs.

We first wrote the story as a musical drama following the death of a young boy in our community. During the six years that the musical was performed, Mary became a voice for people who had suffered. Many people came to us and shared their stories of loss and faith, of courage and healing. After she had seen the play, one eighty year-old woman cried in our arms and told us that she had lost a child sixty years ago and had never spoken of it. As she cried, she said, "Now I am healed."

From the start, the audiences asked for *Mary's Story* in a novel and for a recording of the music. They also wanted to know what happened to Mary after Jesus died. We are now very excited to have completed both the novel and a recording of the music (see the back of the book for CD information).

We have worked to combine biblical history, theological writings, scholarly research, and clinical psychology to make *Mary's Story* both an historically accurate, compelling drama and a personal, inspirational story of sorrow and sacrifice, love and hope. The story of Jesus' life and death is told by Mary as she remembers her son. Passages of her grief and healing are interwoven as a book within a book.

Before you even begin to read, ask yourself why Mary thought that God allowed her son to die? What would any mother do when her son was facing death? What were the roles of those in power at the time of Jesus' death? What were the problems between the factions of the Jewish people? Who really was the beloved disciple at the cross?

This is *Mary's Story*. We hope this book will bring goodness into your life.

Jewish Calendar

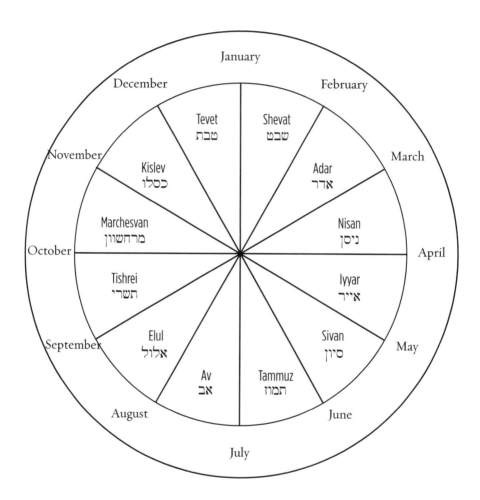

The Seventh Day of Iyyar

I open my eyes and see that I am on a pallet in my own home. Then I hear a loud, loud roar like the wind or the sea, but there is no wind, and I do not live by the sea. I put my hands to my head to make the noise stop, but it goes on and on. A woman comes into the room carrying a cup. I do not recognize her, but the cup is one my father gave me as child. Now, steam curls up and into the room in a tiny wisp. The woman comes closer. I close my eyes and wait for her to go away.

I am Myriam of Nazareth, mother of Jesus, James, Myriam, Joses, Simon, Jude, and Salome, wife of Joseph, and daughter of Joachim and Anna. I am a mother, and I have lost a son. I am not the first and not the last, but now I join those who know this bitter pain.

I have lost my parents and wanted to curl up in the corner and whimper there until they came and found me. I have lost my husband and known a loneliness that surrounded me even in the crowds of greatest celebration. Still, I talk to him as though he is at my side. Years now, after he is gone, I wake up and expect to find him lying next to me, and he is not. But I have gone on, and I have known joy again.

But this time, I do not think that I can survive. When Jesus was a babe, and I cradled him in my arms, the fierce mother love burst forth from the depths of my soul and branded me as his protector. But I did not protect him. I did not keep him from harm. I did not keep him even from death. Now, his absence cannot be filled. My failure cannot be forgiven.

Later in the day, Martha comes by. I say that it is good to see her, that it has been too long. She tells me that she was here with me yesterday. I say, yes, yes, I knew that. But I did not know it. So many things I do not know now.

1

Bethlehem

When we arrived in Bethlehem, every room was filled. I was so tired from the journey that I didn't care if we slept on the street, but we found shelter in a stable. I slid from the donkey and followed Joseph inside. I made my way to a pile of straw, and as I lowered myself onto it, my first birthing pain came. Then another one so sharp that I pressed my hand to my mouth to keep from crying out.

A woman came. I remember her talking, giving directions to me as she attended the delivery, but I do not remember anything that she said. Only Joseph, only that he was there telling me it would be all right. I didn't even begin to believe him. I gripped his hand until my own grew numb, and then I gripped harder. Finally, the child was born, and I heard the midwife announce that it was a boy. Joseph pried my hand from his and took the babe from her.

"A son, Myriam. You have a son," he said. His voice was husky and cracked as he spoke. "Hamashiach hakadosh.¹ The son of our Lord."

The babe was only a bit of a thing, all blue and smeared with birthing. His tiny mouth quivered, and he held his whole body stiff. Then he began to wail loud and long, and I watched him turn a bright pink.

"Joseph, is he . . . is he?" I tried to sit up, but I didn't have the strength.

"He is fine. He is fine," Joseph said, never taking his eyes off the babe. "Just telling us he has arrived. He will make his voice heard in the world. Yes, I believe he will." Then he placed his hand upon the child's head and said, "And you shall be called Jesus."

I smiled at Joseph, but I wished for my mother. I had no idea how to care for a newborn. Joseph paid no attention to the babe's cries. He held him in his large carpenter's hands and wiped the birthing from him with soft cloths. When he had finished, he lifted him to his shoulder and comforted him until his crying stopped. Then he placed Jesus in my arms and wrapped a woolen blanket around both of us. It was finely woven and had a stripe of blue running through it. My mother had sent it with me at my marriage, and we had brought it along on our trip to warm ourselves at night. "You must attend him now," Joseph told me.

I could only stare at him. I did not even know how to feed my own child.

"Do as I say now," he ordered.

I nodded, but I could not bring myself to uncover in front of him.

"I will wait in the outer chamber." He bent his head low and disappeared through the passageway.

I held Jesus, loosened my clothing, and offered my breast to him, but he would not take it. His eyes were closed, so I held him closer so that he would feel the nipple, but he arched his back and began to cry again. His face turned red, and he wailed louder. I thought I might cry with him. Joseph reappeared demanding to know what was wrong.

"I cannot . . . I do not . . ." I sniffled.

He turned and stalked from the chamber bellowing for the midwife as he went. All of Bethlehem must have heard. When he returned, the woman was with him. Joseph was silent then as the midwife scolded him and told him that if he took a young wife, he must help her.

She set Jesus to my breast, and he quieted and began to suckle. But after a short time, she lifted him from me and ordered Joseph to put him to my other breast. I wanted to send the woman and Joseph away, but Jesus was wailing loudly again, and I didn't want him to starve, so I turned and lay there as still as I could.

Joseph held Jesus up against me, but he cried harder. Again, the midwife scolded Joseph, telling him to quit staring at the ceiling and pay attention to what he was doing. He mumbled something about the woman not knowing her place, but he lifted my breast, and Jesus took hold.

As my tiny son nursed, my breasts burned and stung, and pain seared my womb, but Joseph held the babe with one hand and me with the other and made soft crooning sounds, assuring us that we would be safe and fine. I watched my child as he suckled greedily. Eyes closed and hands fisted, he was working so hard and with such determination that I willed myself to calm and give him what he needed.

As he nursed, I dared to touch his tiny face. I had never felt anything so soft. He was softer than the finest cloth, softer than the finest powder. I traced his perfect head and round little cheeks wanting to know every detail of him, and then when he relaxed a little, I placed my finger in his tiny hand. His fist tightened around me, and a glow began in my chest and spread throughout my entire being. Even now, years later, I can feel my first born in my arms.

"Oh Joseph, look at him. He is beautiful. He is beautiful."

"He is handsome. His mother is beautiful," Joseph said. Little tears leaked out of the corners of my eyes. It was the most personal thing Joseph had said to me since our marriage.

Jesus began to slow in his nursing. His eyes were closed and his long dark eyelashes rested on his cheeks. He released my nipple and lay sleeping in my arms. A droplet of milk pearled on his pouty bottom lip and made me laugh. Joseph looked down upon us and nodded his head in a way that told me that he was pleased. He brushed his lips across my forehead and took Jesus from my arms.

"Rest now," he said to me, "and I will care for him."

He held Jesus in one hand, supporting his head with only two fingers, and examined his head, arms, fingers, toes, all of him. Then, he turned him and draped him over his hand like he was made of cloth and inspected him again. I protested that he would break the babe in two, but he did not even hear me. When he had finished, he looked up, sighed, and smiled at me, and my relief was great for I knew that the babe was not marked.

Joseph placed his hand upon Jesus' head and proclaimed, "Hakadosh baruch ha."[2] And then, so infection would not take him, he rubbed Jesus with salt, crooning to him all the while.

"Here's my big boy. Yes, yes you are. Say hello to your abba. Abba loves you. Yes, he does."

When he had finished, he wrapped Jesus in swaddling cloths and placed him in the straw. Then he unpacked the rest of our belongings and made a pallet for our bed. I crawled to the pallet and slid Jesus beside me. He was as light as one of my sandals. Joseph found an old shovel and placed it near the pallet. He took some ropes and stretched them across the entrance of the cave.

"Will someone harm us?" I asked.

"I believe that an angel of the Lord is keeping watch over us right now," Joseph said as he tightened one of the ropes.

I looked at the ropes and the shovel.

"He might want some help, hnnh?" He said and gave a shrug of his shoulders.

I was startled by his boldness.

"Do not worry. We are safe," he said and gave the rope a final tug. Then he stretched his lean hard body out beside me and sighed from the weariness of the last days.

"You have done well," he said and draped his arm across me. I smiled and smiled until my face hurt, and then I slept.

In the darkness, I heard the babe cry and came quickly awake. I struggled to reach Jesus, but I could not move from the stiffness. My body throbbed in pain, inside and out.

"Joseph, wake up!" I said, raising myself.

"What is it?" He sat up and grabbed the shovel in one move.

"No. It's the babe. Turn up the lamp. Hurry, something is wrong!"

"Nothing is wrong. He is hungry. That's all."

"Hungry already?" I asked, not quite believing him. "How often does he eat?"

"Two or three times a night, I would think, until he has grown some."

"Two or three times a night?" I could not imagine how that was going to work.

"Shh . . ." Joseph said as he arranged Jesus at my breast and gathered us both into his arms. Though the pain in my womb was still sharp, my breasts did not sting so much as they had at his first nursing. I was learning.

I lay there between the man and the boy child, and for that time, nothing else existed. I was surrounded by goodness. It radiated from the two of them, seeped into my body and warmed me. I rested the arch of my foot against Joseph's shin, and he tightened his arms around me. I do not remember ever being happier than I was that night in the stable. The three of us were bound together by the laws of the earth and the hand of God.

"The Lord has given to us a great blessing in this child." I whispered in the darkness. I felt Joseph's body stiffen, barely noticeable, so that I knew he did not want me to think something was wrong.

He reached up and stroked my hair away from my face, then said in his low voice, a voice that scared me just a little, "Remember, Myriam. Jesus is God's son, too."

Of course, I would remember. Jesus would serve the Lord, become a great leader. But he was in my arms. I was the one who would care for him. Long after Joseph had fallen back asleep, I lay awake with my lips soft against my child's forehead. Finally, listening to Joseph's snores, I fell asleep.

A fight on the street woke me.

"You bloody cur!" a man shouted. "I'll slice you open and feed you to the dogs. An' then I'll tear your wheat from the ground and sell your wife to the traders."

Joseph sat up, listened, and then lay back on the straw and was asleep again.

Then I heard soldiers ordering the man to move along. The man cursed at them and told them to stay out of his affairs. A whip cracked, and the man bellowed. Again and again it cracked. His bellows turned to moans, and then it was quiet except for the animals stirring in the outer chamber of the cave.

The animals separated us from the street, and listening to them comforted me. To make room for more travelers, they had been turned out from the lower floor of the inn where they were usually kept so that their bulk and breath would heat the upstairs. I thought it was good that we had not found a bed inside. The straw that we were lying on seemed clean and fresh and would be free of lice.

Another group passed by laughing and singing. I knew that they were well into their drink, and I hoped that they didn't wander into our chamber. I did not want anyone to know we were there. I did not want anyone to know about my son, not yet.

When I was a young girl, I would often find my way to my father's shop. While he worked, he taught me the lessons that the young boys learned in school. My mother didn't approve and would call me to the house to learn a woman's work. Often, she would set me to pounding the grain. It would take me until the sun was high overhead to make enough meal to fill my small hand. She would praise me and tell me that she needed three handfuls—her hands—for each loaf that she would bake. I would pick up the pounding stone again, but when I had pounded my fingers instead of the grain one too many times, she would take pity on me and set me free.

I would race away, holding my ears so I would not hear if she called me back, and run all of the way to my father's shop where he would resume my lessons. I loved to listen to my father recite the scriptures and explain their meaning. He taught me of the privilege of being Hebrew, and he taught me about the Messiah to come.

"From the stem of Jesse shall come a shoot," my father's deep voice would repeat the Lord's promise. Then, very solemnly, he would say to me, "We have descended from the tribe of Judah. King David was your ancestor. You must always remember that. You must lead a good life and obey the laws that God has given us."

Joseph and I had been betrothed for a short time when the angel came to me. Now, as I think back to that day, the years have dulled my memories, and I cannot say if I was awake or asleep, but the message was very clear. I would bear a child who would grow up to be a great leader of our people, the people of Israel. I wanted to shout the news from the rooftops, but when I told Joseph that we had been chosen to be the parents of the Messiah, he told me that I had had a dream. At his word, I told no one else.

Many young girls longed to be chosen to be the mother of the Messiah, the one who would lead our people to freedom, but I had not one thought, not ever, that it would be me. I understood from my father the seriousness of our people's future, and I never imagined that I would be chosen for that responsibility. That honor would go to someone who was like Hadassah,[3] the brave and devout young queen who had saved our people long ago.

When my body began to change, I did not understand what was happening to me. I had seen many married women become heavier and grow more womanly, so I thought that my weight gain was due to my betrothal. But Joseph knew. Joseph knew and accused me of being with child. In my excitement, it took me awhile to see that he was angry. I reminded him what the angel had told me. I thought that we must be married immediately. He said that was impossible, that I had shamed him and put my own life in danger as well. He demanded to know what man I had been with. I did not even know what he was talking about.

"Are you free for the taking then?" he raged at me.

"No, I . . ." I tried to speak to calm him, but he wouldn't listen.

"We were betrothed, and yet I denied myself." He stepped closer, and I thought he was going to strike me.

"That night in the storm, did we . . .?" I tried to ask.

"Silence, woman!" he ordered.

The word silence he bellowed, but woman he spit out. His contempt made me burn with shame, and I cowered before him.

"Do you know that if I go to the elders and deny you, you could be stoned to death?"

"Deny me?"

"Tell them that the child is not mine."

"If that is what you wish." I felt the tears burning my eyes, but I would not let him know.

"Yet, you have trapped me so that I cannot." He seethed and paced and turned away and then turned back to me.

"I hold you to nothing," I said.

"The Lord holds me to his commandments!"

I was silent.

"Can you tell me the fifth commandment?" he demanded, staring at me, his eyes glazed and unblinking.

"Yes, I know the commandments."

"Tell me then," he hissed.

I wanted to reach for him and tell him that it would be well, but I didn't dare.

"Tell me the fifth commandment of the Lord!"

"Thou shalt not kill."

"Thou shalt not kill!" he roared. He took in a great gulp of air and attacked again. "If I deny you, they will stone you to death, and the babe, too, will die!" He stood breathing hard. Then he quieted, became deathly calm and forced his words through his clenched teeth. His lips barely moved. "Then your blood will be upon me, and in the eyes of the Lord, I would have broken his commandment. For what you have done, I would have your blood upon me."

And at those words, and on that day, I was to Joseph as so many women are to their husbands. Nothing. My death would mean nothing to him. His only regret would be that I had caused him to sin. I fell to the ground and hid my face.

"Look at me!" he ordered.

2

Married

"Look at me," Joseph demanded again.

I raised my eyes to him, but I didn't move. He stared down at me unblinking, his face strained and bright red against his black beard. I watched as the strength of his fury deserted him. He began to rock back and forth and then to shake as his pain consumed him. He was Joseph again, and I thought that I might comfort him, make him understand. I reached out and held his robe, but he stepped back and pulled it free.

"I will tell no one but your father. But do not speak my name again. Do not ever speak my name again," he choked. Then he said, "May the Lord forgive you," and he turned and walked away.

A few days after that, my mother asked me if I was with child. I didn't answer her. I had not understood Joseph's anger, but I could not see how my mother would take the news any better than he had.

She looked away, said that she would speak to my father. We would have the wedding immediately. From her words, I knew that Joseph had not yet come to them, so I told her he no longer wanted to marry me. She started wailing and clapped her hands over her mouth and ran from the room.

The next day my father did not look at me; when I spoke to him, he did not answer. I was sent away to visit my mother's cousin Elizabeth. Elizabeth was older, and she and her husband Zechariah had no children. I wonder now if it was my mother's plan for Elizabeth to take my child and raise it as her own, though, she did not say so at the time.

When I reached her home, Elizabeth could see that I was with child and asked me many questions. I thought to tell her that I had been married, and my husband had been killed by the Romans, but I was unable to lie, so I said nothing. She kept at me until I told her of the angel's visit.

I waited for her to scorn me like the others, but she did not. She walked over to me and gathered me in her arms, rocked me back and forth, and called me blessed. Then she took my face in her hands, and said, "From the stem of Jesse shall come a shoot. He shall be a light in our darkness and bring peace to our people Israel."

Elizabeth told me that she and Zechariah had also received a great blessing, and she, too, was going to have a child. We rejoiced together, and the days passed quickly. Elizabeth and Zechariah were very kind to me, and I wanted to stay on with them. But after about two months, they told me that I must return to Joseph and everything would be all right. And it was.

In my absence, the Lord made all things known to Joseph, and he told my father that he would marry me the day that I returned. So, when I arrived at my father's house, though I was exhausted from my trip, he sent for Joseph immediately.

I had not seen him since the day of his fury, and when he came up the hill, I cried out at the sight of him. I wanted to run into his arms, and I wanted to run away at the same time.

We married quietly, not the wedding that I had imagined as a girl, not the one that my mother had planned for. There were no guests, just the rabbi who came and said the words that would seal me to Joseph and give him, rather than my father, authority over me.

My mother had prepared a meal, but before we could eat it, Joseph set out and ordered me to follow. I was tired and fell further and further behind. He did not even look back. Finally, we arrived at the place that Joseph had found for us to live, but he did not come to me. That night, I turned my face to the wall and prayed to the Lord that I would be his obedient servant and do his will. I prayed for him not to harden my heart against Joseph.

Joseph was not unkind, but he did not even look at me when he spoke. Many times, I started to ask him to return me to my father's house, but I knew that I had no say in the matter, and my father would refuse me as well. I determined that I was blessed with the child and that I was also blessed that I had not ended up with the tentmaker my mother had wanted me to marry. I didn't care that there had been no great celebration, but I knew that Joseph had taken me to be his wife as a duty only, so pain filled my heart, because Joseph was the one that I loved.

I saw him first when I was fourteen. One day, I went to the well, and there he was—tall and brown and so handsome that to look at him was a privilege. His bare arms were lean and muscled. He wore a full beard, but his cheekbones were set above it. His hair was black and glistened in the sun. His eyes were also black and had fine lines creasing from them, and I knew that meant he smiled often. He lifted the bucket from the well and filled a pitcher for an old woman.

I would come to learn that Joseph had a kindness about him that was rare even to Hebrew men. He would help others when there was no gain for him. It did not matter that they were not relatives or that he received nothing in return. He would help others even when he suffered for it.

That is not what drew me to him that first day, though. No, that day, I was drawn by some feeling within me that I had not yet known. I wanted to place my hand upon his cheek and feel the roughness of his beard. Trace my fingers across his full lips that scared me even when they smiled. I wanted to wrap both of my hands around the muscles in his arms and see if they were as hard as iron, for that was how they looked to me. I wanted to see how he made them ripple up and down by lifting only an empty bucket. That is what I wanted to do, but what I did was to slide backwards into the crowd and hide myself until he had taken his water and left.

I thought of him day and night, and my heart sang the love songs of Solomon. I learned from the girls at the well that his name was Joseph; he was a carpenter and older than me by some fifteen years, but that was of no matter to me. Every day, I offered to carry water for my mother in hopes that I would see him again. And then one day I did. As I drew my water, he came near and spoke to me. I was too shy to answer, but I smiled and didn't run away.

For many reasons, I barely dared to hope that we would marry. Then, to my joy, my father consented. But the marriage was not as I had dreamed. Joseph would go to work early and return late. My time as his wife became lonely days of waiting for him to come home and lonely nights of him turning away from me. But above all else was the child, above Joseph, above me. So I pushed the pity that I felt for myself aside and tried hard to be a good wife. I was glad that my mother had taught me to wash the clothing, grind the grain into meal, and bake the bread. I did those things with great care, trying to bring some ease into his life.

Joseph might give one nod of his head to acknowledge my offerings, but that was all. He never asked me to sit by him to eat the roast quail I had prepared or to share the loaf I had placed before him. He offered his prayers alone, and he ate alone. My mother thought nothing of helping my father with his dress, but Joseph would take the garments I laid out for him and go into the other room. I never approached him, and he never asked me to help. Not so much as to retrieve a sandal or smooth a fold in his robe. Not so much as to tie the straps on his prayer phylactery. And most certainly, not to stand tall for me to admire him in the way that I had seen my mother admire my father when he wore a garment that she had newly stitched for him.

In my loneliness, I had a great deal of time to remember what my father had taught me about the prophecies of the coming Messiah. The Messiah was to be a descendant of King David and would grow up to be a great leader. He would lead by example and inspire all people to live as God desired. He would be the beginning and the end. Through him, Israel would be the glory of God.

Most of the Jewish people believed that the Messiah would come at the end of time, and at his coming, there would be peace throughout the land. The people of Israel would no longer be oppressed, and rather than working all our days to pay taxes and buy food, we would be able to spend our time in study and worship. And at his coming, Jews from all lands would be called home. We would be together again in the Promise Land. In Israel. In Jerusalem.

I asked Joseph about what the priests and rabbis believed. I loved those times because when he answered, he would forget his aloofness and share his wisdom with me. He told me that the priests and the rabbis had many different beliefs among them concerning the Messiah and how the messianic age would come about. Not all of them even believed that the Messiah would be an earthly ruler. The book of Daniel proclaimed that one called the Son of Man would transcend the bonds of this earth, and his kingdom would be everlasting.

I wondered how we could prepare the babe for what was to come, but Joseph told me that we would raise him as any child, taking him to worship and educating him in the word of God, and in due time, the Lord would make known his plan, and Jesus would assume his leadership of the Israelites. He would be a leader greater than Abraham, greater than Moses, greater than all of the kings. I decided that Joseph was right. He was not a priest or rabbi, but he knew the scriptures well and spent much time in prayer concerning our unborn child.

Years later, Joseph confessed to me that he did not know what would happen to any of us once the child was born. He had put his reputation, his family lineage, and even his life on the line, and yet thought that the babe still might be killed as a mamzer[1] or that I might be stoned for a whore at any time by some outraged zealot.

Or, if the world knew of Jesus' birthright, he, or both of us, would be taken from Joseph to be raised in a royal house. But at the time, Joseph never shared his worries with me.

I grew and grew, and it amazed me. I could feel Jesus' knee, or elbow, or foot as he slid them across the inside of my belly. I would put my hand upon my stomach and almost hold him before he was even born. I often wanted to ask Joseph to feel the babe, but I never did. He was always distant, our relationship always fragile.

In the night, though, when he thought that I was asleep, Joseph would place his hand on me and cradle the babe and speak to him, sometimes in Aramaic, but most often in Hebrew, the language of the scriptures. I didn't know Hebrew well, so if he spoke too rapidly or too softly, I didn't understand. But I knew he was saying good things, and I loved to listen to his voice, rich and mellow, resonating deeply as he began and then becoming singsong and lilting as he talked to the babe. Sometimes at midsentence, he would catch himself, clear his throat, and drop to his manly voice.

Often, Jesus would give a good kick just like he was talking back. Joseph would chuckle then, and when that happened, I wanted to lay my hand over his and hold it to me, but instead, I would concentrate on lying still and breathing steadily, pretending to be asleep.

Near the time that Jesus was to be born, the Roman Emperor Caesar Augustus issued a decree for yet another tax census. Joseph was from the House of David which meant he had to travel to Bethlehem to enroll. We didn't have the rights of Roman citizens, so unless it was a sacrilege to our faith, we obeyed the Roman laws exactly. Even if a man could slip through the nets of Caesar, Herod the Great, who was king over all Judea at the time, would track him down and arrest him, even have him put to death. No man disobeyed the summons.

My mother wanted me to stay in Nazareth, but Joseph agreed that I could go along, and she didn't dare argue with him. Looking back, I think that he wanted me along lest Jesus be born while he was away, and some aggrieved kinsmen would try to restore the family honor by arranging for Jesus and me to die during the birthing. The shame of one was the shame of all. Or maybe he just wanted Jesus to be born away from the wagging tongues of Nazareth.

I was in no shape to walk the six day journey, so Joseph led his donkey around, lifted me onto her back like one more pack, and we set out. The babe pounded against me with every step, and I concentrated on the donkey's red plume bobbing before me.

When the caravan stopped for a rest, I found a woman traveler and told her I thought that the babe and I would both die or that I would birth him right there on the road, though I had no real idea of how he would make it from my womb into the world. She scolded me for coming along but said there were plenty of women in the caravan who could deliver a babe.

With the hardships of the trip, the strain between Joseph and me disappeared. He sheltered me from the weather and from the other travelers. At night we huddled together to stay warm. When I was on the donkey, he held the reigns. When I was on foot, he held my hand. The trip was miserable, but my heart sang.

When we entered the gates of Bethlehem, we were swallowed by masses of angry people. They were angry at being called from their homes, angry at the soldiers, and most of all, angry about the unfair taxes. Herod gained money for his building projects by increasing Caesar's tax bill until it reached eight tenths of a man's wages.

Joseph pushed forward, his head lowered and his weight set against the crowd to keep us from being trampled. When a thief tried to lay hands on our belongings, Joseph let out a roar.

The Tenth Day of Sivan

Martha is here again. She has left Bethany and come to Nazareth to stay with a kinsman or to be with me, I am not sure. James said that it's not safe for her in Bethany now. We sit, leaning against the wall, and she cradles me to her. The pain washes over me like waves. As it comes, I tighten all over and pull my shoulders forward around me. I cross my arms to protect myself and bring my legs up to my chest like I am an infant. I breathe through my nose and force myself to take the air slowly as if only my face is above the water, and if I thrash or gasp, I will drown. Tears stream from my closed eyes, but I do not wail this time.

When the wave has passed, I relax my body and try to listen to what Martha is saying. She is telling me a story of Jesus, how he once helped her chase three goats that had gotten into her house. It makes me smile. I love when others remember my son as I do. I try to tell her of the time Jesus wanted to walk to Bethany to visit her, but when I say his name, the waves of sadness come again, and I close my eyes and tighten my face. Instead, I say "I don't know how this could have happened. He was sent to be our leader. I don't know how this could have happened."

"I know. I know," Martha says, and then she tells me in a voice that is soft and kind, not so stern as the one that she usually uses, how Jesus would want me to go on. How he would want me to carry out his work. I try to imagine that, but in my mind, I see the people staring at me while I sit before them unable to speak. I hold onto Martha's arm and tell her that I don't think that I could ever do that.

"You will," she assures me. "Not yet, but you will." Then she talks some more, but I can't hear her words. I keep my eyes closed and keep my breath slow, but I try not to tighten my muscles so much. I try to imagine myself on the waves rising and falling in the sea. We sit together until it is dark outside. The best thing about Martha is that I never have to pretend.

3

First Days

Joseph roared again, and the thief turned to run, but Joseph grabbed the neck of his robe and lifted him off of the ground. He was only a young boy, so Joseph thrashed him around in the air and then dropped him into the dirt and gave him a sandal in the backside. The mob shouted, pushed, and cursed, and we were crushed into its middle. Joseph broke us into a bit of a clearing, and something slammed into my side. He shouted back to me to ask if I was all right, but I didn't even try to answer. The travelers had gone unwashed for days and their body odor mixed with the smoke of fresh manure campfires and rancid and spoiled food. Bile rose in my throat, and saliva dripped from the roof of my mouth. I swallowed and swallowed. I knew if I unclenched my teeth, or opened my mouth, or even nodded my head, I would throw up.

We finally arrived at an inn owned by one of Joseph's kinsmen, but every room was taken. He must have felt loyalty to Joseph or pity for me, though, because he offered us shelter in the cave that he used for his stable. And in that stable, my child was born. My beautiful child.

On the morning after Jesus' birth, I opened my eyes to see a sliver of light coming through a hole in the ceiling of the cave. In the night, I had thought our hideout cozy, but in the daylight, it showed for what it was, a miserable space in a rock, suitable for animal shelter, but not where a mother wanted to keep her child. I wished for Nazareth, for my mother, my cousins, our own home.

Jesus began to cry, and I lifted him, but I hurt so much that I could barely move. I knew he was hungry again, and he was wet. Very, very wet. I blinked my eyes as fast as I could. I had asked to come along, and I had gotten my wish; there would be no whining or crying from me.

Joseph took Jesus from me and wrapped him in dry cloths and held him to warm him. Then he helped me settle myself to nurse. While I fed Jesus, Joseph went into the other chamber and returned with a small manger. He filled it with fresh hay and laid a scrap of blanket on top. When Jesus had finished nursing, Joseph took him from me and laid him in the manger.

"There, that will do until we can get a cradle," he said. Then he lowered himself onto the straw to keep watch over his son, and I was glad that I was there and that Joseph was the one who was with me when Jesus was born.

A woman from the inn brought us food, a large plate for Joseph and warm broth for me. I drank it and lay back in the straw still exhausted from the birth and from the trip. I reached for Joseph's hand. It was large and strong and calloused from hard work, and it was safe. And now, after months of waiting, it was mine to hold, and holding it made everything seem better. I closed my eyes and slept.

Pain in my breasts woke me. They were rock hard, huge, and burning. I thought that I could see them growing as I watched, and I was afraid that they were going to burst open. I sat up and held my arms out like wings. I could not stand it when they pressed against me.

Jesus was crying again, and I said that I wouldn't be able to feed him, but Joseph just shook his head and handed the babe to me. I placed Jesus to my breast and bit my lip to keep still. As soon as he began to suckle, milk streamed from me like I was a goat. I tried to stop it, but I had no control over my body. I had no idea how such a thing happened and thought that I could never go anywhere again, but it felt wonderful, and at least I wasn't going to burst open. Joseph chuckled to himself, relieved that he wouldn't have to be wandering the streets of Bethlehem in search of a wet nurse.

That evening just as we were settling in and I was feeling thankful that we had made it through the day, some of Joseph's kinsmen came to see Jesus. Many still lived in the city, and others had come for the census. I wanted to sleep, but Joseph said that we would receive them, and that began an endless celebration. In the days to follow, so many people came that I barely had time to care for Jesus. They came from everywhere. Even the magi, the wise men who studied the stars, came from far to the east and brought fine gifts. Everyone wanted to see the son of Joseph who had been born in a stable. And they whispered among themselves that this child would grow to become the King of Israel.

Joseph's cousin Labon was one of the visitors, and he came often to discuss Jesus' future with Joseph. The two agreed that, as the scriptures foretold, Jesus would be the leader to redeem Israel. They discussed possible military battles and whether they would still be alive to see the victory. They believed that Jesus would not only be a king, but also that he would serve as a great judge or priest. He would restore the Court of Israel and establish a government that would be the center of all governments for both the Hebrews and the Gentiles. God's law would be the law of the land.

Sometimes, listening to Labon and the other visitors, I would be frightened and take Jesus deeper into the cave where the world did not come. I would press my back against the hard rock and hold the babe to me. I knew my ways were not pleasing to the Lord, so I tried to be as brave as I could and not stay away for too long before I would go out again and share my child. I remembered the words that my father had taught me: "Every head shall bow, every knee shall bend."

All who came to visit our child wished for a word or blessing from Joseph or me. I was shy and wanted to refuse, but Joseph said it was what we must do, and so to each one we said, "Peace to you and to all on earth," or "Glory to God in the highest," and "May God bless you now and forever," or something like that. After the people had seen Jesus, they went away filled with a new spirit.

Though I knew that Jesus did not really belong to me and that he had come for another purpose, he seemed so mine and in so many ways, so ordinary. I loved to bathe him and rub him in olive oil or powder him with crushed myrtle leaves. And I loved to nuzzle my face close to him and drink in his sweet baby smell or swaddle him until little beads of sweat formed across his tiny nose and in the creases of his chubby little neck.

"Give the poor child some air," Joseph would grumble as he took the babe from me and stripped his wrappings away. Joseph was at ease caring for Jesus and knew many things that I did not.

On his eighth day, Jesus was named and circumcised.[1] I had attended such ceremonies before, but as the knife cut into the pure new flesh of my son, I wanted to snatch him away from the rabbi. Joseph stood at my side and pressed me against him. He had his arm around me with his hand circling my upper arm. He looked completely relaxed, but when I jumped, he tightened his grip on my arm and shook his head slowly back and forth in warning to me. His eyes never left Jesus.

When the time of my purification[2] arrived, we took Jesus, as our first born male child, to the Temple to redeem him.[3] We set out at sunrise, and I rode on the donkey carrying Jesus. Our pace was slow, and by the time we reached the outskirts of Jerusalem, the sun was high overhead. We approached the city from the southwest and passed close to the Hinnom Valley and its pit of ever burning fire where the sewage and garbage of Jerusalem were dumped. The horrible place where children had once been burned as a sacrifice to the ancient gods Molech and Baal. King Josiah outlawed the practice a long time ago, so there were no more sacrifices. But those unclaimed for burial and those not worthy to live, were still said to fuel the fires of Gehenna.

In the time that we had been in Bethlehem, I had seen more

people and heard more gossip than I had in my entire life. One of Joseph's kinswomen, who thought that I had deceived him, would gossip to another woman close enough so I was sure to hear. Her worst story was of a young woman named Liat. Though she had no husband, Liat bore a child.

While she was expecting, Liat hid herself beneath her robes, and no one, not even her own mother, knew that she was with child. But when it came time for her to be delivered, great pains came upon her, and she wailed loudly and begged for help. The midwife was called but refused to come because Liat had no husband, so Liat's sister, in her compassion, helped to birth the child. The child was beautiful, so beautiful that when her sister saw him, she held him in her arms and cried and cried.

After that part, the gossip telling the story grew very quiet. She looked at me, and the others who were listening looked away. The gossip stared at me a while more, and then she told that Liat's babe was taken from her, and though Liat wailed and wailed, it did no good. Her babe was placed upon the fires of Hinnom Valley. And as for Liat, everyone knew what happened to her. I didn't. But I wouldn't ask.

The smoke from Hinnom Valley choked us. I got off the donkey and walked so close to Joseph that he tripped over me. He set the donkey to shield the pile from my sight, and I pressed Jesus in between the two of us and covered his face to keep the evil from him. I recited scripture to block the story of Liat from my mind. Still, across the years, I could hear the spirits of the sacrificed children crying out and smell the burning flesh of the poor ones.

We stopped first at the mikvah.⁴ Joseph bathed so that he could enter the Temple and then took Jesus while I bathed. Water was scarce in the stable where we lived, so when I entered the pool to wash away all that was unclean, it felt so cool and wonderful that I wanted to laugh and splash like a child. I reminded myself to be solemn and concentrate on my purification.

After I was cleaned and dressed, we climbed the steps to the Temple. They were endless, and before we reached the Portico, the heat had overtaken me again. We passed through the marble columns and took a short rest in the coolness under the roofed porch before we stepped into the sun again in the Court of Gentiles. From there, we climbed the steps to the most beautiful of the gates. The doors of the gate are Corinthian brass and covered with designs. They are so large that it takes twenty men to open them each day, and the noise that they make can be heard throughout the city and lets the people know that the Temple is open for worship.

Next, we entered the Court of Women, and I waited there and completed my purification while Joseph took Jesus into the Court of Israel where all that was ordered to be done before the Lord was done.

I imagined the priest taking Jesus in his arms, holding him high, and dedicating him to the Lord God, ruler of the people Israel and ruler of all the earth. When Joseph reappeared with Jesus in his arms, I was filled with the spirit. My strength grew and then drained from me, and I wept. I had done what I had been called to do, and Jesus was now in the hands of the Lord where he would remain for all eternity. It is what every parent desires.

Joseph and I made our sacrifice of two doves and gave thanks to God for the child and for all that he had given us. We made our way back to the Portico where we would depart the Temple. There, an old man named Simeon came to us and took Jesus from me and blessed him. Then, he lifted his face and asked the Lord to let him depart in peace for he had seen the child. When he handed Jesus back to me, his voice was sad, and he warned me that one day a sword would pierce my soul.

I held on to Jesus and wanted to run, but an old woman stepped from the shadows, stood in front of us, and held out her arms. I pretended I didn't see her and kept walking, but Joseph ordered me to stop. He took Jesus and handed him to the woman. She was an old prophetess named Anna, who, for years, had spent all her days at the

Temple. Her ears had grown large as those of an old woman do. Her skin was transparent and hung in folds, and her blue veins made trails from her small wrists to her swollen knuckles.

She could not see well and held Jesus up close to her face until her lips brushed against him. I was afraid of her blindness and thought that she might drop him. I hovered close by while she marveled over him and then put her bony hand on his forehead and blessed him. Joseph took Jesus, and I took the old woman's hands in mine and blessed her in the way that Joseph had taught me in Bethlehem.

Then, I took Jesus back into my arms and hurried out onto the street. Joseph warned me to slow my pace before I attracted the attention of the Romans. I turned my eyes down and walked behind him.

4

Joseph's Dream

I wanted to go directly home to Nazareth, but Joseph thought that the trip would be too difficult. He said that we would stay in Bethlehem until Jesus and I were stronger, so we returned to the stable.

Joseph took some of the money we had received as gifts and bought tools so that he could work and earn our keep. He made improvements to the inn, repaired carts and wagons for the townspeople and travelers, and did whatever else he was called to do. When he put his hands to stone, metal, wood, or ivory, everyone marveled at his skill, and more and more work came to him. Jesus and I grew stronger, but Joseph was pleased to be near his kinsmen again, and we stayed on in Bethlehem.

Some of the kinsmen, like the gossip who told the story of Liat, thought I had deceived Joseph and disapproved of me, but most welcomed me into the family. Joshua, an old man with hands so gnarled that they must have pained him at all times, came and brought a cedar cradle. I knew that he had gone to great effort to find the wood and make the beautiful bed.

"All boys," he explained, "must have a gift of cedar." For girls it was a gift of pine.

He lifted Jesus and placed him in the cradle and prayed over him. I smiled at Joshua, and he smiled back with a smile so wide that I could see all of his teeth. He still had many of them.

When he came to visit, he would sit and rock the cradle to help Jesus sleep and tell me stories of when Joseph was a young boy. I loved to hear them, and I missed him and his kindness for a long time after we left Bethlehem.

My favorite of all of Joseph's kinsmen was his cousin Sarah, Labon's wife. She and her two young children came often. Sarah was very bold and dared to speak out to anyone, to her husband, to the kinsmen who wanted to advise me or borrow my husband for the evening, and even to Joseph.

After one of her visits, I told Joseph that I wished I could be like Sarah. She was so brave and sure of herself, while I was shy and awkward. Joseph told me that Sarah would drive him to wine if he had to listen to her yapping all day, and if I wanted to be like someone else, I should pick another. And I named Nava. But he said no, that would not do, for though she was the kindest woman, he could not bring himself to eat the soup she brought or one other thing that she had cooked. He would surely starve to death if I became as Nava.

The time that I wished most to be like Sarah was when Avigail came. Avigail was a widow who called herself a kinswoman of Joseph's because she had been married to his cousin. Even young and naïve as I was, I knew that she did not come to see Jesus. When she thought no one could see her, she looked at Joseph and made her eyes grow large. Then she would let them flutter shut and while they were closed, she would moisten her lips by sticking her tongue out just a little. Often, she would brush herself up against Joseph and pretend that it was an accident. I would stammer and tiptoe around her like an awkward child. If I were like Sarah, I would have dared to tell Avigail that she was fooling no one. But in truth, she fooled Joseph, or at least I hoped that he did not know her plans and still allow her to go on like she did.

When I asked Joseph if he would ever take another wife as men of other tribes did, he didn't even look up from what he was doing and just said that was no longer our way. But it didn't make me feel any better. By then, Avigail was coming all of the time, whining about how hard it was to be a widow, saying anything she could to bring sympathy to herself. And then, she would cluck to Joseph about my age, how it was as if he were caring for two children. Since that was true in many ways, it made my face turn red, and if he attended her, it made my eyes tear. I never let her see, though.

When Avigail looked at me, her mouth smiled, but her eyes were as cold as the night wind of the desert. Once, she offered me a cup of soup, but I was afraid to drink it and poured it out when she wasn't looking. Another time, she offered to stay and help me with Jesus, but I refused her. Joseph addressed me for being unkind, but I couldn't help myself.

After Avigail's visits, the strain between Joseph and me was always worse. He was irritable and would leave our bed at night and sit and stare out into the outer chamber. When I asked what was wrong, he would snap that it was nothing and tell me to go back to sleep.

Then, one evening Avigail came just as we finished our meal. Joseph was going to soak his feet because he had walked a long distance from work and they were blistered and sore. I had to nurse Jesus. Avigail insisted that Joseph let her bathe his feet. Only to help me out, she said. As she walked past me, she patted me on the head the way my father patted the goat.

First, she placed the empty basin at Joseph's feet and went to bring a pitcher of water. The pitcher was very full, and I thought it might spill over, but it didn't. She carried it out away from her body and moved it from side to side with the wave of the water. She swayed her way back to Joseph and never once took her eyes off him. Then, she stood before him and tossed her scarf back so it would be out of the way of the water, but she did it in a way that made my eyes and Joseph's follow her hand and her head. Next, she knelt before him and removed his sandals. She lifted his feet, one at a time, and held them over the basin pouring water over each one with the pitcher and then with the cup of her hand. She did this again and again, until his feet were clean. Then, she took a cloth and slowly wiped each foot. Finally, she took both of his feet in her lap and began massaging them. She closed her eyes and massaged his feet in a way that made me choke out loud. At the sound, Joseph pulled his feet away and reached for his sandal. Avigail snatched it away and laughed. I thought they were going to wrestle to the ground over it.

The night of the foot washing, I lay on the straw far away from Joseph and pitied myself. All the next day, Joseph barely spoke to me. Then, when darkness came again, he lay on his back upon our pallet and offered me his shoulder as a pillow. I lay beside him, and he took my hand in his, lifted it to his mouth, and kissed the back of my fingers. Then he pressed my hand to his chest. I dared to comb my fingers through the coarse hairs until I reached his warm and naked skin. I heard his startled breath, so I kept my hand still.

"To your question of before," he said. "I did not attend you well."

"Yes?" I said. I knew the question and feared that he had set his eye upon Avigail. That he had changed his mind, and would put me aside and take her as his wife or at the least take her to his bed, and in his honor, would not do so without telling me.

"I will tell you what I believe," he said.

"Yes?" I said again. My voice shivered. I sounded like the little girl Avigail said I was.

"I believe," Joseph said and brushed his lips across my palm and then placed it back on his hard chest, "I believe that the Lord God made one woman for one man."

"It is what I hope, but it has not always been so."

"It was with Adam. Did he not have one wife?"

"There was no woman but Eve to be his wife," I said in my little girl voice again.

He placed his hand over mine and slid it to the side of his chest. He took into him a deep breath so that my hand rose and my fingers parted, and then he turned and kissed my forehead.

"There," he murmured. Your hand is upon me."

"Yes."

"And you see how the Lord has made me."

"Mm, hmm."

"So you know then, that just as he made Adam, he made me."

"Yes, Joseph," My heart was pounding.

Then he said in his most serious voice, "Plenty of ribs for another wife if the Lord intended."

"Joseph!" I wailed.

And he laughed, and so did I.

"You are teasing me," I said.

"Yes wife, I am teasing you."

And I laughed again.

"I am most pleased that the Lord has chosen you for my wife," he said and hugged me to him so quickly that he lifted me half on top of him.

"I am pleased that you are pleased," I said. I forced myself to speak quietly, but I could hear my own smile.

He reached up and brushed my hair from my face, and even in the darkness, I could tell that he was looking into my eyes. And then, making his voice low and rich the way I loved it, he said to me, "I will never leave you or forsake you. It is my vow to you."

"Then the Lord has answered my prayer," I whispered and lay against him.

"Yes," he said. "Now you must put your worry aside."

So I did not worry anymore. Except when Avigail was around.

But she was not there that night, and our laughing made me not so shy, so I took Joseph's face in my hands and placed my lips upon his. His beard tickled me, and I used my hand to brush it away from his mouth so that I could feel his mouth under mine. He groaned and pulled me to him. I gloried at the feel of his body, and my heart leaped in my breast. And then he kissed me until I could not breathe, and drums beat through parts of my body that I did not know I had.

"Please," I whispered.

"Yes," he said. "Yes, it is time." And I felt his hands upon me.

After that, when Avigail came, Joseph did not attend her. Soon she did not come so often. Sarah and the children and Joshua did though, and they were good company, and our time in Bethlehem was good.

I liked it best, though, when Joseph returned in the evening, and it was just the three of us. He smiled again like he had when I first knew him and told me stories about his day that made me laugh. I would tell of some new wonder Jesus had performed, lifting his head, smiling, grasping a toy, things all babes did, but new to us. We delighted in everything about our child.

The stable was comfortable and cozy. There was plenty of clean straw, and it was cold enough outside that it even smelled good, good enough anyway. Sometimes, when the night grew too cold, Joseph would bring one of the cattle, or the goat, or some of the sheep into our chamber so that we were warmed from their breath and bodies. The sheep, he would leave free, but the cattle and the goat needed to be tied. The goat was a nuisance because she ate everything she could reach. Sometimes we would feel her chewing the blankets right out from under us. Joseph would mutter something about eating goat soup and get up and tie her farther away.

One afternoon when Jesus was some months, and we were still in Bethlehem, Joseph was outside of the stable crafting a trunk that someone had ordered. It was made of fine Hawthorne wood with special carvings of palm trees on its top to represent the city of Jericho. I was standing just inside the shelter of the rock, holding Jesus and watching Joseph. He had on his carpenter's face as I had come to think of it. His forehead wrinkled in concentration, his mouth opened slightly and was drawn around his teeth so that it pulled his nostrils in, his tongue between his teeth pushing out one side of his lower lip. Generations from now, I believe someone will say, "Now that one has descended from Joseph of Nazareth. I recognize that expression. He wore it all the time."

Then, without lifting his head or breaking his look, Joseph flicked his hand as if brushing some sawdust from the trunk and motioned me inside. I hurried into the cave far enough back so I would not be seen. I heard a sword clanking, leather creaking, footsteps on the cobblestone coming closer. I knew it was a Roman soldier.

I found a chink in the rock and looked out at the soldier. He reached out and ran his hand over the trunk. When he did, I saw that his arm was covered with a tattoo of a green and purple and red fire breathing beast that came alive when he moved his hand. I had never seen such a thing. I walked farther back into the chamber and stayed quiet. The Romans had not bothered us so far, but we kept separate when we could. They could never be trusted.

"I have heard that you are the best carpenter in the city," the soldier said to Joseph.

Joseph gave a snort to acknowledge that he had heard but said nothing.

"A fine carpenter with a fine son," the soldier pressed. "I have heard of your babe."

"Hmh," Joseph responded. I heard pounding and knew his trick of pretending to be very busy with his work when he did not want to talk. I could see his brow creasing a little more and his mouth drawing as if he were thinking so hard about his work that he didn't even know what someone was saying to him.

"I have heard of your wife too," the soldier said, and he laughed when he spoke.

Joseph did not respond. He kept pounding, pounding, never breaking his rhythm, like the soldier's words did not affect him at all.

"I would like to have a look at the child," the soldier announced.

"Not here now," Joseph lied.

"I have been told he was." I heard the threat in his voice.

"His mother took him to visit some kinsmen," Joseph said, his voice still steady.

"Later then, on my way back."

"She will not return until the morrow."

"You would let her be gone the night?" The soldier laughed. This time a leering laugh. "I have heard that she is one that a man would want to keep in his bed."

"The babe is ill," Joseph lied again. "She will get advice from a kinswoman."

More pounding, but neither one said another word. I didn't move until I heard the Roman's receding footsteps.

That night, Joseph was restless. I thought that I was crowding him, taking my half of the pallet out of the middle as he often charged. Then he sat up and shouted something into the darkness. Before I could ask him what he was saying, he lay back down, and I heard him snoring. He was still asleep. Then he called out again, and by the light of our small lamp, I could see that his eyes were open. He bolted from the pallet and ordered me to get up, told me that we would leave at once.

"Shh. You are dreaming," I told him.

"Now!" he snapped. "The Lord has warned me, and we will listen." He was throwing supplies onto the blanket as he spoke. "Herod has learned of the birth of Jesus. He is going to destroy him."

My heart leaped at his words, but still I thought he was dreaming. "A babe?" I asked. "That does not seem believable."

"Believe me and stop your chattering. Get ready now!"

He went out to fill the water skins and bring the donkey. I was frightened by then and worked as fast as I could to gather the rest of our belongings and dress Jesus. I was ready to leave before Joseph returned. Still that did not suit him.

"Hurry! Herod's soldiers may be coming even now," he barked as he strapped our bundles onto the donkey. It was gray. I remember that the donkey was gray.

"What of Sarah and Labon?" I pleaded. "What of your other kinsmen?"

"Stop! Your job is to protect Jesus."

He took Jesus from me, laid him in the straw, and boosted me onto the donkey with such force that I nearly fell off the other side.

"Keep the babe quiet and out of sight, no matter what," he threatened as he handed Jesus to me. "Do you hear? No matter what."

"Yes, I hear," I answered and set Jesus to nurse so that he would not cry out.

We stepped out into the night. The stars shown down on us, and the cold air smelled of freshness and hope. But we smelled of sweat and fear. The donkey's hooves clip clopped on the stone. I wanted to get off and run because I believed that I could travel faster, but Joseph kept his head down and did not hurry.

Jesus was old enough to be interested in the night and would not nurse. I held him tighter, but he squealed and reached for Joseph. The more I tried to silence him, the more he protested. I buried his face in my robe, and he cried aloud. I held him tighter and scolded him to hush, but he squirmed until he was free and lunged for Joseph. I pulled him sharply to me, but it was too late. We had already attracted the attention of a soldier on patrol. As he walked toward us, I strained to see if he had a fire-breathing tattoo.

The Twenty-second Day of Tammuz

Often, when I am alone, I weep. Not the pretty kind, but the kind that hurts and makes me want to throw up. My breath snorts in and out and my stomach convulses. My tears stream down my face and splash on my robe. I weep until my eyes are swollen and my nose stuffs and runs. I weep until my head aches, and I have no more tears.

Or I wander around staring at nothing, touching the things that belonged to Jesus, picking up a robe or a tunic that he wore, holding it, drawing in breaths, rubbing my face back and forth in the garment. I hold the scriptures that he held and studied, and when I hold them, I think that I can feel where his hands were. I want my faith to be as strong as his. I want to know the Lord. I try to read them, but I cannot concentrate, so I hold them and remember.

Near the close of the day, I go outside and look to the hills, past the Cedar Lebanon tree to the boulder where the setting sun casts green and black and blue shadows out onto the ground, and I think that Jesus might be sitting there for a short rest before he comes the rest of the way home, but he is not.

When James comes and bends his head just so as he ducks under my doorway, and the sun is bright at his back, and it is dark inside the house, I am sure that it is Jesus. They don't really look alike, but their builds and their movements are the same.

I long to see him. I close my eyes and softly grip my hands, and I concentrate as if he is in the next room and can hear my thoughts through the wall. I stand very quietly and will him to come back so that I can see him just one more time.

I tell myself that would be enough, and then I could let go and go on. But for a mother to hold her child just once more would never be enough. I know that.

In one way, his resurrection was a miracle that was so overwhelming that I cannot describe it. Jesus came to me, and he was well and whole. His hair was not matted with dirt and blood, but clean and shined in the sun. His face was not swollen and bruised, but lean and strong and beautiful.

My feet rose above the ground. The pain that makes it hard for me to breathe disappeared, and I felt warm sunshine and cool water all at once inside and outside of my being. But Jesus did not rush to me or embrace me. He was not even surprised or happy to see me after what had happened. He stood while I mothered over him, but like when he was a child eager to be off on a boy adventure, his thoughts were not with me. He was ready to be with the Lord in heaven, with Joseph and those who had gone before, and he could not understand why I wished him back. And then he left again.

James, who has been studying with Jesus these last years, tried to explain to me, and I think that he is right, that Jesus needed to come back to assure us that the Lord is triumphant over death, and we must not fear it. We have always believed in a life after death, but the Sadducees have not, and that has been a great divide between the Israelites. Now, there is no doubt.

As a Hebrew, I try to grasp what Jesus wanted me to know, but as a mother, I just want to see my son one more time. Many have told me that this is displeasing to the Lord, that I should accept what has happened, but both Jesus and Joseph encouraged me to speak my mind and to not be afraid of the things that I felt. And so, like all who have lost someone, I will tell you that I want my son back, and if I cannot have him back, I want to see him just one more time. I know that I will not see him again until I no longer walk this earth, but I do not want to believe it.

5

To Egypt

The soldier continued toward us. Jesus hushed and buried his face in my robe. We turned into a narrow passage way. I looked ahead into the darkness, but I heard the soldier's footsteps behind us. He was in no hurry, but he had followed. I was praying hard, trying not to make a sound, trying not to give him a reason to stop us. And then, like manna from heaven, the Lord sent our rescue. I heard shouts and then a fight. I turned, and between us and the soldier, two brawling drunkards fell out of a side door and blocked his path. He had to stop for them.

We walked on, turned through more passageways, and then made our way out the gates of the city. We had not said a word. Joseph stepped back to my side and told me that we would flee to Egypt to escape Herod.

"Egypt?" I had barely heard of the place, but I knew that it was far away and dangerous.

"We will go where the babe is safe."

"I am afraid."

"God has chosen you to be the mother of this child. There is nothing you must fear."

"I do not want to fail our child or God."

"I will give my life," he promised. And I knew that he meant it.

We walked on awhile before I could bring myself to ask, "Do you think one of your kinsmen has told Herod that I wronged you?"

"No. My kinsmen have regard for you."

"Not all. One might have complained to Herod."

"Never! My kinsmen would never betray me, and you are nothing to Herod. It is Jesus that threatens him. It is Jesus that he wants to destroy."

"Why would any babe be a threat to Herod? Especially one born with such a stigma as Jesus was."

"Herod knows that the King of Israel will come from the House of David, and the magi predicted that it will be Jesus. They have made it known that he will grow to become a great king and take the crown from Herod."

"How did you hear this?"

"There was talk when I was working near the Temple."

"Does Herod know?"

"Herod has spies everywhere. One way or another, he has heard by now."

"And from such talk, he would murder a babe?"

"Quicker than he can spit. He will not chance his crown."

Jesus was amusing himself by pulling on my hair, so I found a rattle for him, but when it fell to the ground, Joseph picked it up and warned me that we could not leave a trail.

I became obsessed with Herod that night, and over the next few years, I came to know that he was a man consumed with his own genius who let nothing get in his way. Not in his quest for power and not in his building projects and business ventures. He rebuilt Solomon's Temple in Jerusalem, and it is so magnificent that the people say that even in one thousand years nothing will be greater. He improved the water supply for all of Jerusalem through a system of aqueducts, and just to the south of the city, he built Herodium, a mountain fortress with its own garden city and a swimming pool the size of a wheat field that he filled with water that he piped for miles. Herodium had towers so high that when he climbed them, he could watch over much of his kingdom.

He built a palace in Masada that looked like several mansions layered upon the hill, yet all were connected. In Caesarea, he built the Promontory Palace for himself and the Temple of Augustus in honor of Caesar. I could not understand how one man could require so many magnificent buildings when half the people in his kingdom didn't even have bread to eat.

Also in Caesarea, he built a deep water harbor that was three times the size of the Greek harbor in Athens and could hold 300 ships at one time. He built a great theater and a 20,000 seat Hippodrome where he held chariot races and athletic games. They said men who would go to the Greek Olympic Games trained there.

But what I learned most about Herod was that he was insane, ruthlessly insane.

"He does not even fear the Lord?" I asked.

"He fears everyone," Joseph said, "and that is what makes him so desperate. He drinks his wine by the hin[1] until he fills himself with courage, but that lasts only until the headache comes. I have heard that he sometimes cannot leave his bed for the fear. Trusts no one, they say, convinced that everyone is out to steal from him or betray him. He has rewritten his last testament more times than can be counted. One day he names a man for an inheritance, and the next he has him executed. He made his young brother-in-law a high priest, then had him drowned in a swimming pool.

"He has been wed ten times and has had many children, but none have brought him peace. He banished his first wife and three year old son. Then he had his favorite wife, Mariamne, put to death because he was convinced that she betrayed him. Afterwards, he went mad with grief and tried to call her back from the grave. They say that is when he really went insane. He even had three of his own sons arrested because he was afraid that they would take his throne. Executed every one of them."

"He is a madman," I said and squeezed Jesus tighter.

"He is," Joseph agreed.

"What do you think will happen to Sarah and Labon and the children?" I asked.

Joseph stopped and tightened a pack on the donkey. "I carved my mark and Labon's upon a wood shingle and gave a stable boy one silver shekel to deliver it and warn them to flee."

"For a shekel he will try."

"That and I told him that I would come after him and give him the hiding of his life if he failed."

"I hope that . . ."

"It is all we could do," Joseph interrupted. "Now stop. We must keep moving. The donkey is fresh, and we will be far from here by the time the sun rises tomorrow."

But Joseph was wrong. We did not get far before morning. We walked southward toward Hebron, and as we entered the Hebron Valley, we heard screams, sorrowful, agonizing screams that went on and on and on.

We would not learn until much later what had happened. That night, all we knew was that our son's life was in danger, and it was up to us to save him.

"Hold fast," Joseph ordered.

I swung my leg over the donkey and nearly slid from her back, but it was not a time to be timid. Joseph changed our direction to the west and pulled on the lead. When the donkey brayed in protest, he slapped her on the hind quarters until she took off. I gripped my knees into her sides as tight as I could and twisted my hand through her mane. I bounced up and down to the trotting, slipping from side to side. I was afraid that Jesus would fly out of my arms, and I dug my free hand into him. Joseph slapped at the donkey again and again until she began to gallop and the ride smoothed.

Joseph was running fast beside us and breathing hard. I was afraid that if he didn't fall back, he might drop on the spot like a horse run to the death, but he ran on like a great Olympian and kept pace with the donkey.

Finally, we reached a cave in the hillside. I didn't know how Joseph knew it was there, and I didn't care. He led us down into a cavern, and we were safe. It was so black inside that I could not see one thing, and I was glad because I knew that no one would see us either. We stood holding onto each other with Jesus between us. Joseph had saved us.

In the night, the Lord sent the wind, and it blew so hard that it piled sand into the cave so that I knew it had covered our tracks. After Jesus settled down from his wild ride, he slept soundly. Joseph told me to sleep, and he would keep watch. I tried, but I was past the point of exhaustion. It was cold in the cave, but my skin twitched and burned, and each time I closed my eyes, I was falling from the donkey, and Jesus was falling from my arms. I saw the morning light before I slept.

All the next day, we stayed inside the cave, and I became more and more uneasy. It was not like the stable cave in Bethlehem where the openings were large, and we could walk in and out. As the day passed slowly by, this one closed in on me. I watched the sand blow in and imagined it piling higher and higher until the opening was closed, and we were sealed inside where we would die and be buried under the sand forever. I knew that the place I feared was our safety and that we had to stay there, but it set me even more on edge, and I could not rest. I whispered my prayers over and over.

Sunlight streamed down the opening and allowed us to find our food and care for Jesus, but we moved little and stayed as quiet as we could. Toward evening, Joseph began to repack our supplies, and I noticed that he limped. I examined his foot and found a break across the bridge. I thought that we should stay hidden for a few days, but he insisted that we had to go on, so I tore strips from my robe and wrapped his foot as well as I could.

We set out at darkness following some long forgotten route. Joining a caravan would have made us easy tracking for Herod's soldiers, so we traveled alone and took our chances with the thieves and cut-throats. The Lord guided our way.

As we walked, Joseph told me that we had been hiding in the Cave of Machpela, the burial cave of the patriarchs that held the ceno-taphs, the tombs honoring our ancestors Abraham and Sarah, Isaac and Rebekah, and Jacob and Leah. So perhaps Jesus was the young-est child to ever visit the bones of his ancestors. I don't know if that was really true, or if it was just a story that Joseph told me to pass the miles and give me courage.

After we left the cave, we traveled about forty miles west to the great Philistine city of Gaza near the Great Sea and the place where Sampson was overcome by Delilah, and according to Joseph, one of the very centers of Hellenistic culture.

We traveled parallel to the Mediterranean Sea for part of a day, and then we came to the Wadi Gaza.[2] Gulls, herons, tern, pelicans, and even a Great Cormorant filled the place. Though the birds were beautiful, they squawked and scolded us until I wanted to scream with them. I was sure they would give us away, but we made it through without meeting up with anyone. We bought supplies in a small village and continued south over the plain of Philistia to the town of Rafia which was built on a very ancient battleground.

Finally, we crossed into the Northern part of the Negev Desert, the most desolate part of our trip. Brown and rocky, it looked as if some-one had taken a great knife and cut away all the surface of the land, and then the sun had come and beaten away every drop of moisture. The Wadi Al-'Arish ran across the Negev, but unlike other wadis, this one was filled only when floodwaters came from the Sinai. When we crossed, it was bone dry. There was not a single bloom or blade of grass. And where there used to be mud, the dirt curled like tiles baked into squares by the sun.

That night, Joseph and I sat talking in our camp. Jesus was asleep in a sling that I wore inside my outer robe. It kept him warm and off the ground and away from the snakes. It also allowed my hands to be free. Suddenly, the donkey raised her ears and snorted, and two men stood before us. We had not seen or heard them, and I had no idea where they came from. One had a patch over his eye, and neither looked like he had had a bath in a long time. Joseph stood and welcomed them as though they were invited guests and motioned for me to offer food.

I got some bread and cheese, keeping my back to the men because I did not want them to see Jesus or to see how hard my hands were shaking. When I gave the food to Joseph, he pressed his hand around mine, and I knew that he was telling me to be calm. He offered the food to the men and then sat and ate with them. I knew they were waiting to make their move. I kept my head down, crying and praying but not making a sound.

Joseph rose, saying that he would tend to the donkey. The men ordered him to sit back down and said they would like to see our treasure. Joseph told them that we had none. Then they dropped all pretense of being friendly, accused him of lying, and insisted that for us to be traveling alone, he must have stolen something. They demanded that he show them what he was hiding, or they would find it themselves. The one with the patch stood over Joseph.

Joseph said again that he had no money and asked the men to listen to his story before they decided. The men argued with each other but finally agreed. Then Joseph told them that God had sent him a dream to flee and protect our son, and we were obeying.

They had not noticed Jesus and ordered me to show the child. When I pulled the robe away from Jesus' face, the night air woke him and he cried a little. The man with the patch called us fools for traveling alone with a child. The other one laughed, drew his knife, and stepped toward Joseph. The man with the patch drew his knife as well and shouted something that I did not understand. The first man dropped his hand to his side, and the two of them walked away into the night. To this day, I do not know why they let us live.

Joseph said that we would join a caravan the next day. We would keep our silence, and no one would recognize us. When morning came, we made our way to another village and bought a few more supplies, but when Joseph inquired about a caravan, we found that there would not be one passing through for three weeks. He decided that was too long to wait, and we set out alone again.

Sometime that day, Joseph stumbled and fell, and I saw that his foot was swollen to twice its size. I thought that we should make our way into the next town and find someone to treat him, or at least rest, but he said that it was the town of Rhinocolura, and we would not go there. He told me that legend claimed that long ago, criminals were sent there to be punished. And their punishment was always the same. Their noses were cut from their faces so that they were but skeletons walking about, and there they stayed for the rest of their lives for no one wanted to see the living death, and no other town would have them. And if that were true, the town could never be cleansed, and we would not take our babe to such an awful place. So, once again, we went on.

Joseph's foot slowed us down, and it took us many extra days of battling the heat, the cold, and the sand to reach Egypt.[3] In the day, the sun rose high in the sky growing hotter and hotter until it had baked the life from us. It parched our tongues and burned our faces. Our lips swelled until we could not speak. But the nights were so cold that we longed for its return. We did not dare risk a fire, so we tried to force the donkey to lie with us for warmth. We kept Jesus between us and shivered together until morning.

Though the heat and the cold were miserable, the sand was the worst. It settled in thick layers on our clothing and shredded the weakened fabric with its sharpness so that I could tear my garment with a light pull of my hand. It bit into our skin and scraped away the flesh until we were covered with raw painful abrasions. It came into our noses and mouths so that we swallowed it and choked for air. I kept wet cloths over Jesus' face to keep him from breathing in the sand. When we ran out of water, Joseph made a tent for him using his own head cover because it was more tightly woven than anything else that we had.

Yet for all of the torment that the sand caused us on our journey, our fortune was good. We met no more outlaws, and we did not experience the storm of the sand. Over the next few years, we would meet the storm many times and come to know its fury. A wall of sand would rise so high into the air that you could not see above it, and it would come so fast that unless you were near shelter, you could not outrun it. Even if you could, the sky would turn to the darkest black, and you could not see your way. It would sweep across the desert and destroy everything in its path. When it had passed, people and animals lay dead, buried in the sand. The inside of the house looked no different than the outside. Everything was brown, and the sand was so deep on the floor that it covered our feet. If we had been caught in such a fierce sandstorm, we would not have survived our flight.

Finally, we arrived at the city of Pelusium.[4] "The Lord has delivered us from our enemy!" Joseph proclaimed. "We are safe." Then he bent and kissed Jesus on his dust covered cheek.

We stood there, dirty and exhausted. Foreigners, come back to a land where our people had fled from the Pharaoh and slavery, to a land where we did not even know the language, but we smiled at each other like we had reached the new promised land. Joseph told me that we would not return to Palestine until Herod was dead or had been deposed, so I prepared to spend my life in Egypt. I had no idea how we would ever survive.

I could never ever have imagined such a place as Pelusium. Even Jerusalem at the Passover did not compare. The smell of fish from the fish tanks was overwhelming, and masses of people, many of them with dark, dark skin, and all with strange haircuts and dress, were winding their way through the streets in some sort of parade or religious festival.

I leaned against a pillar to rest and avoid getting trampled, and when I looked up, a giant stone falcon was staring down at me. I cried out before I could help myself and looked away as quickly as I could. Then, I stood staring at the ground until I was sure that the Lord would not strike me down for looking upon a false idol. I could hear how rapid my breathing was and told myself to stop being foolish. I held Jesus over my arm, though, so that he would not look upon the idol. I realized, then, that we were standing at a temple, and I looked down the street for a place we might go and make our plans. But there I saw another temple and more false idols, all of an enormous man. Another turn of my head, and another temple. It was the worst of them all, decorated with idols of a woman with a cat head and bare saggy breasts. I would later come to find out that the falcon was Horace, the Egyptian god of the sky and son of the goddess Isis. The man idol was the Greek god Zeus, and the cat woman was Bast.

More gods than tongues," Joseph muttered.

I had heard that the Romans and the Greeks had many gods as well, but since our people had set their lives against idolatry in Jerusalem, we never saw them.

"Where can I look?" I hissed.

Joseph pointed to a group of travelers that looked like they might have been from Palestine and said that I should concentrate on them. He was pointing to the travelers, but he was looking at the exotic Egyptian women who painted their eyes like the feathers of a peacock and lined them with kohl and wore arm jewelry that jangled when they walked and dressed in clothing that I had never seen. Clothing that did not even cover their breasts. I thought that I was defiling myself, so I tried not to look. I tried not to, but I did. I looked again and again. So did Joseph.

6

By the Nile

I thought that we might settle near the great port of Alexandria. The city was more Greek than Egyptian, and there were many Jews living there, so we would have been among our own. But Joseph said if Herod was still looking for us, that would be the first place he would send his men.

Herod had many connections there because he and Cleopatra, in her reign as the Egyptian Queen, had conducted business together. Cleopatra wanted the mud from the Dead Sea, and though Herod used this mud, or asphalt as Joseph told me it was called, for shipbuilding, he was afraid of Cleopatra's armies and allowed her to gather all she wanted.

Cleopatra used the mud for sealing mummies and making her beauty products. When we were in Egypt, I learned that both men and women packed their faces with mud to keep away age's wrinkles. They also painted their eyes, rouged their cheeks, stained their nails, oiled their skin with cedar oil to keep the sun from turning it to leather, and donned wigs of sheep hair after they had shaved their own heads to rid themselves of lice. I thought they must have devoted the entire day to their vanities. I don't know how they ever accomplished one other thing.

So, because of Herod, Joseph did not allow us to settle in Alexandria. We did not really settle anywhere but moved from town to town along the Nile River so that Joseph could find work, and so there was less chance of anyone getting to know us well enough to realize who we were. Whenever Joseph thought that we were in danger, we rose in the night and moved to a new town. The route along the Nile had many houses that had been built for pyramid workers. They were long abandoned and just waiting for someone to claim them. We lived in twelve of them, and no one ever questioned us.

Our first days in Egypt were the hardest, and we got by on our few left over provisions. I mixed some meal and salt and a spoon of honey with water and made little cakes that we baked on the fire coals. They were dry and tasteless, almost impossible to swallow. The water was brackish and of little use to force them down. I wanted to throw my food back into the fire, but Joseph's watchful eye and Jesus' urgent suckling at my drying breasts made me force myself to eat them.

Joseph had a few shekels that he had brought from Bethlehem, but he didn't want to use them and call attention to us as foreigners.

After a few days, he found work. When he was gone, Jesus and I stayed in hiding. I barely dared to breathe until Joseph returned that first night, but no one even came near. The next day he left us again and went to the market. He bought some figs, vegetables, more meal, a small piece of meat, and a measure of oil.

With the oil, I baked bread that was good to taste and easy to swallow, and we roasted the meat and ate from it until the bone was so polished that it did not interest even an insect. Then I placed the bone upon a rock and with another rock pounded it again and again so that it would give up its marrow and flavor the brackish water. I cooked it for some hours over the fire and added some onions and turnips and peas, and we had a fine soup.

We had enough food so that we did not starve, but I longed for leavened bread. I would dream of fresh loaves, dream that I was kneading the dough just as my mother had taught me, shaping them, and putting them to bake. But we lived on the bread of the Passover because I had left my leavening in Bethlehem. I imagined it fermenting and bubbling over the whole stable and the goat lapping at it until he could not walk straight.

Starter was not the kind of thing sold at the market. Everyone kept some in their own home and would have no need to buy more. It was free for the asking, but I didn't dare to borrow from a neighbor and bring suspicion on us.

After some weeks, when he had found more work and received a wage, Joseph went into the market and came home with a goat. I hugged him and hugged him and thanked him again and again. He laughed, held me to him, and told me that we would do well together and that someday we would be back in Nazareth and have ten goats and some hens for eggs as well. When I grew weepy at his words, he shook his head and said that he had not thought that a woman who risked her life and braved the desert would fall apart over a goat. I laughed and milked the goat immediately. She kicked me hard enough to give me a fine bruise, but I didn't mind. I took some of the milk for us to drink and covered the rest with a cloth to keep out the sand and set it to ripen.

The next day I measured some grain, which I had ground and reground, into the milk and then added the last of our honey. I mixed all of these things together and set the uncovered bowl outside in a bit of shade so the hot sun would not destroy it. It was my hope that the mix would capture the wild yeast in the air and give us a starter for bread, but I was not sure that this would work the same in Egypt as it did in Nazareth.

During the day, I left my treasure outside and guarded it carefully so that no animal would take it. At night, I brought it inside and covered it, and Joseph slept with it near his side of the blanket to protect it. After three days, it was bubbly and pungent and ready to use. I had captured the yeast. That evening, we ate leavened bread. We laughed as we tore the bread from the loaf.

I have kept the starter since, and it still tastes of Egyptian sand. It is our custom to rid our homes of all leavening before each Passover. Many households scatter it to the winds or dissolve it in water, but others, who like my parents were always on the watch to save every shekel, remove the leavening from the inside of the house but store a small bit of it out of doors, either by burying it in a cool place or tending to it daily. I grew into my mother in many ways. The way I handled the leavening was one of them.

My whole life, I had lived among my own people, but in Egypt I was a foreigner. I kept to myself except to go with the neighborhood women to the river to wash clothes. That was a chore too dangerous to do alone. I knew the women were heathens, but they were kind to me. I liked to listen to their stories, and I tried hard to learn the Egyptian language so I could understand them. One woman, Walidah, knew some Aramaic, and she did her best to translate for me.

The women loved most to talk of Cleopatra, their Mesopotamian queen, and to gossip about her glorious life. She had been dead for nearly thirty years before we came to Egypt, but she lived on through her people.[1]

Cleopatra was a name that I remembered. When I was a young girl, I heard my mother and father talking about a strange woman queen, and I hid around the corner to listen. My father saw me and sent me away, but when he left the house, I started in on my mother, and she was more than willing to tell me the story of Cleopatra. She described how Cleopatra had come riding into Jerusalem with a parade of servants that stretched from one end of the city to the other and a golden headpiece so studded with jewels that it must have cost the Temple treasury. She had come to visit Herod the Great at his palace.

Once my mother started to talk, she didn't stop.

"Can you believe it—a woman ruler? And Herod. How can he even call himself a Hebrew after what he did? He claims Hebrew blood and still . . ."

"What? What did he do?" I clamored, afraid that she was going to stop talking.

She looked around the room, maybe checking for my father, and the words burst out. "Hebrew blood and, still, he roasted seven boars for a banquet he held for the Egyptian whore who walked around half naked."

I had no idea what a whore was, but I was shocked about the boars.

"Boars?" I wondered how he would ever dare?[2]

"Well, that's what your father said anyway." She pressed her lips together and nodded her head up and down. Then she said that I must never breathe a word of what she told me, picked her pounding stone up from the table, and set to work pounding the grain like famine was coming tomorrow.

So when the women at the river mentioned the name Cleopatra, I remembered her and could not wait to hear more. Because my Egyptian was poor, it took me awhile to understand the story, but this is the way it went.

Egypt was not always under the hand of Rome. For many years, it was ruled by the Ptolemy family, whose brothers and sisters often married, passing down the reign to the next generation. All stories that the women told were interrupted by oaths and curses against Rome and Caesar Augustus. I was shocked by their language, but I had grown up waiting for freedom from the Romans, so I liked the way they spoke out. Most people in Palestine were not so brave, but in Egypt, Caesar was a sea away, and they cursed him freely.

I think there were as many Cleopatras as Caesars, but the women only cared about the one my mother had told me about. When this Cleopatra was in her nineteenth year, she married her brother. He became the Pharaoh, and she became the Queen.

All of this marrying of brothers and sisters seemed outrageous to me, and I thought that I might not have understood, so I asked Joseph. He told me that was the way of things and reminded me that Sarah and Abraham were brother and sister as well, though like many of the Ptolemies, they did not have the same mother.

The women told me that when Cleopatra ruled, it was a wonderful time for Egypt. She treated all of the people, even the women, very well, and unlike most of their rulers, she could even speak Egyptian. The women also told me that Cleopatra drowned her brother because he wanted to get rid of her. She killed her sister, though I don't know why, and became Caesar's lover and had a child with him. When Caesar wouldn't marry her, she helped to assassinate him. The women always argued about whether or not this was true. After Caesar died, she took Marc Antony as her lover; they had twins, and everyone was happy but not for very long.[3]

Marc Antony already ruled part of Rome, but he wanted all of it. Some traitor must have told Octavian Caesar because he attacked Cleopatra's navy and defeated her. Marc Antony thought that Cleopatra had killed herself, so he stabbed himself. But he didn't die right away, and Cleopatra brought him home to die in her arms.[4] By then she was trapped, and she knew that Octavian would parade her through the streets of Rome in chains, so she ordered her servants to smuggle an asp into her chambers. She laid the snake on her breast, it bit her, the poison went straight to her heart, and she died and became eternally immortal. Or, at least that's the story the women told me.

After Antony and Cleopatra died, Octavian killed his little brother Caesarian and changed his own name to Caesar Augustus, which is what we called him in Palestine.

The stories filled my endless days in Egypt, and I chattered to Joseph about them. I thought that if Antony and Cleopatra were the rulers of Palestine, even if she would have been an old woman by then, she would have never let Herod act the way he did. Jesus would have been safe. Joseph scolded me and reminded me that things were not always as they seemed and that most of what the women said was probably not even true.

"Like what?" I wanted to know.

"Like the snake bite," he said. Augustus would have never let her servants bring a snake into her."

"How did she die then?" I asked.

"By her own hand. She had a poison pin in her headdress."

I did not believe it.

"Did you know that her two maidservants died at the same time?" he asked.

"Yes, Walidah told me."

"How do you think they died?"

"How?"

"The legend says snakebites as well, and I don't believe that any snake could manage three fatal bites."

"Maybe there was more than one snake in the basket. Asps are small."

Walidah had told me that it wouldn't be any problem at all for the snake to bite three people in a row, but if it didn't feel like biting, it could just spit at them from this far, and she spread her arms wide, and they would all be dead. Thirty or forty of them if it wanted. I had not really believed her, so I didn't tell that to Joseph.

Joseph grunted and turned away. He didn't care too much one way or the other about the snake, but when I told him that the women said that Antony and Cleopatra would be one of the great love stories of all times, he lost his patience with me.

"They took their own lives," he said sternly. "That is never the answer to any problem. The Lord forbids it. He has made man, and he will take man. If they had worshipped God and not their idols and warring, they might still be alive. Then it could be a great love story."

I was set back by his harsh words to me as if I did not know that it was wrong for a person to take his own life. And I knew that he had never criticized other leaders who went to war. In fact, I had heard him speak with Labon about whether or not Jesus would need to go to battle. Joseph saw that I was near tears and softened.

"It is all right," he said. "It is all right. But taking your own life is never the answer. Never! You cannot know the plans that the Lord has for you."

Another day, I told him that Walidah said Cleopatra was a great leader, but the men did not like her. They thought she was shameful because she had had many men. And they thought that was different than when a man had many women.

That's when he told me he was tired of hearing about Cleopatra. He called for Jesus, and the two of them went out to tend to the chores.

I could not believe that we spoke like we did, but life was different in Egypt. Women had many rights. They could own property, run a business, or even refuse the man their father had arranged for them to marry. It would never be that way for Jewish women, but we were in Egypt, and we were alone. I was allowed a place that no wife would have had in Nazareth. After that, though, I kept quiet about Cleopatra. I didn't want Joseph to forbid me to go to the river.

The children loved wash day as much as the women did, especially while the clothes were drying and they were allowed to run and play together. During the washing, though, they were required to sit quietly and help watch for the Lizards of the Nile, the large crocodiles that swam hungrily along the banks of the river.

The first time I saw one, I thought it was a log. It was rough and black, floating with only a small part of it showing above the water. I was bending to wash a robe, and when I stood, it had moved. I saw the eyes and knew it was not a log. I did not hear a sound as the great lizard came toward me.

Walidah whispered to me to back out of the water, but I was so frightened, I could not move. She clucked a soft warning to the others and took my arm and moved backwards with me. The other women had moved out of the water without a sound. I went step by step with Walidah until I backed into the bank. My eyes were locked with the crocodile, and I as I tried to step up, my foot slipped, and I sat hard on the bank and splashed into the river. I slid down under the water, and before I could get myself up, I felt something clamp on to my head and shoulders. I screamed and thrashed to fight the crocodile,

not realizing it was the hands of the women as they snatched me
out of the water and onto the bank. I scrambled to my feet and ran
for Jesus. We stood and watched as the creature opened its jaws and
showed its many rows of teeth. Then it snapped its mouth shut and
turned and swam silently away.

The women had warned me that the crocodile could slide through
the water so quietly that even the goddess Isis couldn't hear it. It was
an ambush hunter that might go for days without eating. It would lie
still, barely moving until its prey—fish, or land animals, or humans—
was very close. Then it would lunge for the attack, but by then, there
was no escape.

Only the magic bird, the Egyptian Plover, was safe. I saw it once.
A crocodile came gliding through the water. One of the children saw
it long before any of the women could make it out. He called out a
warning, and all of us ran up onto the banks. The children gathered
round, and their mothers scolded them to keep back. We watched
the crocodile come near and glide straight toward our bank. It pulled
itself onto the shore enough so that its back was in the sun and lay
there warming itself. And then a plover flew down and sat right on its
back. The bird rested awhile, and when the lizard opened its mouth,
the bird hopped inside. I thought that was the end of the plover, but
he hopped around inside that hideous mouth pecking and cleaning
like he was sitting on a flower bush. The lizard never moved until the
bird flew away. Then it slid back into the river and disappeared. We
finished our wash and talked about the powers of the little bird that
could stay the jaws of the Lizard of the Nile.

After we had lived in Egypt for more than one year, and I had
washed clothes in the river many times, Walidah and I were standing
next to a large rock where we liked to lay our clothes. The water was
up to our knees, and we were chattering away, my Egyptian broken
and poor, hers very loud in hopes that I would understand her better.
I was looking down, inspecting a tear in the fabric of Jesus' favorite
tunic when I heard her scream.

The Fifth Day of Av

My family has come for the Sabbath, not James or Simon, but the others. Preparing the food for them kept me busy, and it is good to have the house full. It is especially good to have the children, to hold them, their soft little bodies bending and molding around my grief, soothing it like a cool breeze on hot skin.

Now the children are asleep and Joses reads the scriptures. I smile at everyone, and they smile back, but the pain crackles in the air between us like lightening in a storm. We do not shed tears; they are burned off. It is hot behind my eyes, and the pain radiates. And there is pain in my arms so that they seem stuck to my sides. Finally, the sharpness of it subsides. It becomes mellow and blows about the house like the desert wind, the sand cutting and stinging my face.

When the Sabbath ends, my sons and daughters each urge me to come to stay with them, but I do not want to leave this place where I lived with Joseph, where we raised our children. It is my home, the place of Jesus' life on earth.

So, I watch them leave, and my face grows hot. I put my hand to my cheek, and it is hard as stone. I do not clean the house. I just go to bed. I think that I will throw up, but I close my eyes and do not move.

In the darkness, I lie awake and think how it could have been different. What I could have done. I do not want to fall asleep because something in my sleep must make me forget. Each morning I wake up and think that I have had a horrible dream that Jesus has died, and I am so relieved that it is a dream. Then I remember, and the sword pierces my soul one more time.

I see that the sky is pink in the desert, and I feel my eyes closing. And then the heat wakes me, so I know that it is already midday, and this time I already know.

Outside of my window, I hear the cry of a small animal. On and on it goes with its pitiful keening until I get up to go out and look for it, to see if I can help it. When I arise from my pallet, the keening stops. I go outside and look around, but there is nothing there.

I lie down again, despondent. Sometimes I have lain for days. I know that I should not, and I pray for strength. But there is only bleakness and darkness, so I lie there trying not to think, praying for a miracle. Finally, I have to relieve myself, and I am forced to rise from my bed. As I walk out the door, I laugh to myself, just a little. The miracle I have prayed for is the way the Lord created me. Because I cannot ignore my lowliest of needs, I must rise from my bed and live another day.

7

Danger

Walidah's scream and her body rose into the air as one. The power-ful tail of a crocodile thrashed so that its body twisted and danced in the water. It held Walidah in its jaws like a piece of fruit. Its tail thrashed some more, and Walidah disappeared under the water. One more time, I saw its tail rise and then crash on the water with a sound like falling boulders. Then it was gone. The air was quiet and the water rippled out in black circles from the place where its tail had pounded it. That is all that I remember of that day. Not one thing more.

From that day on, I did not step into the water. Joseph made a bucket for me with a long rope that I could lower into the river and pull water from it without ever stepping off the bank. It was easy to tell the difference between a log and a crocodile on the land.

We had been in Egypt some months before we found out what had happened in Bethlehem on the night we fled. Joseph came home with the news that on that night, Herod had ordered the death of every male child in Bethlehem and the surrounding countryside who was under two years. His soldiers rampaged the city and bathed it in the blood of the innocent children.

I was devastated. I grieved for the parents and children, and I grieved over the part that we had in it. I walked around holding Jesus until he couldn't breathe and weeping until he was covered with my tears.

Finally, Joseph took Jesus away from me and ordered me to stop. He reminded me again and again that Herod was a madman and there was no way anyone could ever know what he was going to do, so it could not be prevented. 'Herod's evil,' he called it. Not a day passed when he did not have someone put to death. "It is best," Joseph said, "if Herod does not know you are alive. His friends and his enemies live in equal danger."

Hebrews gain respect only by living in a way that is pleasing to the Lord, but Herod cared nothing for that. The Pharisees denounced him because he had no regard for what was right. He claimed to be a Jew, but he loved money and power above all else and pledged his loyalties to the Romans who appointed him to govern Judea. He did not live or rule as one who feared God. Joseph said that was why he did not give a thought to murdering dozens of innocent children.

I tried to stop thinking about Herod, but it was impossible. It was like when I was a little girl, and I would pick and pick at a sore so that it would not heal.

"Do you think that Herod is the most evil man on the earth?" I asked one day.

Joseph had a cloth in his hand and was rubbing down the donkey. He did not look at me, but I heard his sigh when I started in.

"Did you know nothing of men before?" he asked.

"Nothing like this," I said.

"It is the way of many."

"Evil?"

"The earth is full of evil men." He picked up the donkey's foot and examined it. The donkey kicked, and Joseph leaned his head into her side to set her off balance and keep her still. "We have been given the Ten Commandments, but most men do not heed them."

"Herod breaks every one," I said.

"Yes."

"And the Romans?"

"God did not give the law to the Romans," Joseph said.

"Does that excuse them?"

"No, it does not. They have their own laws, but even if they did not, all men should have within them the knowledge of right and wrong."

"But the Romans do not?"

"I don't know. I once saw a soldier split a man's skull in two for the pleasure of it. But it is not only the Romans. I have seen a man kill his brother for a plot of land and a thief bludgeon a stranger to death for a shekel. Once, when I was working with my father, we watched a man sell his wife for a slave and take the money to buy himself a whore. Another time, I came upon a man who had just beheaded his own wife because she did not cook his food the way he liked it."

"I do not understand how men can commit these abominations against the Lord," I said as I began to imagine, in great detail, each of the stories that Joseph told. I tried hard to block them from my mind before they could take hold.

"These things have gone on since before the time of Abraham. You have heard the stories. The innocent families thrown to the lions by King Darius because their fathers plotted against Daniel? The many innocent people slain by Jacob's sons to avenge the rape of their sister Dinah?" Joseph pressed his point to me.

"They were so long ago." I protested, but I wondered why I had never realized the horror of them.

Joseph sighed again. "That does not make them right, but it is the way of things. Those in power believe it is better to destroy any number of innocent lives than to let their own house be weakened."

He finished with the donkey and gave her a pat on her shoulder. She nosed his robe looking for a treat.

"But that is not your way," I said.

"No, I despise the destruction of what the Lord has created. A man howls over a broken wagon axle but does not shed a tear over a child cast on the heap of manure to await death or slavery? A rusted piece of metal worth more than the sons and daughters of Israel? We will be the ruin of ourselves." He laughed, but it was not a happy laugh, and turned and looked out across the dessert. "And I stand by while it happens."

"I have never heard you speak this way before," I said.

"No. We have enough worries," he said. "Besides, who would listen to a simple carpenter?"

I took his hand in both of mine.

"Sometimes, though, I dream that the Lord will place a sword in my hand, and I would be strong enough to bring those men to their knees and keep them there until they understand that their disregard for a human life is a danger greater than any barbarian attack."

"No! They would only murder you too."

We stood for a moment, and then he pulled me to him and kissed the top of my head. "Now" he said, "I will tell you again that you must put Herod from your mind. We have work to do."

But I could not, and many nights I lay awake, certain that I heard Herod's soldiers coming after Jesus.

Great caravans passed along the Nile on their way to Alexandria, or Petra, or north to Antioch. Some traveled with hundreds of camels, donkeys, and mules loaded with wares. Camels were tied rear to front to make a chain so long that you could not see from one end to the other of the line. And next to the animals, the rich men rode their horses and shouted orders.

Joseph often traveled to the caravan camps to find work. He made repairs for the merchants or sold some of the beautiful wooden chests that he had crafted. Sometimes he was paid in coin, and other times he traded his labors for things we needed or even some small luxuries. Luxuries that we would never have had back in Nazareth, but Joseph was careful to have us blend in and look the same as other households.

One day, he brought home an Egyptian kalasiris. I stood and stared at him. A kalasiris is nothing more than a piece of linen made into a sheath barely large enough to wrap around the woman who wears it. It is held up by two shoulder straps, sometimes only one. Some women covered their breasts with the straps. Others did not cover them at all. I was long over the shock of seeing the bare breasts, but still, I could not imagine myself wearing any sort of kalarisis.

Actually, the dress Joseph brought me was quite modest, made to be worn high with a cape to cover my shoulders. I couldn't believe that he would ever allow me to wear it, but he said that it would give me some relief from the heat. So when the days became too unbearable, I put it on. But I wore it only at home. I would never have chanced having one of our own people see me in it.

I desperately wanted to go with Joseph to the caravans, but he said that it would be too dangerous, and someone might recognize me. Then, one day he came home with a nomad's garb and told me to put it on. The headpiece was covered with ornamentation, and I thought that it might be a sin for me to wear it, but Joseph said that it was not against our laws. It would be a disguise, and if I wore it, I could accompany him to the market. I had it on before he was finished speaking.

I put on the black robe, black shawl, and black headpiece decorated with hundreds of small metal discs that were meant to attract the attention of the evil eye and keep it from looking upon a woman's face. The headpiece covered all but my eyes, and at first Jesus was frightened when he saw me. Once he realized it was me, he was fascinated with the shiny metal discs and the way they danced and chimed whenever I moved my head.

On the day of the next caravan passing, I dressed in the nomad garment and went with Joseph. He led the donkey, and I walked behind with Jesus on my hip, not looking at anyone as was the custom of the tribe. I hurried to keep up, jangling with every step.

The caravan was a tumult of sound and color. Animals bellowed, bells clanged, and merchants shouted and chattered to each other in strange languages as they displayed fascinating wares from faraway lands. As we walked into the midst of the caravan, I was excited and frightened at the same time. I wanted to hold onto Joseph, but I did not think a nomad woman would touch a man, even her husband, in public.

Jesus laughed and leaned to reach for some bright feathers. I kissed his black curls, and the top of his hot little head smelled of sunshine and little boy mixed together. He straightened then and put one hand on each side of my cheeks so that he could turn my face toward him and have my full attention. "You love me," he said.

"Yes, yes, I do," I said, and I wanted to skip for the joy of being his mother, but Jesus had turned his attention back to the wares, and I had to concentrate on holding on to him. He turned and swiveled, looking at everything and reaching for things he wanted to explore until I thought that I would drop him. Finally, I slipped my free hand around his plump soft little leg and gripped hard enough that I knew that I could hold him if he pitched forward to reach for a bamboo ball or some other thing that caught his eye.

"Owie," he said and pushed at my hand. I looked and saw that I had been holding him tightly enough to leave a set of white finger marks on his leg. I loosened my grip, but only a little. When he grew too heavy, I set him on the ground and held his hand as firmly as I could. Even in the dry dessert it was sweaty, and I was worried he would slip away.

A merchant came past leading a camel that spit at us and curled his lip back, working it up and down over his teeth. Suddenly, the beast lunged toward us and tried to take a bite out of Jesus' shoulder. I snatched Jesus away from the camel and picked him up again.

"It bit me. It bit me," he hiccupped.

I wiped the foamy camel slobber from his robe and face and assured him that he would be all right.

Joseph made some trades that day, and as we were walking between vendors just out of sight of most of the crowd, I saw a man buy a measure of salt. He took out a leather bag from his robes and drew a coin for the merchant. The merchant told him that was not enough. They argued. The man put the salt down and started to walk away.

The merchant stopped him and accused him of cheating. The man denied it.

Then, right as we stood there, the merchant drew his dagger and drove it into the man just below his breastbone. The man grabbed at the knife, lurched forward, and fell into the merchant's arms, his eyes wide open and staring at nothing. He didn't make a sound. They stood as in an embrace while the merchant held the knife in his victim. Blood turned their robes red and streamed onto the ground. Suddenly, another man grabbed the bag of coins and dashed away.

"Stop! Stop! He hurt him. He hurt him." Jesus shouted in Aramaic.

"Hush!" Joseph ordered him.

"He hurt him, he hurt him," Jesus cried. I could not quiet him.

The merchant let the victim fall to the ground and slid his dagger back into the folds of his robe. He signaled for his friends, and we turned and hurried away. The men were right behind us.

"Go on," Joseph ordered. "I will try to speak to them."

"No. They will kill you," I hissed.

"Go!" he snapped.

I saw an opening in the crowd and slipped into it. I walked, looking for a place to hide, but I didn't get ten paces before two men stepped out in front of us and blocked our way. I turned to run, but we were surrounded. One of the men grabbed me, and another wrenched at Jesus. I tried to hang on to him, but I could not. The man wrapped his arm around me so that I was helpless and clamped his other hand over my mouth so that I couldn't scream. He tightened his hand on my face, and I could not breathe. I was suffocating and tried to jerk my head away. The last thing I remember thinking was that I hoped the urine that I smelled on his dirty hand was from an animal.

I woke up on the ground inside of a tent, and Jesus was beside me patting me and crying. I whispered to him to stop, and we huddled together and waited. I saw a huge man with a beard down to his waist sitting near us. I raised my eyes over his enormous belly and saw his gold earrings dangling to his shoulders. He was staring right at us. He didn't even blink. I looked away as quickly as I could, but I knew I was defiled by looking into his eyes. Another man, tall and thin, stood by the opening of the tent. There was no way we could get past them.

Every possible horror flashed through my mind, death, slavery, rape, that my son would be taken from me, that Joseph had been murdered. I forced myself to stay calm and show no emotion. I knew if I made them angry they would kill me without a thought.

A man wearing a turban and a red robe entered the tent. I thought he was the killer, but I was not sure. When Jesus whimpered and huddled closer to me, I knew that it was him, but he had changed his robe. He came close and started screaming at me in Egyptian. I could tell that he was asking questions, but he talked so fast that I couldn't understand what he wanted. He screamed and screamed. We cowered on the ground.

Still another man came into the tent. The killer kept pointing at us and screaming, and the newcomer tried to calm him. Something in his voice caught me. The screamer went on a while more and then snapped an order to the new man who then, speaking in Aramaic, ordered me to stand.

"Thank you, thank you." I scrambled to my feet. "Can you help us? We have no business with this man." I motioned to the Egyptian.

"You are far from home," the new man said and walked toward me.

When he spoke in my own language, I was even more certain that I knew him, and when he got closer I saw his nose sticking out of his headdress. He smiled and made little tsking sounds with his tongue and shook his head from side to side.

I had not seen him for some years, but there was no mistaking him. He clapped his hands, and I saw the same rings on the same scrawny, long nailed fingers. At his command, the thin man who had been guarding the entrance pushed me closer so that I stood face to face with Levi the tentmaker. Jesus hid in my robes.

8

Levi the Tentmaker

"What business do you have with Kafele?" Levi demanded.

"I don't know Kafele," I answered.

"Do not lie," he snapped. "Imenand wants to know."

"Who is Kafele?" I asked.

"The thief," he said. He made a gesture with his thumb as if he were knifing himself and widened his eyes and thrust his head forward.

"We do not know him," I repeated. "We were passing when we saw the fight."

I saw the two guards slip from the tent, but I didn't turn my head from Levi.

"Why did the boy cry out then? You are his accomplice."

"No. I have told you. We do not even know the man."

"Do you think me stupid? He is a nomad." Levi leaned close and glared at me. When I just stood there, he smiled and took a handful of my robe and twisted until it pulled me toward him. "You fool no one," he sneered. "Did he give you this?"

"No. He did not. We do not know the man," I insisted again.

"You are his contact." He kept twisting at my robe until I could hardly keep from falling into him.

"We do not know the man," I repeated one more time.

"Your Aramaic gave you away. Do you think that I would believe a child would care about a thief that he did not even know?"

"It is so."

"Ha!" Levi said and jerked his head back.

"He saw a man being hurt. He felt compassion for him. That is all."

"Do not argue with me," he screamed. Then he lowered his voice and leaned even closer. "No one feels compassion for one he does not know."

"He is a child. He does not like to see someone harmed."

"If he does not mind his own business, he will not become a man. Now, I will ask again. How do you know this man? And tell me the truth. Imenand will find out."

"I do not know him. It is the truth."

"You are lying."

"No. I am not."

"Teach the boy to mind his own business then."

"Yes, yes. I will do that."

Levi turned, then, and spoke to the Egyptian. They argued back and forth for awhile, and before they were finished, the guards returned dragging the murdered man behind them.

"You do not know our friend Kafele?" Levi asked again pointing to the dead man.

"No. We have never seen the man before today."

"For you to enjoy," the merchant said to me, speaking slowly enough for me to understand.

One of the men drew his knife. It was very large and the sun coming through a space in the roof of the tent danced on the metal as he waved it in the air. Then he drove it into the dead man and slit him from belly to throat like he was gutting a ram.

I wanted to close my eyes, but I knew that Levi and Imenand were watching to see if I was lying, if I knew the man. So I did not close my eyes, and I did not look away. I hid Jesus' face in my robe, bit my tongue until I tasted blood, and acted like it was something that I saw every day.

The man cleaned the blood from his knife, carefully, like it was his treasure, and returned it to the sheath. Then he dug into the bowels of the dead man and squashed them through his hands, over and over, like he was working a bucket of grapes. After doing this for awhile, he shouted something that I did not understand. The others shouted back and clapped their hands together. The man rose and opened his bloody hand. I saw what I thought was part of the dead man, but it turned out to be three stones. He gave them to the Egyptian merchant who was called Imenand.

The guard wiped his hands on the dead man. There was still blood all the way up his sleeve. Imenand wiped the stones on his own robe and held them to the light to examine them. They were rubies, and he started laughing and rubbing them together in his bloody hands.

Then Imenand turned his attention back to Levi, and once again they argued. They kept looking at me and shouting, so I knew it was about me. Finally, Imenand pointed to the dead man, snapped some orders, and left the tent. Levi spoke in Egyptian to the two guards. They left, dragging the dead man behind. Jesus and I were alone with Levi.

"You are far from home," he said, giving me a leering smile and looking me over just as he had some years ago.

"Yes," I said. "Will you help me find my husband?"

He laughed at me. "You ask me for help?"

"You are Jewish."

"You are nothing to me."

"No, I am not," I agreed.

"It should not have been up to you," he said.

"It was my father's choice," I answered, making my voice as respectful as I could.

"Unheard of for a girl to dictate her family's future as you did."

I stayed quiet and kept my eyes down.

"Why are you here?" Levi demanded.

"Herod ordered the death of all the male . . . ," I began.

"I know what Herod did," Levi spit back. "I am not asking why you are in Egypt. I want to know why you are here? Why are you at the caravan? Do you not know the danger?"

"I am here with . . ."

"I despise you, you know?" he interrupted.

"Yes," I said. "I ask your forgiveness."

The memories came. I was only thirteen on the day this man now standing in front of me had come walking up the hill to my father's house. The day was hot, and I was tending the grape vines. When I saw him, I slipped into the shed to hide. "Myriam, Myriam," his voice came sharply across the dry air.

I pressed myself against the wall and stood very, very still. I didn't want to risk a sound, even a rustle of my clothing. He leaned his head into the open doorway and swiveled it from side to side, bobbing it back and forth like a bird. I wondered if he could make it go all the way around so that he could see directly behind him like a chicken could. His eyes were not adjusted to the dark so he could not make me out in the shadows, and he withdrew. I let out my breath but slowly, softly so that he would not hear.

Through a crack in the wall, I watched him prance to the stone bench. He sat and held his hands out in front of him and admired his rings, his many rings. His fingers were long, scrawny and boney with nails that grew long. He could have picked up tiny morsels of his food without ever having a bit of grease touch his flesh. He smiled and twisted his rings as he examined them. His fingers were so small that I thought the rings must have been made for a woman. He brought them close to his face to admire them, and I waited for him to peck at the pretty stones like the magpie pecks at pretty bits of things that catch its attention. He had not found me, but he sat there, bobbing his head and blinking his eyes, and looking confident that he would capture his prey.

"I will not, I will not, I will not!" I vowed to myself. I waited, and soon my father walked out from the house to join Levi. They rose, and the two walked away so that I couldn't hear their voices. I didn't have to hear them to know what they were talking about. Levi was a tentmaker. He was more than three times my age and older than my own father. He had an enormous beaked nose that grew from high round little cheeks, few teeth, and beady eyes that darted over me whenever I saw him. I knew he was offering for me, trying to make a marriage contract with my father.

I wanted to scream. But if I gave my hiding place away, my father would call me out, and I would have to stand in front of the old man while he surveyed me like a piece of flesh ready for his taking. He might even touch me. Imagining that made my skin crawl, and I was silent. Finally, Levi clasped my father on the shoulder as a sign of friendship and turned and walked down the hill. He wore a robe made of silken material like a woman might wear, and it slithered around his boney frame. I had heard that he was a gluttonous eater, but I didn't see how he could be. His round cheeks were the only flesh I could see on him. Other than that, he was skin stretched over bone. He looked smaller than me, and I thought that if I ended up with him, he would starve me to death. I slipped out of the shed and busied myself pulling the weeds from the grape vines.

My father walked back to the house, and my mother came out to join him. From where I knelt, I could hear their conversation.

"He wishes to take her for his wife then?" my mother asked.

"He does," my father said, pulling on his beard and looking down the hill where Levi had disappeared. "What do you think?" My father would make the decision, but he often asked her opinion.

"She is a child," my mother said.

"Older than you were."

"He is a pious man," she said nodding her head in approval.

"Hmm," my father said looking down the hill.

"Did you consent?" my mother asked.

The roar in my head was so loud that I was barely able to hear my father's reply.

"I agreed to think on the matter. I did not consent."

There was still hope. I stayed out of sight and made my way into the house. The next day my father set out early in the morning and did not return until late in the day. I didn't dare ask where he had gone, but I listened when he spoke to my mother. The tentmaker was to leave with a caravan for Egypt. He would be back in two seasons to hear my father's decision.

Over the next months, I became obedient onto every wish of my parents. I got myself out of bed early enough in the morning that I had their breakfast waiting for them when they opened their eyes. I tended the grape vines, went to the well for water, and did whatever I could to make them glad that I still lived in their house.

Then I met Joseph, and one day he helped me carry home a heavy jar of water and met my father. After that, he came by when he was able, often with the excuse to help my father with some chore. He was strong and quick, a cheerful worker, but my mother didn't like him there. She wasn't fooled by the reason for his visits. She didn't argue with my father, but when Joseph came, she pounded on the grain so hard that I thought she might break her stone.

My father loved to talk to Joseph. He questioned him about the law, his knowledge of the scriptures, the Romans, and many other things. He approved of Joseph's strong back and quick mind, and I began to dream that my father would turn away the tentmaker and choose Joseph.

But at the end of two seasons, the tentmaker reappeared, and my mother invited him to a meal. It was true. He did eat like a glutton. It was so disgusting to watch him shovel the food into his mouth that I couldn't even eat. When he saw that I had not eaten my food, he took what was left on my plate and shoveled that in too.

After the meal, Levi stayed for many hours. He talked about his great wealth and whined about how he had been deprived of his comforts when he was with the caravan. He talked about his piety and discussed the scriptures with my father. Compared to Joseph, he knew nothing, but still he kept talking. When my eyes closed, he was still talking.

The next day, my father called me to his shop. I dreaded what he would say, so I walked as slowly as I could. Beyond the low door, the dust danced in a beam of sunlight that came through a crack in the wall. My father stood in back where it was dark. My eyes were not adjusted, and I saw only his shadow, stooped in a way that I didn't remember. I stood still and waited until I could see better.

"Come," my father said, holding out his arms. I rushed to him like I was still a small child and buried my face in his robe. He smelled of wood and sweat.

"Levi grows impatient for your hand," he said.

Nausea rose within me.

"He has the means to care for you." he continued.

"He is older than you," I said into his shoulder.

He set me away from him, and held my shoulders so that I had to look at him. "Your mother does not want you to be poor."

"It is done then?"

"It is not what you wish?"

"No," I whispered. "Please, no."

"The carpenter has nothing," he said. His voice was cross.

"He is a good man," I said. I knew that my mother would speak against Joseph. I hoped that my father wouldn't listen. Joseph hadn't even asked for my hand, but it was clear to all of us that he would.

"He would not even be able to provide food for you," my father said examining some tool like it held the answer.

"You don't like Levi," I challenged. I was brave. I had nothing to lose.

My father chuckled. I had been disrespectful, but he did not seem to notice.

"You are right," he said. "And I cannot say why. Your mother badgers me to say why, but I cannot." He shook his head.

"But you would give me to a man that you don't even like?" I pushed.

"He offers a high bride price and asks no dowry."

I knew what it would mean to my parents if I were to make a good marriage. I knew that Levi was a man of wealth, and he would have the money to care for them as well as me.

I lowered my head and walked out of my father's shop. Once I was outside, I grabbed my pitchers and started to run. I was crying and wiping at my eyes and running, the clay pitchers banging together so that I don't know why they didn't break. I didn't care. I kept on running, running to get away from Levi, but I knew I would not be fast enough. I didn't stop until I reached the well.

Joseph was there, pulling the bucket from the water, his arms bare and brown and sprinkled with his sweat. A young woman was waiting to fill her jars, and he poured the water into them. She smiled at him and lowered her eyes, and he smiled back, his teeth white against his dark beard. My face burned, and I wanted to push her over. He saw me and left the bucket and walked to me.

"Will you speak with me?" I asked.

"Give me your pitchers, and I will fill them for you."

I handed them to him and watched while he lowered the bucket and filled my water pitchers. The young woman turned and hurried away. Others crowded around the well, but no one paid attention to us. He handed me the pitchers and waited without speaking.

"The tentmaker has returned," I said.

Joseph buckled forward, then straightened and looked away toward the hills.

"He wishes to marry me now."

"He will provide well for you," Joseph said.

"Do you not care for me at all?"

"Do not speak to me so if you are promised to another." His words were sharp, unkind.

He was right. I should not have been so brazen. I should not have even been there, but I knew that I would never have another chance.

"My father has not consented. He knows that the tentmaker is not my choice."

"It is not yours to make."

"It is yours though. You are a man."

"I do not have the means of the tentmaker."

"It is his courage that you need, not his means."

I turned and ran again. I headed toward my father's house. There was no place else to go.

The sun was setting. We had eaten, and my mother was sitting on the roof. She called for me to join her. I said that I would finish pounding the meal first. I heard her humming to herself as she rested in the evening breeze, content, I thought, that I would make a good marriage.

Through the small window, I saw Joseph coming up the hill carrying my forgotten water pitchers. My mother stopped humming. I kept pounding the grain. I wanted to run to the hills and hide after the shameless way that I had acted.

"Joachim, I have brought your water," Joseph called out. "I will leave it." He set the pitchers by the door but did not turn to leave. My father stepped from his shop.

"Joseph," he nodded to him.

"Joachim, mah shlomcha?"

"I am well," my father said and with a pitch of his head motioned for Joseph to follow him.

He turned, and they walked into his shop. I heard my mother climb down from the roof and knew that she would walk around behind the shop to listen to what the men would say. I pounded and pounded and kept on pounding. After a time, Joseph came out of the shop, turned and walked down the hill. He did not look my way.

The next day, I kept to myself. I was cross because of Levi and Joseph. I had stayed awake most of the night trying to think, but there was no answer to my problem. My father didn't come to the house for the noon meal, so at least I didn't have to face him. My mother was outside at the cooking fire, and I heard her call to me. I wanted to pretend I didn't hear, but I walked out and stood where she could see me, though I stood like a sullen child and didn't speak. She measured out a bowl of soup from her kettle, handed it to me, and told me to take it to my father. I looked at the ground because I was certain that if I looked at her, I would begin to wail.

For only the second time in my life, I didn't want to go to my father's shop. I took the soup to him, but I walked as slowly as I could. When I neared the shop, I saw his silhouette bent over his work bench in the back. He straightened when he heard me and walked out into the sun, ducking his head as he stepped under the doorway. He squinted in the bright light and took a seat on the bench against the wall of the shed. I could not look into his eyes, so I looked down at his robe, the color of the dust beneath his feet. I had always thought how handsome he would be if he were to have a robe with colored stripes. I wished that he would give my mother the coins for the fabric to make one, but he never did. I handed him the bowl. He nodded but didn't speak. It was painful between us, and I turned to leave.

"Wait," he said. I took a few more steps. Then I stopped.

"He will come for my answer when the sun sets," he said.

I cringed and thought of the talon-like hands of Levi the tentmaker.

"It would be a hard life you would have with the carpenter," he said. I did not speak. I did not look up. "That is what you wish?" he asked.

My heart pounded. I could not believe that he would even ask my wish. I nodded my head, only slightly.

"Yes," I whispered. I did not want him to think me disrespectful and dismiss me.

"Your mother wants better for you," he continued. "She would have you . . ."

"Please, please," my words rushed out. "I ask you not to send me to him. Please. I would find a way to care for you." I dared to look into his eyes.

"I have not been firm enough with you. Had I been so, it would not have come to this."

I looked down.

"Leave me be now," he ordered.

I turned and walked back to the house, crushed again. I spent that afternoon scrubbing some garments in the extra water that I had carried. I scrubbed them furiously and hung them on the bushes to dry. The sun baked them, and soon they were scalding to the touch. I watched as the dry air sucked the moisture from them, and they became dry as old bones.

When I finished, my mother sent me with two loaves of fresh bread to the widow Gayla's house. It was nothing more than a hut, really, where she lived on the back of her brother-in-law's property. He would have taken her in, but her sister was so mean spirited that the widow chose to stay in the hut. No one bothered with her. She did as she pleased. She was near starving, but I envied the control she took over her own life. I stayed and visited with her for a very long time so that I did not have to go home.

Finally, I left for my father's house. As I walked up the hill, I tried to will Levi to change his mind. I prayed that the Lord would make him turn against me and rescind his offer. It was beyond hope to think that my father would refuse him. I clenched my teeth together and walked on.

When the house was in view, I saw two people walking across the yard. Underneath my robe, my skin turned cold. It started at the back of my neck and spread across my shoulders and down my arms, over my entire body. I wanted to turn and run and never return, but I walked on.

I saw my father first. And then, I saw Joseph. I did not dare to hope. I stood rooted to the ground and waited and waited while they talked and gestured. Then Joseph broke from my father and ran towards me. I felt as if I were rising from the ground. He stopped an arm's distance away, not allowing himself to touch me in the presence of my father.

"It is settled," he said. "He has consented." And he smiled and smiled.

"To you? To us?" I asked, and he nodded. Then I asked again and again, and my tears came. I cried until I had to wipe my nose on my sleeve, and I was afraid that Joseph would change his mind.

I praised God for many days. I never saw Levi the tentmaker again, until that day in Egypt when he stood looking at me. Looking at me and leering. I was afraid.

The Twelfth Day of Elul

I am awake, and the moon is high overhead, so I know that the night is only half gone. I have dreams in the night now, and I don't want them to take me again, so I rise from my pallet. The wind blows in through the windows. I find my shawl and pull it around me. I look around the moonlit house, but there is no one here to see. I close my eyes and then open them again. Sometimes I do that to check on myself. I move my hand to make shadows on the wall. It is best if I find things to concentrate on. Otherwise, I see the table move, a person at the door, the wall begin to crumble, strange things. I reach for the mint and the basil that I have brought in from the garden. I bring it to my face and breathe in its scent until I feel calmer.

Of all the things that have happened, I do not remember going to Golgotha or anything about his death. The first that I remember seeing Jesus was when someone brought him to me. The soldiers, I think. I remember that he was beaten and bruised, so that when I think of him lying in my lap that day, I do not see how it could have been him, yet somehow I knew it was. His skin was still warm, not like others I have seen who have died. Someone told me afterwards that that would happen to Jesus too, but it was not so when I held him. I thought that he would open his eyes and talk to me, but he did not.

Sometimes now, that is how I remember him—beaten and bruised—and then I have to try very hard to remember how he really looked. How he looked before they hurt him. I do it by going back to when he was little, and then when I can see him, I just let him grow older and older in my mind until I can remember what he looked like when he was a man. When he was not beaten.

I don't remember, and I don't want to. When I start to think of the hill, I am afraid that I can't survive it again. Now in the darkness, I clamp my mind shut, fast like snapping a box. Then I clench down on my jaws so that my mind does not open, and the memories do not come to me. I make repetitive hmm hmm, hmm hmm, hmm hmmm

hmmm noises alternating high and low pitches. I lie down on my pallet again and pull the cover over my face. I rub the sole of one foot back and forth over the instep of the other, back and forth, back and forth, still hmming, until I have soothed myself, until the danger has passed.

I stare into the empty room. I stare and stare, and finally I see Jesus and Joseph. I know that I should not do this. But Jesus is there with Joseph, and I cannot help myself. I tell myself to stop, and I close my eyes. When I open them again, they are gone. I know that it can lead to a sickness if I continue to pretend, so I tell myself that it is time to accept that Jesus does not live upon this earth anymore, and then I cannot breathe.

It is already too late. I think I have lost my mind. I stare again until they come back. If I lie still and don't think, they will let me watch them. The sun is shining, and Jesus is running and laughing, his young body as brown as a nomad in the desert. I watch until my heart aches so that I cannot stand it, and I hold out my arms to him, but he does not run to me. He runs to Joseph.

9

Home to Nazareth

"Are you going to harm us?" I asked.

"Why would I harm you? As you said, I am Jewish."

Levi smirked a little and stepped nearer to me. I forced myself not to step away and anger him more. The laws of Israel would not allow one man to take the life of another, even a woman. But we were not in Palestine, and in the desert, there was no law. No one would blink an eye over a dead Jewish woman who didn't know enough to stay home.

"We are at your mercy," I said, trying not to sound afraid. "I ask your protection in the name of the Lord God who rules over the House of Israel."

"Hmph!" he said ignoring me again. He bobbed his head up and down and blinked and made his loathsome tsking noises. "The carpenter is not the reason that your father did not give you to me. Do you know that?" he asked.

"He did not share his reasons with me," I said. "Perhaps he did not think that I was worthy of you."

"Do not patronize me," he hissed. His hand flashed out from his sleeve, and he slapped my face, hard. I flinched but I didn't cry out, or move, or let myself put my hand to my face.

"I meant no offense," I said. Jesus stepped to my side and held onto my leg. I pushed him behind me again.

"He did not accept my offer for you because someone told him stories of me."

I didn't know what he was talking about.

"Stories of my passions. And now you are here," he taunted.

Bile rose and burned in my throat. I swallowed it down.

"Let me see the child," he said, leaning around me and calling Jesus to him.

I didn't move.

"Let me see the child, or I will take him from you," Levi warned.

I pushed Jesus farther behind me.

"Why do you think that you can disobey me?" he screamed. He grabbed my wrist and twisted my arm up behind my back.

He pushed my arm higher and higher behind me. I bent forward and could see his dirty scrawny feet sticking out from his sandals; his toenails were as long as his fingernails. I tried to concentrate on them so that I did not think about my arm, but he pushed harder. I cried out, and he pushed harder. The pain grew until I thought that my shoulder would snap, and I took Jesus' hand and pulled him to stand beside me. He was upset and crying, but I ordered him to stop, and he did.

"There, now. That is better," Levi said in a sick sweet voice and dropped my arm.

He looked Jesus over and spoke to him in Aramaic, asking his name and other simple questions.

"Answer him," I instructed.

Jesus answered in Aramaic. Then Levi repeated the same questions in Hebrew, and Jesus responded in that language as well.

"He has begun his studies already," Levi said.

"Yes," I answered.

"His father teaches him?" he asked.

"Yes," I said again.

"I have known your mother a long time," he said to Jesus, "but she needs to learn to obey."

Jesus did not understand the meaning of Levi's threat, and then Levi spoke to Jesus in a friendly tone, talking about how big Jesus was and other things that little boys like to hear, and Jesus was unafraid. I looked around the tent as they spoke, but I knew that even though the guards had left, I would not try to escape. No matter how Levi felt about me, we would be safer with him for the time being. I hoped that Joseph was alive and free and that he would find us. I hoped that Levi would put the final fault with my father and release his grudge against me at least enough to spare my life. And I hoped, most of all I hoped, that the Lord would hear my prayers.

Before long, the two guards came into the tent bringing Joseph with them. At first, I thought that he was their prisoner, but then I saw that he stood free. Levi's men had found him and brought us back together. Joseph smiled and held out his arms to Jesus.

"Abba!" Jesus said, and ran to Joseph. I rushed to him as well and stood at his side.

Levi walked to Joseph and embraced him. Joseph thanked him and blessed him and thanked him again. Levi was gracious and humble, very happy and honored that he was able to help. He did not even look at me. I was a married woman; it would not have been proper. And now, in front of Joseph, Levi was proper. Proper, respectful, pious.

"You have a fine son," he told Joseph.

"Thank you," Joseph said. "It is so. He is a fine boy."

Jesus beamed as he stood and held Joseph's hand. I stood behind them with my eyes down. No one even noticed me.

On the way home, I offered prayers of thanksgiving to God for protecting us and made plans for my packing. I wanted to tell Joseph about what happened, but he said that we would not speak of it in front of Jesus. When the house we were living in came into our sight, I looked across the shimmering sand of the desert, where shadows danced and visions rose from the ground, and saw men coming from behind the building. Levi's men, Herod's men. I closed my eyes and opened them again, and the men were gone.

Jesus fell asleep before I could even cut the bread and cheese for our meal, and when I saw that he was asleep, I left the food and started to pack. I wanted to be ready to leave when the moon rose.

Joseph told me to finish with our meal. There was no need for us to move. After he had eaten, he walked outside to catch the evening breeze, and I followed and pleaded with him to let us move. I thought that Levi would have his revenge if he discovered our hiding place. What if he captured Jesus and took him back to Herod?

Joseph could not believe my talk. He assured me that Levi was a friend. Had he not saved us that very day? I agreed that he had, but said that I believed he was still insulted over my father's refusal.

Then I told Joseph about what had happened in the tent that day with the Egyptian and the rubies, but he said that the fight was the way of the desert, and he should have left me home. When I told him more about the things Levi had said and done, it made me sound like a vain woman. Nothing sounded the same as it was in the tent. Again, Joseph assured me that Levi would remember he was a Jew, and he would not hurt us. Joseph was my husband, but he was a man. He took Levi's word over mine.

We didn't move, and Joseph was right. Levi didn't turn against us. Each time his caravan passed, he brought us news of Judea. Still, I could not bring myself to trust him. One evening Joseph brought Levi home with him. I hurried inside, but Joseph called me out and said that Levi would take his meal with us and that I would sit with them. Levi had news I would want to hear. As we ate, Levi spoke of the situation at home in Judea and Galilee. Herod the Great had died. And as he neared death, he had ordered his son and daughter to have several prominent Jews executed, so that the land would be filled with great mourning. Fortunately, Herod's son Archelaus did not follow his father's wishes. So on the day of Herod's death, there was great rejoicing throughout the land. And when Levi told this, Joseph gave thanks unto the Lord.

Still, the situation in Judea was tense. Herod Archelaus was also violent and unpredictable. Some Jews were fleeing north to Galilee, where Herod's son Antipas was in charge. He did not seem to rule with such a harsh hand.

When the meal was over, Levi asked Jesus to walk with him and show him the land. I thought that Joseph was going to consent, but he did not. He told Levi that Jesus was up early that day and needed to sleep. Joseph walked with Levi, and I took Jesus into the house and did not leave his side.

Levi and Joseph talked long into the night, and then Levi made his bed on the floor. He slept there until sunrise the next day. When he had gone, Joseph told me to get ready. We were going home. I was filled with excitement and a little bit of fear. We had been in Egypt for more than two years.

We traveled with several caravans, and the trip back to Judea went more quickly than our escape to Egypt had. We heard the story of Herod again and again, and long before we reached Jerusalem, even Bethlehem, we could see the mountain where Herodium, Herod's winter palace, was built. Soon, we saw the palace itself.

"There you see it," Joseph said pulling on the donkey's halter until she came to a stop.

Jesus started climbing down from the donkey. Joseph ordered him to stay seated, but when he saw that his stout little legs were bright red and raw from the ride, he lifted him and set him on the ground to run.

I watched Jesus for a while, but my mind was on Herod.

"It is hard to believe he is really dead." I said. "Are you sure?"

"Yes. The travelers have told us. Levi has told us. His word is good. Herod is buried someplace under the mountain, and there is nothing he can do to us anymore," Joseph assured me.

"It is hard to believe his power has ended."

"Do you see the tower with the parapet about halfway up the hill? You can see that it is newly built. I would think it holds his sarcophagus," Joseph said.

"Levi said there was a great parade to bear his body to his crypt."

"He would have planned for that before he died."

"He readied his own burial place?"

"There is no one else he would have trusted to choose it for him."

All the way from Egypt, we had searched for Sarah and Labon. We kept on through Bethlehem, Jerusalem and into Nazareth, but we didn't find a trace. To this day, I have never heard one word about them.

Looking back, it's hard to believe that we could have returned to a place ruled by anyone whose name was Herod, but it was our home. Joseph said that we would not mention the circumstances of Jesus' birth, or where we had been, or why to anyone. We would say only that we had been traveling and working. No one, except my mother, would know what really happened. He said that whatever happened would be according to the Lord's plan, but still there was no need to announce our son before his time.

I agreed. I didn't want Herod Antipas to find out about Jesus and succeed where his father had failed. My instinct was that of every mother, to protect my child, and I would do it as mothers do best, by blending quietly into my surroundings and hoping to go unnoticed. Joseph kept his silence to his grave. Now, for the first time, I have told.

Some kinsmen had kept our house in good repair for us, and we settled into it again. Joseph took up work as a carpenter and also tended the adjoining land for a landowner who was a fair man and gave us a good measure of the flax, wheat, and barley that Joseph harvested.

On the days that Joseph worked close to home, Jesus would play outside to be near him. He loved to hide around a corner or inside a doorway and then jump out and surprise Joseph who would always act frightened and hop around in a way that made him look foolish.

Then the two would laugh. Always, they would laugh. And I was happy to know that Jesus was taking on the ways of his father.

When Jesus was in his fifth year, James was born. I thought that he would be named Joseph after his father, but Joseph chose the name James for the babe, saying that we would not set the two boys apart. As James grew, Jesus watched after him and instructed him in everything from how to remember a passage of scripture to how to jump off the roof when I was not looking. James adored Jesus and followed after him imitating everything that he did. Jesus was his friend and his hero, and if Jesus said something was so, to James it was so.

After James, we had a daughter, and she was given my name. Then another son, whom Joseph consented to have as his namesake, and we called him Joses. In the years to follow, we were blessed with two more boy children, Simon and Jude, and another daughter whom we named Salome.

When James and Myriam and Joses were babes, I was nearly too busy to breathe, and Jesus would tag along with Joseph whenever he was allowed. His smooth little brown hand hanging on to Joseph's, he nearly ran to keep pace with his father's long strides. He would chatter away, looking up at Joseph, not paying any attention to where he was going. Often he would trip and sprawl out onto the ground. He seldom cried though; he would just jump up and brush himself off, looking surprised that such a thing could have happened.

"Watch where you step now," Joseph would say to him as they started out again, but Jesus would already be looking up at Joseph, chattering away.

Once, when Jesus took one of those falls, he came up without a front tooth. I gave him water to rinse his mouth, but he took the water and cleaned the tooth instead. He was fascinated by it, examined it, tried to fit it back into his mouth, and asked endless questions: how it grew, how it worked, whether he would lose all of his teeth, and whether he would really grow teeth as big as Joseph's. That was our first sign that Jesus was interested in such things. As he grew, he fed stray animals and tended every injured creature that he could find. He made countless mud plasters and slings for his brothers and sisters and mixed up nasty tasting herbal brews.

Sometime after we returned to Nazareth, Elizabeth and John came here to live with a kinsman. They had been alone for a long time. Her husband Zechariah had died when he refused to give up the hiding place of his wife and son during Herod's murder of the innocents.

One day, when Elizabeth came with John for a visit, Jesus and John disappeared. We went looking for them and found them high up in the Cedar Lebanon tree that shaded our house, John preaching to his imaginary followers and Jesus hanging from his knees. I called them down immediately, but after that, Jesus made his way to the top of the tree every time I turned my back on him. He always tried to get me to climb with him so I could see Sepphoris or Lake Galilee to the east. Instead, I would order him down, smooth my new gray hairs, and warn the younger ones to stay on the ground.

Both Jesus and John were quick learners, but Jesus also loved to play and laughed often. His laugh was like music, like tiny bits of metal ringing together in the wind. I can hear it now, sometimes, when I step out of my door and listen. It comes to me down from the hills across the air. Once the rabbi told Joseph that Jesus smiled too often, that he should be more like his cousin.

John was earnest, debating and philosophizing over every lesson that the rabbi gave to them, and he grew more and more serious, less interested in anything but discussing the scriptures. Jesus and Joseph would talk with him for awhile, but then they would stop to eat or tend their chores. It would insult John that they would let anything at all, especially something like feeding an animal, interfere with their study of the scriptures, and he would storm off for home. More than once, Joseph called him back and gave him a talking to, told him that his behavior was rude and disrespectful, and John would agree to hold his tongue.

Every day, we prayed three times, and every time I prayed, I thanked

God for the blessings that he had given me, for our children, for Joseph, for his kindness. I believe that I loved Joseph since the first day I saw him at the well, but when he set himself aside for the sake of our unborn babe, and when he saved our lives by guiding our escape to Egypt, I became devoted to him in a way that directed every single thing that I did. I revered him, and everything in my life was made better because the Lord had given him unto me. Sharing my life with Joseph, sharing his bed, seemed like it had always been a part of me.

We did not think far into the future as the day's troubles were sufficient to themselves. We were always short of money, water, and time. There were always faces to wash, tears to wipe, and mouths to feed. The crops needed to be harvested before the locusts ate them, my mother needed care, and Elizabeth needed food for John. But then there was Sepphoris.

As a young girl, I had loved the beautiful city that sat high on the hill about an hour's walk from Nazareth. Many people called it the Jewel of Galilee, and I had believed that to be true. Always, though, there was the longing for the city to be reclaimed, for it to be free of the influences that marked it as a Roman rather than a Jewish city.

Then, when Herod the Great died, and the new leaders could not keep the people so well under control, a man named Judah ben Hezekiah led the revolt to reclaim Sepphoris. It was a horror. Hezekiah led his men into the city, stole all the weapons from Herod's own palace, and tried to overthrow the Romans in charge. He also armed men throughout Galilee who staged more revolts. But a few small bands of Jews could never stand against the Empire, so the people watched helplessly as the Syrian governor Varus had the men hunted down and put to death. It was a tragedy to all of the families around. The men who fought were their cousins, their brothers, their husbands, and their sons, and these were the men who Varus had nailed to the trees. These were the men that hung from the crosses that lined the roadsides of Galilee. The city of Sepphoris was burned to the ground, and the people learned to bow to the Romans.

After Herod's death and the rebellions, his lands were divided among his sons Antipas, Archelaus, and Philip. Herod Antipas chose to rebuild Sepphoris and make it his capital. When he moved to the city, my nightmares began.

10

Twelve Years

In my dreams, Herod the Great had come back to life, and I was forced to follow after him and watch while he beheaded his wife and killed his own sons. Then he would always turn and walk toward me. I would stand, a peasant before a king, and beg him to spare Jesus. He would lift his arm and laugh. I would grab onto his forearm and push against it as hard as I could to force it away, to keep him from lowering his hand. I could not let his hand fall. I would wake in a sweat, and Joseph would hold me and try to comfort me, tell me that Herod the Great was dead and that he could not hurt Jesus. I would lie in the darkness afraid to close my eyes.

I prayed and Joseph prayed for the Lord to end my nightmares, and after sometime, the dreams left me. Still, my fear of Herod Antipas, son of Herod the Great, remained. I had convinced myself that Herod the Great had learned that we had escaped with Jesus and had left word for his son to complete the deed and destroy the child the magi had predicted would be the next king of Israel.

I wanted to leave Nazareth, but Joseph said that if Antipas thought to harm Jesus it was better that we keep him in our sights. Then he would tell me that a house on the hill was always seen, and every time he told me that, it would irritate me for I thought he was not paying attention to me. Joseph seemed to believe that with Rome now the unquestioned power, even over all of Egypt, no one threatened Antipas, and he would have no reason to give a second thought to a little boy named Jesus.

I loathed what had happened in Sepphoris and refused to go there, but the city fascinated Jesus. One day he came in from play and asked me to pack a lunch for Joseph and him.

"Did your father send you?" I asked.

"No. It's going to be a surprise for him. I need to pack our hammers, too."

"Where do you think that you are going?" I asked "To help a neighbor?"

"No. Sepphoris. They are building there every day. We will find work and make enough money to buy a new plow."

I wanted to scream that he must never ever go to Sepphoris, but I stayed calm. "You are only in your eighth year," I said. "You are quite young to be hired as a carpenter."

"Abba said I am as good as any man with a hammer," he said, his little chest puffing at his father's compliment.

"I will pack you a lunch, but I don't think you will be going to Sepphoris today."

Joseph found some work for Jesus to do in his shop, and Jesus forgot about Sepphoris. I did not. The construction in the city began before first light and went on until after dark. Even though Antipas did not have the money his father had, his treasury was vast by any other measure, and he set his course to make his own place of government the most impressive in all of Palestine. Once he started building, he didn't stop. He built up the entire city, added theaters, gymnasiums, and always more and more roads. Some years later, he moved his capital city to Tiberius and began his building all over again. But it was Sepphoris that marked our lives.

Thousands of people moved to the city to find work or to enjoy the comforts it offered. It grew more and more crowded, and the markets were always a frenzy of trading. Commerce thrived because of the good Roman roads that ran throughout the Judean desert. The Silk Road passed north of Sepphoris from Persia all the way to the Mediterranean Sea where the ships sailed back and forth to Egypt and Rome. Lesser roads led from that route to Sepphoris and south to Jerusalem.

Endless caravans and trains of packed donkeys passed through Nazareth on their way to the Sepphoris market. Sometimes they would pass our house, try to sell us wares, ask for water, or even beg for food.

Once when Joseph was out in the field, a band of traders stopped by our house. They were leading a string of starving donkeys whose ribs rode up and down under their skin with every step. The poor beasts were packed with heavy loads, and the flies buzzed the sores on their hides. The men were dirty and arguing amongst themselves. The leader, the only one riding, got off his donkey and called out to me and asked for a pitcher of water. He was a wiry, agile man dressed in layers of red and green and purple clothing. He wore so much neck and arm jewelry that I could hear his every move. I could see that the man was a sorcerer, and I was wary of him and his friends, but still, I could not refuse them water.

When I went for the pitcher, the sorcerer began weaving a tale, and Jesus wandered over to listen. I hurried to bring the water, and when I got back, Jesus was sitting on the donkey, and the caravan was moving away. I dropped the pitcher to the ground and ran to catch up to Jesus.

The driver scolded me and offered to buy Jesus from me for two *denarii*. I grabbed Jesus' hand, jerked him off of the donkey, and started running before his feet hit the ground.

"Run!" I ordered him, and he did. I pulled him along behind me, and as we ran, I heard the driver laughing behind us.

"You could come too," the driver called out. "Not for me, though. My eye is on the boy."

I stopped at the cradle just outside the house, grabbed up the sleeping babe, put James in between Jesus and me, and ordered them to hold hands real tight. We all ran until we reached the fields and found Joseph. James was crying, and I was shaking so badly that I could not speak. But Jesus was bursting with news and without a breath told Joseph that the man with the donkey said we could go to Sepphoris with him, but then he scared Imma, and then he laughed at us, and that made her feel bad, and that was why we could not go to Sepphoris with the man. Then Jesus begged Joseph to take us all to the city market in Sepphoris.

Joseph scolded Jesus for getting on the sorcerer's donkey, told him that we would not be going to Sepphoris and that he should not think of it again. Jesus didn't argue, but he remained fascinated by the city. When Jesus was older, Joseph explained to him that Sepphoris had many temples built to honor other gods. Those temples, the Roman way of life, and the public baths made the entire place an abomination to God. After that, Jesus didn't ask to go to Sepphoris again.

For two years, the crops were very poor, and the landowner Joseph worked for went into debt and lost his land. The new owner kept Joseph on, but he was not so generous. We had stored little in the two years of poor crops, so we were growing hungry. Sometimes I ground the barley, which we usually kept for the animals, into flour and made bread. Still, the children grew thinner, and I gave them more and more of the milk from the goats so that we ran low on cheese.

One evening after the children were asleep, Joseph told me that he was going into Sepphoris to work. I could not believe it. I did not want him near the place, but when I protested, he stopped me.

"I will not stand by and watch my children starve," he growled, and he stared at me until I turned away.

"How do you even know that they will hire you?" I asked.

"They need workers. The city is growing so fast that they are running out of water. They need more cisterns to store it, and not everyone can work with stone."

"How long will you work there?" I wanted to know.

"Not long. Only this one season."

"What about the crops here?"

"The boys can help, and I will have time in the evening."

So the next day, long before it was light, Joseph left for Sepphoris. I made many trips to the well that day, and set out water and soap for him to bathe when he returned. When he came walking home that evening, I could see that he was tired, and I knew that he wanted to hurry to the fields so that he could finish before dark. I watched from the doorway, and when he saw the water he looked from the water to the fields, then back to the water again. I heard him sigh, and then he removed the clothing that he had worn into Sepporis and bathed until the city was washed from him.

He called for Jesus and James, picked up the clothing that I had lain out, and was still pulling it on when they set out for the field. That was our pattern for two months, and when they were over, Joseph was as thin as a young boy, but there was food in the house and the children were growing again.

Even when Joseph did not work away from home, the days were hard, and the work was never finished, but the evenings were my reward. After we had eaten, Joseph would call for us to gather near to him. Then he would read to us from the scriptures and teach all those things he wanted our children to know. I would sit at his feet, holding one or more of the younger children, and forget my tired back and roughened hands. I thought that I was the most blessed woman on the earth and would not have traded my place for any amount of wealth.

Joseph taught the children the Ten Commandments and told them of how the Lord wrote them upon stone and gave them to Moses so that the people of Israel might live well and remain a faithful people. He spoke of how the law was not a burden but was a great gift to us. He said that of all the laws given to us, the command to love the Lord your God and the command to love one another were the essence of our lives.

He required that all of the children, not only the boys, commit the scriptures to memory so that they might always carry them with them and be ready for whatever would come. He spoke of the prophets who warned the people what would happen if they did not worship the Lord God alone and obey God's commands. Sometimes he told the children things that I thought they were too young to know, like the cruel ways of the Romans, the ways of the traders who kidnapped people and sold them as slaves, the ways of the Gentiles in Sepphoris, or even of some Hebrews who had broken from the faith. Joseph was very grave when he talked about these things and always made it clear to the children that they must never fall into those sinful ways.

And then, as my father had taught me, Joseph taught our children the privilege of being Hebrew. "Now I will tell you," he said. And there was such awe in his own voice that we all slid closer to him, for though we had heard those words many times, we wanted to hear them again. After we were so close that we were sitting on top of one another, he would begin.

"Now I will tell you of the blessing that you have been given. You are Hebrew."

And all of the children would smile and nod their heads at their good fortune. Then Joseph would go on, "You are Hebrew, and you must never forget that you have been chosen. Hundreds of years ago, the Lord God Almighty made a covenant with Abraham saying, 'I will be your God and you will be my people.' And it has been so. And to be chosen is an honor above all others, above gold or silver, above freedom, even above your own life. To be born of the House of Israel is a great privilege and a great duty."

And then the children would swallow and their eyes would grow wide as they waited to hear what would be required of them.

"You must worship the Lord our God and love him above all others. And when you love the Lord, you will love others. You must use the great minds that the Lord has given you to study the scriptures and all things. You must live your lives to bring good into the world. And finally, you must care for every Israelite as you would care for your own family."

By now, the children could barely contain themselves at the thought of the great deeds that lay ahead for them, and Joseph would say in his most solemn voice, "And I will tell you this. I will tell you that the Lord stayed the hand of Abraham to bring an end to human sacrifice. And so he has made you sacred, and he has made you safe. And he has made you a blessing upon the House of Israel."

Then Joseph would stop and be silent and still. The children would also be quiet, and in that room, I could always feel the hand of the Lord upon us.

Joseph would often end the time by telling the boys that they must be of a kind heart and chose a devout woman to take as a wife. Many other women, he would say, might want to marry them as well, for these women longed for a good Hebrew man who would treat a woman with kindness. But he told them, it would be better if they married Hebrew. They would nod gravely back to him, their little heads bobbing in unison.

We would chose for them, he went on, but sometimes it happened in these modern times that men and women chose for themselves. Then he would lean toward them, waggle his eyebrows, and nod his head toward me with a, "Hmmh?" as if I were supposed to be unaware of their talk.

"Did I really want to marry him?" they asked.

"Yes of course, because I was so handsome," Joseph said with a smile.

They all laughed and laughed. And then one of the boys would take a poke at another, and the wrestling match would begin, and the lessons would be over for the night.

All of us looked forward to the festivals and the celebrating and visiting that went along with them. Usually, we didn't have the time or the money to travel to the Temple and observed them at home. The Passover was our favorite.

The day before it began, I removed the leavening from our house. Then Joseph went on a search to make sure that none remained.

I always hid one small piece of leavened bread for him to find. He began the hunt with great ceremony, the children cheering him on. And while he hunted, he would tell them again the story of the Passover. Long ago, the people of Israel lived in Egypt. They worshiped the Lord and grew strong in body and number. The Pharaoh was afraid that they were becoming too powerful and forced them into slavery. He forced them to work building bricks out of clay and straw and worked them so hard that many died. He was so cruel that he even tried to have all of the newborn boys put to death. But when a boy named Moses was born, his sister hid him in the river where the Pharaoh's daughter found him and took him home to be her own son. Moses grew strong, and when he was grown, the Lord commanded him to lead the Israelites out of Egypt.

Joseph was a great story teller and demonstrated the characters until they came to life. He would take on the role of Moses and petition the Pharaoh to "Let my people go. Let my people go."

But the Pharaoh did not let the people go, so the Lord sent great plagues on the land. Still, the Pharaoh did not let the people go, for the Lord had hardened his heart. Finally, the Lord told Moses to instruct the people to prepare to leave that night. The people needed a meal for their journey, but they were in such a hurry that they could not even take time for the bread to rise. So for their meal, they ate a lamb and unleavened bread. And they ate with their loins girded, their sandals on their feet, and their staff in hand so that they would be ready to go when the Lord gave them word.

That night, the Lord sent the Angel of Death, and all the firstborn of Egypt died. Pharaoh's own first-born son died, and in his grief and anger he sent Moses and the Hebrew people from the land. But when the people set out, the Pharaoh changed his mind and ordered his soldiers to chase after them to bring them back. He did not want to lose his slaves. When the Israelites came upon the Red Sea, the Pharaoh's soldiers were close behind them. The Lord told Moses to cast out his rod. And Moses did as God commanded, and the waters parted so that the Israelites could pass through. When the Israelites were near the other side, the soldiers charged into the opening that Moses had made. As the Israelites hurried on to the shore, the sea closed upon the Egyptians and crushed them. If Joseph found the leavening while he was still talking, he turned a blind eye. Finally, he would finish the story, find the bread and destroy it with as much flourish as if he were slaying a wild beast.

The next day, we would gather with our kinsmen, and Joseph would roast the lamb over the fire, and I would prepare the unleavened bread. With the bread and the lamb we would also eat *haroset*, crushed bitter herbs, and parsley.[1] At the meal, Joseph allowed each of the children to drink a small cup of wine.

When Jesus was in his thirteenth year, Joseph announced that it was time for him to make his first journey to the Temple. He was old enough to enter the Court of Men. He and Joseph and I would make the Passover pilgrimage. I did not think I should leave the younger children, but Joseph had asked a cousin to come and stay with them.

Jesus was wild with excitement, and Joseph walked around with a smile on his face at all times. He coughed often so no one could see how his eyes misted when he talked about presenting his son at the Temple.

I scrubbed the house from top to bottom because I wanted it to be clean when my cousin and her new husband came to stay with the children. I took cloth that I had bought long ago for this occasion, cloth that had beautiful red stripes running through it, and stitched new robes for Joseph and Jesus. Joseph had not had a new robe for more than two years, and Jesus had long outgrown his so that his arms dangled bare beneath the sleeves. Joseph and Jesus dressed in their new robes without much thought, but I was so pleased that I thought the Lord would find me vain in his sight. I could not keep my eyes off my handsome husband and son. I was sure no men in Jerusalem would look finer.

I don't think that Jesus even closed his eyes the night before we left, and Joseph woke me before the sun was up. I lit the lamp, and Jesus grabbed his pack and mine and headed out the door. We met the other travelers and were on our way. We were all too excited to eat.

Jesus ran ahead, and Joseph and I followed along enjoying the walk. Joseph reached out and took my hand, and I smiled up at him. It was wonderful to be alone with him.

"He has grown taller than you," Joseph said as we walked.

"Yes, he will be tall like his father."

It was spring, the time of new life, and trees were leafing and blossoming all over the rocky Nazarene hills. Olive, lemon, pomegranate, and so many more made the early morning walk especially beautiful.

The carriage roads, which the Romans built and maintained for quick travel for their legions of soldiers and for transporting materials for the empire, were an unintended gift for us to use and made our travel easy.[2]

When the sun was high overhead, we stopped for our noon meal. I was tired and worrying about the children at home. I told Joseph that I thought I should turn back and let him and Jesus go on without me, but Joseph said that I would go and enjoy the celebration.

When we started out again, Jesus fell back to walk beside us. Joseph took my pack from Jesus, and he didn't argue. We made our way south to the Plain of Esdraelon and followed it east past Mt. Tabor and Mt. Gilboa. Then we turned south and followed the Jordan River, walking along its eastern bank. This added miles to our route, but it was the route Jews traveled most often. The road to the west would have taken us through Samaria whose people we believed were not true worshipers of God. When we camped that night, the stars sparkled and made everything seem perfect. Jesus fell asleep the minute he lay down.

On the second day, we continued along the eastern bank of the river. The rains had come early and the wild flowers were in full bloom. There were purple irises, royal against the green grasses; huge anemones in white, pink, and all shades of purple; and red, pink, and blue poppies. I thought that I had not seen so much beauty and did not see how one season could change it to lifeless desolation.

On the third day, we traveled through the land of Decapolis and Perea. We were well into the desert, and that night it was very cold, so the three of us huddled together to stay warm. Something in the desert sky must have given Jesus thought of Egypt. He wanted to know why we had lived there? How had we traveled there? What was it like? What was the language? Joseph spoke to him in Egyptian, and Jesus answered back immediately. I could remember little of it. Jesus laughed, saying that he did not even know that he knew the language. Joseph said what is learned as a babe is known far better than what is learned as a scholar.

The fourth day, I do not remember. It must have been more endless walking. On the fifth day, we reached Jericho. Jesus ran ahead with friends that he had made on the trip, and Joseph and I trailed behind.

"We do not speak of his future," Joseph said.

"No," I agreed. "It seems that now is the time for him to be a young boy."

The circumstances of Jesus' birth and his destiny had come to seem almost unbelievable to me. When I remembered the things that had happened to me and what was ahead for Jesus, I often put them out of my mind. Living in Nazareth, far away from the Temple, I worried for his safety, but it was easy not to think of his calling.

"He is twelve years. A man in the eyes of the Lord," Joseph reminded me.

"Yes."

"Once he has made his covenant, he will be responsible to keep the law for himself. If the Lord calls him, I will not interfere."

"He does not seem ready to leave us."

"I will not ask him to break his covenant just to keep him at my side. He must be ready whenever he is called."

"Now? At twelve years?"

The Third Day of Tishrei

I lie on my pallet and look at the hand on my cover. It is a small hand with an old scar by the wrist. I know the scar, so I understand that it is my hand, but it does not seem to belong to me. Finally, I trace the hand where it joins to the wrist and then I follow the line of the arm up higher until I know that it is connected to my body and is a part of me. I look back down at the palm and the wrist, and other than the small scar, there are no injuries. I close my eyes and wrap my arms around my chest to try to stop the pain.

Lately, I have been so tired. Myriam and Salome are here. They tidy things, take the bed out to air, sweep the floor. I tell them to let things be, that I will have plenty of time to do the work after they have gone and that we should just sit and rest awhile, but they keep on. Myriam nags at me to take down my braid and replait it. I put my hand to it and know from the looseness that I must not have combed my hair for days. When I start each day, I think of the things I will do to take care of my house and myself, but in the evening when the sun sets in the sky, all of these things are still left undone.

For a time, my thoughts jumbled together and nothing made sense. If the rain fell upward, it would not have surprised me, but now the emptiness has come. Always, my mind has been busy, busy making up songs, thinking of ways to help others, making plans for a new day, but now my mind does not even work.

The pain has lifted some, and I have given up trying to bargain with God. At first I would make a promise of things that I would do if he would bring Jesus back, but he did not. I'm not sure why. Maybe because I didn't do the things that I promised. I try, but I am tired. I am empty, without anguish and without joy. I am nothing. It is easier.

Salome combs out my hair and braids it again. Then, quietly and patiently, she sits by my side. Myriam brings me a bowl of stew. She must have set it to cook over the outside fire when she came. I will myself to feel hunger and swallow three spoonfuls. I do not want her to start in again.

I look at my daughters. They are me. They have more beauty and wisdom, but they are like me, like I was before this happened. At first, I wanted to cling to them at all times. I didn't want them out of my sight, but now, I have grown more distant. Some days I want to reach out to them, but I never do.

Myriam pushes, tells me that I am alive and that it is time that I join the living again. I take her hand in mine. I mean to tell her that I am glad she is with me, but I say nothing.

"Oh Imma," she says and lays her head on my shoulder and cries. I pat her back, but I have no words for her. I cannot comfort my own child.

James is here. I hear him tell his sisters that I have gone to ground to heal my wounds. He walks over to me and is talking to me now like I am a child. He tells me that I want to hang on to my grief. I want a reason, I tell him. He tells me that he cannot give me one. He tells me that whether there is a reason or not, I must let go of my grief, let go of my anger. I don't know what he is talking about. I don't answer him.

I have decided that maybe the Lord of the Israelites does not exist. That the suffering of the Jewish people has been more than he could bear, and he has left the heavens. Maybe he is tired also. Maybe the Romans have sent him away.

James and my daughters talk about me like I can't hear them. He tells them that I am ill. I feel my stomach and my head. My ribs are sticking out. I am thin like a starving woman.

I want James to stay, but I don't think he will. What if he is the leader and it happens again? He says that for now Peter is in charge. I wonder if it is hard for him to have someone take his brother's place. If it is, he keeps it to himself.

"Imma, Please try," he says, and then he leaves.

11

Favor with the Priests

Joseph was agitated and walking at a near run. I hurried to keep up and reached for his hand, but the companionship we had known on the journey was gone, and he would not close his hand around mine. Finally, I dropped his.

"He will go when he is called," Joseph said.

"Yes," I agreed, and fell silent to save my energy.

That night we had a campfire, but we didn't cook. Joseph gave Jesus some coin and sent him to one of the vendors who had ventured out from the city. Jesus came back with three skewers of lamb, and we sat together and bit into them like we were the wealthiest of people. I could not eat all of mine and gave the rest to Joseph. I watched while he finished the meat. Jesus chattered away, and we laughed at some story that he told about one of his brothers. An adventure they had kept from us at home.

On the sixth day, we entered Jerusalem. The Temple stood before us, and Jesus saw it for the first time. "Abba, look. Imma, look," he repeated over and over.

The Temple is more enormous than all of the buildings in Nazareth put together,[1] and to see it for the first time is always an experience beyond comprehension, but on that day, the sun shone on the gold on Solomon's Porch and reflected great dazzling, piercing beams of light into the air so that it was hard to look upon it in its magnificence.

Jesus could not contain himself and started to run towards it, but Joseph took a firm grip on him. We would have never found him if we had gotten separated in the holiday crowds. It seemed to take forever to make our way through the busy streets, but Jesus' attention never left the Temple.

When we reached it, I stood and trembled in fear to be in the presence of the Lord God. I cannot describe the feeling even now. I had been hesitant on the trip, but standing so near the Temple, it seemed like the whole of Israel waited for Jesus. I thought that I might be lifted from the ground.

The shofar, the choirs, and the music of trumpets, cymbals, harps, and lyre all sang out and seemed to be proclaiming that our son had been chosen to lead the people of Israel. I was humble, obedient in spirit, and solemn. Jesus was filled with new energy. He placed his hand upon the wall and called, "Allelujah! Allelujah! Glory to the Lord." Then he wept.

We stood there together, for a time not uttering a word, and then Joseph wrapped his arm around Jesus' shoulders, and the two walked ahead of me. We climbed steps more than three stories high to the top of the Temple mount. We passed through the Portico and I could not resist placing my hand on one of the columns.[2] We crossed the Court of the Gentiles, and came to the lattice wall. I shivered when I saw the inscription on the marble screen warning foreigners that if they passed within, they would hold the guilt for their own death. We climbed higher and passed through the bronze and silver gate into the Court of Women. There we stopped, for I could go no farther.

"Why do we wait?" Jesus asked. "Let's go, Abba. Hurry!"

"I will wait here," I called to their backs.

I did not see Jesus again for two days. He joined us for the Seder, but he didn't stop talking of what he had seen until the meal was served. He slid in beside Joseph, ate his food without chewing, and returned immediately to the Temple where he stayed until it was time for us to leave for Nazareth.

Joseph told me that Jesus was wearing him out. He had climbed thousands of steps following Jesus as he explored the Temple day after day. Then he looked as pleased as any father and told me that when the priests questioned Jesus, they were amazed at his answers and his knowledge of the scriptures. Joseph did not say it, but I knew that the priests would be very surprised that a boy from Nazareth could be so brilliant.

Our group met at the Damascus Gate for our trip home, but Jesus did not want to leave and pleaded for us to stay in Jerusalem awhile more. Joseph refused. He needed to be home to tend the crops, and I was eager to get home to the rest of our children. Jude was still a babe. But when Jesus asked if he could go into the Temple just one more time, Joseph consented. Though, he said that he was not climbing anymore steps; he needed his energy for the trip home. He told Jesus that we would start out, and Jesus should travel with other pilgrims leaving later in the day. He could catch up to us when we stopped to camp for the evening.

My mind was on home. I didn't even worry when Jesus didn't catch up that first day. When we made camp, and he wasn't there, I was a little cross that he hadn't obeyed, but still, I didn't worry. Joseph passed word through the caravan that Jesus of Nazareth must be sent forward to his parents, but he didn't come. No one had seen him. We searched and searched, but he was nowhere to be found. By then, I was in a panic.

If Jesus had stayed in the Temple, the priests would watch over him, but if he had missed our caravan and set out alone to catch us, he would have been taken by a slave trader or some man who wanted him for his pleasure, maybe the sorcerer. Maybe he had been murdered. If he were alive, he would be frantic. He had never been apart from us. How had I let him out of my sight? I would never forgive myself. Joseph would never forgive me. The younger children would never forgive me. I spoke sharply to myself not to give in to my fear and imaginings but to get myself under control and concentrate on finding Jesus.

Joseph and I left the caravan and started back toward Jerusalem. I knew that if anyone could find Jesus, it would be Joseph, and I held on to that thought as we traveled into the night, running until we couldn't breathe and then walking until we could.

When we came to a camp of travelers, Joseph made us stay with them until morning. It wouldn't do anyone any good for us to meet with trouble as well, he warned. In the darkness, I prayed to God to help us find Jesus.

And then very clearly, as clearly as if he were standing next to me, the Lord spoke to me, "Remember, Myriam, Jesus is my son too." I shivered in the night and pulled the blanket around me.

We were off at first light and reached the Temple early in the day. We searched for some time before we located Jesus in the Portico of Solomon. I saw him through the great columns sitting on the ground with other young boys, the priests on the bench teaching them.

He was safe. I cried and laughed and ran to him. He stood, and I threw my arms around him. Then I set him back from me and looked him over to see if he was hurt.

"What is wrong?" he asked me.

"I just want to know that you are well," I said.

"I am not a babe, but you treat me like one in front of the others."

"You should have come with us. Your mother is sick from worry," Joseph said. He put his hand on Jesus' shoulder.

"There is no reason for her to be," Jesus said. "Do you not know that I am about my Father's business?"

The slap of his words burned my cheek. Joseph withdrew his own hand and dropped his head. Immediately, Jesus realized what he had said and asked our forgiveness. He looked at us, then at the priest, then at us again.

"I will come with you now," he said.

But Joseph did not move. "Tell me," he directed Jesus. Jesus was silent. "Tell me!" Joseph said again.

"I was listening to the priests. They were studying the Torah and discussing the exodus," Jesus said. "Then one of the priests said, 'Even the boy would know that to be true.' I told them he was right and explained why I thought as I did. They asked what else I knew on the matter. I spoke again, and then I was summoned to the high priest. He questioned me and was pleased with my answers. He said that I should come to the Temple to live, and he would speak to my father about it. I said that I was needed at home, and he said that was not for me to decide."

Joseph ordered us to wait for him in the South Portico and went into the Court of Men to find Annas. I wanted to call him back. Instead, I called upon the Lord, dared to plead with him. I asked him not to take Jesus from me so soon. I reminded him that he was still a young boy, and that he was studying faithfully in Nazareth. But the Lord did not answer me. I knew I had agreed with Joseph that Jesus would go when he was called, but I didn't think that it was the time. He was young, too young to live away from us.

It was a long time before Joseph returned. He set out toward home without a word, and Jesus and I followed after him. He kept a furious pace until we found another group returning to Galilee. A few rode donkeys, but most walked as we did, so it was easy to keep up. We were glad to avoid the danger of traveling alone. We fell in with them, but still Joseph didn't say a word about the Temple. When we camped that night, I had to know.

"What will happen?" I asked.

"The boy will stay at home for now."

"And go to the Temple when he is older?"

"If Annas will require him."

I could not wait to get home.

After our pilgrimage, Joseph spent great amounts of time with Jesus preparing for his call. All of our lives became centered around it.

Joseph took Jesus and his brothers more and more often to the synagogue and the Temple. He and I had times of fasting and prayer. We would get up early in the morning before the children woke and go to the rooftop. Joseph would pray aloud, and I would listen and pray in silence. He prayed for us to be obedient to the will of the Lord, and with his prayers, my spirit grew more submissive, and I listened to hear the voice of God giving us the direction that we needed.

But Jesus did not go to the Temple to live.

Annas was deposed as High Priest, and in the sixth year after Jesus made his covenant, Joseph died. We were devastated, and without Joseph, our lives started to crumble. As the oldest son, Jesus assumed responsibility for our family, and we went on. I relied on him for so many things, and the children looked up to him and did as he asked. He became the undisputed leader of our family, of me. We had traded places.

Jesus grew more serious by the day as he shouldered the burden of caring for us. Like Joseph's, his carpentry work was perfect, and he used his skill to earn money for our support. Sometimes, I would watch him as he stood in the sun, lifting his hammer again and again pounding out his restlessness, tiring himself out until he didn't remember that he had a family of seven, but no wife to sit by his side and no child to hold upon his lap. He pounded until the heat overtook him, and then he would strip his shirt from himself to find relief. I would see his back, brown and strong and beautiful, narrow at the waist with muscles that rippled when he moved his arms. And I would think about the weight that we had placed upon it. He didn't complain, though; he never complained, and I was grateful that I didn't have to live as a charity widow or marry someone I despised.

Jesus and James often went to Jerusalem for the festivals. When the time came, they presented Joses and later, Simon and Jude, at the Temple. I did not go again for many years, but I heard from my sons that even though Annas was deposed, he was often present at the Temple, and from time to time, he and Jesus spoke together and discussed the scriptures. No mention was made of Jesus going there to work and study. I don't think that Annas' sons, and later his son-in-law Caiaphas, wanted Jesus around. They would not have liked to be displaced in Annas' eyes. The old man always maintained power.

After some years, Jesus took work as a shepherd, and it agreed with him. He became more carefree again as he wandered about the hills with the sheep and the goats. No roof, no walls, few people. Sometimes he would take one of his brothers with him, but mostly he did not allow them to miss attending the synagogue. He demanded that they do well in their studies and drilled them relentlessly until they had committed many scriptures to memory.

But out in the hills, without Joseph's presence in his life, there also came a recklessness about Jesus. When he would come down from the highlands, and we would join with others at some celebration, he would run the fastest, swim the farthest, and climb the highest. The people were caught up in his wildness, and he would draw men and, especially, young women around him. I hoped that he would marry and settle down, but he did not. He would smile at the girls, laugh with them, sometimes even walk with them, especially one named Rebecca, but that was all. Fathers hinted about marriage contracts, saying that they would not ask a high bride price. But Jesus brushed them aside before they became too serious, telling them that he had other responsibilities that must first be met. I think about that now and wonder how much he knew of what was to come.

One night, Joses came home late from working just north of Nazareth. Like Joseph and Jesus, he was a carpenter. He washed the dirt from his hands, took the plate of stew that I offered, and ate in silence. He was growing into a fine young man, more like my father in looks and temperament than he was like Joseph.

"There is a celebration in Sepphoris that I could hear all the way from Ezra's place," he said.

Jesus and his cousin Eli were days late in coming from the pastures, and immediately, my heart began to pound. Even after all those years, in the back of my mind, I still feared that Herod would assassinate Jesus, and I imagined him celebrating the deed.

I paced the floor and prayed through the night. The next day was the same. In the late afternoon, James said that he and Joses would go and look for Jesus and Eli. I insisted on going along. The younger boys would not be left behind, so the five of us set out.

We found Eli leaning over a cliff, hanging on to a rope that reached to Jesus far below.

12

Oldest Son

A sheep had fallen and was stranded on a ledge. Jesus had jumped down to rescue it but slipped and fell another ten cubits before he landed on a ledge below.[1] He had injured his ankle and was sitting on the narrow shelf with his back pressed to the rocks working to fasten the rope around his waist. I saw that the fire they burned to keep the wild animals away was almost out, so I knew that they had been this way for some time.

Jesus finished tying the rope and stood to scale up the cliff wall while Eli lifted. I watched, and as Jesus stood, I saw the ledge giving way. It broke loose, and Jesus plunged through the air, jerked to a stop, and then hung, suspended. There was nothing but space for a long, long way below him. Unable to bear the force, Eli slid toward the edge of the cliff.

James and Joses each dove for one of Eli's legs, and their collective weight held. By this time, Jesus was tipped head down, spinning slowly. Somehow, they swung him near the cliff, and he got enough of a hand hold to right himself. Eli hoisted, the boys pulled, and Jesus scaled one footed back to the ledge where the sheep had fallen. He untied the rope from himself and tied it around the sheep. Eli lifted the bleating sheep to safety and then sent the rope back down for Jesus. Jesus tied the rope around himself, and the three pulled him to the top. Eli stayed behind with the sheep, and the rest of us set out walking.

Jesus threw his arm over James' shoulder, and James held him around the waist, lifting as Jesus limped his way to the road. We had not gone far when a bigga currus[2] thundered past us. The driver reigned to a stop and waited while we made our way to the chariot. The magnificent horses pranced in place, their decorated harnesses and breast plates sounding out their importance.

"Climb on," the driver ordered. I kept my head down.

"No." I whispered to the boys, but Jesus climbed on and nodded permission for them to follow.

They scrambled on and stood beside the driver looking down at me. I shook my head no. James stayed behind, and we walked home together.

When we reached the house, Simon and Jude rushed out to meet us and tell about their ride. They were fascinated by the horses, and for the rest of the evening couldn't stop talking about them, their speed, their power, their beauty. Joses knew they should not have compromised themselves in such a way and kept silent. I fretted and scolded.

"Imma, the Romans are God's people too," Jesus said quietly.

"You count them as the House of Israel then?" I heard the sharpness in my own voice.

"Yes. No. I don't know. It is what I struggle with," he answered.

He stood by the basin and washed himself and the water ran off his handsome face, through his fingers and down his strong brown arms. "Imma, I am sorry that . . ."

"No. It is all right," I said. "I didn't mean to be so harsh."

Late that night, I went up to the rooftop to enjoy the coolness and to pray. I was retreating there more and more often, becoming my mother without even knowing it. After awhile, Jesus pulled himself onto the roof favoring his injured ankle. I knew that he had a power to heal, but he did not seem interested in using it on himself.

"Your ankle?" I asked.

"It is fine," he said.

"James can cut you a walking stick."

"No. Don't worry about it."

"It's good that you weren't hurt more."

"James said the scribe returned the final contract for Ariela," he said changing the subject. He referred to his cousin.

"Yes. It was a good match you arranged for her. And a strong contract."

He laughed. "With you remembering just one more thing and then another one more thing that had to be put in the ketubah."[3]

"It is strong."

"She will be protected," he agreed.

"Her mother will sleep well," I said, but Jesus did not seem to hear me.

"I saw a woman . . . when Eli and I were in the hills, a young woman lying dead. I could tell that she had taken her own life. I found out that she had been attacked and raped by five men when she walked home from the well. She just walked to the hills and took her own life."

"May the Lord have mercy on her soul."

"No one even tried to stop her. No one even went after her."

"She didn't want to shame her family."

"The shame was not hers. The shame was her attackers," his voice rose. "And yet she would be held to blame. It is not right."

"No. It's not, but it is the way of things."

"I think almost every day of the man in Egypt," he said.

"At the market?" I knew that was the one.

"Yes. The one who was stabbed to death."

"I didn't know you remembered. You have never spoken of it."

"I was not always sure if it really happened. I remembered the arguing, a man standing by the camel, a man falling. When I was older, I thought that he must have been stabbed. Then, I remembered inside the tent."

"He was a nomad. The one who killed him was an Egyptian from a higher station."

"No one is above another in the eyes of the Lord," Jesus stated.

"No," I agreed. "But on earth some men have the power to take another's life."

"They sin against God and man. Life is sacred."

Again, I agreed with him. We fell silent and sat watching the night, the moonlight reflecting off the white limestone houses of Nazareth, the stars brilliant and twinkling. Then Jesus pointed out how a man could find his way by studying the heavens. How he could be guided by them, how they were unchanging over all the years. How those very stars had shined down on Abraham and how they would shine down on generation after generation of my children. He did not speak of his own children but of those of his brothers and sisters. I had not heard that about the stars, and I didn't know if it was something that he had learned from the rabbis or if it was something that he knew, but the rest of the world did not.

"A star led the Persians to your cradle."

"Yes, Abba told me that." He flexed his ankle as he spoke. "Why wasn't I born in Nazareth?"

"Caesar had issued a new tax decree."

"I never knew why you traveled there when you were . . ."

"We wanted to be together. That is all."

"Everything has been different since his death. Harder to understand."

"Your father was very wise."

"Wiser than some of the leaders, I think. My rabbis do not always agree with me, nor do some of the priests."

"You question them?"

"They often have a different interpretation of the scriptures than Joseph or I. The will of the Father has always seemed clear to me, and Joseph understood it in the same way."

"What is your disagreement with them?"

"They use the scriptures as a way to gain power over others that the Lord did not intend them to have."

"Most feel they abide by the laws."

"The law is for the one who is sinned against as well as the sinner. It cannot be applied to the transgressor only. The law says an eye for an eye, but they take an eye for a loaf of bread or put a man to death for refusing to bow down."

"Should the Romans obey Jewish law?"

"The law is a gift to every man. Without it, we would live as barbarians. Men should not stop with the law only, but embrace the spirit of it. If a man steals a loaf to end his hunger, forgive him his debt; if he steals in greed, make him repay the cost twofold, but do not take his life for such a thing."

"Yes," I agreed. "Joseph told me that is what God intended."

"You know that as well."

"When I was young, I wished to be a boy so that I could study the scriptures." `

"I have seen you read them."

"In truth, they go on until I lose my thought, and I cannot understand them. I do not understand even all of what you say."

"If you follow only two commandments, you will live in the way God intended. First, you must love the Lord your God with all your heart and all your soul, and second, you must love your neighbor as yourself. All else depends on these. Really, only the first must be known for if the first is in you, then so is the second."

"Only two?"

"Yes. Take these two commandments into your heart, and goodness will follow. Almost all else in scripture is a history of our people and stories of how they listened or did not listen to the Lord."

"Is it easy for you to follow them because you are . . . ?"

"I follow them because it is what I know. You have made it so. You and Joseph. For me and my brothers and sisters."

"By his teachings?"

"Even before that. When a child is born, if his mother shows him the way of love and mercy, and his father does not turn him against his mother, he will almost surely grow to follow these great commandments.

"What if he is not given these things?"

"Still, it is not impossible. Everyone is a child of Abraham, a child of God."

"It doesn't seem that it could be that easy."

"It is. If all men would follow these two commandments, everything would change. All would return to the ways of the Lord, and justice and peace would come to the land."

He was excited when he spoke. I thought that he was young, too young to understand the hearts of men. He rose, winced when he stepped on his ankle, but walked to the side of the roof. Then he returned and sat by my side.

"Do you think that would ever come to be?" I asked.

"It is why I have been called. I want to begin my work now," he said. His voice was impatient.

"The work of Hamashiach?"

"Teaching, first."

"In the Temple?"

"Nazareth, I think."

Our brief sentences were separated by silences. I tried to think of the right things to say to him.

"James could tend the sheep now, or Joses and Simon."

"No. Joses and Simon will stay at home with you." His order was sharp, final.

"You have worked so hard since your father died. I know that we have been a burden to . . ."

"The burden is not you or my brothers and sisters."

I sat and waited, but he did not continue. "What else troubles you?" I asked.

"Many things." He rose again and walked to the edge of the rooftop, limping enough that it was noticeable in the sound of his footsteps. He stood at the edge and stared out into the night. "Many things. What is to come? When it will come? How I will accomplish my purpose?"

"Will you lead a rebellion?" I blurted it out. I had not intended to ask, had guarded against it, but the question popped from my mouth. He turned to me, his brows drawn together, shook his head and frowned a little.

"You know that is not my way," he said.

I sighed loudly and he lifted one side of his mouth into his indulgent smile and shook his head again. We had a moment of relief. He returned and sat again.

"If I lead with force, there would always be someone who thinks that he is stronger, someone who thinks he can rule better."

He took my hand in both of his, lowered his head and held our hands to his forehead. I put my other hand on his shoulder. He was growing thin. I wanted to get up and fix him something to eat.

"I am impatient, but I do not believe my time has yet come."

"You are young to lead so many."

"Or it may be that I am not ready to accept what I will face."

"I do not understand," I whispered. I whispered because I didn't want to irritate him. I didn't want him to leave. And maybe I whispered because I didn't want to know.

"What will happen in my life will transcend our life on this earth. You must remember that."

"Yes." I agreed, but I didn't know then what he meant.

"My work and that of my followers will be to bring change, to begin something that will not be stopped."

"Like a windstorm?"

"Like the leavening that you put into your bread dough. It permeates the loaves. The kingdom of heaven will not be stopped."

I waited.

"Not only heaven as you believe. The kingdom of heaven is also upon the earth. It is everywhere, in all places and all times. In Judea, and in all the lands, even Egypt and Persia."

"You will bring this?"

"If through me the world knows a greater love, a greater truth, my work is done."

Then without stopping, he asked if I thought it was right that we have so many sacrifices at the Temple when so many people are starving. He would often shift his thoughts and comments from subject to subject like that. At times, so quickly that I found it hard to understand him.

"It is not something that I have thought about," I said. "I didn't think that we should put anything before our sacrifices to the Lord."

"The Lord wants our lives, not our blood offerings." His words were almost harsh. "The Lord stayed the hand of Abraham and accepted the ram, so that a father would no longer sacrifice his child, male or female. But the sacrifice of the animals is out of hand. Do you think that a rich man who is able to buy a better dove or lamb will find more favor with the Lord? No, he will not. The endless parade must stop. It is a waste of food that could feed the poor."

I was silenced by the sharpness of his words.

"It is not something to worry about now," he said. "I should not have mentioned it." Then he looked out into the distance and said, "The Cedar Lebanon tree is dying."

The Eleventh Day of Marchesvan

I have been trying. Each day now I prepare food. Mostly though, I cannot eat it, and I feed it to the goat so that it is not left to waste. My hair is braided, my clothes are washed, my garden is weeded, and my fire is lit. I force myself to do one thing and then one thing more until I have gotten through the day. I only pick at things a little now. It is one of the things that I do when I am afraid. The threads of a blanket, the bits of mud plastered between the stones, anything will do. Over and over until I quiet myself. I have a fear that I have lost my mind. There are so many things that I can't remember.

My neighbor, Rebecca, is here. Most of the people have gone now, but she still comes. She tells me that I am doing well, and I agree so that I do not inflict my grief upon her. Like so many others, she does not know what to do with my pain and is relieved when we can pretend that it has passed.

She marvels at my strength, and she is right. I am strong and bold in ways that I never would have been before. Things that once frightened me are of no consequence now. But in living, I have no strength at all. I have not taken even a single step on my own ever since it has happened. Over and over, I repeat The Psalm of David, "Unto Thee I cry, O Lord; be not silent to me: lest I become like them that go down to the pit."

Today, though, I cannot even remember my prayers, and I cry out to the Lord like I did to my own father when I was a frightened child. In my anguish, I do not worry what will happen to me if I say the holiest of names. But my prayer is a secret. I cry out in silence, and Rebecca and the others do not even know. She sits and smiles and cannot hear me. I have learned to do this so that no one hears. No one knows. It is too hard for them.

This time the Lord has heard me, and for now I am safe. He lifts me in his mighty arms and holds me, and I am safe. Rebecca leaves, and I fall against the door and slide to the floor and stay there until the last bit of sunshine disappears.

Now the night has come. The darkness has fallen, and I am alone and afraid. I cry out again, but the Lord has left with the daylight, and He does not answer my prayers. Again and again, I cry his name, but He does not hear me. Then I see him in the darkness, but he turns his back and walks away.

Finally, I sleep. In my sleep, it's not too late, and I plead, "Save my child Lord, save my child. Place your hand upon his brow. Lift him up and save him from this evil." Then terror wakes me, and the mountains fall upon me, and I know again that my son is gone.

13

A Teacher

Jesus waited until his ankle healed, and then he returned to the hills. After that, we saw him less and less. He began leaving the sheep with Eli and James and traveling to Capernaum or all the way to the Mediterranean to work or study. Sometimes he stayed away for weeks or even months at a time.

I worried about him when he was gone, but it was hard to live with him when he was home. One day he would be enthusiastic, exuberant even; the next, brooding and sullen. When I asked what troubled him, he would walk away. He caused a tension in the room, and no one knew what to expect, so our days were centered on trying to humor him or trying to avoid him. Sometimes, when he would sleep, I would stand and watch him or pray over him. In sleep, he was my son again. I would look back over my time with him and hope that I had not wasted it. I realized then, that the others did not even know of Jesus' future. Joseph and Jesus had spoken of it many times, but we had not really shared it with his brothers and sisters. Now it seemed past the time. On occasion, I brought it up, but I could never find the right words, and it didn't go well. I prayed for the Lord's guidance. I wanted to help Jesus in whatever was ahead for him, but I grew more and more confused about what it would be. I thought that he would return to the Temple to work, but he was very troubled with the way things were going in Jerusalem, with the things that were happening to the Jewish people.

He would often withdraw to pray, and that would settle him. But soon, he would grow restless again, upset by some new political or religious happening.

James began spending more and more of his time with Jesus, traveling with him. Myriam married and lived some distance away. Joses was taking over many of the responsibilities at home, but then Jesus would appear from out of nowhere and assume command of the family again. Simon would not listen to Joses as he listened to Jesus, and he sometimes ran away and followed after Jesus. Joses resented being left as the man of the household but then having Jesus give orders to everybody when he returned. It was becoming unbearable.

Elizabeth's son John had now joined the Essenes and begun teaching and preaching. He was gathering large groups of followers who were eager for the coming of the Messiah. John was growing wild, more rigid in many ways, condemning anyone who did not repent and live as he thought they should. He was making the authorities nervous, and some of them were turning against him.

Jesus and his brothers spent time with John. But John was not satisfied, and he assailed Jesus, demanding that he come and live with him. Jesus refused, telling John that the time was not right. He was the head of our family since Joseph's death. He would fulfill that responsibility first.

Then Jesus announced that he was going to move us to Capernaum. I didn't know why he would want to move there. It was close to Herod's new capital in Tiberius. I worried that Jesus would do something to attract Herod's attention or even do something to challenge his authority. Capernaum was filled with Gentiles, and I didn't see how that would prepare Jesus for his work as the Messiah. When I asked for his reasons, he said only that it would be better for Joses and Simon. That way we would all be together again.

Joses did not see it that way. In the end, I moved to Capernaum with Salome and Jude, because Jesus wanted them with him, but Joses and Simon stayed at our home in Nazareth. I missed my sons, but both Salome and Jude, as the youngest in the family, had ended up with a wonderful calmness about them, and it was a peaceful time for us.

We were not long in Capernaum before Jesus moved us north to Caesarea Philippi near the start of the Jordan River. It was far from our kinsmen, and Salome did not want to come along. Jesus allowed her to return to Nazareth and wed. By then, Simon came to Phillipi and began traveling with Jesus. He had grown wild, zealous, always ready for an argument. I worried about him constantly.

In Caesarea Phillipi, Jesus attracted a group of Pharisees, and I thought that he might come into his leadership with them, but that didn't happen. He was troubled by how they demanded exactness in every small detail of the law and then disregarded more important matters. Strained the gnat and swallowed the camel, Joseph would have said. So Jesus left them, first to join with James as he worked to raise money for the poor, the widows and orphans, and later to spend more time with John. Jude and I returned to Nazareth to live. I never knew where Simon was.

When Jesus came home, especially after he was spending so much time with John, he was thin and tired and troubled. He would sleep a few hours and then be ready to leave again.

"Not a place to lay his head," Joses mocked.

Joses was ready to take a wife, but Jesus thought that he was too young and that he had obligations to his faith. I agreed with Joses that he should marry, and Jesus relented. Joses' wife must have softened both of them because the arguments between them ended, and they sought each other's advice and help on many things. Still, I knew that Joses shared my worries over Jesus and his other brothers.

Then miraculously, Jesus settled on his course and was at peace. He left his carpentry, turned the sheep over to Eli, and became a rabbi. He began traveling and teaching full time. His personal turmoil seemed to be resolved, and he went ahead with a confidence I had not seen in him since he stood by Joseph's side with his hammer in hand.

When he entered a room, peace came with him. Instead of avoiding him, we all gathered round him. He still had his concerns about what was happening in our faith, and he still spoke against some of the practices, but he was different. When John came to visit and began to rant about the evils of the nation, Jesus would say a word to him, and he would calm down. Jesus assured John that all things would come in the fullness of time, and for once, even John seemed content.

There was a presence about Jesus. People wanted to be near him, wanted to listen to him. He was patient and kind, and the joy of his boyhood had returned to him. His followers grew in number, and the people invited him into their homes to eat and sleep and into their synagogues to teach. I praised the Lord for the peace that my son had found and for the strength that seemed to be growing within the Jewish people under his leadership.

One evening, when the air was chilled, I sat with Jesus by the fire. We spoke of our family, of Joseph, and of things to come. It was one of our last times together that I remember.

"The grapes will be good for wine this year," he said. "They are just sweet enough."

"Will we pick tomorrow?"

"Another two days will be better. I will stay and see to it."

"You are the perfect son," I said.

He smiled, and fine lines crinkled from his eyes. "No one is perfect, but God alone," he said.

But he was. Everything about him was goodness. "You are," I said. "There is no mark against you."

"It is what I have tried to be. To be pure and undefiled before God."

"Tell me what you have learned," I said.

"Yes, Joseph," he teased, for Joseph had always required a report from the children when they returned home each day.

We laughed together at the remembrance.

"It is a bad time for the people of Israel," he said. "I fear we are losing our way."

"What makes you think that?"

"We cannot serve two masters. The people do not realize that they are replacing the Lord with their luxuries and their love of money. It has become too easy to accept the ways of the Greeks and the Romans. They will entice us with their conveniences, and then, when we cannot live without them, they will own us. They have divided us already. When the time comes to pay the price, it will be great."

"The Essenes have already taken a stand against that."

"Yes, but their stubbornness only spurs the infighting. We should stand together against those who defy the Lord. Instead, the Essenes, the Zealots, and the priests all quarrel with each other and weaken the people. It is our strength that we can disagree with each other and therefore, see all sides, but when we extend it to the Gentile world, it weakens us. I will tell you this. If we continue this way, they will find our divisions and break us. When the House of Israel becomes so divided, it will fall. We must return to who we are before it is too late. That is the only thing that will save us."

"Can you do that?"

"I know the will of the Father, and I will tell it to anyone who will listen, anyone who has ears to hear. If they don't, we can't stand against the Romans. We divide ourselves, and they stand by and laugh."

"I pray always for you in your work."

"Pray that I do the Father's will."

When I knew that he was not going to say more on that subject, I stood and stirred the fire. "What else?" I asked.

"How quickly life passes. How short our life upon this earth is," he said.

"You are young."

"There are things that cannot be changed, and no matter how much you want to, you can't protect me from what I must do."

"It is what every mother wishes, to care for her child."

"Imma, I am not a child anymore."

"I know."

"A mother has two great gifts to give, first a nest and then wings. You have given me the first, now it is time for the second. It's time for you to let go."

I didn't answer.

"You have given me everything I have needed, you and Joseph." He picked up a pebble and threw it into the night. I didn't hear it land.

"Maybe if Joseph were still here, I wouldn't be so . . . ," I hesitated and then whispered, "I wish him back."

"He lives in eternity, and he lives on through all of us he has left behind. If we had had another hundred years with him, it wouldn't make us miss him less when he was gone."

"I know that's true, but . . ." I didn't want to get weepy so I changed the subject. "Will you stay home awhile now?"

"No, I cannot. Even if I wanted to, I could not stop myself. I must answer my calling. I want to answer it."

"We miss you when you're gone."

"In spirit, I will be with you always. Even onto the end of the age."

"You are at peace now. With your calling, with the Lord."

"Yes. What I do now, I do in love. The wind of heaven is the power within me."

"Who will go with you?"

"I will have some close followers, both men and women, but some things I alone will be called to do. My time has come now. We cannot wait for the end time and claim that we have faith. My brother James is an example to me. He has already given his life to good works. I tell him that he has grown up to become his mother."

I laughed.

"It's true," he said. That's what I remember about you. How you cared for everyone, providing food and clothes, tending the sick. Sometimes I didn't know who my own brothers and sisters or cousins were. The house was so filled with people you were helping."

"There was always enough, though. And Joseph didn't mind so much."

"He worked as hard as two men to provide for your flock."

"He was a servant of the Lord."

"In more ways than either of you have ever told us."

I didn't answer.

"He who is greatest shall be a servant. Whoever exalts himself will be humbled, and whoever humbles himself will be exalted," Jesus said, his voice soft and kind, but also urgent like Joseph had been when he taught us.

"Joseph is exalted then."

"Even now, he is exalted in heaven."

"Do you know? Can you see him there?" I wanted to grab Jesus' hands and say tell me, tell me.

"Let your faith sustain you," he said and bent and kissed my brow. Then he banked the fire, and we went into the house.

And I was at peace from that time until . . . until the darkness came.

For a short time, Jesus was in Nazareth, but things didn't go well for him there amongst his friends and neighbors. Because of Herod, I was pleased that he didn't stay here. After leaving Nazareth, I believe that he drew large crowds wherever he went, and many of the people followed him from town to town. I knew that he was causing some ripples with both the Roman and Jewish authorities, but my faith was strong at that time, and I didn't really worry about him.

Joses and his wife remained in Nazareth. They brought my water, shared food with me, and helped me with repairs around the house. Jude had also married and lived nearby. He came and planted my garden and tended the grapes. Both of them wanted me to come to live with them, but I wanted to keep a home for when my other sons returned.

Salome and her new husband sometimes traveled with Jesus. James was always with him. Simon seemed to split his time between Jesus' friends and another group of wild men that he had found. A group that I wished he would stay away from.

When it was the time of this last Passover, I had not seen any of the three boys for some time, so I decided to travel to Jerusalem to celebrate with Martha in hopes that Jesus and James and their friends would join us, and that I would find Simon with them.

Joses told me that it wasn't safe, that Jesus wouldn't have time to spend with me anyway. But I had it in me to go, so finally, he relented and arranged for me to travel with some kinsmen.

The journey was long and tiring. My years were telling on me. Each morning I could barely rise from the ground because of the pain in my hips and knees, and it took me until the sun was half way over-head to get rid of my limp. Finally, we reached Be-eroth, some eight miles or so north of Jerusalem, and I thought that the worst of the journey was over. Then the accident happened, and I didn't know if I would make it the rest of the way to Jerusalem. But I concentrated on each step and on the thump of my walking stick on the pavers to take my mind from the scene. My hand was hot and sweaty and cramped around the wood. I didn't loosen my grip, though, because the blisters had broken leaving tender red circles across my palm and in the web of my thumb. Every time they touched the stick, they stung like a fire ant bite, so I held on and ignored the cramps.

Finally, I could see Jerusalem in the distance, but like walking to the rainbow's end, I never seemed to get any closer to it. At the side of the road was a meadow covered with the wild flowers. The green of the grasses was so much kinder than the desert, the perfume of the purple iris was intoxicating, and I wanted to give up and lie down. I heard my breath exhale in a steady hunh, hunh, hunh, matching my steps.

Just a short rest, I thought, was all I would need, so I started to make my way across the road to the meadow. Then from across the valley, the shofar wailed, loud and long, echoing across the hills, calling the people of God to prayer. My heart raced. My strength was renewed.

My stick clattered, barely touching the pavement as I ran then to keep pace with my fellow travelers. The wall of the city was only a fur-long away. In a final surge, we passed through the Damascus Gate. We had reached Jerusalem, and in shouts, whispers, and fervent prayers the songs of our souls rose to the heavens.

I stood tall and drew a breath. The city pulsed with excitement, and my heart pulsed in anticipation of the blessing that I would receive from it. People came from all over the lands to worship in the holy city, in the Temple, and that day I was one of them.

Before me, the Temple stood tall, magnificent, and immaculate, white marble adorned with gold. King Solomon built the first Temple for worship almost 1000 years before Jesus was born. The Babylonians destroyed the Temple and sent the Jews into exile. Then about 500 years before Jesus was born, the Persian King Cyrus defeated the Babylonians, and our people returned to Judea and rebuilt the Temple. By the time King Herod came to power, that second Temple was badly in need of repairs, so in the eighteenth year of his reign he began to repair and enlarge it to nearly twice its size.

The leaders of the people did not trust him to complete the project. So to appease them, Herod had all of the materials for the new Temple, including the massive stone blocks used in the base, brought in before the first stone was removed from the old Temple. The project took many, many years, so Herod also allowed the priests to continue to offer sacrifices to God on the Temple site during the building period.

One thousand men work continuously to keep the Temple clean and in good repair so that it will remain through generations of lives, through hundreds, even thousands of years. That day, I asked God to let my children and my children's children come there throughout the ages to worship him.[1]

I thought that Jesus might soon enter the Temple proper, a place where no one but the priests were allowed. The rule was fast. When the Temple was being built, the priests themselves had to learn to be stonecutters and carpenters, so that law was not broken.

Though I would never see the inside of it, I had been told many times of its beauty. Above the gate to the Temple proper are golden vines as large as a man. Inside the gate, the entrance to the holy place is covered with a veil embroidered in blue, white, and scarlet purple. And within the inner Temple stands the altar of incense, a menorah, and a table for the show bread. Separating this room from the Holy of Holies was the curtain of the Temple. Since Jesus' death, that is no longer so.

Only the high priest himself can enter the Holy of Holies and only one day each year, on the Day of Atonement which is called Yom Kippur. This place now stands empty because the arc of the covenant was destroyed in long ago battles, but the Holy of Holies remains our most sacred place.

My traveling companions broke into my thoughts and invited me to go with them to buy food, but I declined. I had to keep a straight path. Already it was midday, and I not only had to make my way through the city but travel three miles more to reach Martha's house. Roman soldiers, patrolling to keep order during the festival, ringed the portico of the Temple and stared down at us. Even so, I felt a sense of freedom that I had never experienced. I knew there were over three hundred thousand people in the city, more people than I could ever count, and yet as I stood in the midst of them, I felt for the first time in my life that I was completely alone.

I had, at times, wandered from my house or my father's house, but I had never done anything like this. I was on my own, and I knew I would not forget it. I stood alone, and the world did not come to an end. I told myself to look purposeful, but I could not get the smile to leave my face.

In one glance, I saw things from all over the world. The city market is located by the Damascus Gate, where we entered from the north, and extends well into the city. The stands spilled out onto the streets and reached back into the houses. Everything was for sale: sacrificial animals, beautiful fabrics, wonderful pastries, fresh and pickled fish, jewels, spices, pottery, bronze, and perfume. The merchants were as assorted as the wares that they sold. But they were all smiling as they jingled the coins that filled their purses and counted the money in their overflowing coffers.

14

Jerusalem

I had lived in Jerusalem for my first years, and since then I had been back to visit many times, so I inspected it with a proprietary eye. I noted which buildings had been well kept, which ones needed repair. After I studied them awhile, I could distinguish the individual stands. I saw the stand of Ezra the priest where I would buy my fowl offering. I picked out Zebedee's fish stand, run now by his sons, and Paz the jeweler.

Next to Paz was Ma'or, a weaver who had crowded her stand into a space that was no wider than my outstretched arms. I laughed remembering how Paz grumbled that her constant complaining was driving all of his business away. I saw Pina at work by the doorway of her house. She was a fuller and bleached the woven woolen fabric until it was almost white. My favorite spice stand, where I would buy gifts for my friends back in Nazareth, was still there. I heard my mother telling me to watch my shekels just as if she were standing beside me.

The pilgrims were jubilant and crowded the stands eager to find a bargain, eager to spend their shekels for a good sacrifice, a good meal, a useful tool, or something to impress their neighbors, something to serve as evidence that they had made the required pilgrimage and give them a place of respect among those who had stayed behind.

But once back home, whatever they had bought was just a reminder of how gullible they had been to spend their last bit of money on worthless trinkets. The excitement of the festival, the air of holiness that surrounded the Temple, the awe of standing within its walls, or even within the outer court, was not for sale.

A few of the travelers ignored the food, the scarves, the baskets, and the tools waved in front of them. They had learned. Some, I thought, did not even feel the holiness of the Passover in this city. They were here only because the pilgrimage was required. Their hostility against the Romans for taking our land and freedom was great, and as much as the Temple stood as a sign that the Israelites were the chosen people of God, the ever present soldiers were a sign of Rome and the complete power that it held over each and every one of us.

So the merchants circled, and what they did not collect, pickpockets would. I saw them, looking innocent while they worked the unsuspecting crowd. It was an easy day of profit for them. My coins were tied inside my robe, bound against me just as my mother had taught me. They would not get them.

I had not heard such celebration for years. Sometimes the voice of a child stood out to me, or the familiar accent of a Nazarene. But mostly, the noise of the city was just one loud din. Clanging, barking, Hebrew, Aramaic, Greek, and sounding trumpets all combined into the chorus of Jerusalem.

The smells were the most overpowering. The heat baked the entire city and intensified every smell as an oven does a loaf of bread. They blended together, and yet, in turn, drifted to me in distinct waves. Skewered chunks of roasted lamb made my mouth water, fresh steaming camel dung stung my nostrils, and hot wet feathers from thousands of fowl, hot cattle, hot goats, and especially the hot blood, roiled my stomach. The blood was sacred, but it smelled of rotted flesh, and it was nauseating. Then the wind gusted from the south, and the smell of the burning dumps from the Hinnom Valley mixed with it all.

I held my shawl to my face and crossed the street that I might be nearer to the Temple and walk in its shade. The rainy season was just ending and the full heat of summer was some months off, but it did not feel that way that day. The sun burned through my head cover as if a hot stone had been taken from the fire's edge and placed perfectly on top of my head, and it hurt. I touched it to relieve the pain, but the heat of the cloth seared into me. I wanted to pull my head cover away and pour water on my head, but, of course, I did not. It would not have been proper. The rabbis would have had to have a talk with my sons. It would have brought shame upon my family.

I walked along the Temple toward the southwest corner where I would meet young Micha, a kinsman of Martha's, who would escort me to Martha's house. Since he was not a kinsman of mine, it was not completely proper for him to be my protector, but Martha had sent me word that he had offered, and I accepted.

I remember that the walls were cool in the day's heat, and I slid my hand along the rough stone as I walked. I slowed my pace and enjoyed my nearness to the Temple. I did not climb the steps of the mount that day, and I could not see into the courtyard over the high walls, but I have been in the Court of Women many times, and I have heard the Passover stories from the time I was a little girl, so I knew well what was happening. High above, I heard the breezes blowing through the pillars. When I closed my eyes, I could feel the wind on my face and see the priests at work.

They had been getting ready for the celebration for weeks. Every-thing had to be cleaned. The Temple mikvah had to be filled. Hun-dreds of thousands of offerings needed to be accounted for, so census and treasury rolls were prepared to record the half shekel donation that was required of every Jewish male. All of the musicians needed to practice, the Levite choir, the hatsotsra,[1] psalter, harp, and lyre players. Even the cymbal players practiced long hours. The vendors and the money changers readied their stands. The lucky ones had been assigned spots in the Court of the Gentiles. The others would be left on the street.

But the most daunting task was the sanctifying and slaughtering of more than 100,000 animals on that first day of the festival. The priests would work without pause, without even looking up. The heartbeat of the festival, they work in a steady rhythm, as they slaughter the fowl and beasts for sacrifice and the lambs for the Passover meal itself. The cut is made sure and swift across the throat of the sacrificed bird or beast. Death comes in an instant. There is no suffering. The law forbids it.

As he makes the cut, the priest holds the animal's head so the blood pours into a golden *Mizrak.*[2] Not a drop of blood will spill. The bowl, filled with blood, is passed through a line of priests and the blood is splashed on the Temple altar. The bowl is passed back through the line and the process begins again. The animal is passed to another priest who flays the carcass, and the vultures and carrions swoop in and out pecking up any animal flesh that falls.

From high above me, near the southern arch at the place of trumpeting, came the voice of a priest, proclaiming the familiar words of "Shema Yisrael" from the scroll of Deuteronomy.[3] These words are our confession of faith: "Hear O Israel. The Lord our God, the Lord is one."

The priest went on to recite the story of the first Passover celebration when our ancestors left the land of Egypt and slavery behind: "Praised be his name, his glorious kingdom is forever and ever. Hear O Israel, the words of the Lord and observe the festival of the Passover. For when the Israelites were held slaves by the Egyptians, the Lord sent great plagues to the land that his people might be freed. And after he had sent nine plagues, he said to Moses, 'At midnight, I will go forth and all of the first born in the land of Egypt shall die. You may know that I the Lord will make a distinction between the Egyptians and Israel. Tell all of Israel that they shall take every man a lamb for their household, and on the fourteenth day of the month, they shall kill their lambs. Then they shall take the blood and put it on the doorposts of their house. And they shall eat the lamb with unleavened bread and bitter herbs, and they shall let none of it remain. The blood on your doorposts shall be a sign, and the Angel of Death shall pass over your house, and no plague shall fall upon you to destroy you. And this day shall be for you a memorial day and you shall keep it as a feast to the Lord; throughout your generations you shall observe it as an ordinance forever."

At his words, I felt the collective worship of generations of Hebrews surge through me. I stood in silent worship unable to move. Then I heard the young lambs bleat.

A man, who was an old friend of my father, walked slowly toward me. "Myriam." He nodded in greeting.

"Samuel." I nodded back.

His white hair and stooped back made me think that I should offer my arm, but he bent and lifted a trunk onto a cart like it was no heavier than a loaf of bread. I braced myself. Samuel had never approved of me. I had often heard him chastise my father for allowing me too many freedoms and privileges.

"Why are you alone?" he scowled, his eyebrows meeting at the deep wrinkle in his forehead. "Five sons and you run around alone like a whore on the street. What is wrong with you? What is wrong with them that they let you?"

My face burned at his words, but I kept my voice steady. "I have just arrived and am meeting a kinsman," I said.

I would not have survived Joseph's death if I were the weak and helpless widow that Samuel thought I should be, but I thought that it rankled him that I had chosen to live a thorn rather than die a flower.

"You should not be alone," he barked. You invite an attack. If it befalls you, you will be blamed. I tell you this as Joachim's friend." He gave a hmmph before he continued. "Your son is out of control."

"Simon?" I asked, thinking of his zealot friends.

"No, Jesus. Rein him in, and the others will fall in line. Unless it is already too late for Simon."

"Is Simon here? Have you seen him?"

"No, not for some time. I have heard that he has gone to the hills."

"Good. There is less chance for trouble. Where is Jesus?"

"Laying low, if he has any sense."

"Jesus is a grown man, thirty three years. He knows God's plan for his life." I didn't dare to look Samuel in the eye, but I didn't back down.

"God's plan? He had a near riot going on last Yom Ree-Shon.[4] People cheering, throwing palm branches and clothes on the ground for the ass he was riding to trample over. He is attracting a lot of attention from our religious authorities, and I have heard that Herod has taken notice as well."

I had heard from some of the travelers that Jesus made an entry into Jerusalem on a donkey instead of walking as he usually did and that he had drawn a crowd.

"Herod is here then?"

"Yes, the drunken fool and his women, pretending he is here for the Passover." Samuel's eyes burned into me as he spoke. His voice did not waver. "If Jesus had those people howling because they thought he was planning a rebellion, he had better forget it. He will never win against Rome. It will be a bloodbath. Jerusalem is a hot bed, and the Romans are ready to put down anything that looks like trouble."

"I don't believe that he is planning a rebellion."

"He should remember that Rome is not all bad for us. Their aqueducts bring us fresh water, and their good roads make for easy travel. Besides, if Rome did not hold the power, there would be someone else trying to take the land. There is too much money in the Temple for anybody with an army to ignore this city. At least now we have a place where all Jewish people can come. And we have the Temple for worship. It may not be like it was under King David or King Solomon, but the Temple stands. It is what we have until the coming of Hamashiach." Samuel pulled on his beard and shook his head back and forth.

"At least there is order," he went on. "You were not yet born, so you can remember nothing of the war after Julius Caesar was assassinated.

The battles that went on between the traitor Marc Antony and Octavian. If Octavian had not restored order and brought the empire together, we would be a battleground for countless nations who want to control our land."

There was no good will for Marc Antony in Palestine. He had written in his last testament that he wanted to be buried next to Cleopatra in Egypt, and Octavian used that to turn the people of Rome against him. He convinced them that Antony was a traitor, and he, Octavian Caesar Augustus, the hero.

"I don't think that he will go against Rome," I said again. "He abhors weapons and violence."

"He does not mind striking with his tongue."

"He teaches what he believes."

"He antagonizes the Chief Priest, the Sadducees, and the Pharisees. They even fight amongst themselves over what he teaches. We do not need more dissention among our people at this time."

"Our leaders have always debated amongst themselves".

"This goes beyond that, and now is a time we should stand together."

I was growing weary from standing in one spot. The straps of my sandals were cutting into my swollen feet, but I would not lift my robes to loosen them in front of Samuel. I thought that if I did not walk soon, I would not be able to. I took a few steps to leave, but Samuel had more to say.

"He is making claims that the Pharisees adjust the law every time the wind blows from a different direction. That they are so busy telling the rest of us what to do that they have no time to keep the requirements of worship, and that they misunderstand the spirit of what God intends. He has no right to question their authority!"

"The Sadducees make the same charge," I said. I swatted at a horsefly that buzzed my head and Samuel scowled at me.

"Yes. If he could side with them, he would be all right, but he attacks them at every turn as well. He accuses them of giving into

Hellenistic ways,⁵ says that they are soft on living as God commands. That they care more about staying in the good graces of the Romans than serving God. And if it were only that, they might ignore him. It is nothing that they do not hear from the Pharisees at all times, but he cannot be still. He can never be still."

"He does go on once he has started," I agreed.

"Yes," Samuel said tiredly, and I saw in his eyes that perhaps he did care for Jesus, even for me. "Now, Caiaphas has installed the priests as the merchants in the Temple and pretends that he did it to assure that the sacrifices are pleasing to God, but others believe that the House of Annas is not right in taking such a large share of the market, even holding a monopoly on the doves and the oil. Jesus seems to be in the group that believes there is corruption."

"And you?"

"It does not matter what I think. Jesus is a rabbi with a message some do not want to hear, and others do not want told. He does not know when to stop. He has made outright accusations, said that it is clear to all that Annas is charging too much for the sacrifices, and in so doing, he is taking food from the mouths of the poor. He told the people that Annas is skimming the money."

I wanted to weep at the foolish ways of my son. Samuel stood shaking his head again. "Do you think," I asked, "that you could speak to him? Tell him that he must not be so outspoken?"

Samuel stared at me. He narrowed his eyes and stared some more.

"As Joachim's friend, I have tried. I have tried, but I have failed. He told me that he could not be silent, that he must speak out even more, speak out until his voice has been heard. He told me that the Lord grows weary of the endless sacrifices. People are starving, and we are wasting food and money on sacrifices and then burning the food that is left."

"I will try to speak to him," I said.

Samuel gripped my arm and leaned close. "Listen to me. If Jesus threatens the authority of the priests, it will not go well for him. Neither Caiaphas nor the rest of the leaders will stand for some young rabbi coming in and bleeding the power of the Temple. They will not sit by while he convinces the people to follow him instead of the Temple laws. I will tell you again, they will not stand for even the thought of Jesus destroying the power of the priesthood that God ordained!"

"How can you say that? The priests know that Jesus obeys the laws. How can you say those things?"

Samuel ignored my question. "I bid you to turn back to Nazareth, now," he said.

"I will stay," I said.

"Your father is dead. Your husband is dead. Your sons have abandoned you. As Jochaim's friend, I order you to leave this city."

The Seventeenth Day of Kislev

I have been thinking about what James said to me before about my anger. It surprises me because that has never been my way, but I think that he may be right. I feel the iron in me so that I am unable to bend, or move, or sink to the floor. And when I grind the grain into meal, I pound so hard that I feel the shock of the two stones hitting together all of the way up my arm. I pound and pound until the grain turns into powder. Or I pluck the weeds from my garden with fury. And then I tear out the good plants as well because they offend me.

I think about our leaders and how they could have protected Jesus. Sometimes when I am pounding, I tell them. But if I do see any of them, I cannot say a word. I try to let the anger go as James has told me, but I think that if I am not angry, I might dissolve into the ground. Maybe my being is made up only of my anger, and if it were not there, the rains would wash me away.

Now it creeps through me and builds to rage. Rage at the Romans, especially the Romans. But the others too—the priests, and even God. They have taken my son's life, and they have destroyed his brothers and sisters as well. This anger is the very opposite of everything my son gave his life for. He did not give into it, but I do.

There is a dream that I have. I am falling into the pit, clawing at the sides and trying to stop myself, but I am sliding, sliding. Finally, I give up and let myself go until I reach the bottom. I want to get back to the top because Jesus and the others are up there, and I want to help them, but I cannot climb out. There are guards. Annas is there. Caiaphas too, but he is pacing, looking around, waiting for Annas to tell him what to do. Herod is there, and Pilate. And the Roman soldiers who do not care what happens. They just stand and do what they are told. In my dream, I keep asking them what will happen? What they are going to do? But they won't answer me. I try to remember every-thing that happened to Jesus that day, but even in my dream, I cannot remember. I do not want to.

I am helpless in the pit. I call out for Jesus to perform a miracle before it is too late. To perform a miracle and save himself and his brothers. He calls down to me that I must not fight, that I must not be angry. He leans low over the pit like he could pull me up, and we could get away, but he calls down, "Forgive them, Imma. Forgive them." My throat closes and chokes me. In my dream, I am even angry at Jesus for not stopping this. And the dream is always the same.

The rage burns through me, through my covers. Why did it happen? Was it Rome? Was it Annas? Was it Herod? Was it Pilate taking a bribe from Barabbas so the marker against his own life would be called off? How many times do I go over the same questions? Ten? One hundred? One thousand?

I lie in the darkness and think that my anger cannot be pleasing to the Lord. But still, it is there, hot and choking in my throat. I touch my face, and my cheeks are burning, but they are hard, carved of stone. No child or man would allow his lips to touch me lest he too be turned to stone by my wickedness.

Then, I hear Joseph, so real that I want to reach over to his side and touch him, but I do not because I know that he will not be there. I don't know if I am really awake or if this is part of the dream. I hear Joseph saying, "Stop it! Stop it! Stop it! The Lord has made you the mother of this child, called you to be angry at the injustice of the world. Go and use it to bring good. Do not fear the anger, but do not let it consume you, and do not let it turn you to stone."

And so I have been thinking more and more about the goodness of Jesus, wondering if there is any good left in me? Wondering if I could share it with the world?

15

Micha

"No," I told Samuel, "I will not leave. I have come for the Passover and to see my sons. I will stay." His sun browned face turned red.

"Your boldness does not become you," he stormed. "I am an old man, and I have never been disobeyed by a woman. Yet, you do so without hesitation. What has become of you that you think that you can run the streets on your own, that you can speak so and survive? Well, Jochaim is reaping what he sowed."

"I meant no disrespect," I stammered. I turned to leave.

"He is gaining too many followers," Samuel said. "And he is causing disturbances, Lazarus and now even in the Temple."

The name Lazarus, he no more than whispered, and at the time, I did not even hear it. It was the Temple that caught my attention.

"Have you seen him there?" I asked.

"In the Court of Israel? No. Do you think that they would let the troublemakers that travel with him past the Court of the Gentiles?"

"They are good men."

"Good men? Matthew is nothing but a robber bleeding everybody dry, collecting taxes for Rome. There are charges that some of his Galilean followers are Zealot terrorists.[1] And Peter is as big as an ox, so all he has to do is look at people and they get nervous. All of the authorities want to drive his band out of the city."

"You sound as though you despise my son."

"I do not condone the ways of his friends. Look at John the Baptizer. Any Essene can keep his silence for months, but this one couldn't keep his mouth shut long enough to save his own neck."

Samuel talked on, but I didn't hear him. I walked away with my mind on Jesus and John. John, the little boy who ate at my table, climbed the Cedar Lebanon tree, and discussed the scriptures with Joseph. John, the little boy who grew into a preacher and preached all the way to his execution.

John had a power to his words that could not be ignored. His ideas often consumed him and offended others. We might be sharing a meal, and he would begin to argue a point with such intensity that I could not swallow my food. It didn't matter to him if the bread was freshly baked and the meat perfectly roasted. I could have fed him the sawdust from the carpenter shop. Nothing of this earth was a comfort to him.

He should have followed in his father Zechariah's footsteps and taken up a position in the priesthood, but he did not have the patience for that, so he went off on his own. He wanted everyone to repent and be baptized to prepare for the coming Kingdom of God, and he often shouted wildly at people, condemning them for their sinful ways. He gathered droves of followers on the one hand and drove them away with his venomous tongue on the other. I have mentioned that this was his way even as a young boy, but Joseph had been able to temper him somewhat. After Joseph died, no one had control over John, and he spoke out without giving a thought to the consequences. When Herod married his niece, Herodias, John condemned them both for their sinfulness. As Samuel had said, he would not be still.[2]

Herod took his revenge and had John beheaded. There was a rumor that Herodias was the one who could not take his judgment, so she ordered her maidservant to dance for Herod and request the favor of John's head as a reward. The maidservant danced and asked,

and Herod obliged. John was beheaded at Herod's Fortress Machae-
rus, and at a banquet that followed, the maidservant wove a spell over
the guests by carrying John's head on a platter as she danced her way
around the exotic floor mosaics until she came to the table of Herodias and presented her with the head of John the Baptizer.

I didn't think this was really true, but I could not be sure. I had
heard that Herod wanted to be rid of John because he was afraid of
John's powerful sermons, afraid that John could stir the people to
a revolt if he was left unchecked. What did it matter, though, if it
was Herod or Herodias, dance or no dance? John was dead just the
same. I was glad that Elizabeth was not alive to know what had happened to him.

I put John and his execution from my mind. I had decided at the
time of Joseph's death that I would not let my life be defined by trag-
edies. I had learned from the stories of the persecution of the Israelites.
If my people did not hold on to hope when death came, they would
spend their lives in a wailing heap. Seven days are given to mourning,
and then it is time to go on. Seven days to pray for the soul in its cleansing. John's soul was in the world to come. That day, I was in Jerusalem
for the Passover, and that was enough.

Jesus was not like John, I told myself. He did not create the strife
that John did. I thought about what Samuel had said. I thought that
he was being too harsh in his judgments. To know Jesus, to touch his
hand or to have him touch yours was to know love. I do not say this
because I am his mother. Many others have told me that it is true.

While Jesus had been traveling and teaching, he had also been
healing, and his reputation for this had spread throughout Palestine.
He had done amazing things in the name of the Lord. His healings
were beyond what any physician could do. His touch or even his word
could restore health to someone. His works did not surprise me.
His faith had always allowed him to do things that others could not.
Joseph taught me to accept Jesus' gifts from the time he was a little
boy, and I had, but I did not speak of them to others. I knew that

many were jealous, and some were fearful. It was better that I kept still, especially since John's execution.

I knew that Jesus had been criticized for breaking bread with sinners and for helping people on the Sabbath. At one time, the law forbidding work on the Sabbath was so strict that we were not even allowed to defend ourselves against an enemy attack. Almost none of the leaders were that extreme anymore, but still, they would see no reason for Jesus' actions, and they would condemn him. I would speak to him and ask him to be careful.

I saw Micha then, and he lifted his hand in recognition and walked toward me. It had been many years, and he was not the child that I remembered. He was, after all, older than Jesus and had been a widower already for seven years. Martha claimed that he had not remarried because of a dispute with his father. The old man forced him into a marriage the first time and was now trying to do so again. This time Micha's resistance was stronger.

I understood his feelings. I have had offers since Joseph's death, most of them from older widowers, but I could refuse because I had children who could take care of me. I knew that whatever their flattering words, most of my suitors had wanted me to care for them in their ill health or for my sons to support them.

Micha was tall and handsome. His hair was cut shorter than most Jewish men, but not so short as the Romans. Shiny and black, it curled around his ears and neck. He had a moustache and a beard, but it was also trimmed so that his smooth brown throat showed below it. His teeth were white and strong. His eyes black. Now they flashed with anger, and I could see that behind his beard, his jaw was clenched. He grasped my arm so that it hurt.

"Why are you alone?" he demanded, exercising an authority over me that I did not intend to give him.

"It is safe enough in the city," I replied. "What is wrong that makes you act in this way?" I tried to pull my arm away, but he held his grip.

"I have heard what happened on your caravan. Were you hurt?"

"No, no. I am fine," I assured him, pulling at my arm again. This time he let it go.

"Tell me."

"It was just as we were finishing bathing at Be-eroth this morning. The Romans came thundering up in their chariots, and one of them drove right into the crowd of people. It was horrible. An old man died, and a young boy was . . ." I couldn't go on and struggled to control myself.

"Tell me," Micha said again taking hold of my arm once more and turning me so that I faced him. I looked at the ground.

"When we heard the chariots, everyone tried to run off the road. Some of them got knocked down, so they rolled or crawled into the ditch. I didn't see what happened to the old man. But the young boy . . . I had my eye on him because he had so much energy compared to the rest of us. The boy was on the ground . . . he was on his stomach trying to get himself up . . . I saw that he got to his hands and knees, his little behind sticking in the air. The horses veered and missed him, but the wheel of the chariot. . . ." I shuddered and held onto Micha's arm, ". . . the wheel cut his leg right off. It was just lying there on the road all bloody and dirty. It looked like a little dead animal. His whole robe turned red before anyone could make the ten steps to reach him. The Romans didn't even stop."

Micha pulled me to him and squeezed so hard that it hurt, but it helped to block the sight of the little boy's leg. I had not had the comfort of a man's arms for many years, and strangely, I started to weep. It was not something that I usually allowed myself to do.

"What happened?" he asked, his jaws clenched tight again. He relaxed his arms, but held me to him. I made myself step away.

"They tried to stop the bleeding," I said. "It slowed, but I don't think they could stop it."

"Did someone sear it?" he asked.

"I think someone tried. There were still coals in some of the fires. I don't know what happened. He couldn't be moved. His family will camp there until . . . Some stayed with them. The rest of us went on."

"There was nothing else to do."

"The Romans knew there would be travelers there. They could have watched."

"They don't care," he seethed.

"They will answer to God."

"They do not believe in God."

The streets were crowded, and some travelers pressed against us, so that we had to move backwards with them to keep our balance. Micha gripped my elbow and headed us in the right direction again.

"Don't they believe that their own gods would care?" I asked.

"About a Jewish child?"

"Is there no goodness in them at all?"

"Like Jesus teaches, you mean? That all men are good, even the Gentiles?"

"Yes, I suppose that is what I mean."

"I don't know. If they are, it is hard to see it in this city. It seems that the Romans thirst for violence, not goodness."

"I have heard that they hold innocent men in dungeons and then put two of them who have no quarrel with each other, brothers even, into the arena and make them fight to the death. Fine strong men who have no crime, one begging the other to slit his throat and end it so that he is not eaten alive by the lions or the dogs."

I didn't think that any Jewish person had ever witnessed such a fight, but we had heard. I had also heard that some religious men had been thrown to the lions, like Daniel in the scriptures, but I didn't know for sure.

"You cannot let anyone hear you speak like that," he said, his voice sharp again.

"I am a woman. No one will take notice of me."

"You are Jewish. They will."

"Are you my father?" I laughed to lighten the mood.

"No, Myriam, I am not your father. I am anything but your father."

My heart pounded a little. I looked at him, and his eyes held mine for just a few steps. Then I looked away again.

"You need to pay attention," he said. "Do not fall into danger. This is not Nazareth. Many are put to death here every day. Not just accidentally like you saw today, but deliberately sentenced to death for some small infraction."

"I will try to be silent," I said.

He smiled at me, and we headed back along the Temple wall towards the Golden Gate and Martha's house.

"Have you seen Jesus?" I asked.

"No. Not for some days."

"I hope that he will come to Martha's," I said.

"I am worried about him. He makes the authorities uneasy."

"What has he done?"

"He doesn't have to do anything. Pilate's men talk too freely because they think that we are simple peasants and do not understand them. I have heard that Pilate put some of his men to death for speaking of his business in front of Jesus, giving away political secrets."

"He knows that Jesus understands Greek?" I asked.

"Most know that about him. It's not only that, though. There is major trouble in the city."

"More than other times?"

"Yes. Barabbas has struck again. He and his band were involved in a riot, and five men were killed."

"Who?" I asked.

"I don't know. I heard that one was a Roman guard."

Barabbas stayed hidden when he could. But I had learned from my sons that unlike most Jews, Barabbas and his followers didn't want to wait for the Messiah, nor did they bother with an organized uprising. They identified their targets and struck, swift and lethal. They could walk into a crowd and never cause a stir. When they exited on the other side, they had left someone dead. Their daggers already sheathed and out of sight in their robes.

"He is tired of the oppression," I said.

"Yes, but there is word that he and his band have broadened their attack. Yaniv the priest was murdered, and his death has been blamed on Barabbas."

"A Jewish priest? I can't believe that."

"Some say it was a robbery, but others are not so sure. The word is that Yaniv was collecting bribe money, and Barabbas had him assassinated to make an example."

"I thought Barabbas was a man of God. I don't understand how he could take any life so easily. But a priest?"

"An eye for an eye."

"The priest would not have harmed a man."

"If he takes a bribe, he is hurting good men."

"So it is true? Barabbas will do anything for his cause."

"He is going to do something for it now," Micha said. "He is about to die for it."

"What do you mean?"

"He and some of his men have been captured. He and two others are scheduled for the tree tomorrow. That is what I hear."

"May the Lord have mercy on his soul," I prayed.

"Enough of this," Micha said. "You're here for the festival, not to manage Barabbas and his rebellion."

We walked in silence, and I prayed that the Lord would spare the life of the rebel Barabbas.

"How is Lazarus?" I asked.

"Lazarus?" he whispered.

"Word came to me on my journey that he was very ill. Has Jesus been to his house?"

Micha pursed his lips and shook his head slowly back and forth so that I knew to be silent. "Lazarus is well. He is at work again." He spoke softly so that only I would hear.

"Martha must have cured him with her oils and herbs" I said and heard myself give a nervous little laugh.

"He is well and making up for lost time. Works me from first light till after dark."

I smiled, relieved. I had been worried about what would happen to Martha.

We headed out the gate onto the Jericho road. The road is always busy, but that day it was solid with travelers coming into the city. Roman soldiers patrolling to keep order wove between them, and Roman chariots on official missions sat unmoving in the crowds.

We made our way against the traffic, sticking to the side of the road. Just outside of the city, the crowds thinned so that it was easier to walk. We passed by the Mount of Olives and then met a group of travelers singing the song of the exodus.

"Sing to the Lord a song.
Trumpet His victory.
He is my God and I will praise him."

"Death has passed over our house.
Baruch Hashem.
Israel shall not be harmed.
Our enemy is crushed by the sea.
Sing to the Lord a song.
Trumpet His victory.
He is my God, and I will praise him."

We waved to the group as we passed but did not stop to speak. Everybody was in a hurry. The sun was merciless. The dust covered my skin, coated the inside of my nose and throat, and seemed layered between my eyelids and eyes so that I could not even blink.

Micha handed me a skin of water. As I drank, I saw that he looked at me in a way that made me turn from him. I didn't think he meant to insult me, but he appraised me in the way a man appraises a woman, and I saw his interest. I handed the skin back to him; our hands touched, and I pulled mine away. He took a drink and I watched his smooth brown throat as he swallowed the water. My breath caught. He tied the water skin shut and let it drop to his side. He stared at me while he wiped the back of his hand across his mouth, and, again, I looked away from him.

16

Martha's Story

Without a word, we started out again. Micha's stride was graceful and relaxed; his arms swung loosely at his sides. After a short time, we were again at ease with one another. He bantered. Told me stories of his work. Complimented me. I pretended that I didn't notice his attentions. I asked him if he had a young woman. He said young women were foolish. Then he reminded me that when he was a boy, he told me that he would ask me to be his wife when he was grown.

I was twelve years. Micha and his father had come to get cuttings from my father's grape vines to plant in their own vineyard. While the men were working in the orchards, I watched after Micha. He picked a bouquet of wildflowers, presented them to me, and told me that when he grew up, he would come and ask my father to make a marriage contract.

I laughed to remember it, only it didn't seem as funny now as it did when he was a child. I told him that I was afraid he had missed his chance, that I was an old woman. He told me that I was still beautiful. I stepped in a rut and stumbled. No man had ever spoken to me like that except Joseph. Micha caught me.

"When I heard of the trouble at Be-eroth, I was so afraid that you were hurt," he said.

"No. I am fine," I assured him again.

He released me, and we walked on. He began to sing. His voice was deep and rich, and beautiful. I heard his strength and thought of Joseph. I wanted to take Micha's hand and pretend. Or maybe I just wanted to take Micha's hand. I pulled my own hand into my robe, so that I did not act foolishly.

At the bottom of the hill, he left me. He had to return to the city to work most of the night. He promised that he would try to find Jesus when he had finished. I thanked him. He smiled, bright and strong. I returned his smile like I was a young girl. It doesn't seem possible now.

Martha's house stood on the edge of the town of Bethany. The walls were made of thick clay and the roof was covered with layers of palm branches to keep the house cool in the heat of the day. Behind her house was her grove of olive trees, their leaves the lime green of spring that day. In the fall, when the olives were ripe and bursting, Martha would shake them to the ground, then gather them and remove the pits. After that, she would place them in her olive press[1] and bruise them until the pure oil was released and flowed into a container. She would sell all of this purest of oil to the priests to be used for holy anointing oil. They would mix it with myrrh and cannabis, cinnamon, and flowers to make it just so, like they had done since the time of King David.

After the first press of oil, Martha would gather the pulp into baskets, crush it again, and then hang them until all of the oil dripped from the pulp. She kept a share and sold the rest for table use. I think this year, though, that Martha's olives just fell to the ground. Maybe the birds or animals ate them, or maybe Annas sent men to harvest them. With Lazarus and Martha both out of his way, he could have done whatever he wanted.

As I came near the house, a barking dog charged across the way and planted himself in my path. Martha had made friends with this mongrel scavenger, feeding him scraps from her own table, and now

he never left her. I stood motionless. His neck hair bristled, his ears
flattened, and he growled deep in his throat. I lowered my eyes so he
did not think that I was challenging him. He came toward me, teeth
bared. I stood, letting him catch my scent, telling myself not to run
and awaken him to the chase. Most people would have run the ugly
mutt off, but Martha was alone much of the time, and he made the
perfect guard for her.

Martha lived with her brother Lazarus, whose work was to prepare
the city for the Passover. He did this all year long, but the month
before the festival, starting around the 15th of Adar, he worked night
and day. He supervised the repairing of bridges and roads, ready-
ing the camp sites, cleaning and inspecting the mikvahs, marking
the graves, and whiting the sepulchers to prevent any travelers from
unknowingly making contact with them.[2] And with his own hands,
he helped to build the many clay ovens needed each year to roast the
Passover lambs.

All of the lambs had to be roasted between the seventh and ninth
hours on the day of the Seder and then eaten between the ninth and
eleventh hours. Anything left at sunset would be burned. Those who
lived in Jerusalem or had relatives in the city held their feasts in private homes. All others used the public ovens that Lazarus made.

If Passover came after the rainy season, everything worked well. If
it came early or the rainy seasons continued longer than usual, there
was trouble. The ovens melted away, and the streets ran red with the
clay. Or, if the rains caused the ovens to heat unevenly, they erupted
into grotesque shapes and did not hold the heat to roast the meat.

Martha had invited me to spend the Passover with her. Her sister Miriam would wait and celebrate with Lazarus the next month,
which was the scheduled time for the festival workers. I had hoped
that Jesus and his followers would bring the lamb and join us. If not,
Martha and I would share a meal with a neighbor.

The dog was still growling at me when Martha made her way

through the narrow passage beside her house and the neighbor's. She was holding the baking shovel, and I knew that, in spite of the heat, she had been standing at the ovens preparing the unleavened bread that we would eat.

I waved, and the dog growled louder. She called him off, dropped her shovel, and ran toward me bouncing up and down inside of her robe. She looked around, and around again, and then grabbed me and hugged me until I couldn't breathe. The dog wagged his tail.

If there is a way to recognize Martha, it is that she is never still, not her person and, as Joseph used to say, not her mouth. She is up before the light of day, attacking her chores like they are her life's mission. She solves every problem by cleaning.

"Did you know that he could do such a thing? Have you ever seen that happen before? Did you know?" she asked one question after the other. I had no idea what she meant.

"What thing?" I asked, trying to eye her and see if she was out of her mind.

"Lazarus. How did Jesus do it?"

She looked fine to me, so I scolded her. "Martha, stop this! Tell me what you are talking about."

"Hush," she said. "Listen!" She jerked her head and rushed to look behind the house. I followed her, but there was no one there.

"Tell me, Martha," I said. I could see that she was bursting with her news.

"I will, but inside."

I tried to stop to wash my feet, but she wouldn't wait and pulled me through the doorway. The air inside the house was cool. It felt wonderful, and I wanted to sink to the floor and rest, but Martha was racing.

"I think there is someone here," she said, running to the small window and looking into the back again.

"There is no one," I said.

"I think they are watching. I must take care."

"Tell me," I said again, sternly this time.

"I saw it." She was nodding her head up and down as she spoke. Her eyes were wide.

"Saw what?" I asked.

"The nefesh . . . God's own breath," she whispered.

I was shocked and backed away from her. She was speaking of something so sacred that even the great prophets are not allowed to envision it. In the beginning, the nefesh of the Lord entered man, and there was life. I stared at Martha and could not speak. "Lazarus," she whispered again.

"Lazarus?" I asked. I felt a prickling on the back of my neck.

"Lazarus died," Martha clutched my arm and shouted in a whisper.

I dropped down to my knees. "Oh, Martha. I am sorry. I am sorry. Micha said that he was well and at work."

"He is Myriam. He is. Didn't you hear what I told you? It was a miracle. A miracle beyond any that he has performed."

"Where is Lazarus now?" I demanded.

"He is at work. Like Micha told you."

"Tell me what happened, Martha." I put a little bit of threat in my voice like the one I had used on the children many times. Sometimes that was necessary with Martha to keep her on track.

Martha sighed, sighed again, then sighed one more time and began. "I will tell you because you are his mother, and it is right that you know, but Lazarus has forbidden me to speak of it."

I waited. She waited, wanting me to assure her that she was right to disobey Lazarus. When I didn't, she leaned close to me, perhaps so Lazarus, who was in the city, couldn't hear her speak.

"Oh Myriam," she exclaimed. Then she burst into tears.

I held her in my arms and waited for her to continue.

"You know that Lazarus has not been well for some time."

"Yes, I have heard."

"He was getting worse. He came home one night and went to his pallet without even eating. The next day, he was too sick to go to work. I think that he was poisoned."

"Martha, I don't think that anyone poisoned Lazarus. Perhaps he ate some bad meat."

"No. They are watching him. I saw two men following him when he left for the city this morning."

Martha was suspicious of everyone, so I was not surprised that she came up with a plot against her brother, but I didn't really believe it.

"Tell me what happened to Lazarus," I said.

"Over the next few days, he got worse." Her voice wavered, but she went on. "I tried every tonic, but nothing worked. Two different healers came, but they couldn't help him. We sent word for Jesus, but he didn't come. That night Lazarus started moaning so loud that he made the dog bark. He was burning with fever, and he became delirious. I bathed him with cool water all night long, but it didn't do any good. By morning he was, he was . . . he was dead." she finished, her voice a whisper.

"Dead?" I asked.

Martha nodded her head.

"But Jesus . . . ?"

"Jesus didn't come for three more days, but when he did . . ." she stopped.

I waited, not breathing.

"It was a miracle," she said, still whispering. "Jesus performed a miracle. It was beyond any of the healings. It was a miracle. He just commanded Lazarus to come back to life and he. . ."

I looked around the room. It was neatly arranged. I looked for signs that Martha was not in her right mind.

"Why didn't I hear of it on the caravan?" I asked. "Surely news like this would spread everywhere. Are you sure that he was dead?"

"Four days. I have told you. Four days dead."

"I can't believe that I haven't heard of it. How could something like this ever be kept a secret?" I stood up and paced around the room. "Doesn't anyone else know?"

"The ones who came with Jesus do, but Lazarus forbid them to speak of it."

"They will never keep silent about such a thing."

"Myriam, stop and listen," Martha warned. "Lazarus is afraid for his life! For his own life and for Jesus' life as well. You cannot tell anyone."

I clutched onto Martha's hand. She pulled it away and hurried to pick up a bowl that had been left out.

I followed her and took her arm and turned her so that she had to look at me.

"Those who have witnessed it will do the telling Martha. You are wasting your breath warning me."

"Even so, the less people who find out about this, the safer Jesus and Lazarus will be."

"Why do you say that?"

"Not even the high priest has the power to resurrect the dead. The Sadducees would not tolerate such a thing from a simple rabbi. They can be very jealous."

"Of a healing?"

"It was not a healing, Myriam. Jesus brought a dead man back to life, and Lazarus is a walking reminder of what happened."

I was exhausted, but I paced the floor and thought of what Martha had told me. Jesus had performed great works before, but that he had breathed life into someone? It was a wonderful thing for Lazarus, but I didn't know what it meant for Jesus. Word would travel. People would tell, and soon everybody would know. I thought of Jesus' entry into Jerusalem. They probably already knew. Those crowds had cheered him; others would condemn him. That was the way of the people.

Martha remembered that I had just walked a great distance and ran for a dipper of water for me. Then we went outside to the bath. On the way, we saw smoke rolling from the oven. She squealed and ran to it, her arms pumping, and her robes tangling around her all of the way. She pulled the bread from the oven with her baking shovel, and I watched the black smoke rise into the hot air. She stood looking at the charred ruins as if she couldn't believe the bread would dare to burn on her, and I lowered my head so that she couldn't see me laugh.

She harrumphed and flipped the loaves to the ground. I clucked my sympathy. We looked at each other and laughed aloud. She had spoken of miracles beyond belief. Failure at a simple task brought us back to daily life.

I stepped behind the wall and washed my face, my arms, my feet, all of me. The water took the dirt and heat and soreness away from my body. When I had finished, we carried the water to the orchard for the trees.

Martha brought me a clean loin cloth and a clean dark red robe. The clothing slid easily over my clean body, and I swished myself around a little just to feel it move against me. Water is a miracle. We went back into the house, and Martha gave me some figs and dates to eat.

"Now, tell me about your journey," she said.

I didn't want to. I wanted to ask her the thousand new questions that I had about Lazarus, about Jesus. But I kept them to myself. Martha sat beside me and fanned me with a palm branch. I told her about the young boy, and she railed against the Romans. Then I started to tell her about the rest of the trip, but I could not help myself from stretching out on the pallet that she had made up for me.

I rubbed my cheek against the clean muslin, and breathed in the smell of sunshine, and thought I would rest for just a few breaths before I sat up and talked to her some more. My eyes closed. I heard Martha talking and someone snoring softly. I knew that it was me, but I couldn't make myself stop.

The Fourth Day of Tevet

In my sleep, Jesus comes to me. This time, I stay very quiet and feel his presence. I look at him, but I can't see his face. I remember it though. I remember it in its beauty, not as it looked in the end. In the end after his torture. He doesn't talk, but I know that he wants me to go on. He wants me to understand that time is not the same as I have always thought of it. Whatever pain that we endure now will be washed away in eternity.

When I wake, for the first time since his death, I feel a great peace within me. My face has been misted with the dew. I touch it, and it feels soft. The stone hardness is gone. I run my hand through my hair, which has been newly washed, and the silk of it soothes my hand, and then I do it again.

I still have not opened my eyes. I am lying on my right side and my face is in my hand so my right eye is covered. I open my left eye slowly. The glow is still there. I see that I am in my home and know that it has been a dream, but I do not startle awake. I know what has happened, and I do not cry out. I lie still and the glow stays. Then slowly I close my eye and let the peace reclaim me. I lie there for some time and remember the feel of a mother's arms.

Then I remember it is the month of his birth, and I feel myself crumbling. "Why God? Why? Why? Why?" I start in again, but this time I stop. For just today, I will not take it upon myself to feel responsible or to question. For just today. And so I thank God for this moment of peace. I thank him for the rains and the new season to come. And I thank him for my children. All of my children.

17

No Return

I was sleeping soundly when the death knock came. My journey was over, and I had the safety of a roof overhead. It came loudly and rapidly, pounding, pounding. My heart matched pace. The dog barked, and it echoed in the night.

"Martha! Martha, open the door. I am looking for the mother of Jesus of Nazareth. Is she here with you?" someone called from outside.

I remembered where I was and reached for Martha's hand.

"Who is it?" Martha demanded.

"It's me, Deborah. Let me in."

Martha was on her feet, fumbling in the darkness to unbolt the door. I found the lamp and raised the wick. My tongue was parched and stuck to the roof of my mouth so that I couldn't speak. My heart still pounded.

Martha pulled open the door, and a girl of about fifteen years stumbled through. She leaned against the wall, panting hard and holding her side. I could see her in the lamplight. Her face was covered with dirt, her head piece was gone, and her black hair was wild and tangled.

"I . . . I . . . they . . ." she gasped.

Martha drew a stool to the wall, and the girl slid onto it.

I imagined one hundred ways that Simon had gotten himself into trouble.

"What is it?" Martha asked. "Are you hurt?"

"I . . . I . . . they . . . hmm, hmm," the girl whimpered.

"Tell me if you are hurt." Martha commanded.

The girl shuddered, drew in her breath. "No," she said. "No, I'm not hurt."

Martha patted her shoulder.

"Are you Myriam?" the girl asked me, her eyes locking with mine.

I nodded that I was.

She delivered the news in one swift blow. "They have arrested your son."

"Please, God," I prayed. "Simon?" I asked. He is a hothead. There is no other way to describe him.

"No. Jesus."

I couldn't speak. I heard Martha's breaths, short, rapid.

"Who?" I demanded. "Who arrested him?"

"Temple guards, priests, Romans. I don't know. It was a mob."

"Romans?"

"Yes. Yes, I told you."

Horror stories of what Roman soldiers had done to Jewish prisoners flashed through my mind. I tried to remember what Samuel had said. Nothing that would warrant an arrest. Jesus disagreed with the laws of Caesar, but he would never disobey them.

"He has done nothing wrong," I said. "It's dark. It would be easy to mistake one man for another.

"It was Jesus."

"No," I said, but fear had its hand around my heart, massaging it, squeezing it. Firmly so that I knew it was there. I struggled to push the fear away, but it tightened until I could feel pain in my chest.

The girl stood up and looked at Martha then back to me. She was breathing easier, and she spoke in soft, measured tones, but I felt the force in my stomach. I pressed my arm across my middle and bent forward a little more with each word.

"I saw it with my own eyes."

"No," I said again.

"Priests and Romans together? Martha was holding her chest and thrusting her head forward. Never!" She gave her head a final thrust. "Never!"

I thought that she was right. The priests would never defile themselves in that way.

The girl's black eyes flashed. "I know what I saw."

"The others? Simon? James?" I asked.

"I think they got away."

"Tell us," Martha said.

Deborah sat again and wiped her hand across her face leaving one clean streak.

When the sun was high, she saw Peter and John roasting a lamb in the courtyard of the house next to her father's. Jesus arrived with the rest of the men at dusk. They were laughing and singing. Then one man asked why they were celebrating the Seder that day. It was the first day of the festival, and the feast was ordained for the second day. He insisted that they should wait until tomorrow. Deborah did not hear what Jesus answered.

"They should not just change the date of the Seder," Martha huffed.

Deborah ignored her and went on with the story. She had gone to bed at sundown and gone to sleep. Sometime in the night, she heard men shouting. It was coming from the upstairs room where Jesus and his disciples had eaten. She thought there was a fight between the disciples, but she didn't recognize any of the voices. She listened for Jesus but didn't hear him. Then the shouting grew louder, and she heard crashing sounds, like breaking pottery.

It went on and on, and then she heard someone say, "You said that you would lead us to Jesus. Things will not go well for you now, Iscariot."

A reply she couldn't make out. She sneaked across the courtyard to get closer.

"Thousands of people to keep under control, so we can't get an hour's sleep at a time. Now they drag us out in the middle of the night to arrest some peace-preaching rabbi." She thought that it was a Roman's voice.

Then a priest or a Temple guard demanding that Iscariot find the Nazarene.

The Roman again, "You think that you can lead us around on some empty chase and waste our time. You'll pay for this!"

"Jesus? Was he talking about Jesus?" I demanded.

Martha slipped her arm around me, and the girl just stared at me.

"Jesus was gone then?" I asked.

"Yes," Deborah said. She went to the jar and dipped a cup of water for herself.

"They will not catch him," I assured her.

"You don't understand," she shouted at me and stamped her foot. "Iscariot."

Finally, I recognized the name. My stomach clenched tight and hard, and cold sweat pooled in my hands. Iscariot was one of Jesus' followers.

"The disciple?" I whispered.

"Yes! Judas Iscariot." She glared and enunciated each word.

"Go on with your story, then; we want to hear." Martha ordered.

"They all left together," Deborah said. "I followed but stayed far enough behind so I would not be seen."

I was sick to think of her out there alone in the night, but it was over. She was safe.

"The soldiers were angry. They wanted to get back to their drinking. The Temple guards were nervous and kept asking Judas if he was sure he knew where Jesus was. Judas told him that Jesus and his disciples would be where they always were. Then he led them to the Garden of Gethsemane.[1] Led them to Jesus."

Deborah wanted to go ahead and warn Jesus, but the moon kept everything too bright, and she didn't dare. She saw some of the disciples lying on the ground sleeping, but she didn't see Jesus. The guards and the soldiers walked through the garden toward a cave in the back. Finally, Peter must have heard them and shouted for the others to wake up.

Deborah stopped talking.

I urged her to go on. She was shaking so hard that she could barely speak, but she told us that finally she saw Jesus. Peter was yelling at him to run. But Jesus never moved. He just stood there and waited. He just stood there and waited, and Judas walked up and kissed him on the cheek. Then the mob surrounded him.

Martha reached out and took my hand. We stood next to each other pressing our shoulders together.

"A kiss is a greeting of respect!" she shrilled.

"Not this one," Deborah said. This was a kiss of betrayal and a sign to the guards and the soldiers."

Martha exploded. "Judas is a traitor. I knew he could not be trusted. What did Jesus do? What did he do?" she demanded.

"Nothing," Deborah said. "He just stood there. Peter pulled out his sword and tried to hold off the mob, but Jesus did not do one thing. Peter was yelling at Jesus to run and swinging his sword. Someone screamed that the giant had cut off his ear. Then Jesus ordered Peter to put down his sword."

Deborah was crying, now, trying to blink away her tears, but she could not. She gathered in a breath and looked at us, her forehead wrinkled, and her eyes squinted. Her nose pinched, and her voice like an insulted little child. "Jesus just stood there and let them arrest him."

"He did not even try to get away? Why, I, myself could have outrun those old buzzards," Martha screeched.

"It wasn't just the priests, Martha. There were Temple guards and soldiers, too," Deborah stormed.

"Well, he could have outrun them. You know how fast he runs. Why did he not even try?"

"I don't know," Deborah said. "I don't know."

"He just stood there?" I asked again.

"He didn't even move when they tied him," Deborah whispered, staring across the room.

"Maybe he wants to talk directly to the high priest. Yes, yes, that is it," Martha said, jumping on the possible explanation.

But I knew that was not the reason. I pictured my strong young son standing there letting himself be bound and arrested without even trying to escape. I could think of only one reason, and in my mother's heart, I feared that my secret nightmare was coming true. I was growing warmer and warmer and pulled at the neck of my robe.

"Please, Lord, protect my son," I prayed.

"Where is James?" Martha asked.

"I don't know," Deborah said. "I ran away when I saw Jesus chained. I ran away before they saw me." She started to cry.

"It will be all right," I assured her. "I'm sure there is a misunderstanding about something. Jesus will be able to settle it."

"Do you know anything about the ways of this place?" she asked, still crying. "His life is in danger."

"His life has been in danger before."

"We are not talking about some mountain lion," she said, her eyes fixed upon me. "We are talking about the court of the Sanhedrin. We are talking about Rome."

"No mountain lion. It was Herod."

"Antipas?" Deborah asked.

"His father," I said.

"Herod the Great?"

A chill ran through me, and I wrapped my arms around myself. "Jesus was born in Bethlehem. There was a massacre."

"The Slaughter of the Innocents?" Martha asked.

"Yes."

"You were there? You escaped?"

I nodded.

"All those babes," Martha said and shook her head back and forth and back and forth. "All those babes."

"Herod the Great?" Deborah asked again.

"He went by that name, but he was not great."

"Nothing great about him," Martha snapped. "He was a puppet. A Roman puppet and a despot." Then she scowled at me. "I never knew."

"It doesn't matter now," I said. "We need to pray that the Lord will keep his hand upon Jesus and that he will help us find him."

"Where do you think they have taken him?" Martha asked. She was already sweeping the floor, digging hard with the straw broom. "We have to know where to go. We can't just go running out into the night."

Deborah was standing looking at us.

"Is there more?" I asked.

"I . . . It was hard to hear, but I think that he has been accused of . . . They say that he made claims . . . He has been accused of . . ." Deborah hesitated.

"Have out with it," Martha demanded.

Then the mongrel dog let loose with a stream of barking so vicious that we all swallowed our words and stood motionless.

18

John

"Someone is out there," Martha whispered.

The dog was snarling now. We heard a man's voice. The dog growled low in his throat, and I could see the ugly beast, his neck hair standing straight up.

"Martha. Martha, are you there?" The man yelled. The dog growled again. "I am John. I'm looking for Martha."

Martha went to the door and called down the dog. John, Jesus' disciple, pushed his way inside. Martha barred the door behind him.

"Myriam," he gave one sharp nod of recognition and looked at Deborah standing to the side of the room. The light was dim. "Deborah?"

"Yes."

"Are you . . . ?"

"I'm fine. What happened to Jesus?"

"She told you?" he asked me.

"Yes. Where have they taken him?" I asked.

"To Caiaphas and Annas, I think. Peter is following them."

"The House of Caiaphas?" I was so relieved that I collapsed onto a bench and sat there with my head in my hands. The high priest was charged to keep order among the Jews. If Jesus had been taken to Caiaphas, the Romans must not have had a charge against him.

"James?" I asked.

"When he saw Jesus was not going to resist, he ran. They caught his robe, but he slid out and kept running. Some soldiers chased him, but I don't think they could ever catch him. I'm sure he escaped."

"Where do you think he is?" I asked.

"I'm not sure. He may have circled back and followed them. He wouldn't let Jesus out of his sight for long. I know that."

"Why was Jesus arrested? What did you do?" Martha demanded.

"Nothing!" John glared at Martha. She glared back. "We didn't do anything," he insisted.

"Who else was taken?" I asked.

"No one."

I couldn't believe it. I couldn't believe that all of them were not bound and lined up beside Jesus. If the authorities were afraid of a disturbance, they would have arrested them all.

"Every one of you, except Jesus, escaped?" I asked.

"We didn't escape. We could never have escaped." John tipped back his head, pulled at his hair with both of his hands, and moaned. "No, we didn't escape," he said. "Jesus ransomed us. He told the soldiers to leave us, and he would go without a fight."

"No one tried to help him? His own men deserted him?" I asked. I concentrated on my breathing so I wouldn't pass out.

"We were sleeping. They took us by surprise. Peter tried to fight, but Jesus ordered him to stand down."

"And James got away? You don't think they went after him?"

John shook his head. "They could never catch him."

That James had gotten away gave me hope. I wanted John to take me to Jesus immediately. He refused, said it was too dangerous. He had only come to find Deborah. She had screamed out for them to let Jesus go, and two of the soldiers went after her. She ran, and Peter sent John to try and help her.

"I lost them in the olive grove," Deborah said.

"You lost me too," John said, his voice edged with anger, "but I hoped that you had come here. What were you thinking, going out there? You're a fool. The whole band of drunken soldiers would have passed you around until they wore themselves out and then left you to bleed to death."

John was right, and if that had happened and she had survived the night, she would have taken her own life anyway, and everyone would have thought that she deserved it for being out alone at night. Like the woman Jesus saw in the hills.

"I was trying to help Jesus," she said, glaring at John.

"Then help him by using your head." John glared back.

"Caiaphas will have to release him," I said.

They all stared at me.

"At the most, keep him safe until after the festival," I added.

"Myriam, there's more danger than you think," Martha said. "The whole city is a mess. Half of the countryside has no land, no jobs, no food, and they have all come here looking for work. They hear that there is always labor at the Temple and always pilgrims to buy their wares. Then they get here and find that isn't so. Pilate's got his soldiers so worried about a rebellion that they are jumping at their own shadows. A man reaching for his purse might be mistaken for a terrorist reaching for a dagger and get himself run through with a Roman sword."

"I knew that Judas was no good," John fumed. "I could tell that the first time that I ever saw him. We all knew that. A thousand times, we warned Jesus."

"Jesus was never concerned about his own safety," Martha said. "Lazarus warned him too. But he wouldn't listen to him either." She went for her broom again.

"I'd kill Judas with my bare hands if I had the chance," John said. He clenched his fists and the cords on his neck strained.

"That is not what Jesus would want," I said.

"Judas was one of you," Deborah said.

"Judas is a traitor," John seethed. He paced the floor, went to the door, unbolted it and looked out. The dog started in, and he slammed the door shut. "Judas was never one of us. We didn't want him. Nobody wanted him, but Jesus insisted that he could stay."

John's voice was pitching higher. He was still a boy.

"Was there a fight?" I asked.

"With Judas? Always. He always wanted something. Wanted Jesus to act now. To move on Jerusalem. To do it this week. Jesus said that wasn't the plan, and Judas took off. Judas has been talking about Barabbas for a long time. He said Barabbas wasn't afraid to do anything, and he wanted us to gather an army to help Barabbas overthrow Rome."

John's anger filled the room.

"An army? How could you afford that?" Martha demanded.

"We couldn't. You know that. But Judas got it in his head. He held the purse, and he was always counting the money. Stingy with every shekel, figuring out how we could save enough for it. We couldn't even buy food. He would say that we needed the money for a higher cause, told us that we could do without or get ourselves invited to someone's table. Then he got the idea to get Annas involved."

"Annas?" Martha asked. "Annas?"

"Judas was always impressed with his money," John said. "He thought that Annas could help us finance an army and convince Jesus to move at the same time."

"An army of untrained weaponless Jews against Rome? Judas is a fool. Annas would never, ever chance acting against the Romans." Martha said.

"Judas swears Annas is sick and tired of Rome, or Pilate, telling him every move he can make," John said.

"That could be," Martha agreed. "Annas has been around a long time. Pilate wasn't here a month before he started taking control of Annas' commerce. And the young bull barely knows a fig from a grape. But no matter what Judas has done, or how much our people hate the Romans, Annas won't jeopardize his own interests by offending Rome. You're a fool if you think he will."

Deborah bent to examine a cut on her foot. She wiped away some of the dirt with her robe, and it started to bleed.

"I don't see that Annas would have anything to do with Judas," I said.

"Why did you celebrate the Passover tonight?" Martha interrupted.

John sighed. "Jesus said that we would not be together tomorrow, so he wanted us to eat the Seder tonight."

"Why wouldn't you be together tomorrow?" I asked. The fear crawled back through me again and crowded my heart up into my throat so that I could barely speak. "Why wouldn't you spend the day of the feast with Jesus? You would all be welcome here."

"What difference does it make now when they celebrated the Passover?" Deborah asked. Then she moved closer to John, and they hissed back and forth just quiet enough so we couldn't hear what they were saying.

There was nothing left to sweep on the floor, and Martha went for the grinding stones. 'Click-clack, click-clack, click-clack,' the grain fell in little piles. Then 'clack, clack, clack,' she pounded them for emphasis. Her face grew redder and redder as she worked faster and faster, 'clack-clack-clack, clack-clack-clack.'

"Jesus and the rest of you should have more respect for our ways, our traditions. You go around creating trouble," she burst out.

Deborah and John reeled.

"How can you criticize Jesus like that?" Deborah shouted at her.

"Do not take that tone with me!" Martha screeched. "He cannot go around challenging the leaders and angering the Romans."

"The priests need to be challenged. They act as if God belongs to them alone," John shouted back at her.

"If the priests don't keep the people under control during the festival, they'll answer to the Romans. Now is not the time to go against them! You won't settle a difference of opinion between Jews by creating a riot." Martha was still grinding hard.

"There was no riot," John defended himself.

"He can't be so outspoken. People will think he is with Barabbas," Martha said.

"He is nothing like Barabbas. Jesus never allows violence. None," John argued. "Jesus is the leader that we need. We will do as he commands."

"Barabbas has been arrested, and now Jesus," Martha warned. "Barabbas is going to be put to death. Do you want Jesus to be next?"

"How do you know this?" Deborah asked.

"It's good that Jesus has been turned over to Caiaphas," I said.

"That's the only good thing about the night," Martha said.

"We have to get to the priests and try to intervene," I insisted. "Tell them that he is not well. Tell them that we will bring him here and keep him in his bed until after the festival. Then they won't have to worry about him offending the Romans. We can't chance having him come to Pilate's attention."

"I will try," John agreed, "but I don't think that they'll let him go. They won't believe that he'll stay away from the festival. Besides, they're afraid of him."

"How do you know?" My heart pounded faster again.

"There's no reason they would have let the rest of us go if they weren't."

"I have warned him," Martha started in again. "I have warned him not to be so free with his criticisms outside of our group. He makes the authorities nervous." She paced back and forth and shook her finger for emphasis.

"Martha, stop," I ordered.

"I'm going now," John said.

I reached for my shawl.

"No," John said. "You'll only slow me down."

"Please," I said.

"I cannot take you," he said. "I believe that this is all part of Jesus' plan. Deborah will stay with you. If you don't," he said looking at her, "you and I will both have to answer to Peter."

"Plan?" I asked.

"Jesus hasn't told us everything," John said, "but I think that he knew this was going to happen."

I looked at John's smooth face, with only a few stubbles of whisker, and knew that he was way too young to understand what could happen, how many things could go wrong. I didn't know what Jesus' plan was, but I had one of my own, for him to return home with me. He would be safer in Nazareth away from the political disputes, and if I could convince Jesus to leave with me, he would order his brothers to follow.

John opened the door. Martha stopped him and gave him some bread and cheese, telling him to eat, telling him he was so boney that even the crows would not bother with him if he fell.

"John, wait," I called. "What are the charges?"

His body jerked, and he stopped short, his back still towards me. I could see him clearly in the moonlight. His robe was brown and coarse, tattered and too short for him, so that his thin legs stuck out too far from the bottom of it, like he had not been done growing when he came by the garment. His shoulders were thin underneath the cloth.

"I don't know," he said.

But I could tell by the way he had jerked at my words that he did. "Tell me," I said.

"It is not true," he said and started to leave again.

"Tell me," I repeated.

He turned to me. "Blasphemy," he whispered. Then he fled into the night.

שבט

The Twentieth Day of Shevat

Today for the first time since his death, I do not think of Jesus until the sun is high in the sky. At first, when I realize it, I think that it is good, but then I am filled with remorse, terror even. Terror that I am forgetting my son. I close my eyes and picture him, his face, his hair, his hands. I hear his voice. Still, that is not enough. What if I am forgetting him? What if I forget my son? What if the world forgets my son? And I am back in the pit. Alone in the pit.

Then I remember Hagar. I was at her house with my mother when I was a small child. Someone came to the door and told her that her son was lost to the seas. I remember her bellow. She bellowed like a mother cow separated from her calf. She bellowed like her very heart had been carved from her. I was a small child and afraid of the sounds that she made, but I went to her. I feel my hand patting her now. I wish that I could see Hagar again to tell her that I know now. Many people must know. I pat my own hand.

I start walking and find myself in the hills where I have gone so often since his death. I stand high upon the cliff and look down into the ravine. There is a small chunk of rock near the edge that has a crack running through it so that only a small corner secures it to the hillside. I reach out with my foot and work at it until it breaks loose and cascades down the rocks. First a long fall, then it hits a ledge and it bounces and rolls down a steep wall, then it is in flight again bouncing, ping, ping, ping, before it comes to rest far, far below me. I watch it and step a little nearer to the edge. It would be so easy to slip. So easy.

When I have been in my deepest anguish, I have wondered how many more days I would endure before I was allowed to die. I longed to be with my husband and son. Some nights I really thought that I would die in my sleep and was surprised when I woke in the morning. Now I look to the edge and to the ravine far below where no one would see, where no one would ever know. I have known widows who have done this.

But I hear Joseph's voice. "It is never the answer. Never."

I could not anyway. It is against the word of the Lord, and I could not do this to my other children. I step back and am happy to know that I do not want to fall. I may not want to dance yet, but neither do I want to die.

I turn and walk toward home, and as I walk, I come to believe that the Lord will not allow Jesus to be forgotten. I want the world to remember my son, but not just as the Messiah who led the people and performed miracles, not even as the one who atoned for sins or who watches over them from the heavens. I want the world to also know about the boy who brought me flowers from the desert, the boy who swung his hammer and fed the animals and tended the sheep, the boy who would run fast and swim and laugh for the pure joy of living. I want the world to know about his kindness and about the way he loved and about how he always, always thought about other people and did whatever he could to show them how God loved them. And as I walk, I take a tiny skip.

19

Blasphemy

Blasphemy . . . death. Blasphemy meant death. Hysteria was swallowing me. I fought to breathe. I had to help Jesus. Breathe, think, breathe, think, breathe, think. I repeated over and over. Deborah was beside me. We were sitting on the floor, leaning against the wall, and my legs were bouncing up and down under my robe. I gripped her arm and tried to get myself under control.

"Tell us," I ordered.

Deborah closed her eyes and didn't speak. We waited. Finally she whispered, "I am . . . I am not sure. I heard talk."

"What talk?" I demanded.

"I heard that . . . that Jesus is accused of . . . They say that he is guilty of blasphemy and should be stoned. Stoned to the death."

"Don't be ridiculous," Martha barked. "No one is stoned to death any more. The Sanhedrin works to preserve life. Not end it."

"Blasphemy?" I whispered again.

"Yes."

"Blasphemy?" I asked, still whispering like someone would overhear. Like no one else would ever know if we didn't talk too loud.

"Yes."

I looked around the tidy room with its earthen floor, its clean scrubbed furnishings, its sense of peacefulness and waited for the walls to crumble in on us. When they did not, my head cleared, and I knew that the charge was outrageous. No man loved God more than my son. He had a reverence, an understanding that most men couldn't even understand. Outrage replaced my fear.

"Jesus would never, ever blaspheme," I nearly shouted. "Who would dare to say that about him?"

Blasphemy, disrespect of God, mocking him, might be the most serious crime of our faith. It is punishable by stoning, but Martha was right. It was no longer done. I could not remember the last time that that had happened.

"Did you hear what I said?" Deborah asked. "They said he claims he is the . . ." She opened her eyes and looked at me. She held herself perfectly still and whispered. "They said he claims he is the Son of God."

Martha gasped. She clutched her hands into fists and held them to her mouth. "No, no, no," she moaned. She moaned, but her eyes screamed as they darted back and forth. "What has gotten into him? Why would he say such a thing?"

And immediately when she asked her question, I knew. I knew exactly why he had made the claim. I felt a calm come over me. Thirty-three years of waiting had come to an end. Years of wondering when Jesus would be revealed, years of being so on guard that it became a part of me. Sometimes it had consumed me, made me unable to think of anything else. Other times, I had pushed it so far back into my mind that I hardly knew it was there, did not even know that I was thinking about it, but I always was. I was always guarding myself so that I wouldn't say the wrong thing. Worrying that I should tell, worrying that I shouldn't tell. Wondering how it would happen. Until that night.

I thought it must be like falling from a cliff. Outside, I was calm, floating to the bottom. Inside, I was chaos. I would never be back on the ledge again. The waiting was over. I could not think what would happen. Jesus had revealed himself.

"Joseph," I whispered. "His time has come. His time has come." I became weightless again and felt a glow all throughout my being. I reached for Joseph's hand, and of course, he wasn't there, and then I felt myself return, and I was in the room with my friends.

"Myriam, Myriam." That was all Martha could say.

"Myriam," Deborah looked at me as if I had lost my mind. "Did you hear me say blasphemy?"

"Everything will be all right," I assured them. "Jesus would never blaspheme or say things that aren't true. Men who hate him have tried relentlessly to trap him, to get him to say things to anger the authorities, but his wisdom is great and he has refused their word games. He cannot be tricked. But he will not deny the truth."

"Myriam?" Martha gripped onto my arm until it hurt and jerked it like a pull cord.

"Martha," I went on, "you've known from the time that Jesus was a little boy how different he was."

"Different? Why? Because he had a great love for the Lord? Because he was wise for his age?" She drew a breath. She was so agitated that her words came out in a squeak. "He has great powers of healing. He is filled with the spirit. But that does not make . . ."

"You are one of his most devoted followers," I said.

"I am."

"Then why do you doubt him?"

"You do not know how dangerous things have gotten in the city."

"I need to go to Jesus now," I said. "His disciples may not understand what the scriptures have foretold. The priests may have questions for me."

"Are you out of your mind?" Martha gasped. "You can't travel alone at night! You're not going out there."

"I will go."

"If you even try to interfere, you're going to make it worse for him. A woman telling the chief priests what to do? They'll throw you out before you get your mouth open, or worse, arrest you too."

She was talking faster and faster and looking at Deborah. Deborah just stood there looking at me.

"It is not a woman's place," she said.

"It is a mother's place," I said.

She nodded her head, and I saw her relent. "You're right. It is."

"I don't think that either of you understand what I'm telling you," Deborah interrupted. Her eyes were wild. "Didn't you hear me?"

I tied on my shawl, and Martha scooped hers from the peg on the wall.

"I'll go with you then," she said, ignoring Deborah. "They know me. I can speak for you." She pulled her shawl around her and headed toward the door, then stopped. "Do you think . . . ?" she asked. "Do you think that this is because of Lazarus?"

"It doesn't connect to blasphemy in my mind," I said. "But I am sure that they have heard by now."

"Maybe the priests just want to perform a rite of purification," Martha said. "Maybe they're afraid that he'll go on teaching in the Temple while he is still unclean. If they know he's been with a dead man, with Lazarus, they would call him in for purification."

"That was true then about Lazarus? I didn't believe it was true," Deborah started.

"Not now," Martha barked.

"I think that Caiaphas and Annas are nervous, and they want some answers from Jesus about what's been going on, but in the end, they'll deal well with him," I said.

"Deal well with him?" Deborah shouted. "Deal well with him? Didn't you hear anything that I said? Some want to stone him to death! They want to stone him to death for calling himself the Son of God."

"We are all children of God, Deborah," Martha scolded. All of Israel has been chosen."

"That's not what they mean," Deborah snapped. Her hand jerked up, and I thought that she was going to slap Martha, but she dropped it again. "They are saying Son of God like he doesn't have another father."

"Of course he has a father. Joseph was his father. Tell her Myriam." They waited.

"Yes, that is what I had the world believe. That is what I believe myself most of the time."

I tried to remember the angel, but it was so long ago.

"Myriam, tell Deborah that Joseph is Jesus' father."

"There are so many signs, Martha. Why do you still refuse to see it?"

"Tell her Myriam. Tell her that Joseph is Jesus' father." Martha was almost hysterical.

"Martha, listen to me. Jesus is the Son of God."

"The Son of God? The Son of God?!" Martha clutched at her heart, and started going down.

Deborah and I reached her in a single step. One on each side, we lowered her to the bench. Deborah pressed against her to keep her from falling to the floor. Her eyes rolled back into her head, and her mouth fell slack. I thought that she was dead. Deborah was shouting her name. I was leaning over her to see if she was breathing. When I felt her breath on my cheek, I backed away and slapped at her face a little to see if I could get a response out of her. She opened her eyes and stared at me. The corner of her mouth was frosted with spittle.

"The Son of God?" she whispered.

"Yes," I said. He is the Son of God and the . . ."

"The Messiah? Hamashiach?" She was off the bench now, on her feet, holding onto the wall to keep her balance, but the pallor had left her face, and it glowed pink. She fastened her eyes on me. "Yes. I have wondered that he might be . . . if he could be . . . Hamashiach. But the Son of God? A man would be the Son of God?"

"He is, Martha."

"Did Joseph . . . ? Did he know? How did . . . ?"

"He'll be a great warrior," Deborah said.

"He's not a warrior," I told her.

"How will he lead us then?" Deborah demanded.

"How do you know this? Did he tell you that he is the Messiah?" Martha asked. She stood still now.

"I have always known," I said. "Since before his birth, and then when he was born and everyone came to see him, because . . ."

Martha interrupted, her head moving back and forth as if she were following her own racing thoughts. "Were you? Was Jesus? The child in Bethlehem? Was that . . . ? Was he the reason Herod . . . ?

"Yes."

"You have never told me," she said.

"It wasn't my place to tell. It was my place to keep him safe."

"It wasn't just that you escaped Herod. It was that Jesus was the reason for it all in the first place. Where did you go? How did you escape?" Martha pressed.

"We will talk about it some other time. I have to get to Jesus now."

"How could you not tell anyone? Didn't you want to share it at the well? Didn't you want to tell everyone you knew?"

"I learned early to keep my silence. It was not my place to make his identity known. He would be revealed only at the appointed time. And now it has come."

"Hamashiach? Hamashiach?" Deborah asked again and again.

I remember her face. It was beautiful, radiant. She was already one of Jesus' devoted followers.

Deborah was certain that Jesus had come to overthrow the Romans and drive Caesar from our city. They would leave at his command. Our people would reclaim the Promise Land. We would be free from our oppressors. But Deborah's hopes would not be answered that night.

"I'm not sure what is going to happen," I cautioned. "Jesus hasn't told me everything, but he never speaks of his kingdom in the way we have imagined it would be. I don't think that he has come to overthrow the Romans."

"Do the priests know?" she asked.

"I don't think that they want to know."

"Why wouldn't they?"

"Maybe they're afraid; maybe there is some other reason. But I cannot waste time thinking about the priests. I need to leave now. I've wasted too much time already."

I'm going with you," Deborah insisted. She danced around the room when she spoke.

"And I," Martha announced. "We will all be at his side when he proclaims his kingdom. When . . . when the world sees that our God, the God of the Israelites, has sent Hamashiach. It will be a glorious celebration."

"I do not think there will be a celebration tonight," I said, and I could hear the dread in my own voice.

"Myriam, how do you know this? Martha took my hand.

"Tomorrow then." Deborah said. "We will celebrate in the morning. It will last for days. It is the perfect time."

"Myriam?" Martha said. "Myriam?" She walked to the window and stood looking into the night.

Everyone is here already for the Passover," Deborah chattered on. "Do you think Jesus planned it for this time? He'll send Pilate right back to Rome. And the soldiers with him. Yes! This is what we have waited for!"

Martha wheeled, grasped Deborah by the shoulder, and shook her. "Oh for the sake of God!" she blurted. "For the sake of the mother of Jesus, still your tongue. There has been a terrible mistake. The priests will never admit that they're wrong."

"What, Martha? What?" Deborah asked. Her black eyes had grown to half the size of her face.

"If the priests had him arrested, they cannot welcome him as the Messiah," Martha said. Her voice was shaking so that it was hard to understand her.

"We don't know that," I said. "We don't know that the priests were involved in his arrest. It may have been just the Romans wanting him off the street."

"The priests were involved. They sent the Temple guards," Deborah said, grabbing onto Martha's arm.

"We don't know why they arrested him," I insisted. "They may have just wanted him off the streets until after the festival so that there was not a disturbance that would bring the Romans down on him. Jesus will have to tell them who he is tonight." I opened the door. "I am going now."

Three women alone in the deep of night in a countryside bursting with revelers, thieves, murderers, soldiers, and more. I was not sure how we would survive the dangers and make it to Jesus, but my friends never hesitated to come with me, to help me. Deborah thought that she could lead us, and if we could find her Syrian friend, Chavala, she would be able to help us get the rest of the way to the House of Caiaphas.

"Everybody knows Chavala," Deborah said.

"Chavala?" Martha choked. "Chavala the . . . ho . . .?"

20

The Night

"Do you mean to say Chavala the whore, Martha?" Deborah asked.

We were trying to get out the door, bumping into each other because we couldn't decide who was going to go first. I listened for the dog, but now that I wanted him, he wasn't around.

"You are Jewish," Martha gasped.

"Tonight is not the night to judge," Deborah chided her. "Besides, you will like her."

"A Gentile?" Martha muttered, and we stepped into the night.

We left the lantern at home, but Martha carried a small oil lamp that she could hide under her robes if we didn't want to be seen. We didn't really need it because, from high in the sky, the Passover moon lit our path.

"The Lord is my light and shield; whom shall I fear? The Lord is the stronghold of my life, and I shall not be afraid," Deborah said.

We joined her and repeated the psalm again and again. It helped me block out the terror that was claiming me again. The terror that was pushing aside the joy I felt when I realized that Jesus' time had come.

In the night, everything was a threat—a night bird, a small fox looking for food, a bat searching for insects. We fell silent and concentrated on reaching Jesus. I was in poor shape from my journey. My feet were blistered, my joints stiff, and my limp so mean that I had to force myself to keep moving over the uneven terrain.

"We will trust the Lord," Martha said.

"Yes," I agreed.

"Because I do not trust Annas," she added.

"It doesn't matter. Caiaphas is the high priest," I said.

I knew that Jesus and Caiaphas had some disagreements, but they were religious matters between Jewish teachers. Nothing that would be of concern to the Romans.

"Annas is the one with the power. Mark my words; he is the one with the power, and he will have his say.[1] Old and half dead most days, but he still overrides Caiaphas whenever he pleases. I do not trust him," Martha went on. "I think both of them are too close to Herod."

Now you sound like Joseph."

"He was right. The Romans sell to the highest bidder."

"I don't remember him saying that."

"He said they sell to one they can control. And he was right about Annas," Martha said. "We're used to it around Jerusalem, but the people in the rest of Judea have never accepted him. Now I think that they are right, and I've been wrong." She was shaking her head from side to side, and the moonlight bounced off it with each turn.

"Jesus is the Messiah. Caiaphas and Annas will have to support him. They will want to," Deborah argued.

"The whole Ananus family is a pawn of Rome. They will not support anyone who challenges the Roman's power." Martha said. "All those groves of olive trees he owns outside of Jerusalem are on some of the best land," she continued. "Between his farm harvests and what he sold in the Temple, Rome would have expected a good pay off. I heard that he cheated them, so they stripped him of the office to punish him."

"He must be back under their thumb because the priesthood is back in the family," Deborah pointed out.

"And that's why he won't go against them again," Martha said.

"Is the office only political then? Not sacred? Is that what you're saying?" I asked.

"I have always been taught," Martha said, "that the Lord gives the high priests knowledge that we do not have, and that their wisdom and dedication have been what has held the Israelites together throughout history. Without them, our heritage would never have survived, especially in Egypt and Babylonia. But I will tell you, since Lazarus has been at work, I have seen more of what goes on, and I am not so sure anymore. I believe that in matters of faith, the Ananus family does as the Lord calls them to do, but in matters of commerce, they are as ruthless as any merchant can be."

"He is a priest, Martha. Whatever happens in the olive orchard doesn't discharge him from his sacred duty to the people," I said, but my mind was on Jesus. "Maybe it would be better if Jesus would wait until after the Passover to announce himself."

"It would be better," Martha conceded.

"Why would he wait?" Deborah demanded. "Why should we wait? It has been thousands of years already."

"It makes the most sense that he was arrested, because he has gained too many followers, and the authorities are afraid of the festival crowds," Martha said. "If he announces himself now, they'll have to consider that the people will riot, and that will bring the Romans down on us all."

"Jesus might be ready to retreat to Bethany or even Nazareth," I said.

I thought that we could stay with Martha until after the Passover and Sabbath. Then travel would be allowed again, and we would leave the city.

"Not everybody is going to want this," Martha warned.

"Not want the Messiah to come?" Deborah's voice was filled with impatience. She quickened her pace. Martha and I hurried to keep up.

"Some won't," Martha said, "and we don't know who is for us or who is against us. We run to one for help, and he might be the one who is controlled by the enemy. Move the wrong olive and the whole pile topples."

"Yes, Martha," Deborah muttered.

Martha decided that we should speak directly to the high priest, and I agreed with her plan. I hoped that Caiaphas would listen.

"Annas has admired Jesus since he was a boy. I believe he will welcome him. He has no reason not to," I said.

"Except that he won't want to lose power, and he wants to live out his days building his financial empire, not spending them in prayer and study," Martha said. "Who knows? Maybe he thinks he can be the one to finance a movement against Rome and get all the credit. Maybe he even believes himself to be the Messiah."

"There's something else," Deborah said.

"What? What were you and John whispering about?" Martha demanded.

"Let her speak," I said.

"There was almost a riot at the Temple. Jesus chased some of the merchants and money changers out of the Court of the Gentiles, and things turned mean."

"Why would he do that?" I asked.

"He went to the Temple to make a sacrifice and saw that the money changers and sellers had overrun the place. The stones of the Temple were being used as slaughtering blocks, and the whole place had been turned into a stock pen. He ordered it stopped, but . . ."

"It's true," Martha said. "He shouldn't have done that, but it's true. The animals, especially the oxen, splatter all over everything when they are herded through. Manure and urine streaming and splashing, staining everything. It's filthy. They can never get it clean. The mosaics are ruined."

"What happened?" I asked.

"That is all I really know."

"What happened?" I asked again.

"There are stories. I don't believe that they're all true, but the gossip is that he went on a rampage, tipped over tables so the coins rolled all over the court for anyone to pick up. The merchants didn't get half back. They say he let the animals loose, and they near stampeded. After that, he grabbed a bull whip and started chasing after the merchants shouting that they were nothing but a brood of vipers and a den of thieves. When the merchants were running from the whip, the people helped themselves to whatever they wanted. They say it took the sellers most of the day to capture the animals and get their tables back in order."

"Why would he do anything like that?'

"He said that was not the purpose of the Temple. It is a place of worship, and the moneychangers have turned it into a market place, and then they cheat the people besides."

"What?"

"Some of the merchants cheat the people by overcharging them. Everybody knows that," Martha said.

"Then his anger was just. Caiaphas should be pleased with him," I said.

"No! He should not have done that. He must know he should not have done that," Martha nearly shouted.

I defended him, but I was shocked that Jesus, would do such a thing, especially now. Perhaps in years past when he had been so restless and volatile, but lately he had been so patient.

"Some of the tables belonged to Annas and . . . ," Deborah said.

"He must have known that," Martha interrupted.

"Let her finish," I said.

"I heard that some of the rabbis stood up for Jesus, but Annas brought them back in line in a hurry by threatening to take away their seats on the court if they went against him. Caiaphas stayed out of it."

"Why are you just telling us this now?" Martha demanded.

"I didn't think . . . I didn't want . . . I don't know, I . . ." Her voice trialed off.

"How would Annas even know that Jesus was really the one to

upset his tables?" I asked. "With the Passover crowds in the Temple, how would he even know who it was? It could have been anyone."

"There is talk that Jesus has already angered Annas, so the old man would be glad to blame it on him no matter whose fault it really was."

"How would he even have had time to see him during the festival?" I asked.

"It was not direct, but when Jesus told the crowds that one could not serve two masters, everybody knew that he was talking about Annas trying to serve the Romans and God, or money and God."

"There are more possible reasons for his trouble than I can count," Martha said. "And who knows what else could be going on. We need to think of everything if we are going to help him."

And so as we walked toward the city, Martha questioned me about everything including Jesus' birth and our trip to Egypt.

"Did Herod Antipas know that you escaped?" she asked.

"I don't know. I have never told," I assured her.

"You wouldn't need to," she said. "If he looked, it would be on the census. All he would have to know is who Jesus' parents were. It would be easy for him to trace it back."

That had been my fear for many years. If Herod Antipas knew how the world had bowed to Jesus when he was a babe, what the magi had foretold, he would never welcome him as the Messiah. He might tolerate a military leader, but a king, never. Antipas wouldn't stand for that and neither would Pilate. The more I thought about it, the more I thought that there might be a battle when Jesus came into power, and I didn't want that to happen before he was prepared.

"If Herod was worried, he would have assassinated Jesus long ago," Deborah said.

"How could you stand living so close to him all of these years?" Martha asked.

"I could not," I said.

"Herod is born a Jew. Not that he acts like it, but when Jesus announces himself as the Messiah, he will follow him like all of Israel," Deborah said.

The clanging of metal rang out in the night. We stopped talking, and made our way down a steep incline in silence. A rock broke loose under my foot, and I twisted my ankle. Sharp pains shot through my ankle and up my leg, but I hopped around on one foot and bit my lip to keep quiet. Deborah jerked my arm, and we stood and listened.

More clanging and then voices. We went on, trying to stay as quiet as we could and maybe sneak past them. When we came around a bluff, we saw a group of men squatted around a campfire. The dancing flames lit their faces, and I was sure that I could see that they were covered with dirt. A camp of ragged tents or tarps spread out from the fire, and silhouettes of men walked among them.

"The outlaw nomad tribe," Deborah whispered. "From Syria."[2]

I wanted to turn back and take a route around them. Desert dwellers live by the tribal code of "I and my brothers against my cousins. I and my brothers and my cousins against the world." All of them are dangerous, and this tribe was the most dangerous.

Everyone knew about the legendary band. It was the most feared in Judea. Mostly, they roamed the wild Decapolis area on the other side of the Jordan River, but they had come to Jerusalem to work the festival. I had heard that any one of them could bend numbers faster than a priest could add two and two, so they did well buying and trading.

Martha agreed with me that we should leave before they saw us and started back around the bluff, but Deborah thought that her friend Chavala might be there, and we should wait. We argued.

"They are only outcasts pretending to be fierce to protect themselves," Deborah said.

I didn't believe her. After that night, I have asked people about them. Simon mostly. He has told me that years ago, a tribe of Syrians had a feud among themselves. The blood ran so red that the tribe was nearly wiped out; then part of them broke away. There were not enough of them to live safely in the desert, so they stayed in Judea. Over time, slaves who escaped the Silk Road traders, other outcasts, and even some disheartened Jews joined them.

They turned into a band of vicious cutthroats who would skewer up an intruder like a lamb on a spit, or slice up their victim like so much calf liver and feed him to the wild dogs. Better not to leave evidence. There were other stories, too, about how some in the band were demon possessed, about how they fought to the death even among themselves. They welcomed a fight for any reason.

One who I would come to know as Gillaro came to the band. He and his family had been attacked, and his parents were brutally murdered while he watched. He was taken as a slave to Rome and trained to be a gladiator. In the arena, he refused to be defeated and finally won his freedom, citizenship even. But he hated Rome and her soldiers. He hated her for forcing him to bear the blood of his innocent competitors, and he hated her even more for the murder of his family. So he found his way to the outlaws and challenged one after another of them until he had established himself as their leader.

Then he remade the band with fierce discipline. He instilled in them the ancient code of honor, calling for total loyalty to the clan and tribe. He demanded obedience and trained the men relentlessly in the ways that he had learned in the arena. They all knew how to kill a man quicker than they could blink. But if they knew they were going to lose, they would walk into a sword with a smile on their face.

Roman soldiers were required by law to round up any derelicts and vagrants who might be a nuisance to the land, but the Romans never caught up with this group. The band was gone before the legion arrived, and if a soldier was brave enough to sneak in alone, he wouldn't live long. So the soldiers stayed away, and for that, Gillaro kept his outlaws off the streets of Jerusalem. Most of the time.

I didn't know all of those things that night, but I knew enough to be afraid of them. "We need to leave now," I pleaded.

The Seventeenth Day of Adar

Today I am tending my garden because it is what I want to do. I pick the weeds and pat the dirt carefully back around the plants so they are not disturbed. I breathe in and feel soft inside, but then it turns to sadness. I feel Jesus with me and remember him. Not in my sleep or in my dreams but right here, right now in the daytime. I think that he might be sad to see me suffer and want to tell me something. I look up and expect to see him. Of course, I do not, but I feel him, I know he is there. I smile at him, feel him smile back. I think that he wants more from me, but I don't want to listen. Not right now. I reach for the basil that I carry with me and breathe in its smell. Right now that is all that I can do.

I smell the basil and watch as a small insect makes its way across the sitting rock at the edge of my garden. It takes a long time, but finally, it reaches the other side. I don't know what made it keep going, but it did, and now it is resting in a bit of shade.

Peter and John and some of the others are here now. John has grown, become stronger. There is sadness, but also a presence about him that is beautiful to see. He is filled with the spirit as he tells me of Jesus' victory, his triumph over death. He tells me that now no man must fear death. The price has been paid, and we are all equal in the eyes of the Lord.

All of the men are bold now. Not like on the night when they ran. They lay their hands upon me and ask for strength and healing, and my stomach tightens to know they are here taking my son's place and he is gone. I want to pull away, but I do not, and I am renewed. Not enough that I rejoice as they do, for my journey is different, and my healing will not come in the same season, but I feel better.

There are still times, though, when I do not believe I will ever be healed, but I do not say that out loud anymore like I have no faith or have given in to self-pity, but it is a fear I have. Jesus told me before died that his spirit would be with me always, but sometimes I am not sure.

One day I feel strong and think that I will join the men as Martha has, but the next day I am tired, too tired to leave my home. I scold myself that I do not do more, but Martha tells me that I must be kinder to myself. "Surely the Lord has made you in this way, fashioned you in his image. It is not for you to judge your grief." I think she is right.

21

Outlaw Camp

Deborah ignored me and took off toward the camp. She was light on her feet, quick enough to run for safety as she had done already that night, and she could squeeze her small self between the rocks if she needed to hide. Martha and I were older, slower, larger, but we followed and somehow managed to keep up. I was so afraid that I tried not to even breathe out loud.

Finally, we came to a small cave with the opening so low that I didn't want to go in, but Deborah pushed us through. It wasn't any higher inside, so we had to squat. My knees gave out, and I let myself fall back and sit on the ground. I hoped that I had enough room to get up. We could see the men from our hideout. Sometimes, I could make out an oily face in the firelight, or a bright piece of clothing, usually so ragged that it was barely hanging on the man wearing it. The men lifted their cups and drank, and drank some more. From our cave, we could hear their songs and their curses very well. They spoke in Aramaic and Syrian laced with strings of angry, vulgar expressions directed at the Romans, the Jews, and each other. I was shaking in fear, but still, I was haughty.

I remember the camp and the people and how I thought that they were not my kind, how I thought that I was above them, that they were nothing more than a pack of thieves. They had no class status as Roman, Jew, or any other, so they had little chance of making an honest living. They might earn a few shekels for some kind of menial work or take up a trade that no one else wanted. Simon told me later that many of them had skills that were in high demand, and they could charge their own price.

Skills like the blacksmith had, the blacksmith we saw working in the camp. He was going back and forth between the fire and a barrel of water on a plank wagon. I could see that it had only two wheels so that one man could pull it easily. The kind of wagon a man had when he could not afford to feed a donkey.

The blacksmith gripped a piece of iron in his tongs and placed it in the fire. He turned his head away and waited until it was red hot, and then he took it from the flames. It glowed in the night, and he laid it against a rock and pounded it over and over with his hammer. Then he inspected it, pounded some more, placed it back into the fire, pounded again, inspected it one more time, and was satisfied. Then he plunged the hot iron into the barrel of water, and it hissed and sputtered its warning into the night.

The blacksmith was named Hasaan. He looked older than the others but as strong as two of them. He was not tall, but I thought that his arm must be of a greater size than my waist. He hammered on and on. Fire, hammer, water, fire, hammer, water. The fire leapt, the hammer clanged, and the water sizzled. One of the drinking men beat out the rhythm on wooden sticks.

In the light of the fire, I could see that the blacksmith wore an armband made of bronze and studded with an enormous green gem, maybe an emerald. It looked like a magnificent work of art, as fine as anything in the Temple.

Joseph had shown me works like that in Egypt and told me that the Syrians could make fine jewelry and artwork, a trade that had been passed down for hundreds of years. I knew the pieces made in that country were priceless.

This man could never afford to have such a piece. At first, I thought that he had stolen it, but I didn't know why he wouldn't sell it for the fortune it would bring. I decided his father had made it, or maybe he even made it himself.

I think that he was a free tradesman who was captured as a slave and somehow escaped. His owners probably had him digging in the quarries or plowing fields not knowing that his skills could have brought them measures of gold.

The hammering went on. I wanted to leave, but Deborah said if we turned back, it would add too much distance to our route, and we would be much safer if Chavala was with us because she knew many men and could call favors from them. With her, we could pass where we needed to. I was horrified to think that we would be relying on such a person. How could I compromise myself in that way? I would jeopardize my children and my children's children with such behavior, but it was a chance I would have to take. Only Chavala could offer us the protection that we needed. She was known. Deborah said that women feared her because she was tough, and men feared her because she was under the protection of many men. Men who might be far more powerful than them. No one would harm us if we were with her. She was our only chance, so I agreed. If I displeased the Lord, I would suffer my punishment, but I had to try to save Jesus.

The hammering agitated me until I couldn't think. Ominous endless clanging. It was a sound I had heard all my life, but that night, I could not tolerate it.

I closed my eyes and again called for God to spare my son. But I did not pray like I had been taught; rather I begged, and what I could not put into words, I moaned, "God of Abraham, God of Jacob, protect my son. Lift him in your arms. Protect my son, your son." I did not often say the words *your son,* but I was bold in my prayers for Jesus. There was no hope but the Lord.

We waited, the blacksmith hammered, and the nomads drank and sang. Then, just at the moment when there was not one other sound, a man let out a scream and ran out into the night. He was round and jowly and ran with his arms pumping and his backend swaying.

"Hesbuhla, Stop! Stop that you old hag! Stop that!" he screamed. "In the name of Ilaha Gabal[1] or whatever god you bow to, you stop that right now."

An old crone was walking the perimeter of the camp and sprinkling something on the ground. When he reached her, she turned and flung whatever she had held in her hand. I could not see her face, but I heard her hissing at the fat man like a cornered Egyptian cat.

"You stop that right now," the man screamed and pumped his way into the shrub, obviously searching for whatever she had thrown.

The men by the fire broke out laughing. "She made off with his perfume again," one of them said.

"Warding off the evil," another one added.

The crone disappeared into the shadows, and the man, whom I guessed to be a perfumer huffed his way back to the group. He looked far better kept than the others, cleaner, dressed in expensive clothing, well-fed. Well-fed enough to have several chins.

"She's a sorceress, I tell you. We should stone her," he bellowed.

The rest of the men laughed again. The perfumer took a drink, waved it in the air, talked loud and pointed his finger, and lectured that something needed to be done about the crone. The men only laughed at him.

"You ungrateful reri,"[2] shouted an old man. She has kept the trespassers away and saved your sorry hide more than once with her vigilance."

"You don't belong here, Cassim." A man with one sleeve ripped from his robe scorned.

"Go back to your wife," another one added.

"Never," The fat man promised. "She nags me to give up my talent, and I will not. I make a fine living with my perfume, and she gives me no respect at all.[3] She nags me not to sell to the Romans because they give the perfume to their whores. She nags me to find a more godly trade, and then she nags for more money. There is no pleasing her."

"The tanner came lookin' for you today, Cassim," the man with only one sleeve said.[4]

"The tanner?" he squawked. "What did you tell him?"

"Told him you weren't here."

"What did he say?

"Said he'd be back. His wife had a vial of your perfume."

"She needed it to stand the smell of the man," Cassim huffed. "He stinks."

"Well he's lookin' for you, and he's not happy. Said there is no way his wife had the coin to buy that perfume and wanted to know exactly how she came by it."

"Perhaps someone gave her a gift," said Cassim.

"That's what he thought. And he thought you were the one to give it to her."

"I felt sorry for the poor woman. And that is the truth I speak."

"That's not what the tanner thought. Said she must of give you somethin' in return, and he is goin' to kill you."

"Big man," One Sleeve's friend, who was called Raji, goaded. "Very big man."

"What did you tell him?" Cassim squealed.

"Told him he didn't have to worry about you. You were but an eunuch." All the men laughed and raised their cups to One Sleeve.

"A good story, I believe," Cassim said. "A very good story. Did that satisfy the man?"

"It did. It made him smile. And then he said, 'You tell him, if he's not now, he will be soon enough.'"

Cassim yelped and clasped his hands, one over the other, between his legs, and then he yelped some more. All the men roared with laughter.

"Hasaan," a man who stood drinking on the sidelines called. "Hasaan, put the hammer down and let the night begin."

Hasaan ignored him and kept hammering. Then the man on the side lines took a whip from his waist and cracked it into the air. Two more times he cracked it. Then he raised it and sent it snaking out through the night until it wrapped around Hasaan's hammer. The hammer jerked, but Hasaan's grip held, and the hammer did not leave his hand. He glared at the man, unwrapped the whip, and went back to work.

"The Gladiator," Deborah whispered. "His name is Gillaro."

His strength announced itself in the way he stood, in the way his garments draped over him like he was made of granite, even in the way he lifted his drink, but he walked toward Hasaan like he had not a care in the world.

"Yes, it is time for some pleasure before the sun comes up again, and the streets are overrun by those Roman bastards," Gillaro mocked.

"I have an order to fill, and I'll have to work all night to complete it," Hasaan said, plunging the hot metal into the water. The Jews have come from everywhere for the Passover. They've taken over the city." He laid his finished nail out onto a plank. "Get too close to them and they turn their heads and carry on that they have been defiled. And they think they own the streets. I wasn't able to get close to the well today, so I had no water to cool my nails."

"Hmmph," Gillaro grunted.

"The Jews know as well as you," scoffed the perfumer, "that it's the Romans who own the streets. They own the streets, they own the Jews, and they own us. Oh, this is the city of Jerusalem in the land of Judah, but it belongs to the Romans. No, no, I am incorrect. Gillaro would say in the land of Yihudah. Gillaro, what does Yihudah mean?"

"Of God," Gillaro answered.

"Yes, yes, of God. Given to the ten tribes of the ten sons of Jacob," Cassim continued dramatically.

"Twelve," Gillaro corrected.

"Twelve?"

"Jacob had twelve sons," Gillaro responded curtly.

"Oh, yet again, I have erred," mocked Cassim, "and my learned friend has corrected me. This is the land of Yihudah, given to the twelve sons of the twelve tribes of Jacob, but owned and ruled by the Romans."

"Still, the Roman soldiers are afraid of the god of the Jews," Hasaan said, holding his next piece of iron deep into the fire, leaning back to try to keep away from the smoke. "They pretend not to be, but I have seen it in their eyes. They know if the high priests don't keep the Jews in line, there will be an uprising, and they'll have to kill them all to restore order, and Yahweh himself may take revenge on them. The Roman gods may reign in Rome, but here it is the god of the Jews, and every soldier fears that."

"The Romans pity the Jews because they have only one god, but they envy them because of his power," One Sleeve observed.

"The god of the Jews has no power," taunted the perfumer. "If he did, why would he let his people suffer?"

"You pale, Gillaro," Raji observed. "You run, but the God of Abraham still rules over you."

"The God of Abraham has nothing over me, if he even exists," Gillaro sneered.

Hasaan spoke again. "You are who you are, Gillaro. A man can change his name, but his soul remains the one he was given."

Gillaro spit and raised his cup.

"And does his lot?" asked Raji. "We are free men now, Hasaan. And still you work like a slave. How did your mother raise you to be such an honest man? Such a stupid, honest man. I will make more in one night of stealing than you will in a week of pounding nails."

"Ha! Hasaan will not steal," sneered Cassim. "He has a trade. He is a blacksmith. He could make fine art if he would steal a bit of gold, but now he makes nails. All day, he suffers from the smoke and the burns as he pounds hot iron into nails, all so that he can call himself an honest man. He works very hard. He makes the nails, and then he sells them to the Romans."

Cassim hoisted himself onto Hasaan's wagon and waved his knife. The metal flashed in the light of the fire. "And do you know what the Romans do with the nails?" He looked to the crowd.

"Tell us. Tell us," they demanded.

"They murder your brother!" he bellowed.

"Enough!" Hassan warned.

But the crowd howled, and Cassim went on. "Some poor bastard doesn't bow low enough or jump high enough, and the Romans pin a crime on him. Taking a piece of bread for food or defending himself against a soldier, and they put him to death in the most hideous way they can think of. They nail him to a cross and let him die."

In a flash, Hasaan leaped onto the wagon, and the weight of the two men tipped the cart to the other side. The water poured over them, but they ignored it. Hasaan was sure footed and sober, and when Cassim stumbled to catch himself, Hasaan picked the knife from his hand. He gripped Cassim by the neck of his tunic and leaned close, their faces almost touching. Hasaan pressed the knife against Cassim's throat, and Cassim whimpered and leaned further backwards.

"I will cut your tongue from your mouth if you cannot keep it still," Hasaan warned. "My nails are the best they can find. They are used for the wagons and the gates."

By now Cassim was leaning so far back that he had no balance. Hasaan was holding him up with one big blacksmith hand.

"Come on, come on, come on," the onlookers chanted. "Cut him, cut him, cut him."

The rhythm of the sticks quickened, but Hasaan released his grip, and Cassim fell to the wagon. Hasaan threw down the knife and turned away.

"No one, Jew or Roman, can make a better nail." He spewed out his words. "They despise me, but they beg me to sell them my nails. Curse them all." Then he let lose a string of words so that my face burned.

The girls were so quiet that I smelled their perfume before I even saw them slip into camp. They wore bright flashy clothes that were cut low and tight across the bosom so that their breasts rose high and fell out of them like round melons. They surveyed the camp, and when they saw no danger, they started singing, shouting, cursing, laughing, and making more noise than I ever knew women could make.

A thin one made a line for Gillaro, but another cut her off and stared her down. The winner wrapped herself around him and pressed and squirmed until he told her to be still.

"Why do you ignore me, Gillaro? Does my beauty not please you?" the girl pouted.

"Your beauty would please any man, Yari," he said, but he didn't look away from his drink.

She tried to lead him away from the others, but he wrapped his arm around her to anchor her and they stayed in the crowd.

"You are all talk, Gillaro. You would not put down the drink long enough to take a woman," goaded Raji. He was older, and his face had a crooked look to it like his nose has been moved over to one side. He moved in on one of the girls and draped his arm over her shoulder. "But if the lovely Chavala would fill my arms, I would give up wine and spend the night bringing her pleasure."

"Chavala. He said Chavala," Martha whispered in the darkness. Only her whisper was almost a shout. "Is that your friend? Is that the same Chavala?"

22

Fire Dance

"Shh," Deborah hissed and clasped her hand over Martha's mouth. "I am not sure."

I heard a soft cackle and followed it to the crone who was again making her way around the perimeter of the camp. She had her arm outstretched, palm out warning the enemy to come no closer. She did not want him to look upon the camp in the darkness and cast the evil eye upon them.

I could not see it, but I knew that the old woman's hand would be painted with blue and white circles to stay the power of the evil eye. She must have been a stone or sun worshipper, maybe both. Tireless in her duties and ignored by the group, she made her way around the camp.

"And what would you give up for me, Raji?" a short round girl asked as she slid herself up against him and positioned herself into the crook of his free arm. She lifted the cup from his hand and took a long, long drink.

"Tonight! Tonight the gods are smiling on Raji!" the old man, hooted.

Then a shrill voice pierced the crowd.

"RA jee, RA jee!"

An older woman, layered in drab clothing, clothing that would warm and protect, not attract attention like that of the young girls, advanced to the fire. She descended on Raji like a sand storm in the dessert swinging a gnarled walking stick as she came. There was nothing wrong with her balance.

"Do I have to do everything myself?" she shrilled. "You cannot even bring home a simple bucket of water? I ask you to do one thing and you cannot part from your bragging and drinking long enough to do even that."

Raji immediately freed himself from the two girls and backed away from the woman. "Hannah, stop. Hannah . . . Hannah."

She kept coming, and he kept backing away.

"Stop before I back hand you," he ordered. Stop it now!"

She didn't even slow down. When she reached him, she poked her stick into his chest and backed him across the dirt.

"You are in trouble now, old man," Cassim heckled. "The woman is angry, and she hunts you down like a jackal hunts a rabbit. You have been caught, so bare your throat and end your misery. I am sure the beautiful Chavala will cry the rest of the night for you."

"Whee Haw!" One Sleeve sang out.

Raji paid no attention to them. "Oh Hannah, Hannah, Hannah. Do not be so cross with me. I was on my way to you right now. Do you think I would stay the night away from the one I love?"

But Hannah would have none of it. "Ah, save your foolish jabbering for the young girls. I have heard it all before." With that, she cracked him on the shoulder with her stick and turned on the girls, going from one to the next looking them over and shaking her stick at them. "I sent you out to steal some bread. Not for a night of whoring with the Romans. Get to your tents, all of you!"

"You heard her. Get to your tents!" Hasaan roared.

"We have to leave. We have to leave," Martha insisted. .

"Shh," Deborah hissed again. We were still wedged into the cave.

"The blacksmith is right," Cassim said as he continued to ogle the girls. "You are all far too beautiful to waste on the Romans."

"Do not be so cross, Hasaan," the girl who had been hanging on Raji coaxed. "We please the Romans, and they treat us well."

"I have heard that you like the Jews as well as the Romans, Chavala," Cassim said, groping at her, trying to get his arm around her.

"At least they bathe,"[1] she laughed. "You should learn a lesson from them, Cassim. Your perfume does not cover your smell. Maybe that is why your wife nags you. Maybe that is why you can only get the tanner's wife." She slid away.

"You have no chance with her, Cassim," the girl with Gillaro shouted. "You do not have what the Romans have to give."

"You are wrong, Yari. You are wrong. The Romans are the ones who do not have what we have to give," Gillaro warned.

When Gillaro spoke, everyone turned toward him. I could feel the power that he had over them. I could feel his draw all the way across the darkness.

"They do not have our spirit," he continued. "We have more trouble than the Jews and the Romans put together. Yet we are the happier ones. And do you know why? We are happy because we do not remember yesterday; it is over. And we do not worry about tomorrow; it may bring a fortune that we do not want to face. We survive and keep a dance in our hearts because we live when we have a chance to live. And that is now, my princess. That is now!"

Then he swooped the girl into his arms, and she laughed with such music in her voice that all the men turned to her.

"We all remember, Gillaro," Hasaan countered, his voice bitter. "We remember. We just pretend to forget. Would we want to remember that we were free men in a faraway country that we will never see again? Or the years that we spent as slaves before we escaped? Or would we want to remember the horror of our people hung on the tree to feed the crows and the dogs? Oh, we remember, Gillaro. We just try to forget. But what about you?" Hasaan went on. "You and Hannah, and Raji? You come and live on the streets with the foreigners and the laborers and the despised perfumer. What about you?"

"Ahh, we grow too serious for the night," Raji interrupted. "It is time for pleasure." He clapped his hands, and the man who sat by the fire beating out the pulse of the night on his small *tof*² doubled the time. The rhythm sticks and rattles matched him. Talk stopped, the men sang, and the women gave their bodies to the dance and, with brass finger cymbals that they pulled from their pouches, made new music that laughed into the night.

I was mesmerized. I had heard stories of Miriam, the sister of Moses, dancing after the Israelites escaped captivity, but I had no thought that it could have been like this. I had never seen anything like this, shameful and beautiful at once. And then the women sang.

"Dance, dance, dance! Dance the dance of fire. In the fire burns your destiny."

"It is her. I can tell," Deborah whispered as Chavala danced by the fire.

She motioned for us to follow. Deborah and Martha took off, and I somehow got my knees under me and stood enough to duck walk out of the cave. Once out, I stood and ran after them into the camp. I had to force myself not to run the other way. I hoped that I would not die at their hands.

Hannah stopped, tilted her head, held up her hand and everything stopped. The only sound in the night was the crackling fire. She clucked to Hasaan.

"Show yourself, now." Hasaan commanded.

"I am looking for my friend, Chavala," Deborah called out."

We stepped into the light. Gillaro was right behind us. I clasped my hand over my mouth to try to stop my cry.

Chavala stepped forward. She was beautiful. Even in her awful clothing, she was beautiful. We stood still. The perfumer strutted around us jingling the coin in his pocket like we were on the auction block.

"Oh great, Chavala," he said, "how is it that you are of such influence that three Jewesses seek you out? And even more mysterious, they come in the middle of the night."

Chavala ignored him as she faced Deborah. "What are you doing here? Who is with you?"

"We need your help," Deborah said.

"Such proper women as you out in the middle of the night? You couldn't take care of yourselves if your lives depended on it." Yari, the girl who had claimed Gillaro, sneered. She was not laughing anymore, though, and she drew her brows into a scowl and walked toward us until I backed away.

"Their lives do depend on it," another girl said, flashing a knife. "I don't like sharing." She glided toward us, cutting her blade through the air like she was waving a pretty scarf. She smelled like wine, perfume, and the kind of oil the Roman men wore, and she smelled like a woman who has lain with a man.

Then Gillaro slid around us so we were face to face, and he was standing between us and the girl. She stopped and draped her arms around his neck. He ignored her and stepped closer to me dragging her on his back like a sack of grain.

"You have made my desert flowers jealous," he said. "They know my men would like you. Bad men like modest women, but you would not like them." He stepped closer and brushed a strand of my hair from my face. I would treat you well, though."

He laughed and stepped even closer to me, so close that I could feel his breath mix with mine and smell faint smells of wine and garlic and fresh mint leaves.

"I have waited a long time for a pretty Jewess of my own," he said, his voice soft and private. "Not so old that she could not warm my bed, but not so young to want children. You have no need for more children, do you?"

I kept my eyes down. He rested his hand on me, and I forced myself to stand, hoping that he couldn't feel me shaking. He laughed, and the men clapped and whistled for him. "You don't want me to get too close to you, do you? Do you think yourself defiled just to look upon me?"

He dropped his hand and turned away. As he did, I saw him and Deborah look right at each other, and then quickly away. They were not strangers. I looked at Martha, but her eyes were on the girl with the knife.

The old crone was back now, and she whimpered and cowered next to Hannah. Hannah brushed her away and waved her stick at Gillaro. "Sha! Enough!" she snapped. Gillaro smirked at me and stepped away from us.

"Chavala, do you know these women?" Hannah asked.

"I know one of them."

Deborah stepped forward. "We need your help," she repeated. "This is Myriam. We're looking for her son, Jesus. Jesus, the teacher who arrived in Jerusalem just a few days ago."

"Thousands, even hundreds of thousands, have arrived in Jerusalem in the last few days," Hasaan scoffed. "Is he so important that he would be noticed?"

"The Galileans follow him."

"Galileans? Ha! He can be of no account at all if he is followed by the Galileans," Yari sneered.

We didn't even take notice of her insult. Everyone who lived in Nazareth or anywhere in Galilee had heard many.

Hasaan approached me. He smelled like iron and fire.

"Mother of Jesus, I have heard people speak of your boy in the city. He seems to be making quite a stir around here with the prominent Jews."

"Chavala, can you help us?" Deborah asked again. "We need to get to the house of Caiaphas."

"Oh, Chavala," Cassim taunted, waving his cup and slopping his drink on himself, "not only are you a friend of the Jewesses but the high priest as well?"

Chavala ignored him. "What business do you have with Caiaphas?"

"Jesus was arrested earlier tonight," Deborah explained, "and we believe that he is being held at the house of Caiaphas."

"The priests have arrested a rabbi?" Hasaan laughed. "I have heard that they are turning against their own."

"Ah, the priests. Men of God. Men of God, all right," the girl with the knife sneered. "Men of God as long as it gets them what they want."

"Ouu. Do not be so hard on the poor priests, Julia," Yari mocked.

All the women laughed and heckled and winked at each other. I was shamed at the thought but sure that it couldn't be true.

Gillaro walked over again and stood right in front of me. Now he did not even pretend to be carefree. Like before, his eyes smoldered, but now it was with anger. "Your son has not found favor with the priests, or with Rome."

"How is it that you know so much about my son?"

"I have heard him teach. He is careless and has no regard for his own safety."

"What do you mean?"

"He is right in his thinking but foolish in his speaking. He is too bold. He must learn to play the game or pay the price."

Again, I asked, "What do you mean?"

"Jesus of Nazareth has a brilliant mind, good enough to keep him alive, but he does not use it to help himself. His wisdom does not serve him."

"You speak with authority. Do you know why he has been arrested tonight?"

"Because he escaped all of the other nights."

I wanted to slap his sarcastic mouth.

"Can you help me find him?"

"No. I cannot. This is a matter for your people, your leaders. And if the Romans think it will get out of hand, they will put an end to it. No one can stand against them." Gillaro spit on the ground again and turned away from me.

"The Romans are swine with the power of gods," Raji bellowed.

Hannah agreed with her husband.

"No one is above them. No one is safe from them," she lashed out. Then she twisted and turned, stamped the ground, and spewed her contempt.

The group had gathered round her show, and they agreed with her every word and cheered her on whenever she stopped to catch her breath.

"It does not matter. You follow their laws; you break their laws. They do as they please. They take our men, take our sons. Cast us to the gutters. No more regard for us than the dogs that run the streets. We are nothing to them! Nothing!" The fury was spilling from her. "If I had my way, I would spit in their eye and be proud of it. Nothin' more they can do to me. Nothin' more." She slammed her walking stick into a rock, it shattered, and the group gave a final cheer.

It was getting later and later, and the nomads weren't going to help us. We started to leave, but the old crone came and stood in front of me. She reached out and rested her palm on my cheek. It was gnarly and grimy and calloused, and my face grew hot where she touched me.

I didn't want to offend her, so I stood still as she slid her hand under my head piece and scratched her long sharp nails through my hair. When she grasped a fistful of my hair and drew it out, I was frightened and tried to pull away, but she pulled harder. Her free hand snaked out of her robe, and I saw the knife that she had been hiding slash towards me. I cried out and pulled away. The knife cut through my hair, and I fell against one of the other women. The crone did not try to touch me again.

She walked to the fire, dropped the handful of my hair into the coals that ringed the flames, and began to chant. The hair sputtered, sizzled, and burst into flames. After it had burned, she took a stick and drew a large circle on the ground all the way around the fire. She clapped sharply, twice, three times, and the music began.

The girls danced around the fire, and the crone danced with them jerky and slow so that they bumped against her, and she stumbled between them. I was afraid that she would fall into the fire, and I reached for her robe to pull her away, but the dancers surrounded me.

The crone stood in the circle with me and stared into the fire. I drew my nostrils together to keep out the scorching smell of my hair and pushed hard on my head where she had cut the hair because I felt the fire burning there. The crone began chanting, croaking. Faster and faster. The music, the dancers, the song, all kept up with her; they whirled, blurred around me. I was afraid that they would push us both into the fire. I held on to the crone and tried to keep us upright. Instead of trying to help me, though, the crone swayed and pitched and then went limp, and I could barely hold her from the flames. I heard the girls laughing. The fire licked at my robe. I called to Martha and Deborah.

The fire was searing hot, and it was hard to breathe. I didn't know how much longer I could keep the crone away from the flames. I thought that if she caught fire, she would let herself burn. Finally, the dancing and the music stopped, and the crone stood and shook off my hand.

She leaned over the fire, staring into the flames. "Vada satana!" she howled, and the fire leaped "Vada satana!" Again and again she let out the blood curdling howl. "Vada satana." Then her howls turned to moans, and she folded into a heap of rags.

Finally, she lifted her head, pushed herself up from the ground, and walked to where I stood. She looked at me, her face close to mine, but not touching. I have never seen eyes as old or as tired as hers were that night.

"Why are you staring at me?" I asked.

"Go to your boy now," she whispered. Her raspy voice scraped over my skin. "Go to your boy, and may your God be with you."

I wanted to run. I wanted to run and run and not stop until I reached Jesus.

"Please, please, we must leave," I pleaded with Deborah.

She agreed, and Chavala started to walk with us. Hasaan forbid her to go and let loose with some curses about the Jews and their religious skirmishes.

But he offered us some direction. "Go by the way of Cogi's. His interest is in gold, not women. Our kind and Jews traveling together will only make more trouble for everyone."

Then he reached inside of his shirt and brought out a piece of gold neck jewelry with a beautiful emerald stone and pressed it into my hand. I wanted to refuse it, but I did not. I took it from him and hid it inside my garments. The sin of it burned my breast.

"Please, Hannah," Chavala said.

Hannah looked at Hasaan and then back at Chavala and made her decision. "We will help them," she announced. "Jew or not, slave or free, we are all sisters."

Only from Jesus, had I ever heard such thoughts. I vowed to stop judging others.

Raji made a weak attempt to control his wife and order her to stay, but she didn't hesitate.

"Do what pleases you," she said. "We are going."

Then from the distance, we heard a lone cock crow. The crone bristled and shook her head slowly back and forth and peered into the darkness.

"It is not yet close to the light of day. No good can come of this," she warned. "No good can come of a cock crowing in the black of night. It is not natural." And then she turned to the west and began to howl again and did not stop.

We set out. Far ahead of us, I saw Gillaro running into the night.

The Ninth Day of Nisan

It has been a year. I know that, because it is the time of the Passover. The rains are over now and the first wild flowers are here. I lift a purple iris to my face, and I breathe in the sweet grape smell. I breathe in more deeply, and then I cannot push the air out. I am suffocating. Again and again I try before I realize that I have already expelled the air. I breathe in again, and once more feel like I am suffocating. I cannot breathe. A pain spreads in my lungs. I gasp and claw at my robe. I cannot breathe out, and I am afraid. I see it, and I do not want to. I sit on a rock and try not to take in more air because I don't want it to suffocate me.

When I can breathe, I hurry into my house. There is a knock on my door, and I want to hide and not answer it. Someone is coming to tell me that something has happened to one of my children. My mind races to each of them. The knock comes again, and stiff and slow, like my body is made of wood, I make my way to the door.

It is a woman who tells me that she is my neighbor, and her name is Lydia. Nothing has happened to my children. I sigh, and thank the Lord for protecting them. I try to ask the woman in, but my face trembles. It is often physically painful for me to be around others because I think I will cry, not from sadness but from the pain. This is different though. My face doesn't hurt, but my eyes well up, and my cheeks sting, and it stings inside my nose. I can't speak, so I blink back my tears and step back to let her enter.

She is holding a cloth wrapped around a fresh loaf and offers it to me. I can smell the yeast. Smells have a power over me. It is not just like they make me remember, but like I am right there again. Sometimes it is good, sometimes not. For some reason, the yeast is Egypt, and it is good. I wrap my hands around the loaf, feeling the warmth from the bread and from the stone that she has placed in the cloth.

I thank her and say that I will put a pot on the fire for tea. She smiles and tells me to sit; she will make the tea. I sit and watch, comforted by her woman movements. She reminds me of my mother when I was a child. We drink the tea before we speak.

"I have not come before," she says.

"You have come now," I say. "Thank you."

"I wanted to."

"It is not easy. It was a shameful death. Many have shunned me and will not come at all."

"That is not my reason," Lydia says.

"Many will not come," I repeat. "Some of the priests have come to give prayers for my son, but many have shunned this place." She doesn't deny it, and I continue. "It's just as well though, because I don't want to see them. I don't want to listen to the reasons that it happened, how Jesus should have been obedient to the laws." I am surprised that I say these things to her. Usually, I don't say them out loud.

"I have not lost a child to death," she says.

"You are blessed. Your children are well."

"No, I have no children."

It is very still in the room. I make myself look at her. I who have lost a son in this basest way, and she who has never had a son at all. I thank God for the time that I had with Jesus and reach out and cover Lydia's folded hands with both of mine.

"Tell me your stories," she says.

She listens while I talk about Jesus, telling her of when he was a young boy, telling her of the things he has done, telling of his death. And then she asks me about my other children, and I tell her about them.

When it is time for her to leave, I think that I will cry again. I want to ask her to stay, but I do not. She says that she will come again. It is good to tell your stories.

23

Trial in the Night

Caiaphas is our high priest. He has been chosen to oversee the people of Israel. He knows all the right things to say. He can nearly recite the entire Pentateuch[1] and endless oral tradition. His name is on the seal. But he is blind, as blind as a stone. When Annas rearranged commerce to suit the family, Caiaphas did not see it. When Pilate built great aqueducts to update the water supply in Jerusalem and keep the people happy, and our taxes were raised to pay for it until we were too poor to buy bread, Caiaphas did not see it. I didn't think or care about any of this that night, but now I see how it played into what happened.

Caiaphas lives in a palace high on a hill in the upper city. As we climbed toward it, I could see down the deep ravine of the Tyropoeon Valley and east to the Temple that glowed white in the moonlight. The road narrowed into a steep path of stone steps carved into the rock shelf of the hill, and by the time we reached the top, I was breathing so hard that I could not speak. Stone walls surrounded the house, but I could see it well through the gate, serene, majestic, awash in the moonlight like only good could happen there. Beyond were the more modest homes of other priests.

The house is of three levels, the top above ground, the middle built partially into the hillside, and the lower almost completely carved from the rock. The lower level of the house holds the guard room and prisoner cells, underground stables, and many storage houses filled with the choicest harvests of grain and the purest of oils. The living quarters for Caiaphas and his family and the servants are on the top level. The Court of the Sanhedrin sometimes met on the middle level.[2]

The Romans allow the court in an attempt to let us govern ourselves, at least in Jewish matters. This frees Pilate from dealing with our religious issues and also keeps the priests under the thumb of Rome. In return for the power of the court, the priests are expected to keep the Israelites firmly in line and do as Rome tells them.

I tried to think if I knew any of the Pharisees who had been assigned to the court. They knew Jesus infinitely better than the Sadducees who, in all their wealth and power, kept themselves separate from the common man. At the time, I didn't think that Jesus would ever be brought before them, but I knew that they might discuss him at their next meeting which I thought would be in two days. We would be gone by then.

I knew that Annas would be at the palace that night. Caiaphas would make all of the public announcements, but as Martha had said, he would take his directions from Annas. I reminded myself that these were God's chosen leaders. Surely, they would serve God first, have more loyalty to him than to the Romans or even themselves.

It was the deep of night; all should have been quiet, but it was not. Guards flanked the gate and swarmed throughout the courtyard. Three small fires burned and men huddled around each one. I saw scribes and apprentices, heads low, talking and gesturing, arguing among themselves. Servants trotted back and forth between the fires, the house, and the groups of men. I saw a ragged man summoned from his place at the fire and led inside.

"How are you going to get to the priests?" I whispered to Martha.

"When I see someone I know, I'll send word that we must speak to Caiaphas. Be ready."

The guards allowed no one to enter, so Deborah led us past the main gate around the western perimeter wall. Footing was slippery, and the path showed little sign of travel. Caiaphas discouraged use of the rear entrance. The east or front was more convenient, and it allowed him to see everyone who came to the Palace.

We found a small gate in the wall, overgrown with vines and unguarded. We squeezed through and hid ourselves between stacks of firewood and some of the larger ovens that had been set away from the house because they put off so much heat. We waited there while Deborah went to see what she could learn. We had a fairly good view of the courtyard but could not see the entrances to the front or to the lower levels.

I didn't see a single person that I knew. Not James, not Simon, not John, not even one of my son's followers. Worst of all, I did not see Jesus. Many times I watched the back of someone and thought that it was him. But then the man turned, and my heart fell, and I started my search again.

I was restless. The other women told me to have patience, but I wanted Martha to ask to be brought before Caiaphas. We were wasting time. I believed that Caiaphas would set this matter straight. I was sure he would free Jesus and reprimand all of our people who were involved. I stepped out of the shadows hoping to see over the hill. I thought that if I could just see Jesus, not even speak to him but just see him, I would know what he intended to do.

I took one step into the light, and a guard stepped out of the shadows and stood in front of me. I tried to get away, but his hand clamped my arm and half lifted me from the ground.

"State your business," he demanded.

I wanted to tell him that we had come for Jesus, that there had been a mistake, ask him if Jesus had already been released, but I couldn't speak.

"State your business," he growled.

Hannah stepped from the shadows and slipped between the guard and me.

"Same as yours," she replied, making her voice husky so that I felt his hand jerk. "Working my fingers to the bone to serve the priests of the house." She had shed the outer layers of her clothing and stood in a simple robe. She brushed her head cover back and looked up at the guard.

"Doing what?" the guard demanded. He straightened and tightened his hand on my arm again.

"I have been ordered from my bed to prepare a late night meal for them."

"I have never seen you here before."

Hannah was calm, bold even. She leaned toward the guard and rested her hand on his chest. I could see her face now, and I could see that though life had carved away at it, she still was very beautiful. The guard released me.

"You see only the young girls," she said, "but it is my cooking that you would like. Come back near the end of the watch, and I will set a bowl for you."

He turned to her and spoke softly. He placed his hand on her back and drew her closer to him in a possessive way like they had just sealed a bargain, and she was his for no reason other than that he decided to take her. I lowered my eyes and hoped that we would be out of there before he came back. The shame of women burned through me.

"Till later," he said and disappeared into the shadows.

"Wait," she called to him. "Word has come that one called Martha wishes to speak to Caiaphas. Perhaps she is a kinswoman of his. Quite taken with herself, so she must be of some importance. Shall I send someone to ask him?"

"I hope you make a tasty dish, because you know nothing of the workings of this place. If you try something that foolish, you'll land on the street. No man would dare to ask to be taken before the priest in the middle of the night, and a woman . . . ?" He laughed at how ridiculous it was. "Caiaphas will never see her, not even if she is his mother.

Get rid of her. She wouldn't want to see him anyway," the guard went on. "Caiaphas is furious. Gotten himself into a mess that no one can clean up for him."

"How do you know?"

"I've got eyes to see and ears to hear. Now get on with your cooking. It's no concern of yours."

"I have heard that a rabbi was brought here in chains," Hannah pressed.

"It's politics. Nothing that matters to you. Don't spoil your mind."

"But is it true?"

"Hmph, true enough."

"Did you hear his name? Do you know who it was?"

"Jesus of Nazareth. But I'm warning you, keep your nose out of it!"

There was a shout in the courtyard and the guard took off on a run. Hannah pushed me back into the shadows. "Do not ever show yourself again," she seethed. "If I had wanted to whore, I wouldn't have picked this place. Now stay out of sight, before you end up on your back or get us all killed." I stepped further back and did not even whisper.

In the darkness, I remembered when Jesus was a babe, and we took him to the Temple to redeem him. I remembered Simeon and his warning to me that a sword would pierce my soul. I tried to think what he had meant, but it was so long ago. I started shaking and couldn't stop. Martha put her arm around me and pressed me to her.

Of all the fears, and worries, and even nightmares that I had had for Jesus, I never once thought that he would be threatened by our own leaders. The men charged with the safety of Israel. The men called to protect us.

I was getting so tired that I had to let myself sit on the ground. I tried to clear my head and think of everything that had happened. The donkey, the moneychangers, the Seder on the wrong day, Judas, the Temple guards and the Romans together, Jesus not even trying to defend himself. Would they really try to make a case for the charge of blasphemy? Would the priests allow him to be stoned? How could they? He was a rabbi just like many of them.

I went over and over the problem to try to see what I was missing. I thought of every chief priest I knew. Was there one who had motive? What would it be, jealousy? Who was in line to be the next high priest? Was Caiaphas in poor health? Did someone know something that the rest of us didn't? Did Caiaphas think that Jesus was taking away his influence with the people? What else could be threatening Caiaphas? What part did Annas have in it? Why didn't they take the rest of the disciples? All those guards and soldiers to arrest one man? There had to be more to his arrest than the priests keeping order. Who had Jesus offended at the Temple? Or was one of those things, just HaKash SheShavar et Gav HaGamal[3] as Martha would say?

I tried to think the way Joseph would think. I pretended he was there, and I was talking to him. He would look at all the parts of the night like he was fitting the pieces of wood together for something he was building. He would look at all of the pieces and come up with an answer. While my mind jumped from one thought to another, Martha's got stuck on details. I thought that Joseph could have seen the problem clearly and then the solution. I could not. I leaned back against one of the cold ovens and kept trying.

Deborah came back, shivering so hard that her teeth were clattering together. I scrambled to my feet to hear what she had to say. The news in the courtyard was that the Sanhedrin had assembled. It would be very serious for them to be called out in the middle of the night. Martha protested that it was unlawful. Deborah knew the slave girl named Naomi who worked in the palace. If Naomi could get away and come to us, she would know more.

Then I saw Judas coming from around the front of the house, and I started to run to him. I wanted to rip his throat out, do things that I never in my life thought myself capable of doing. Martha held on to me.

"Stop it," she said. "Stop it now, before you get us all killed."

I struggled to get free of Martha. I saw myself attacking Judas. I hated him. I prayed for the Lord to strike him dead on the spot. Then I prayed for the Lord to take my hatred from me. I knew that my thoughts would be a shame to Joseph, a shame to Jesus. As he came closer, I saw that Judas was strangely beautiful, and that made his betrayal all the worse.

"The traitor! The Roman-loving heap of dung, mamzer, traitor!" Chavala hissed. "I hope he hangs for this."

Of all the horrible things that happened that night, I remember that that was the first time I had ever heard a woman say that word. It was a word that always stuck with me because I had first heard it used about Jesus, and I had had to ask Joseph what it meant. It was vile to me then, and it was vile when Chavala used it.

I wanted to call to Judas, but Martha squeezed my arm harder and harder. Then a man catapulted from behind the low stone wall, tackled Judas, and brought him to the ground. Judas was on his back, and the man was on top of him going for his throat.

"You will help me free him, or you won't see the light of day," the attacker hissed.

I knew the voice. James. It was James. I wanted to run out and help him, but Martha gripped my arm and warned me to stay out of sight.

Judas laughed. "Why would I fear your threats? You're not allowed to raise a hand against anyone."

"Why did you do it? Why?" James demanded. He was breathing hard, pinning Judas's shoulders to the ground with both of his hands. Judas stopped struggling.

"I did it for your own good." Judas turned his head to the side and spit.

"What did they give you for it?" James demanded.

"Thirty pieces of silver," Judas said and waved a pouch in James' face. I heard metal clanking softly together.

"You betrayed our master for thirty pieces of silver?"

"No. I betrayed him for nothing. The silver was an extra reward."

"Why? I want to know why?"

"It was the only way to save the rest of your miserable hides."

"You are a liar! You've never cared about any of us," James growled.

"More than your brother did," Judas sneered. "Running off his mouth till he brings the Romans down on the whole city, and he hasn't done a thing to position himself to overtake them. He let us believe that he'd drive them out and then refused to do it."

"That is not his way." James was panting. Judas must have been struggling.

"We got the wrong brother in charge. Simon is ready to fight. Now get off me if you want me to help you get the loser out of here. Maybe he's learned his lesson."

James rolled off Judas and stood brushing the dirt from his robe. It was rough and course, unlike the linen that he usually wore. I didn't recognize it.

Judas leaped to his feet. I saw a flash as he thrust the dagger and then stopped just short of running it through James' belly. He gave an evil laugh.

"If you want to follow him to his death, let me make it easy on you." Judas laughed again. James didn't so much as take one step back.

"Get that away from me!" James pushed the dagger away. "Now honor your word and help me free our master."

"It was the word of a traitor. Remember what I have done and never, ever lay a hand on me again," Judas warned. He shoved James to the ground and ran into the night.

James stayed low and made his way to the front of the house. I had no chance to speak to him.

Naomi, the slave girl, came to us. She stood in one spot for a moment, trying to make sure she had not been followed.

"It is terrible. It is terrible," she shrieked, but it was a whispered shriek.

"Tell me! Tell me!" I shouted at her, shaking her shoulders.

"They have called for his death," she shouted back.

I threw up on the ground. My head roared. I tried to speak, and I choked on my own vomit.

"I'm going into that house," I gasped. "I am going in right now. Annas will intervene. He will not let Caiaphas make this mistake."

We argued among ourselves. Martha wanted us to stay hidden. I insisted that we go to the priests. They might have thought Jesus outspoken, even radical at times, but they knew about his work, how he loved Israel and her people. They couldn't impose a death sentence without an inquiry by the Romans, and an inquiry always meant more deaths. We had all witnessed it before.

Then the nomad Gillaro was beside us.

"You were there," the slave girl bawled. "You were there. Please, don't report me! Please, don't report me!" He ignored her and stood in my path.

"You're not going anywhere," he warned me.

"You were inside the palace? How did you get in there?" I demanded.

"A different robe, and I am my uncle's son again," he said.

I recognized him then, as I should have earlier, a Hebrew with a new name, but a Hebrew still. Gillaro, the wildest of the outlaws, had been born into a family of the Pharisees. When he returned from Rome, his uncle wanted him to take up his rightful place in the family course,[4] but Gillaro had, in his own words, been defiled by the blood-lust. There was no going back. Neither did he want to. He denounced his faith and was exiled. But even after he had found his way to the band, his uncle never gave up hope that Gillaro would return to his heritage. He longed for his nephew's repentance and never refused his visits, even on that dreadful night.

Gillaro had observed the events from inside Caiaphas's own palace. This is what I have remembered of what he told us or what others have told me since. The story has been repeated many times.

The collection of priests and teachers gathered in a room where they often met in the daytime, but this was the first that they had

been there in the night. They had been called from their beds some-
where around the third watch.[5] The room was dark, lit only by the
torches on the walls and those held by a few slaves wandering about.
The Pharisees, and Sadducees stood clustered in one corner of the
court, pacing a little and whispering among themselves, questioning
why they had been called; they looked nervous and stayed near the
perimeter, near an exit.

They had many complaints. They were exhausted. They were
angry. They had barely gotten to sleep after working late into the
night to prepare for the festival when they were called from their
beds, and in a few hours, they would have to be up and working again.
The men were only half put together, missing their prayer shawls or
other parts of their dress so it was hard to tell who was a Sadducee
and who was a Pharisee.

Jesus was sitting on the floor in a small adjacent room. He was heav-
ily guarded, but he didn't look like he was hurt. He seemed to be just
leaning against the wall, resting. No one was allowed in the room.

Benjamin, the giant Sadducee, who was always hanging around
Annas, sat in a chair eating some greasy hunk of meat. Annas would
talk to him from time to time. Daniel, the scrawny seer, crouched in
the corner writhing and keening.

The Sadducee Caleb looked terrified and hung onto Caiaphas's
arm jabbering about following the laws, jabbering about not getting
them into trouble until Caiaphas shook him off. Then he went from
one to another cluster of priests and teachers warning them that this
was business for the stone chamber, and they should convene there.
He was referring to the Chamber of Hewn Stone in the Temple
where the Sanhedrin usually met. No one seemed to pay attention to
him. All eyes were on Annas.

Annas was on a rampage. He was ranting about Jesus riling up
the masses and making the high priest look bad to the Romans and
the people. He was ranting about how if Caiaphas could not control
the people, he might be deposed, and Annas would be out with him.

Annas was not going to chance losing his power or his monopoly on the Temple trade, and he was not going to answer to Jesus. He was personally furious with Jesus for going after the money changers and the merchants in the Temple, all of whom he and the Ananus family controlled. He was raving and pacing so that his turban was sliding half off his head, and that seemed to make him as furious as anything.

Finally, Annas stopped, and when everyone in the room was silent, he announced that Jesus had claimed to be the Son of God, and that was the charge they needed. He proclaimed that Jesus was guilty of blasphemy and ordered Caiaphas to have him stoned or hung before morning.

That's when things went wild in the room. Gillaro tried to get to Jesus but could not get past the guards. The priest's talk grew to a roar, the seer started wailing, and Caleb started out the door until Annas ordered him back. Even Benjamin quit eating. The consensus was that Annas was possessed, and he had gathered up this small group of priests to lay the blame on them if things went wrong. Gillaro waited for an opportunity to get to Jesus.

Joseph of Arimathea, Micha, Caleb and others in the room called for Caiaphas to halt the travesty. Caleb shouted that no man could be sentenced to anything without a trial. No trial could be held at night. The members of the court could not alertly and intelligently hear that case at night. If a man was arrested for a capital crime, he could never be arrested at night, and on he went until Annas ordered him to silence.

Benjamin was back to eating his mutton chop but told Caiaphas to send Jesus down to the cells and keep him locked there until morning. Annas turned on Benjamin, but he seemed to be the one man in the room who wasn't afraid of him.

Caiaphas agreed. He would hold Jesus until after the Passover.

Annas had calmed down somewhat and tried to reason with Caiaphas. He told Caiaphas that it was easy for him to keep his holy ways when he had him, Annas, protecting the very lives of the people. He explained again that if the Romans thought Jesus was going to lead a rebellion, they would round up everyone they thought was involved and nail them all up. It had happened before. Caiaphas argued that the Romans would not murder innocent citizens. Annas changed tactics and asked if Caiaphas thought that the Romans would let them keep the court, even the office of the high priest, if they could not control their wayward prophets? It was time for Caiaphas to wake up. Time for him to understand what happens to one asleep at the watch. Caiaphas was still unsure.

Annas went on. Did Caiaphas not see what was happening between Herod and Pilate and how the office of the high priest was going to get caught in the cross fire? If Pilate heard Jesus talk about destroying the Temple, he would raze it just to goad Herod.

Caiaphas was still unsure.

Annas let loose and started ranting again. He said Caiaphas was spineless. He didn't have the manparts to do his job. He only got the job as a gift from Annas and got Annas's daughter in the bargain. Annas mocked him, asked him if he enjoyed life as a eunuch, asked who his wife, Annas's own daughter, took to her bed. He was relentless. No one said a word. No one tried to stop him. Annas raged on and on, and when he had finished the whipping, Caiaphas was shattered and agreed that Jesus should be put to death.

One of the others spoke up in agreement. They shouldn't risk retaliation from the Romans just because some Galilean couldn't stay in line. Another agreed. Jesus had been warned. He should have left the city long ago. Still another one said some of the crowds following Jesus were proclaiming him the heir of David, saying that he would be the new king. The Romans wouldn't stand for it; neither would Herod. And finally one of the priests standing with Annas announced that word was out that Jesus and his men were in with the zealots. That would bring the Romans down for sure. None of the priests or Pharisees were safe around him.

Some of the Pharisees defended Jesus. Said he spoke the word of

God and his message was one of peace. He was not a zealot, and he had gained thousands of followers. True, Jesus was often lax on following the law, especially the oral traditions, but that was no reason to put a man to death.

Micha stepped in again and told Caiaphas that he could not order a death sentence, that he, Micha, would take it to all of the priests and not just the handful Annas had called. Caiaphas, usually one to remain in control, was furious. He had been kicked by Annas, and now he had a target. Micha was not a priest. He was only at the house as a Temple laborer. He had no right to interfere. The seer started wailing and telling Caiaphas to listen to the pup, but Caiaphas ignored him. Then he ordered Micha locked up, and the guards hauled him away.

But Joseph of Arimathea warned that an execution without a trial would be an abomination against the Lord. The priests agreed. The Sadducee had finished eating and got up and made his way to Annas. A man could not be put to death because he threatened someone's authority, he told him. There had to be proof of the crime. Annas was furious, but he consented. Caiaphas set the trial for after the Passover. But that was not good enough for Annas.

Annas ordered the court to be seated and the witnesses to be brought in. Three men were ushered in looking frightened enough that they might have been on trial themselves. Caleb protested against a trial in the night and against one with only a half court. Annas said it was night or not at all. The Sadducees and Pharisees took their places in the half circle so they could see each other. Two scribes readied themselves, one to record the evidence in Jesus' favor, one to record the evidence against him. Joseph of Arimathea stepped forward and offered to make the defense case. Annas told him to sit down and ordered Caiaphas to make the case against Jesus. The seer wailed again, and Benjamin told Annas that he was out of order, that the case for the defense had to be made first. Caleb was on his knees praying. Annas roared and ordered them all to silence.

Caiaphas had Jesus brought into the room. Joseph of Arimathea asked Jesus if he had anything to say. Jesus stared right at the court, showed no humility, and did not ask for mercy. Caiaphas slapped Jesus. Jesus did not even flinch, and he did not cast his eyes to the floor. The priests were nervous and whispered that Jesus wasn't doing himself any good. He should be asking for mercy. That was what any prisoner would do, any prisoner who wanted to live.

Caiaphas cursed and started in. He called the witnesses. Their testimony was poor, nothing more than the same accusations that Annas was making. Caiaphas called Jesus and asked him if he had destroyed the stands at the Temple. Jesus did not deny it. Asked if he had been healing people and stirring the crowds. Jesus did not deny it. Finally, he accused Jesus of saying that he was the Son of God. And one last time, Jesus did not deny it.

"Blasphemy, you have heard his blasphemy! What more proof do we need? What is your decision?" Annas roared.

And then Annas walked up to the youngest priest and ordered him to stand and give his verdict. Caleb protested that Annas was required by law to send the priests home overnight to contemplate their decision. Annas ordered him to be silent. The young priest stood but could barely speak. Annas was nose to nose with him. Finally, the priest voted guilty. One by one, youngest to oldest Annas called for the priests to stand and give their verdict. Several delivered the guilty charge that he wanted. Some voted not guilty, and Annas started shouting that Jesus was guilty, Jesus had gone against his own, and he must be put to death. The court was in chaos, some calling for death, some calling to free him.

Joseph of Arimathea called for a count. Annas needed a majority by two.

24

Caiaphas and Annas

Annas fell short of the votes he needed. He singled out the holdout priests and started in on them, but a man is forbidden to change his vote from innocent to guilty, so it was done. Jesus would live.

Annas turned purple, and Caiaphas ordered Jesus taken to the guard house. Annas struggled to calm himself and tried to reason with Caiaphas. Now that the court had found him innocent of blasphemy, only Pilate could impose a death sentence, and maybe that was the best answer for the people. Jesus' supporters urged Caiaphas to do what was right and keep Jesus locked up until after the festival if he wanted to and then release him. Caiaphas agreed.

It was then that Annas took Caiaphas into the ring. He assured Caiaphas that he had never been in charge, and he never would be. He told him that if he did not take care of Jesus he, Caiaphas, would lose his office by morning.

Caiaphas opened his mouth and closed it without speaking. He had been broken. And in the end, Caiaphas did what Caiaphas always does, took the path of personal gain. And he, too, began to wonder aloud if all should die for one man's foolishness? He ordered Jesus taken away. Gillaro did not know where.

Through all that Gillaro told, I did not see one drop of sympathy or kindness in him. He ended by ordering us to leave. I refused. He cursed profusely, words that I had not heard before, even from the camp, and walked away.

I wanted to go into the house, demand that Caiaphas let me see my son. Demand that he release him to me. Then I saw James across the way. I didn't care anymore who heard me, and I shouted for him. He saw us and ran over.

"Be quiet," he hissed, clamping his hand across my mouth. "What are you doing here?" I knew he was angry at me.

His hand was hot, burning. I pushed it away. "I've come to see Jesus. Can you take me to him?"

"No. That's not even possible. No one can get to him."

"Where have they taken him?"

"Caiaphas ordered him to the guard house, but no one can see him there."

"Where do you think that he is?"

"I don't know. I don't know. Maybe they are hiding him someplace."

"Will he be brought before Pilate?" Hannah demanded.

I felt the darkness closing in on me and reached for James.

"Pilate won't dare sentence a man that the court has found innocent," Martha stormed. "It's no secret that his position is not secure. That Caesar is just waiting to replace him."

"Why would he even risk becoming involved?" Deborah asked. "The laws of the Jews are of no concern to him."

"There has been no charge to do with Rome, so there is no reason for Pilate to enter into this. He will see that and free Jesus," Martha continued.

"You talk like old women and fools," James warned. "Pilate doesn't care at all about the reason. He'll kill a Jew as easy as another man would swat a fly."

"Pilate will release Jesus after he speaks to him," I said.

"Imma," James said and gripped my shoulders, forcing me to look at him. "Listen to yourself. Pilate will never even consent to see Jesus."

I knew that James was right. Even males of position were rarely allowed to address Pilate. A Jewish rabbi would never be. If I could speak to Pilate, I would tell him of the goodness of my son, but I knew that would not happen. Women are less than chattel to Pilate. He would never grant me an audience. I could never even get a message past his gate.

"If Jesus cannot speak to him and plead his own case, his fate is sealed," James warned.

"Can Simon?"

"No. Jesus will not allow it."

"Where are the others?"

"Peter is in the courtyard. John is here also. That is all."

Even then, I thought that James might get to Jesus and talk to him, convince him to do whatever he had to end his arrest. I realize now how foolish I was. How powerless we were against Rome. Against the priests, even. But at the time, I didn't let myself think of failure.

James ordered Martha to get us off the streets, to take us to the house of his friend. He would go to the Praetorium[1] in case they had taken Jesus there. We started out and met up with Hannah's guard. A Pharisee, whom Martha seemed to know, was with him.

"Jacob," Martha nodded. "Can you tell us what happened to Jesus?"

The Pharisee shifted around and looked away before he answered.

"He has been exiled."

"On what grounds?"

"Many, including insulting the priests, tempting others to sin, desecrating the name of the Lord. He will need to repent to regain favor."

"He didn't commit a single crime." Martha laid her hand on his arm. I reached out and pulled it away before anyone saw her, but she shook my hand off.

"He claims to be the Messiah," the man whispered.

"He is not the first. There is no crime in that." Martha's voice was cold and controlled. She didn't argue Jesus' claim, only that it was not a crime in the eyes of Rome or Israel.

"He calls himself the Son of Man," Jacob went on.

"Are you not also the son of man?" she asked. "Adam is father to us all."

"That is not what he meant. Now I order you to be silent."

Martha ignored him. "What will happen to Jesus?" Her voice was pitching higher, and people were gathering around us.

"Pilate sent a warning to Caiaphas that he will not tolerate even a hint of a disturbance during the Passover. Jesus could spark a riot by a word. That is why Caiaphas ordered him brought in."

"Why were the Romans there?"

"Annas said that he would escape. He has powers. He would have used them to get away."

Martha harrumphed.

"Caiaphas wanted him off the streets." Jacob twisted the fringes of his shawl. I wondered if he was praying. "It is no longer our concern."

"Where is he? What is going to happen?" Martha demanded.

"Caiaphas will decide."

"You mean Annas."

"Do not speak with such disrespect for the high priest," Jacob warned in a harsh whisper, shaking her arm at the same time.

"Did you even speak for him?"

"I argued to wait for morning, but Annas explained that . . ." Then he stopped. "Nothing will happen until morning. Go home, now."

"That I ever called you friend," Martha said.

"You have no regard for the safety of the people."

Martha did not answer. She began to walk, and we left unnoticed through the gate we had entered.

"Who was that man?" I asked. "How did you dare to speak to him like that?"

"He is no one."

I asked again. "Who was that man?"

"I have told you, he is no one. No one at all."

I learned later that Martha had planned to marry him.

We began to make our way back through the streets that were still filled with the night people. I felt sick from fear, from lack of sleep. We fell in with a crowd that was traveling in our direction. I could see by the light of the small fires that burned along the way that we looked as wild as the rest of the group.

As I walked, I tried, through the distance, to will Jesus to announce himself, to take his place as leader. In all of the things Jesus had done, I had never known him to use his powers for himself. He had healed others, fed others, saved others, but he had never done one thing for himself that any other man could not do. I tried to send my prayer to him through that night air. I tried to will him to help himself.

A soldier approached us and stood with his hairy legs sticking out under his short leather dress, and I wondered, as I had so many times, why they did not cover themselves. They were vulgar. One of his sandals was untied and his metal helmet tipped to almost cover one eye. He waved his oversized bullwhip and shouted, and it was clear that he had had plenty to drink. He swayed and then righted himself again. He looked like a fool, but I was still afraid of him.

"Clear the streets. Clear the streets all of you," he bellowed, snapping his bullwhip. He had to try two times before he got a good crack out of it.

People jumped away and skirted wide around him. I lowered my head and hoped he wouldn't notice us, but the nomad girl called Yari wouldn't back down. "Go back to Rome where you belong." she shouted at him. "You don't own these streets."

The challenge must have sobered him. He straightened and snapped his bullwhip again. It hissed through the air snaking out and coiling around her legs so that she screamed in pain. He jerked hard and tightened the whip, and she fell to the ground. He walked over and stood looking down at her, panting. Slowly and deliberately, he readied his whip again. That whip could have shredded her skin to bits or separated her head from her shoulders. She whimpered in the dirt.

"Now you are in the gutter where you belong." He laughed as he stood above her. "And now I will give you what you deserve."

I shut my eyes and waited, but I didn't hear the whip. I heard Hasaan's voice. I don't know where he came from, but he was there.

"Is this your sport after you have had your wine?" he demanded. He placed himself between Yari and the soldier, and stood like a little bull, ready to take the whip for her. "Are we to admire your strength then?" he demanded again.

The soldier raised himself up and looked down at the blacksmith. "A wicked tongue is yours, old man," he snarled. "But it is a poor match for my whip. Do not even think of using it again, or I will strike you down like a dog until you bleed and howl for mercy."

By then, the soldier had his hand around Hasaan's neck, squeezing, squeezing tighter and tighter. I could hear Hasaan choking.

Hasaan did not fight back. Maybe he couldn't. Maybe he knew it would make things worse.

"I will whip you until you bleed like a dog and howl for mercy," the soldier warned, "and then you will beg me to let you die."

With that he let go of Hasaan's neck and butted his stomach with his whip handle so hard that he knocked the wind from him. Hasaan fell to the ground and lay still and silent. I thought to go to him, but through her teeth, Deborah ordered me not to move, not to speak, not to even look up. I stood where I was and kept my eyes to the street.

The soldier paced through the crowd and threatened us one after another, ranting louder and louder.

"Now hear me. Here me all of you. If I tell you not to move, do not move. If I tell you to clear the streets, clear the streets. If I tell you to go home, go home and be glad that you have your lives. If I kill a peasant or two to keep order in the streets of Jerusalem, no one would even shed a tear!"

We stood still and silent while he cracked his whip and laughed and cracked his whip some more. Then an old man in the crowd stepped forward and addressed the people.

"From the stem of Jesse," he sang, "shall come a shoot to lead the people Israel."

His voice quavered. The soldier stepped towards him and raised his whip, but the man did not stop. "Oh people of Israel, do not be afraid, you shall not be hurt nor destroyed." The soldier towered above the frail old Hebrew man. He stood with his whip raised, but he didn't strike. One by one, the people stepped forward until the old man was surrounded. The soldier could whip us all, and we would not move.

"The calf and the lion shall dwell side by side, and the wolf of the forest shall lie with the lamb," they all sang. And then, "Every head shall bow. Every knee shall bend and they shall call him Lord."

The soldier glared for a while more, cursed us all, and then spun on his sandal and stalked down the street. And the Israelites sang and waited for the Messiah. They waited for Jesus.

The Sixteenth Day of Sivan

For the first time in my life, I did not celebrate the Passover. Not here and certainly not in Jerusalem. I didn't want to go back. I am tired again, and I am afraid. Not just because of what happened, but everything. The soldiers, the trip, getting sick from the food, a storm that might come, everything. For a long time afterwards, I did not care what happened to me, so I didn't worry about earthly dangers. Now the wind can scare me. So I did not celebrate the Passover, but I have survived a year.

I still find myself bargaining with God or waking to think that it was all a very bad dream. I still want to tell Jesus things, or ask him questions, but I am not so sad anymore when I remember that I cannot. I just tell him anyway. I think he hears. I often find answers to my questions by thinking what he would have said or done. I talk more of him now with his brothers and sisters, of our lives together when they were younger.

I don't pretend very much anymore. I know that is good, but now I don't see Jesus or Joseph at all. I remember them, but it is not the same. It makes me teary sometimes.

When I am half awake and half asleep, it is the best. I am not anxious and afraid like when I am awake, and the nightmares do not take me like when I am asleep. In between, I drift in safe waters, looking at clouds, smelling the sea breeze, humming to myself. In half wake, half sleep, I am lost in the moment. I do not remember, and I do not think ahead.

One thing that is hard is that I never know when I will fall into the pit again. I may be only a little lonely or a little sad, or I may be even feeling pleasantness in the day, and then something happens and I am bent low with grief.

The seasons of the field are a year. One passes into another and then after a year they begin again. Planting, tending, reaping, and turning, but the seasons of grief may all come within a single day. Joy in the morning is cast out with the grief of the noontime. And long ago sadness, even long forgotten sadness, returns.

It has been many years since Joseph, my mother, and my father have died, but since the time of Jesus' death, I grieve again for them. I remember them more, miss them more, want to see them again. It is not like before though. I know that I cannot, and I hold to the promise that we will be together in heaven. And now I turn more to my family and friends who have been with me. I don't remember most of their visits, but I know they were here.

25

Morning

Martha and Deborah and I made our way to the house where James had directed us. Martha led me to a pallet, and I fell onto it. When I opened my eyes, dawn was breaking. I heard the street noise; business had started. It was the second day of the Passover, the day of the feast, and all of Israel would be celebrating.

I rose from my pallet, but when I put my weight on my injured ankle, it buckled under me. I limped my way to the window willing Jesus to be coming up the walk, but he was not. Martha was there and the merchants and some travelers.

I was miserable from days of walking and lack of sleep, and once again, the sand had conquered me. My eyes burned, my throat was raw and dry, and it was hard to breathe. I lowered myself to the floor and leaned against the wall. My head hurt, and my back ached across my shoulders and at the base of my spine. And fear pounded all throughout my inside. I tried to think what I should do, how I should look for Jesus.

Martha came in, offering me a cup of tea. I knew when I saw her that the news was bad.

"What did you hear on the street?" I asked. She did not answer. "Tell me," I said. "Tell me."

"They have taken him to Pilate."

"The Praetorium?"

"No one knows for sure."

The house we were in was close to the Praetorium, and I wanted to leave right away to find Jesus. Martha said Deborah had gone to find news. We would wait.

I took the tea from Martha. The cup was warm in my hands. I held it close and drew the steam into my parched throat all the way into my chest.

"We should go to the Praetorium," I insisted.

"We don't even know if he is there. We need to wait for Deborah." Martha swirled her tea in the cup and sighed.

"Micha?" I asked. "Will someone send for his father?"

"I don't know.

We sat and sipped the strong hot tea. When Jesus was born, we received a gift of tea from one of the visitors. "The king," they had called him. They came and brought gifts to the king who was born to save Israel from the Romans.

"Where is Lazarus?" I asked.

"I have not seen him for days."

"Will he come?" I shifted my weight. The pain speared hot in my spine, and I felt needles prickle all the way up my leg.

"How would he even know what has happened?" Martha asked.

"We need to get word to him."

"Yes," Martha said. She rose and went to the door, called out to someone on the street, and gave him instructions to go to where the last of the ovens were being finished to try to find her brother Lazarus.

She returned and sat beside me. I was not grateful to her though. I was angry at her rightness. I was angry because I saw in her eyes that she knew this would not go well for Jesus.

"Martha? Do you believe that God has turned his face from Jesus?" I knew that my boldness shocked her, but I didn't care.

"Myriam." She choked on her tea, but I went on.

"At every Passover since his birth, we have spread the blood of the lamb on our doorposts. I ate every Passover meal and sang praises to God for the deliverance of our people from the Egyptians. The God of Moses made a promise that the angel of death would pass over the house of every Israelite and that every firstborn would be spared." I squeezed my cup harder and harder. "Am I not an Israelite? Will the blood of the lamb not save my son?"

"Myriam," Martha gasped again.

But I was not finished. "If God will break a promise, then there is no one to trust."

Martha's cup slipped from her hand and shattered on the floor. I sat very still and waited for God to strike me down.

Martha made a funny noise and sat still beside me. After a time, she turned her head to look around the room. Then she sighed, wrung her hands, and sighed some more. She rose and went to the table, cut a piece of cheese, took some unleavened bread from a clay bowl, and brought the food to me.

I refused it, told her that I was not hungry. But she had no sympathy for me. She was cross and told me that if I did not eat, I wouldn't have the strength I needed to help Jesus. Then, she turned with a sweep, so that her robe billowed behind her, and marched out of the room. I thought that I would throw my cup of tea at her back. She turned back to me one last time and said, "Pray, Myriam. You need to pray."

I looked at the food and bile rose in my throat, but I broke off a piece of the bread, put it in my mouth, and forced myself to chew. I ate most of what she had given me, and the pain in my head lessened.

I have prayed many times each day since I was a child. That morning, though, I could not remember how. I closed my eyes and tried. I heard Martha in the other room, but I did not hear God.

Then slowly and trembling, I began. "Hear my prayer, Lord, hear my prayer," I could not tell if he was listening. "Adonai, Adonai," I whispered, "Will you not save my son? Will you not place your hand upon his brow? Lift him from the net his enemies have laid and save him from this evil?"

I confessed that I had sinned. That I had loved Jesus more than I had even loved God, and if I had not loved the Lord above all else, I had broken the first commandment.

Then it came to me that my sin had brought this suffering upon Jesus. That he was being punished because of me. I was filled with shame and begged God to turn his wrath toward me. I begged him to strike me down and let Jesus live. I was selfish, though, and what I most wanted was for God to return my son to me.

Martha returned, and I told her that I believed I should go to Pilate and ask to be punished instead of Jesus.

"Why would you be punished? You have no crime."

I was resting on the floor again and she lowered herself next to me. She was not so cross anymore, and that made me want to lay my head on her shoulder and weep.

"Jesus has no crime. I have sinned against God many times. Jesus has never," I told her.

"Myriam, Pilate would not care about that."

"Maybe he would listen."

She drew in a big breath to begin one of her lectures to me but exhaled without saying a word.

"I believe that is how I could save Jesus," I said.

She placed her hand on my shoulder. "Do you think that you could sleep a while more?"

"Do not desert me, Martha." I was angry again at her dismissal of me.

"I am here, Myriam. I am here," she soothed.

Outside, the noise was growing louder. The merchants called out their wares. Fresh eggs for sale, best to be found in the city. Gold spun fabric. Priceless. The travelers didn't believe it. Worthless. The merchant is a crook. High prices. Cheap goods. Everybody shouted and bargained. Then one voice rose above the rest.

"Have you heard? Have you heard? A trial going on at the Fortress Antonia."

I hurried to the door. The morning sun blinded me. I squeezed my eyes shut and then opened them again, but slowly this time, and did not look into the sky. I saw that the voice belonged to an old woman, so short that I could scarcely pick her out in the crowd.

"I say a rebellion is brewing," she cackled.

"That bastard Pilate, what's he up to this time?" asked a merchant selling spices. He waddled over to the woman, and the rest of the group gathered round.

Talk flew. It was about Jesus. I backed out of the doorway. I didn't want to be recognized. I listened to the voices.

"Whatever it is, there will be bloodshed. Of that you can be sure."

"They say some crazy Galilean is proclaiming himself to be the Son of God."

"Who is the Galilean?"

"The one they call Jesus. Jesus of Nazareth."

"Jesus of Nazareth is at the Praetorium, not Antonia. Get your story right old woman, or don't bring it here."

"Shut up and let her talk."

"This is not the first time he has gotten himself into trouble. Ha! He has shown himself to be a crazy one all right. But this time, he has gone too far. Proclaiming himself to be the Son of God."

"Zeus or some other?"

"Zeus begat a Jew?"

"No, the God of Abraham."

"Son of God? King of the Jews, that's what I heard about him."

"He will learn a lesson today. Just like the zealots before him, cruci-fied for sure."

I held my stomach. "Please, please, God. Please God," I begged. My headache was back again, pounding hard. I pulled my clothing away from me and pressed my head against the cool wall.

"Noooo, I doubt that his boasts will warrant that," someone

interrupted. "Stoning maybe. Scourging, even quartering, but I'd not bet on a crucifixion on the day of the Passover."

Then I heard a young man, a new voice, say, "Pilate has refused to address the matter."

"Gave him the death penalty without seeing him then?" someone asked.

"No, no, no, you braying ass. I did not say he refused to see the man. I said he refused to attend the matter. Sent him away."

"Martha," I called. Martha, did you hear?"

"Yes. That is good news," she said. "Listen now."

"Freed him or sent him back to the priests?" someone else in the crowd asked.

"If you want to hear from me, be silent. I will do the talking." It was the young man again.

"Tell us then."

"He sent him to Herod's."

"All the way to Tiberias?"

"Next door. That is all. Herod is in town for the festival."

"Pilate and Herod living under the same roof? Dangerous. Very dangerous."

"So Pilate will not deal with him? His hands are full enough with the Passover crowds and Barabbas, I suppose. Put his work off on Herod then. Better for the Nazarene to go to one of his own and all." It was the spice merchant. I recognized his voice.

"Herod won't have time to deal with it. He has an orgy going on that would put the Greeks to shame," someone shouted.

They argued among themselves about why Pilate and Herod would work together at all. They talked about how the two men hated each other. One after another they talked so fast that I could barely understand them. Herod hated Pilate because Pilate maintained his residence in the palace Herod built and because Pilate ruled the land that should all belong to him. He hated Pilate so much that he was always sending letters to Caesar telling of Pilate's incompetence and complaining that Pilate could not control Jerusalem, that the city was a mess, overcrowded, filthy, no water. The crowd agreed that the only reason Pilate was even keeping his job was that his wife Julia was related to Tiberius.

Pilate hated Herod because he was not a Roman and because he would not put down his wine long enough to help keep order during the festival. He was a Jew. He should have some sway over the masses. Jesus should fall under his rule. He was a Galilean from Nazareth. Galilee was Herod's territory.

26

Pilate and Herod

The merchants got so caught up in the debate that they forgot to tend their stands, and a thief made off with some goods. They all gave chase, caught the thief, beat him until he could not walk, and left him lying in the dirt. The merchants were quiet then, and time was passing.

I insisted to Martha that we had to go to Herod's palace and find Jesus. She said again that it would be better to wait for Deborah, that travel in the city was impossible with the Passover crowds. I pointed out that we were not so far from the palace, but she made another excuse. Then I knew that she was stalling, because she did not believe that Herod would release Jesus, and my heart seemed to stop beating altogether.

"You believe Herod will sentence him then?" I asked.

"All these years, you are the one who did not trust him, Myriam."

"I know, but all the years in Nazareth . . . it would have been so easy for him there."

"Herod likes to make a spectacle."

"What sentence do you think he will give him?" I smoothed my neck with my hands.

"Does Herod know of your escape from Bethlehem?" Martha was

tidying things in the room. It was not even her home and she was arranging the dishes and wiping the dust from the window sills.

"Martha, you have asked that so many times. I do not know. I just do not know." It seemed we pounded out the same things over and over and over.

"I cannot believe that I didn't know that you escaped with Jesus?"

"No one did, except my mother. We agreed to take the secret to the grave, but now I have told you."

"I cannot believe I didn't know." Martha shook her head back and forth, back and forth.

"I have lived for longer than I can remember under fear of the Herods."

"Antipas does not have as much power as his father did," she said, "but he enacts the death penalty without Roman intervention just to show his strength."

"Do you think that Jesus is a threat to him?"

"If he knows that Jesus is connected with royalty. Herod the Great married into the House of David, but Mariam was not Antipas's mother, so he has no claim. If he understands that Jesus is the legitimate heir for the line of David, he will fight him. But it may be that he has never heard. I don't think that he goes looking for trouble like his father did."

The street people were growing louder again.

"No Jew would want to trust his life to Herod," a woman screeched.

"He's no Jew himself, that's why. Some other blood in the mix."

"No, not him. That was his father."

"Grandfather."

"Still not adding up to a whole. Still not to be trusted."

"The Jews think Herod no more Jew than any other heathen. That's why they don't trust him, because he's a heathen."

"Neither one will claim the other."

"It is of no matter what Herod is," a new voice said. "He sent the rabbi back to Pilate."

"No." I protested.

"We do not know if that is true," Martha said.

"They would not say it otherwise." I was holding onto her hand as hard as I could.

"They are gossips. Nothing but," Martha said.

I listened to the crowd again and hoped.

"Herod said if the man committed a crime against Rome, it would be in Pilate's hands. If it didn't have to do with Rome, it could wait until he was back in Tiberius.

"Not right," someone said, "Herod and Pilate, a Jew and a Roman, scheming together like brothers."

"They're scared for their own hides. That's why. Scared of this one called Jesus, and they want him put to death."

"Because he will be the king," someone else agreed. "It is the Nazarene who has the rightful lineage. He will take the throne and put them both on the street."

Yes, I wanted to shout. Yes! Yes! He will.

A new group of travelers came.

"I heard Herod sent Pilate a message warning him to end it," a woman said.

"What I heard," another said, "is that Herod is cursing himself mightily for not pushing the little mamzer off the cliff when he had the chance or better yet, tying him to the end of an oar."

They all laughed and laughed. I knew that these people had no concern for Jesus. His arrest was only sport and gossip for them.

"I think I know the reason for it," the spice merchant said. "It's all clear to me now. It's not just that Herod is scared. It's that he is jealous, jealous of the Nazarene and his adoring crowds, jealous of his miracles."

"He's right," said another. "It's a poor king that can't perform a miracle, and Herod has not performed a single one. Tried and tried, but it never happened. Every time he fails, he goes into such a rage that people hide from him for days."

"That's right," said the first woman. "I've heard that it was the Nazarene's last miracle that had Herod's face throbbing red. The one where he brought the dead man in Bethany back to life. Four days dead and stinking too, and the Nazarene brought him back to life."

Martha was too late in her secrecy. The news of Lazarus was already on the street.

"That must have really unknotted Herod's loins," someone laughed. "Not jealousy, but fear. Herod must think that the rabbi will bring his lunatic father, Herod the Great, back to life."

"Impossible! No one can bring the dead to life."

"It is true as I stand here," the first woman said. "If a man believes, this Jesus can bring him back to life."

"How could he do that?" the spice merchant asked. "Could he bring me back if I fight the bastard Kinya, and he runs a knife through me? If it's true, I'm gonna give it a try."

Everyone laughed.

"They say it can happen."

"Now there. That's the real reason Herod did not order the death of the Nazarene himself. He is afraid. Afraid as a babe."

By now, I could barely make out the voices. I pulled myself up to the small window so that I could hear. The street was so crowded that the people were packed tight against each other.

"Not a one of you has it right," an old man hooted. "Not a one of you."

"What then?" the crowd demanded of the old man. "What then? You tell us."

He puffed himself up with his importance and waited until his audience was silent, and then he began. "This is not just any Nazarene we are talking about," he said nodding his head slowly, "and Herod knows it." He paused and nodded his head some more and pulled his beard. "This is the one called John the Baptizer."

"No, no. It is Jesus of Nazareth," they called back to him.

"No, mark my word. It is the Baptizer himself. Herod had him beheaded, and here he has come back to life. Herod knows his days are numbered now."

And the crowd roared again and told the man that he was not right at all. Not the same man at all. Did he see a ring around the Nazarene's neck to show his head had been attached again? No it was not the same at all.

"You may be right," the man conceded to the crowd. "So I will tell you the real reason."

"Tell us," the crowd chorused, again. "And tell us the truth this time."

"I will," said the man, his voice so low that his listeners had to lean close to hear the secret he would share with them. I held onto the window and stood on one foot to keep the pain from my ankle.

"And now, this is the way of it." And everyone was quiet as the man spoke. "Herod has not the sense to worry about one of the things that has been told this morning. Not the sense and not the brains. He spends his days drunk with wine and cannot bring a thought to mind. He is not right, for his brain has been eaten away by the disease."

"What disease?" someone asked.

"The disease," the man was near whispering, and I could see the silent crowd leaning close to hear him. "The disease that a man gets from too many whores. That is what Herod has got himself. And there is not a cure in all of the land. He will watch himself rot away now part by part, and not a thing to do."

The crowd laughed and squirmed, looked at the ones next to them, and tried to back away from each other.

"Unclean! Unclean!" someone shouted. "Curse of the Greeks and the Romans."

"Changes women faster than his bed linens," the man went on. "And now he needs a miracle to save him. Needs a miracle as great as the ones the Nazarene performs."

"Will the Nazarene help him?" the old woman asked.

"Why should he?" demanded another.

"Let the king rot," someone else said.

"No," the story teller said. "No, the Nazarene will not help him. He will raise a Jew from the dead, but he will not raise a hand to cure the king. No matter what Herod threatens or how much he begs, the Nazarene will not save him from his rotting disease. So you can see why Herod sent him right back to Pilate."

"You haven't told us a word of truth," someone accused the story teller. "Herod doesn't have the rotting disease at all. He won't deal with the Nazarene because the man has too many followers. Learned his lesson with the Baptizer. He almost had a riot on his hands then."

"What will Pilate do?" someone asked.

"What will Pilate do?" the story teller repeated. "Pilate will do just what Herod warned him to do. He will give the Nazarene the Roman end."

And then, the shouts went up from the crowd. Cursing Pilate, cursing Herod. Betting if Pilate would dare to order a crucifixion on the day of the Passover Feast.

I could not stand to listen anymore. I would not have the crowd speak so of Jesus. I flew out the door, Martha behind me.

"Get away! Get away all of you," I meant to yell, but my voice was a whisper. "What harm has he ever done you? You are not worthy even to say his name!"

"Do you know the man?" the storyteller asked me. "If you do, best keep it to yourself. It will do him no good, and you would be risking your life."

"That is true," added the short woman. "The Nazarene's fate is with Pilate. Whatever he has done or said, he must have known the risk he was taking. Everyone in this city knows how Pilate deals with the Jews. Forget your friend. He has chosen a foolish path, and now he will pay with his life."

And then a Pharisee entered the crowd.

"You are a follower of this rabbi, Jesus," the spice merchant called to him. "Have you seen him?"

"I have tried," the man replied, "but no one can get to him. He is back at the Praetorium under the guard of Pilate's soldiers."

"They hold him because he will not give Herod his miracle?"

"I have heard nothing of that. They hold him because he has been charged with treason."

"The charge is false," I shouted. "The charge is false!" But I saw the heavy hand of tyranny reaching for Jesus, crushing the life out of him.

"He committed the crime that the common man cannot afford," the Pharisee said. "He gave in to his own anger, and now he has been charged for it."

"What is it that he has done?"

"Took a whip after those that defiled the Temple."

"He will have the Lord himself on his side then," the spice merchant declared, slapping at the hand of a shopper who was reaching for a spice.

"The Lord, but not the House of Annas," the Pharisee said.

The crowd roared. Everyone knew that it was not right the way the Temple had turned into a bazaar. And then they repeated what I had learned from Deborah and Martha. Money changers in the Temple court, livestock running loose until the whole place was filthy. They agreed that if Jesus and a few of his men went in with a whip and drove the buzzards out, that was good.

"What would that have to do with Rome?" someone demanded.

"Everything has to do with Rome," the Pharisee said. "Everything." Everyone started shouting again. Shouting and calling on the Lord to smite the Romans. Calling for a rebellion. I thought that they might take up whatever weapons they had and march to the Praetorium to free Jesus. I wished they would. I wish that they had.

"Treason?" Martha choked. "Treason? That is an outrage. Pilate will not care what happened in the Temple. Pilate has got to find him innocent. He cannot condemn a man unjustly. That would be a mockery of the Roman law. A mockery of Caesar. Pilate would never chance that."

"Pilate will condemn any man for any reason," the spice merchant said. "Only a fool would believe otherwise."

"Irritate Pilate and you'll pay with your life. He'll make an example out of any man. No getting off easy with an eye for an eye with Pilate," someone lectured.

A fight broke out in the crowd. Someone knocked a man to the ground. Someone else tipped over a merchant's table, but the debate about Jesus never stopped.

"Why would Pilate care what happened in the Temple? The Temple belongs to God, not Caesar."

"Caesar believes that he is God."

"Of all the gods the Romans have, he is the one to fear. He is the one to give the orders of who lives and who dies.

"Everything in the empire belongs to Caesar. The Temple, you, me, even God must belong to Caesar."

"The crowd at the Praetorium is wild. They are out for blood," the Pharisee said.

"Someone must speak to Pilate; make him see," I cried. "Where are my son's followers? Do they stand mute and not speak for him?"

The Pharisee told me that he had not seen any of the disciples. Even if they dared to speak, Pilate would never hear them, and the crowd was beyond reason. The crowd called for Pilate to come out, but so far he had not.

I asked about our leaders, the other priests. Why weren't they stopping this travesty? Why weren't they speaking for Jesus?

Some had, the Pharisee said. But a lot of the crowd was made of Barabbas's men. Pilate wouldn't listen anyway and ordered them all away.

No one wanted to upset Pilate. They knew how he dealt with troublemakers.

The fight was growing, and the rest of the people were dividing into camps, fighting, throwing things at each other. Food, rocks, whatever they could lay their hands on. Something hit Martha on the back of her head. We held on to each other and pushed our way back into the house.

The Fourteenth Day of Av

I have spent so much time thinking about that night. Not just that Jesus died, but the rest of the night, the nomads, everything. How it was so different from the way I have been expected to live. Outwardly, my world is peaceful and calm again now, but inwardly, I don't fit. Everything that was proper and respectful in me was made a mockery of that night. To keep the peace, though, I still try to act like a woman is expected to.

At first, whenever I thought of our own leaders being involved, I would take to my bed for days. I could not hold on to my faith with such a betrayal. But as the time went on, I thought about it more and more. I kept thinking about it because I wanted someone to blame, someone to be angry at, and then later, I thought it would help me understand, and finally because it had become such a habit, I could not stop. I have named almost everyone at one time or another, but now I have come to believe that the death of my son is not only upon the Romans, or Annas or Caiaphas, or the Pharisees, or Pilate or Herod, or even God, but the death of my son is upon us all. The rulers, the disciples, those who ran away, the Gentiles who thought that it had nothing to do with them. Upon the Roman soldiers who would not stand up to their leaders, and upon me his mother who did not teach him to be wise. Greed, envy, power, even love has played a part.

Yet, I see now how I have to stop blaming, how I have to stop punishing myself. I see how the forces were beyond me. That all I have done or not done has been forgiven. I see how the world is good, and the goodness will not be stopped. I see that to have Jesus as my son was worth any pain, beyond any treasure. I see how my son loved all of humanity. I see how his pain was temporary and why he did not fight. And I see how there is no good answer to the "Why?" How there are countless answers, and there are no answers.

Some of Jesus' followers have reminded me that Jesus was the servant, the suffering servant of Isaiah's prophecy, that gave his life for the sins of the nation. I think his sacrifice was even greater.

Many people have offered many reasons. Everyone is more sure of the answers than me. I do not think that it had to happen this way. I believe that God sent Jesus so that through his human form, people would know God. Know that he is a God of love, not fear. A God who gives men free will. Free will to do many things, even to crucify. My son was taken from this earth too soon, but it does not change the love that God has for all people. The love that Jesus has. The unself-ishness and forgiveness of that love is beyond human understanding, but I believe that is how the Lord wants us to love. At least to try, and keep trying.

27

The Sentence

"Do you think that Herod did send a warning to Pilate?" I asked.

"I don't know."

"But what do you think, Martha?"

She was weary in her answer. "It is what they have in common, their fear that they will be deposed."

For some reason, I started believing that I could go to Pilate and demand that he release Jesus to me. God would send a miracle or Jesus would proclaim himself. I had to go there. I had to make him release Jesus to me.

Once he was in my care, I would get him to Martha's house. He would be tired from his ordeal. I was tired. We would rest. It was the day of the Seder, but there would be no meal for us tonight. It would be alright to wait. Martha would also be required to wait one month more to celebrate. She had been with Lazarus. She had been with the dead. My mind raced. I pictured us all together. Martha, Miriam, Lazarus, Jesus, James, even Simon. This would be behind us by then. We would all sit together and give thanks that death had once again passed over the house of an Israelite.

Martha was sitting in the corner weeping softly, and it alarmed me. To block her out, I concentrated on the scene I had created. Then

Deborah burst through the door. She had been recognized and fled. I ran to her and held onto her hands. "Tell me that Pilate has found Jesus innocent," I pleaded.

"He has, but he . . ."

Then energy surged through me, and I twirled about the room, singing, babbling, hugging my friends. I could dance like Miriam after she had crossed the Red Sea. I was laughing so that it was hard to talk.

"Yes. He will come home. He will be here tonight for the Seder," I announced. "And we will celebrate the Passover. Sing to the Lord! Jesus will be freed."

I tried to settle myself down, think what I must do. Jesus would be famished, and I had no time to waste. I must prepare a meal for him. Fresh fruits, and vegetables, and lamb. I would get lamb for the Seder. No, a simple soup would be better after his ordeal. My friends urged me to come and sit with them for awhile. But I was not tired, and there was no time. Why did they sit there looking at me? Why didn't they help? Well, they had stood by me all night, so perhaps, they were exhausted. They could rest, but I would make ready for the celebration.

And Jesus would want a bath. I would draw water for his bath. He would be tired and dirty . . . but he was innocent. Innocent! Innocent! My son has been declared innocent!

"No, No. You must listen to me," Deborah demanded.

She was wiping her face with her hands and laughing or weeping. I wasn't sure which. She and Martha were clutching at each other.

"Pilate found Jesus innocent, but the crowd wants him crucified."

She was shouting at me, and that made me angry. Not that I didn't appreciate all that she had done, but it was over. Why would she taunt me? Why would she talk about Jesus and crucifixion at the same time?

Crucifixion was vile, shameful, for the worst of criminals. Or insurgents, like all those men who had tried to reclaim our land from the Romans. Living so close to Sepphoris, I knew about crucifixion. It was whispered, gossiped, and lamented about. Everyone knew someone who had met that fate. But not my son, not my son.

I did not want to think about it. I wanted to prepare for Jesus to return to me. Why had this girl uttered that cursed word? Now I couldn't get it from my mind. Crucifixion. How the Romans kept a thousand uprights permanently in place. How they nailed the condemned to a cross beam. How the man would then be lifted onto the upright, and his feet would be nailed. A block of wood placed between his forefoot and the nail or between his ankles and the nail. How this assured that, in his agony, he would not rip the nail head through his foot and release it. There might be a small seat to support the criminal so that the torture would be prolonged.

"Stop, Stop," I begged myself. But I could not. When the man died, they did not remove him. They left him nailed there for the buzzards and the wild dogs. Pecking and gnawing. Shamed and defiled, they left him to feed the scavengers. I heard someone laughing and laughing. Maybe one of the merchants in the street. Martha held one of my wrists in each of her strong hands and would not let go. Her hands were so little, but she was so strong. She drew my arms up to her and held them so that I was forced to stand still. I did not want to look at her. I wanted to get ready for Jesus, but she stood there and held my arms until I looked at her.

"Myriam . . . , Myriam." Her lips formed my name, but I only heard the laughing. The hysterical laughing. I felt a sting across my cheek, and another.

Then everything was quiet. I picked up a mat from the floor and saw that the woven threads were separating. I started to reweave them to make the repair. It would have been easier if I had had a needle, but I thought that I could manage with my hands.

Martha and Deborah were talking, but they ignored me. I thought that they didn't want to interrupt my work. Deborah said that John would come, but the others were in hiding. She was crying that she hadn't gotten to Jesus on time. Martha kept telling her that there was nothing she could have done. I could not understand what she meant. I kept asking them, but they couldn't hear me.

I had the green thread worked almost all of the way through the warp of the mat.

I was sitting on the bench. I didn't want them to leave without me. I thought that they were going to go someplace, but I didn't know where. Then I remembered that I was going to go to Pilate, but I thought I would finish my work first. I had the green thread all the way through and was working on a brown one.

Martha and Deborah were not leaving anyway, they were just talking. Martha was drinking something. Tea or water. Maybe wine. I didn't know.

"It has been decided then?" Martha asked.

"Yes."

"And the order has been given?"

"No. It is the Passover."

"Pilate would care nothing about the Passover," Martha said. She sounded angry to me. I couldn't think why.

"He offered to release Jesus in honor of the Passover," Deborah said.

"But he did not do it," Martha argued. She was being mean to Deborah.

"I think he wanted to," Deborah persisted, "but the crowd is filled with Barabbas' men. They're chanting 'Barabbas, Barabbas, Barabbas.' And they're not afraid of anything. Pilate threatens them, and they threaten him right back of what will happen if he doesn't free Barabbas."

Then they lowered their voices and thought that I could not hear them, but I did. Deborah told Martha that Jesus had been flogged and scourged. Martha started weeping. I wanted her to stop. Deborah was wailing, too, like she was a hired mourner. They were both annoying me. No one would scourge Jesus' back. It was beautiful. Anyone could see.

"If Pilate wanted to release Jesus, it would take him that long," Martha paused and snapped her fingers in the air, "to do it. No. No, he is up to something. He is up to something."

"It is the crowd. There is no reason left in them," Deborah insisted.

"Why would the crowd turn against Jesus?" Martha hammered.

"They are angry at Jesus. He used his powers to get them to follow him, and then he did nothing to stop his arrest. He is far too peaceful for them, so now they think Barabbas is their hope.

"Pilate would not free Barabbas. The Romans are always his target," Martha said. She tipped her cup up like a man and swallowed. I liked it that she was thinking again.

"What does it matter to us anymore?" Deborah asked.

"Everything matters," Martha said. "Everything matters until the end. Until then, there is still hope."

"Every Judean rebel in the country must have come from the hills."

"That would not influence Pilate," Martha said. She set her cup on the bench. She did not clean it like she always did. I went and picked it up for her and wiped it and then went back to repairing the mat.

"There must be some gain for him to consider it," Deborah said.

Martha was up from her seat pacing back and forth across the room.

"Oh Almighty God no," she whispered. Don't you see? Don't you see what is happening?"

It was hard for me to hear her because the thread that I was working on had slipped out, and the cross strands were separating, and the whole thing was turning into a mess.

"Pilate. Pilate knows exactly what he is doing." She punched out her words. "He did not have Jesus scourged to quiet the crowd. He did it to feed their frenzy. He wants to be rid of Jesus, or he would release him. He is afraid. Afraid because Jesus has gained so many followers."

"Jesus has never raised a hand against Caesar, never even said a word against Caesar. Why would Pilate fear him?" Deborah interrupted.

"No army is so powerful that it cannot be defeated, but ideas cannot be stopped. In the end, it is our faith that will be far more dangerous to the Romans than Barabbas and his band."

I thought Martha was right. Jesus had said as much to me years before.

"How could that be?" Deborah persisted. "Barabbas and his men will be fighting again within days. Jesus stands there and does not even raise a hand to protect himself."

"Either way," Martha continued. "Pilate has set himself up to be the innocent bystander. If the crowd calls for the release of Jesus, Pilate will crucify Barabbas and be rid of him. If the crowd calls for the crucifixion of Jesus, Pilate will silence a thousand political rebels by condemning someone that innocent. So it matters little to him who lives and who dies. Whatever happens, he will be rid of at least one thorn in his side. But more important to him is the political victory he will gain by splitting us right down the middle. He has turned Jew against Jew. Two men will love God but hate each other. The Romans will split us down the middle. Then they can murder us all and blame it on us."

She dropped her head and her body shook with her little sobs, and she kept muttering over and over that Pilate would split all of Israel right down the middle.

John burst through the door, and at the sight of him, I started weeping. I waited for him to address Martha and Deborah. It was not the time for political talk. He would silence them. He would tell us that Jesus had been released and that would silence them.

"Is Jesus with James?" I asked. "Has Pilate released him?"

"Pilate has ordered . . ." John stared straight ahead, not looking at me. "Pilate has given the order for Jesus to be crucified this day."

Everything went black. When I opened my eyes, Deborah's face was a hand's width from mine. I reached up and pushed her away. I was on my back on the floor, and I rolled over and crawled to the door. I wretched on the street. People shouted, but I didn't look up. I wretched again and again, and when there was no more but empty spasms, I pulled myself to my feet and made my way back into the house.

"Pilate has washed his hands of Jesus' blood and delivered him to his death. Deborah wailed over and over. "The worst has come. The worst has come. There is no more hope." She went on and on. I can hear it still to this day.

Martha did not say a word.

John said that he was going to Jesus. Deborah argued, said that he should not be seen. John said that he would not stay away. If there was a price on his head, he deserved it. Jesus had ordered them to keep watch, and they had fallen asleep.

I retied my sandals and retrieved the necklace that Hasaan had given me. I was going along. I stood by the door waiting and whimpering. Martha told me later that I did not make a sound, but in my head at least, I was whimpering for Joseph. John was a child. James would try, but he was not . . . I just wanted Joseph.

John tried to move around me to go out the door. I stood in his way until he agreed to take me, but I couldn't let go of the doorpost.

"Can we help him? I just want somebody to help him," I pleaded.

"We need to go now if you want to see him," John said. He gave me another push, and I stepped out on to the street.

We were together, the four of us. We did not look at each other. We did not talk. We walked, and we walked. It seemed like hours. The sun was hot and beat down on us. My ankle hurt, and I could not feel my legs move, but I was keeping up with John.

The swish of our clothing spoke the same words over and over. 'Every head shall bow. Every knee shall bend. Every head shall bow, and they shall call him Lord.'

I knew the words. The visitors sang them to him in the stable. The men had sung them on the street in the night. 'Every head shall bow. Every knee shall bend, and they shall call him Lord.'

Just walk. Just walk. 'Every head . . . shall . . . bow . . . Every . . . knee . . . shall . . . bend . . . and they . . . and they shall . . . call . . . him . . .' Oh Jesus. I am sorry. I am so sorry.

I knew that I was going mad. As I walked, I felt the insanity overtaking me. Stones rose out of the pavement and mocked me. The wind taunted me. Animals stared at me. They knew my horror. Some of them looked at me with sad eyes; others laughed at me. I could see them, tipping their heads back and opening their mouths, pretending to yawn, but I knew they were laughing. They were laughing at the trick. They knew it all along, and I did not. I would have this child to fulfill the prophecy of Isaiah, but before it could come true, his greatness would be stripped away, and he would be put to a death? Did he know? All those agonized years, did he know?

28

Golgotha

Deborah and John pulled me forward. They were talking, but I could not understand them. They talked louder. Did they think me deaf? I could not understand them. I tried to tell them, but they didn't care. Their voices got louder and louder so that I could not stand it.

I looked at the ditch. I looked for the irises. I was tired, and I wanted to sleep. I started toward the roadside. I would let my friends go on without me. Elizabeth never knew. She never knew. It was better that way.

A priest came up and spoke to John. When I looked at him, I could not breathe, so I looked away and searched for the irises. He took my arm even though I was not his kinswoman. He should not have touched me, and I looked at the ground and waited for Martha to tell him his behavior was not proper.

"Myriam?" he spoke to me. "Myriam," he said again. I looked at the irises. "Myriam?" he said one more time.

"Yes?" I reached up and pushed his hand off of my arm.

"I am sorry. I tried to speak for him, but it did no good," the priest said.

I began to shake, and I could not stop, and I clutched John's hand.

"I have heard Jesus teach many times," the priest continued. Then to Martha he said, "Her hair is showing. Adjust her head cover."

I reached my own hand up and pulled at my scarf. I started walking toward the irises again, but John pulled me away, and then we were past them. I looked for Martha, but I could not see her. Everyone was talking louder and louder again, shouting so that each one covered up someone else's words, and I could not understand anything until I heard my own name.

"Myriam . . . Myriam . . ." It was Joseph, speaking like he was at my side. My hand burned, and I felt his fingers lace with mine. I straightened and looked around trying to see where I was. I would find my way to Jesus. I would do this for Joseph. I would do this for Jesus.

The wind blew and brought smoke from the burning piles. The stench of camp garbage was so revolting that I had to force myself to breathe. I could tell when a new pile caught fire by the way the smell erupted. What had been stagnant and heavy suddenly billowed and spread, like the flames allowed it to burst from a wrapping. I remembered when we had passed there so long ago, when I had learned the smell of burning flesh, when I had learned the fate of the lesser children. I was far away, but my flesh stung like I was next to the flames. John handed me a skin of water. I drank until Martha took it from me.

We headed north and wove our way through the narrow, crowded streets of the city, through the jubilant pilgrims who had come to celebrate the Passover. "Shalom," they greeted us. "Shalom," I answered. To the east, the Temple gleamed, beckoning as before, but that day it called to someone else, not to me. That day I would offer my prayers from another hill.

We turned and headed west toward the gates. The crowds were even heavier, and travel was desperately slow.

"Jesus of Nazareth? Jesus of Nazareth?" John asked.

"Gennath Gate, nearest the hill," a man answered. I swallowed hard and held my hand over my mouth. I did not cry so much until afterwards, but all through the ordeal, my traitorous body kept trying to pass out or throw up. I could not waste time on either.

"If he makes it that far," the man added.

"Have you seen him?" John asked.

"Oh, I have seen him. The stinkin' Romans tried to get me to carry the cross for him. Not me. Far better if he dies on the way to the hill. No, if they want his cross carried, they can carry it themselves."

We reached the gate, and I was lifted off the ground and carried along by the mob of people trying to pass through. I clutched on to the robe of a stranger to keep from falling under and being trampled. John held my arm and pulled me to his side. We squeezed through the gate and the crowd spread out. I felt the road, solid beneath my feet, again.

The Roman soldiers were calling out to each other, cursing the Jews, threatening the crowds, trying to keep control. We pressed on along the west wall of the city, heading north. The crowds thinned.

I saw the hill only a furlong away, covered with rocks and upright posts that loomed skyward. Some twined and gnarled, but most empty still, waiting for the victims. One waited for my son. It was a horror to see, and I vowed that I would not allow Jesus to be nailed to it. I still thought, even that day, that I could stop it, that he would stop it.

Martha told me that I must pray for strength and accept God's will. But I did not believe my son's death was God's will. I would try to be obedient to the Lord, but it was God who gave me the wrath of a she lion when someone threatened my children. I felt Joseph's strength within me. I had strength, I had anger, I even had rage, but I did not know what to do with them.

"The world is ruled by men," Martha announced to John.

He nodded his head, opened his mouth and then closed it without speaking.

"Is life not precious to them?" she demanded. "Do they not understand that the death of one is the death of all?"

John opened his mouth again, but Martha did not wait for him to speak.

"Do they not understand that one mother's grief is the grief of . . . ?"

"Stop to breathe, Martha," Deborah said, "or you will pass out right here."

We searched for a path, and John led us down an embankment into the valley and onto a trail that led toward Golgotha. That day, unlike most, there were also Hebrews going to the hill. Followers of Jesus, who were willing to go, willing to defile themselves to be with him.

But mostly, we were surrounded by Persians, Babylonians, and Greeks who had come to town to market their wares and wanted to witness a Roman crucifixion while they were in Jerusalem.

"Who is on the tree today?"

"Three of them together. Two thieves and yet another messiah."

"Is that Jesus the carpenter they are talking about?"

"Yes. The Nazarene. He has angered the priests and the Romans, and he will pay."

"Not all the priests. Only Annas."

"The Nazarene is a magician."

"A jar of wine and a rooster says that he will come right down from the tree."

A man, unwashed, uncombed, and with bloodshot eyes, made his way to us, grabbed John's robe, and bellowed out that John was a fol-lower of the rabbi who would be crucified. John shook him off.

The man turned to me. "Stay with me and drink my wine. It will ease your pain. Stay with me. This coward cannot protect you."

I didn't look at him, and we kept walking. He followed us, taunt-ing John for not helping Jesus. The crowd called for a fight, and the man grabbed onto John's robe again. The back of it this time so that it jerked on his neck. John stumbled and turned on the man, grabbed his hand until he released the robe. The man called John a coward one more time, and John took the bait.

They circled, eyeing each other. He was a head taller and solid, but

John dove for his legs and knocked him to the ground. John came up fast and stood with his fist raised above the man's face. The man blubbered, and John dropped his fist, and we went on.

Near the hill, the soldiers paced in their metal cuirasses,[1] too few of them for such a crowd. John warned me to stay clear. They would be jumpy, quick with the sword because of all the Jews in the crowd. The soldiers knew these men would die for a principle when a simple lie would save their lives. I knew, though, that having so few soldiers increased our chances.

Several of the soldiers stood at the foot of the single, boulder strewn path that led to the top. If they controlled that, they controlled the hill. Wide at the bottom, the path narrowed about a third of the way up to the width of about four climbers. A soldier stood at the narrowest spot. From there, the hill became very steep, steep enough to discourage most people who made it past the soldier.

The nomads were climbing just ahead of us. The blacksmith staggered and fell to the ground. "We should have tried to help the woman last night," he moaned. "We should have tried to help her when we had the chance. The Romans have made cowards of us all." He sounded drunk on morning wine.

"You did help, Hasaan. They are using your nails," someone taunted.

"Mother of Jesus," the blacksmith called as we passed, "you should not have come here. Mother of Jesus . . . Do not go there . . . Do not go there. Take her home. This is not for a mother to witness," he ordered John.

"I will go to my son," I said.

"My nails were meant for the wagons and the gates," Hasaan moaned. "We should have helped the woman when we had the chance. I make my nails for wagons. My nails are meant for the wagons. We should have helped her." He laid his face in his hands and sobbed.

"There is nothing that you could have done, Hasaan," Hannah bent down to him, helped him to sit, and wiped his face with her robe. "You are just one more Roman pawn."

"I have done this. I have done this," he went on. "My nails were for the wagons. We will leave here. We will go where the nails are used only for good."

"No. No. You would not hurt any man," Hannah insisted as she helped him to his feet.

"Get back or you will be arrested," a soldier barked.

"Bravo. Bravo." Cassim mocked. "Let us know that you are in charge. You are diligent in your work. Caesar would be pleased that his soldiers know how to preside over a crucifixion."

"I do as I'm ordered," the soldier growled.

"Does it bother you?" Raji goaded, "Nailing a man . . . ,"

"Get on with your business before I lose my patience," the Roman barked and jabbed at Raji with his spear.

"Your temper is short for a man who has drawn this lot for the day," Gillaro sneered. He reached out and rested his hand on the spear. "You could be out building roads with the other soldiers. Then your back would ache and your hands would bleed. But to do this? You should have no complaints. It is easy labor for you today."

Martha slipped and hit her knee on a jagged rock. A wet, dark patch showed on her robe and grew until it reached from her knee to the hem, but she paid no attention to it.

I searched for Jesus' disciples, but I did not see them. I looked at each man as we passed and tried to determine which ones might be there for Jesus. I prayed for an uprising of the people.

When we reached the narrowing of the path, the soldier stepped in front of us and ordered us to turn back. I searched the hill for a route that would take us closer to Jesus. Most were steep and rocky. Some were impossible for all but a young boy or strong man to climb. I knew that I would not have the strength in my arms to pull myself up to the next rock without a strong foothold. I had to stay on the guarded path.

John asked permission to pass to the top of the hill. The soldier refused him and again ordered us to leave.

"Please!" I said. "We must pass."

"Shut her up," he ordered John. "I will not be swayed by a woman."

John ordered me to silence and asked one more time for permission to pass. The soldier refused him and laughed at us for wanting to see a crucifixion. I felt an energy surge through me. It must have been what soldiers experience when going into battle. I thought that I could move the soldier out of the way myself. I was so sure of it that I could feel his breastplate on the palm of my hands as I knocked him over.

"Myriam, don't!" John snapped.

But God had used me before, and I thought that he would use me again. I was ready for it. I was no longer a shy young girl. I wondered what my part would be. I remembered Hannah and how she had distracted the guard. I looked to see Deborah behind me. The soldiers would welcome the company of a young girl. Then John could get to Jesus and convince him that he had to walk away. He could not let this happen. He would not have to use violence against the soldiers. I . . . we all understood by then that Jesus would not raise his hand in violence.

I felt a conviction that God would use us to rescue his son from this fate. That would be the glory, to snatch Jesus from the powerful Romans. I would stay ready.

Voices came from the top of the hill.

"Jesus, you have to stand up for yourself."

"Why do you let them do this to you, Jesus?"

"Put him out of his misery, you base born cowards."

The soldier turned his head, and I ran past him, but he grabbed onto my robe and snapped me back against him. Then he wrapped one of his thick arms around me and pinned both of my arms to my sides. I gave him one kick, and he squeezed so that I could not breathe. I stood still.

"Let me go! Let me go!" I screamed, but it was a silent scream, only in my mind. I had failed. I knew not to rile him more. I looked down at his hands, cracked and calloused, all of the little lines filled with grime. Beneath the coarse black hair on his right forearm, he had a cut about three dactyls long. Puss seeped out between the breaks in the scab, and red lines spread up and down his arm. I knew that if he did not treat the infection soon that it would spread, and in the days to come, he would have to choose between his arm and his life. Another day I might have offered to help.

He laughed and told me to be still, told me that his hands were strong from years of carrying limestone, and if he wanted to, he could snap my neck. With his free hand, he reached around me and traced his fingers up and down my throat. He closed his fingers around it and laughed. I did not react, and he slid his hand across my breast and gripped my upper arm. He pressed his thumb against the underside of my arm and squeezed until my hand was paralyzed and the pain shot up through my neck and lodged at my ear. He rubbed his arms against my breasts and whispered more insults to me.

I ignored his words, but I could not ignore his smell. He stunk of rotting breath laced with old wine and strong garlic; he stunk of days of sweat mixed with Roman oil; and he stunk of death.

I eased back, and when he did not feel my resistance, he loosened his grip.

Clang, clang, clang. "Jesus!" Clang, clang, clang. I leaned forward and bit the soldier's hand. He bellowed, and I bit harder, bit until I tasted blood.

The Twelfth Day of Tishrei

Martha says that I cannot go on and teach with the others unless I climb the hill. I do not really want to remember because only now, I think I can manage my life again. But even if I do not want to, I have been remembering more.

Micha is here. What happened to him that night is another story, but he is here now. It is not proper for him to visit alone, but such things do not bother me anymore. He has come many times before. Sometimes we have wept together; sometimes he has tried to explain to me the plans that he thinks the Lord has for us, what he thinks Jesus would like us to do. How we could travel together and teach. I have sent him away. He is young and needs to marry and have children. I am a thousand years old. Sometimes he has teased me. Today he does not.

"You believe in what Jesus taught?" I ask.

"Yes, very much."

"Why do you not travel with the others then?"

"Perhaps I am needed here."

"Perhaps," I said.

I am moving my garden, and now we are in the new space that I have chosen. I have shoveled great clods of dirt. Not a woman's work, my sons tell me, but I do as I please now.

Micha picks up the rake and begins raking out the dirt that I have turned. Soon he is catching up to me, and I shovel faster and harder to keep ahead of him. The rain has stopped, and the sun is hot overhead even on this cool day. The sweat drips down my face and stings my eyes. Still, I do not stop. Micha catches up to me. He does not take the shovel from me, though. He stops and waits while I turn the rest of the earth. I finish and laugh. It is a strange sound. Then I plant my shovel and watch while he rakes. Micha reaches for his skin of water and hands it to me. I drink and drink, and then I smile.

When I crawl into bed, my legs cramp, my hands cramp, I am exhausted. I cannot move. I close my eyes, and I cannot control my mind. I cannot stop it. I have not a single defense. I squeeze my eyes tighter and reach out for the hand of God. Very tightly, I hold God's hand and let the memories come. I am absorbed into them like the water into the sand. I do not know if I will survive, if I will ever be able to open my eyes again, but I face the horror and go to this place of Jesus' suffering.

29

An Old Soldier

The soldier bellowed again and jerked his hand. I let go and ran.

"Jesus," I called. "Jesus." I ran up the hill. The clanging sounded again. I clawed the dirt, slipped, and kept climbing. Someone grabbed my foot. I kicked and climbed more until my legs were pulled out from under me, and I fell. A foot dug into my back and pressed me into the rock, harder and harder until I tasted the dirt. I tasted the dirt and my tears. I had failed again.

"Please, I must get to my son," I begged the soldier.

"He will be long dead before I am through with you," he laughed.

"Leave her," barked another soldier as he passed.

"You defend the Jewess? Or only so you keep her for yourself? I say she'll put up a sporting fight."

I heard him spit and thought that it landed on me, but I didn't feel it, and I didn't care. Then he lifted his foot from me. I sat up, and saw Deborah.

"Filthy Roman!" she scorned.

The soldier laughed again. "Roman filth and a Jew whore. We are a match." He reached out and ripped her clothing so that she was bare on the top. She pulled her garment back around her, but the soldier gripped her hand and bent it back until she released her robe and it fell away from her again.

John pulled me to my feet, and I started up the hill. The soldier turned from Deborah and knocked John to the ground and held his spear to his neck.

"Go ahead; give me an excuse to watch your blood flow. And then I'll take care of the women for you." He prodded John with the spear.

We all stood, afraid to move.

"It is my turn to teach the Jews a . . ."

There was a crack and Gillaro's whip snaked around the soldier's neck cutting off his words. Gillaro jerked him to his knees, and the spear dropped from his hand. There wasn't a sound. The other soldiers did not even turn.

I knew that Jesus would have wanted Gillaro to stop. But if he did, I would not see my son alive again. If he did, the soldier would live, and Gillaro would die. I looked away. I asked God to forgive my sin and did not look back.

We made our way up the narrow path. It was so steep that I could no longer see the top. The day was hot and still, the buzzards circled in the sky, and the horseflies were so thick that a new one was biting me before I could get the old one off. They stuck on me in a way that was so offensive, not caring that I could kill them. The soldiers shouted at the people to get back, to go home; warned them that they would be next to try the cross if they did not obey. We ignored them and kept climbing.

I made my way on to the plateau.

"Jesus, Jesus, Jesus," the crowd chanted. "Save yourself, Jesus. You saved others. Can you not save yourself?"

"If you are King of the Jews, save yourself."

I broke into a run. But I could not get close enough. I did not see Jesus. There was an area in front of the crosses where no one but the guards was allowed to enter.

The others were with me again. Hasaan was there. He told us to take the path to the west and come in from behind. There were rocks that would shield us. We saw the path, but a young soldier stood in front of it.

"You are making a mistake that can never be undone," Hasaan called to the soldier. "Let the man go."

"Rome does not make mistakes," the soldier growled.

"She has made many," Hasaan said. He sounded sober then, maybe from seeing the men on the crosses.

"She did once, or we would not be here today," an old soldier said. He was sitting on a rock just to the side of the path.

"Pilate would nail you up if he heard you," the young soldier warned.

"Better us than . . ."

"Do not say another word, or I will make a report on you."

The old soldier threw back his head and sounded a bitter laugh. "Then you would not see another sunrise."

"Why are you here? This is not your garrison?" The young soldier demanded. He looked around, caught the eye of a Roman across the way and signaled him over.

"To see the king, of course."

"King of the Jews?" the young one laughed, and he signaled again for the soldier across the way to come. "He has been crowned already."

"Crown of thorns, crown of jewels, it does not matter. It is his birthright, and no man can take it from him. Not Herod, not even Caesar."

"How do you know this?"

"It is what I know. That is all."

"You know nothing, or you would tell."

"I don't think you want to know."

"I told you. I do!" the young soldier screamed.

"Some time ago," the old soldier began, "a king was born in Bethlehem. When Herod heard the news, he was jealous, afraid he would lose his throne. He was so worried that he set out to destroy the child. Murdered every boy not yet two. Just to make sure. Now Antipas and Pilate are doing the same. They know."

"Why worry if the king was murdered?"

"He was not. He got away."

"How do you know that?"

"I know; that is all."

"It is a lie. You are lying!" The young soldier screamed again.

"Believe what you will," the old soldier said. He rose from the rock and stretched himself, and, on his arm, the green and purple and red fire breathing beast came alive.

"How do you know it is not Barabbas that is to be king? He has many followers."

"Barabbas was not yet born. The records of the census will tell you so. No. It was not Barabbas who was to be king. It was Jesus of Nazareth."

"Is that Barabbas they are crucifying with the Nazarene?" someone in the crowd asked.

"No. Not him. Two of his men though," the old soldier answered.

"Where is Barabbas?"

"Pilate has freed him. He lives in fear of Barabbas and his dagger men. Watch, and you will see that Pilate does not go anywhere without a garrison for his own protection. He knows there is a price on his head."

"Why would he free Barabbas, then?"

"The zealots, the rebels, and many others are all tied to Barabbas. Pilate could hang Barabbas today, and the contract would still be made."

"So he freed his own killer?"

"It's the best deal he has made since he came to Jerusalem. Barabbas's life for his. Barabbas is the only one that can lift the contract from Pilate."

"Barabbas will lift the price from Pilate's head, but let his own men be crucified?"

"He could not bargain for his men. Or he did not. I don't know which. I only know that Barabbas will not be crucified this day."

"Where is he now?"

"Gone to ground, but he'll be back."

I remembered my prayer.

A fight broke out some way from us and the soldiers ran to put it down. We headed for the path on the back side of the hill. It was no more than a narrow ledge. My foot slipped from the edge and I grabbed onto the hillside, but I could not find a hold. Deborah reached me and pulled me back on. I was surprised at how strong she was. Thunder rumbled.

"We have to save him. We have to save him," Deborah repeated.

"I will give my life for him," John vowed.

Thunder rolled in, loud and close. Gray clouds swirled one after another until there was not a streak of sun left to show through. Lightning crackled. The soldiers looked at the sky, at the crosses, at the crowd. They stomped their spears on the ground and slapped their whip handles in the palms of their hands. They paced and cursed, looked to the hills.

I heard Hasaan's voice across the way badgering the soldiers, telling them that even Caesar could not help them for what they had done. They shouted at him warning him to shut up, but he did not stop.

The thunder was continuous. I could feel it all through me. The lightning came and brightened the sky like day. Then it ceded and the sky was black, black like a night without the moon so that I could not see one thing. In the darkness, we crept along the path. We were climbing again, and I could feel more level ground with my hands. I thought we were at the top of the hill. Then the sky turned green, and I could see the crowd. They were frantic. Grown men held hands, clutched on to each other, fell to the ground and hid their faces.

Prophets and future seers wandered the hill casting warnings, making predictions.

"This time they have started something that they will not be the ones to finish. There is nowhere to go, nowhere to hide. The earth will open up and swallow them into her belly."

"Born to rule the world, now struck down like a sheep at the slaughter. Mocked and scorned, bruised and tormented. Hanging like a common criminal."

"Jesus of Nazareth is crucified today. It is written in the scriptures, and the scriptures must be fulfilled. Isaiah has foretold that the Lord would send one to suffer for us all. His enemies say he will die this day because he says he is the Son of God. They condemn him for speaking falsely. But, lo I tell you, he will die this day, not because he claims he is the Son of God and is not, but because he is the Son of God. Behold . . . he is our Messiah, and today he is led to his death."

"They have crucified the Son of God. May the Lord have mercy on their souls."

Lightening flashed bright and lit three crosses, each twined with a man. In front of them, soldiers squatted on the ground, laughing and arguing, casting lots. One shouted out that he had won the purple robe. He put it on and paraded around while his friends laughed. Then another won a tunic and held it high and examined it, dirty, covered with blood, but it had no seam. It would only need to be cleaned, he said, and then it would bring a good price.

Then lightning and thunder hit and cracked as one. The winner dropped the tunic on the ground claiming he had no use for it.

"Pick it up. It is only a storm," a wiry old soldier jeered. "You are as superstitious as the seers."

"The whole Roman army cannot save us from what we have done this day," the winner moaned.

The sky turned black and then green again. The tunic lay on the ground. The tunic without a seam, like the one Jesus wore.

The old crone was there. I did not know how she had made the journey, but she was there, watching the soldiers.

"Sky of light, dark as night. Hell will swallow all who follow this wickedness," she chanted, and then she howled, "Vada satana! The blood will be upon us!" She howled and howled like a wolf in a trap.

Chavala dashed in and snatched the tunic from the ground.

30

Woman, Behold Your Son

We walked until we were directly behind the three crosses and sheltered from the crowd by a bank of rocks. Close enough to smell the blood, the hot raw flesh, the soiling from one who had already died. Close enough to hear another begging for mercy, begging for death in his weak, weak voice. The buzzards had gathered there. They circled, flew in, and pecked at him. He made pitiful sounds that I thought he meant to be yells to scare the buzzards away. They ignored his feeble threats and pecked away.

Only the sides of the men's backs and part of their arms were visible past the posts and crossbeams. I looked at one and saw that his back must have been laid bare by the flagrum.[1] Blood dripped, and the flesh hung in clumps. I stared and stared at the man's back. I could tell that it had once been beautiful. Strong and beautiful.

A soldier came and lifted his skirt to relieve himself. We waited until he left and then followed the path that wound around to the front of the crosses.

"Woman of Nazareth," a man's voice called, soft and toneless, so that only someone who was called so, would hear him. I looked up. His face was hidden by his cloak, but I recognized him. He closed the twenty paces between us and embraced me. My tears came, and I wrapped my arms around James. He looked just like Joseph.

"Get her out of here," he ordered John. His voice was still low, but sword edged sharp.

John ignored him. "Where are the others?"

"There is no one," James said.

"Deserting bunch of whimpering whores," John hissed.

"They will answer to me," James assured him.

"Let's get him down," John said. "I know men here who can help us. From the tribe."

"We would not have one nail out before they'd hang us at his side and rape her while we watched."

"Get her out of here!" John ordered Deborah. "Now!" he barked when she didn't move, "We need to get him down."

"No. That is not what he wants," James warned.

"You think this is what he wants? For us to watch him die?" John shouted. People turned to watch us.

James landed his elbow in John's side and warned him to be quiet. "He does not want us to interfere," he said through his teeth. The people turned away again.

"Is this what you want?"

James did not answer.

"I asked if this is what you want?" John demanded, his voice rising again.

"What I want?" James said, looking around the hillside, looking at the Romans. "What I want is to kill them all."

"Then let me get the men," John said.

"No. We will not raise a hand."

John paced, looked at the Romans.

"Do you hear me?" James threatened.

"I hear a coward," John said. "You want to stand and watch? He is dying."

"Then do not let him die in vain."

"It was all talk. He would want us to fight."

"The killing will stop."

"Even if it means his death?" John's face was red, his eyes wild.

"Yes. Now tell me why you brought my mother here."

"I wanted Jesus to see her. I thought he might then save himself."

"Get her out of here, now," James ordered.

"Please, James," I begged.

"No," he said. You will leave here now." But I saw tears in his eyes. I had not seen that since Joseph died.

"Please," I said again.

He cursed to himself, closed his hand around my arm, and pulled me along the path toward the crosses. John fell back to help Deborah and Martha. The path was studded with tripping rocks. No footprints showed in the hard ground.

"How will the kingdom come if he is dead?" John challenged.

"He has told us that his kingdom is at hand. It is a time for faith."

A soldier came and blocked the path. We stepped to the side, and he stepped with us, stood legs apart with his spear planted in the ground holding it like a shepherd might hold his staff. I reached into my robe for the neck jewelry Hasaan had given me and held it out to him. He took it from me and turned it over and then over again in his thick, cracked hand. I knew that the gold, the stone, and the workmanship made it a very valuable piece. He slid it into his tunic and turned his back on us. We walked right up to the front of the cross.

I looked up at the man hanging above me. James wretched on the ground, and I heard the others cry out so I knew that it was Jesus, but I could not even recognize that it was him. His hair was matted together and hung in thick, dirty strands over his face, over the bruises. He wore a crown made of thorn bush, the thorns long and sharp, the kind that drove into your flesh like nails and stuck there so solidly that you had to pull them out, the kind that hurt as much coming out as they did going in. The crown was pressed onto his head, and blood from where the thorns cut streaked down his forehead and joined with the blood from a deep gash above his right cheekbone. All of it mixed with the dirt that covered his face.

His face, where it showed above his beard, was purple and swollen. His left cheek pressed against his brow, so it looked as if he had no eye at all on that side of his face. His right eye was shut. Gnats swarmed around him in little clusters. Each cluster dancing in the air by a different wound.

When I looked away from his face, I saw that his clothes had been stripped from him. His legs and feet were caked in dirt except where the blood circled wet and dark on his feet . . . around the nails, hideous square iron nails, the size of a man's thumb, pounded through his feet. More nails were driven through his wrists so that they made his fingers curl and shaped his hands like bird claws.

I wanted to climb up and rip the nails away, and I begged James to help him. I begged God to help him.

James refused. God did not help Jesus either, but he did make me strong. I focused on Jesus' face, squinted my eyes a little, and let my tears blur his wounds. I imagined him strong and whole.

"Jesus," I called softly. "Jesus."

"I don't think he is conscious," James cautioned. "Stay back by me."

"He knows that I am here," I insisted. I could feel that he did. "Jesus," I called again. His right eye flickered and opened, just barely, because of the swelling, but a little. "Look. He is opening his eyes. He can see us," I said.

"Myriam," Martha said quietly.

"I know he can." I insisted. "He opened his eyes when he heard my voice."

"We are here." James said.

"Jesus. We are here," I repeated. I spoke softly, like I had when he was a babe, so that I did not startle him. His breathing grew stronger. He lifted his head and opened his eyes again. He tried to speak. No sound came out, but I was sure that he recognized me, recognized James.

"Jesus," I said again.

"Imma? Imma?" Jesus said. His voice was barely a whisper, but I heard him.

"Yes."

"You . . . have . . . come," he said. Then he closed his eyes. I thanked God for the sound of his voice.

"We will help you," John said.

"No. That . . . is not . . . your . . ." But he did not finish. He looked at James, "First pillar," he whispered. I thought he was delirious.

I stepped forward and buried my face in his feet. I kissed them and cleaned them with my hair. I wanted to gather him in my arms. I wanted to hold him and comfort him until he was well again like he was still a small child ill with fever. I wanted morning to come and have him be well again.

"Can you not end this Jesus? Will your Father not spare you?" I asked. I could not stop my tears, but I did not surrender my voice to them.

His chest heaved, and his mouth opened trying to grasp air. His weight trapped his breath in his chest, and he could not exhale, so there was no room to take in the new air that he needed. He extended his legs by forcing pressure on the nails that were driven through his feet. His arms quivered, his legs quivered. He moaned but kept the pressure on until he raised himself. He expelled the air from his chest and slid back down the cross drawing in new breath.

"Today you do not understand my Father's will," he said. "Today you are a mother losing a child, but when your grief has passed, you will remember my purpose."

Then he could not speak. He just looked, looked down on me with those eyes that had been so bright and alert looking up at me from in the manger, so bright and alert when he was at play, but they were not bright that day. That day he looked down on me and wept.

Now, I cannot even bear to remember it, so I don't know how I found . . . how I could even speak, but I wanted to be there for him. If I couldn't help him, then at least to give some comfort. There has to be something locked inside of every parent, something God releases when we . . .

"I love you Jesus. I have loved every minute that I have had with you," I said.

"Because I leave you today, you will be with me for all eternity," he said. His words came one at a time. Sometimes there was sound, sometimes none. Jesus could talk before he was in his second year, but that day he could not.

"Now, I think of today."

"James . . . will care . . ."

James stepped forward. I felt his arm around my shoulder. "I will care for her always."

"Beloved," Jesus whispered.

"Master," James choked.

Jesus lifted his head, looked upon the two of us, and commanded, "Woman . . . behold . . . your son. Son . . . behold . . . your mother."

"It is so," James vowed.[2]

"Jesus," I whispered.

His eyes opened and he looked at me again and tried to speak. Mostly there were no words at all anymore, but I watched his mouth and I knew what he was saying.

"Go now. Go . . . so . . . I can do . . . what I have come to do."

"Jesus."

"My everlasting love I leave with you," he whispered.

He closed his eyes again. His chest heaved in and out, in and out, but no air left or entered.

"Jesus, Jesus. Help him, James. Please help him," I pleaded.

Jesus gasped and then was silent.

"James? James, is he . . . ?" I asked.

"No, but he . . ." James pulled on my arm, but I did not want to leave Jesus' side. "You make this worse for him. We will do as he wishes," James said. His voice was low, but hard. "You will spare him your grief."

The soldiers were there again pushing us away. James held onto me, and I held my fist to my mouth and concentrated on silencing my scream.

"Please, James."

James did not answer, just put his arm around me and let me rest my head on his chest. I cried, but not so loud that I could not hear Jesus. The sky darkened again and the thunder rumbled through me. We stood there waiting.

31

The World Will Not Forget

The nomads were there, Hannah, Chavala, and some of the others from the night. Chavala stood lost, weeping. Her movements were no longer graceful, but abrupt and disconnected, her clothes dirty and torn. She looked like a scared little girl, not a woman men would desire.

"You have seen death before girl," Hannah scolded her. "Did you think it wouldn't happen this time?"

"I have seen the death of a man before, but . . ."

"But now you see the death of a God," Hannah finished.

"The blood of the mother, the blood of the Son on you all," Chavala screamed at the soldiers.

"The blood will be upon us. There is a curse upon us that will follow us to the end of the earth. I have done this. I have done this," Hasaan moaned. He was sitting on the ground with his head in his hands again.

Martha was standing close to the cross again. Somehow the soldiers did not bother her. I heard her ministering to Jesus. I hoped that he could hear her.

"In thee, O Lord shall he seek refuge . . . ," she recited the Psalm, her voice strong until the end.

John came running toward us. I don't know where he had been.

"They have recognized you," he warned James. "The two that walk this way. Hide yourself. Let me stay with your mother."

"I will not leave him,"

"Please James," I begged. "Do not let them take you as well."

"He is my brother, my master, and my Lord. I will stand by him."

"Please. I beg you to leave," I said, and I was crying hard.

"I cannot. He will not let me fight for him, but I will not desert him. Stop now. Your weeping will do no good."

"He has given the care of our family to you. In the name of the Lord and for all of our sakes, do not make us lose you, too. Do what he has asked you."

James leaned toward me and grasped my arm. "Listen now and obey me. You will leave at once with John. Find safety. I will come when I can." He hugged me roughly and slipped into the darkness. I did not see him again for many days.

The thunder was continuous. The earth shook beneath my feet. People were wailing, afraid to stay, afraid to leave on the dark treacherous path. Some knelt before Jesus, weeping and moaning his name. No one taunted him. No one mocked. Even the soldiers were quiet.

"We need to leave. I gave my word," John said.

But I was not leaving. He tried again, and I ended it with my mother look.

"Jesus. Jesus, please do not die," I whispered over and over.

"Death is not his enemy now," John said.

Martha and Deborah were near, holding on to each other. "He is suffocating, he is suffocating," Martha wailed.

As every mother, I believed and desired that I would have my son with me always, even unto my own death. As I watched him on the cross and saw his chest heaving uncontrollably, I knew. I knew that there was no more hope. I knew that my son would leave this earth before I did. Still, I tried to deny it. Pretend that it would end in some other way. Believe that God would save him, that he would save himself. I longed to help him, to end his suffering.

Then as I stood and watched Jesus hanging on the cross before me, I could not stand it any longer. I did not care that he was willing to die. I did not care what would happen to me, only that I try to help him. I could not call myself his mother if I did not try, if I did not get him down.

I walked straight to the soldier. I was not afraid. I stood before him and ordered him to give my son back to me. There was a fire in my throat, and it hurt to speak, but I could not quiet myself. I railed at him, but he did not answer, did not respond at all, so I beat on his chest. Harder and harder, I beat on his chest.

"In the name of the Almighty God, give my son back to me," I commanded. "What more can you want? You have destroyed him, now can you not at least have the decency to let him die in my arms?"

The soldier took my wrists in his hands like Martha had earlier that day, but he did not look at me. He looked away, and he did not speak to me.

"I want him down from there. I want him down," I sobbed. I pulled my arms free and turned to the crowd. "Who will help me?" I pleaded. "I want my son down from there. Who will help me? Who will help?"

But no one helped. As Gillaro had said, no one could stand against the Romans.

I asked again. "Who will help me? Who will help me?" But my voice was pitiful and small. I did not expect an answer, and I did not get one. There was no one to help me, and I could not help Jesus. I could not help my own son.

The soldier ordered John to take me away. It would be over soon.

"They know now," John said. "Those who have spit upon him and mocked him. They know now that they have crucified the Son of God. They have crucified the Son of God, and the wrath of the Lord will be upon them."

Then the crone was there and attacked the soldier with a fury. Clawed and kicked, cursed at him for murdering my son in front of me. He ordered her away, ordered her to silence. He was larger by three, but she kept on, her head not up to his chest. Finally, he struck her to the ground, and she did not get up. Gillaro ordered some of the outlaws to take her away. They picked her up like she was a weightless child. I don't know what happened to her.

Gillaro walked over to me and took my shoulders. He ordered me to stop. I was more afraid of him than the soldier, so that helped me get control of myself. When he looked into my eyes, I could not look away.

"You are the mother of my Lord," he said. He stated this without question.

"That is my son. That is my son. The Romans have crucified my son."

"Since my boyhood, I have lived to curse the Romans for the death of my mother," Gillaro said. "I ran from the sight of God, and he turned his face from me. But now I can run no more, because I have met God. I have seen the living God in your son."

"You love him too."

"Yes. Yes, I do. Today, the sorrow in my heart is not for my own mother but for you. Today, I grieve for you."

I reached out and placed my hand upon his cheek. He was crying. I would not have thought that he knew how.

"Do not forget my son," I pleaded. "Do not let the world forget my son."

"The world will not forget your son," he said. "They have stripped his clothes, crowned his brow with thorns, and crucified him as the vilest of men, but the Son of God will never be forgotten. That is my promise to you."

Again the thunder roared, and the lightning flashed.

I pushed my way past the soldiers, back to Jesus. John was already at the cross.

"Jesus, Jesus," I said, but he did not open his eyes. "If I could just hold him. If I could just put my arms around him and hold him one more time," I pleaded with John.

"Myriam, your arms cannot protect him now, and he is not afraid of death."

"I just want . . . I just want to . . ."

"Let him go." John spoke firmly to me.

"I know. I know I must, and yet in my weakness, I cannot let go. I feel his suffering. And yet, I cannot let go."

"It is time."

"Do you think that he knows that I should be holding him now? Do you think he knows?"

"Yes, he knows. He knows . . ."

Then the thunder stopped. It was eerie and still. The crowd was quiet. Waiting, only waiting was left. The wind did not blow, but the sky swirled a sickening green. I do not know what moved the clouds.

32

From Your Mother's Arms

Jesus' breath came in short gasps. He made awful choking sounds. I kept my eyes on him, praying that somehow it helped him to know I was there. Praying that I could find the courage to release him. Praying that it would end for him.

And then . . . those words, those words that I will hear until I have no more breath within me. "Eloi, Eloi, lama sabachthani?" My God, my God, why have you forsaken me?

My son was a child of the earth. Sent from God, but a mortal being. He did not suffer as God on that day, but as a man.

"We will hold him, Myriam. We will hold him," John said, he was crying hard. "Come now. We will hold him. We will hold him."

But we could not. We could not hold Jesus, so we held onto each other, and I sang to Jesus. The song from when he was born. "In your mother's arms, in your father's arms we will keep you. In your mother's arms, in your father's arms, we will keep you safe and warm." Then, "From your mother's arms to your Father's arms, he will keep you . . ."

On and on I sang. And his breathing calmed. It was not strong, but it was peaceful. I could feel him in my arms.

"Let him go now, Myriam. Let him go."

"I . . . I . . . I am. I will."

"I will stay with you." John said.

I did not want him to suffer anymore. I had to release him. John urged me again to let go. I agreed, but still I did not. I just sang on and on. I sang until I heard my name.

"Myriam, Myriam."

At first I ignored it, but it came again, and as clearly as he had that day at the Temple, God spoke to me.

"Remember, Myriam, Jesus is My Son, too."

"Then let it be so." It was time. I would not do one thing more to interfere. "Goodbye, my son, my Lord."

Jesus lifted his face to the wind, "Father, into your hands I commit my spirit." The wind roared, and Jesus lowered his head onto his chest and breathed no more.

The air was sucked from me. I stood in the green black afternoon and did not speak or breathe. The clouds swirled, but there was no wind. Just a suction as trees were lifted from the ground. Then all was quiet. All was black, and all was quiet. And then the rocks on which we stood split and crashed in two. Later, I learned that the very curtain of the Temple was torn in two as well.

Then the lightening came, and the thunder. The crashing of the rocks continued, and the people wailed. I stood with my face to the heavens and hoped again that God would end my life. But he did not. Everything grew still again, even the wailing stopped, and the light returned to the sky like it was morning.

I could see Jesus on the cross. Some of the people were cowering on the ground, but most of them were trying to make their way down the hill. Some of the soldiers were leaving with them. One was on the ground, not moving. I looked and saw that he had fallen on his own sword. I wondered if anyone would tell his mother.

After a while, John said that they would bring Jesus to me. They had murdered my son, and I remember that I was grateful to them that they would bring him to me and not leave him for the scavengers.

I sat on the ground and held him. His skin was still soft and warm, but when I touched him, he did not move at all, and his not moving made him so heavy. Someone gave me a cloth and a bowl with water. I wet the cloth and wiped the blood and the dirt from his face. It was still swollen, but I wiped it over and over again until it was clean. I wanted him to be clean. Like when Joseph wiped the birthing away from him. Wiped the other world away, wiped the time before he was born away.

There were so many cuts. Dirt, bruises, and a wound on his side that I did not think had been there before. I tried to clean it, but I kept making it worse because there was so much blood. I cleaned where the nails had been. I massaged his hands to try to straighten them. I could not reach his feet, but the water was gone, so I just held him in my arms and sang to him. The soldiers did not bother us.

Martha told me that someone was coming to take him for burial. He had to be buried before the Sabbath. I knew that I had to give him to them. I drew in one more breath to smell his smell. I thought that it was like when he was a baby again. So I sang to him.

"From your mother's arms to your Father's arms."

I thought I heard the angels. When he was a baby, the angels sang for him.

"Do you hear the sweet songs that the angels are singing for you, Jesus?" I asked him, and I thought he smiled. He didn't, but his face looked happy, not like when he was on the cross. "The heavens are waiting and the angels are singing for you, Jesus. They're singing for you," I whispered.

Then it was time. "Take good care of my boy, God. Take good care of my boy. You are going to love him. You are just going to love him."

And then they took him away. They took him away.

Martha was there. She was talking. "Out of the darkness shall come a great light. The Lord has made a new covenant with his people. And it shall be so forever." She is my friend. She always tells the truth.

It was over. Jesus was gone. He had been born to unite the people of the earth and to offer to all the hope of the God of Israel. I knew then that in his life and in his death, he had done this. His work on earth was over.

"Hear O Israel, the Lord, the Lord our God is one."

The Sixteenth Day of Tevet

Once again, it is the month of Jesus' birth. This year I will rejoice in it. As the seasons pass, I grow stronger. God the Father and God the Son are my constant refuge. Still, at any time, when I least suspect it, I will see someone who looks like Jesus, remember something about him, or smell some favorite food and be brought low again.

There are times when my grief is still so physically unbearable that I double over from the pain. Most days, though, his death has lost its sting, and I feel myself embraced by Joseph and Jesus. I feel their love rain down on me, perfect warm gentle drops of water drifting down from the heavens.

I try to be governed by love, to do good to all, and to live in a way that will honor my son's life. I try to remember his commandment to love one another. A commandment that is not so much. A commandment that is everything. That is the way I do not slip back.

Peter is our new leader. It is still painful for me sometimes to have him take Jesus' place. But he is wise and kind, and it is right, and I strive always to embrace him without jealousy or resentment.

I am rarely afraid anymore, and I do not neglect my other children to mourn for Jesus. I know that he would not want me to. I have devoted my life to carrying on his work, but I know that I receive more than I give, so I do not allow myself to become obsessed about it.

I see the rabbis and many of the priests and take comfort from them. It is still a troubled time for our faith. James spends much of his time at the Temple. There are many problems.

I am still haunted by the sight of Jesus on the cross. But now, mostly I remember his beauty. I see him in his brothers and sisters, in his nieces and nephews. I see how his kindness and love live on.

Today when I opened my eyes, the winter sun was shining warm upon my hand. That is not unusual, because the sun shines often in the desert, but it was warm and kind, and the dust danced in its light.

I reached out my hand to catch the ray of sun. I could not catch it. I could not hold it. But I could feel it. I knew it was there.

I am a mother who has lost a child. Not the first, not the last, and I have gone on. I am a mother who has lost a child, and I have lived to know joy once again.

I live and I work and I pray, and it is my constant prayer that the Lord will bless you and keep you in every step you take, and that he will comfort and protect you through every tear you weep.

NOTES

Chapter 1: Bethlehem
1. Hamashiach hakadosh: The Messiah, the Holy One.
2. Hakadosh baruch ha: Holy One, blessed be he.
3. Hadassah: Hebrew name of Queen Esther.

Chapter 2: Married
1. Mamzer: One born of an illicit sexual union.

Chapter 3: First Days
1. Jewish males are circumcised as a mark of the covenant God established with Abraham (Genesis 17:9–14).

2. After a Jewish mother gave birth to a child, she was considered ritually "unclean" (Leviticus 12:1–8). She had to stay home seven days, and on the eighth day, a baby son was to be circumcised. Then the mother had to stay home for another 33 days. Then she was to offer a sacrifice and make herself "clean" again.

3. During the exodus, the Lord spared all firstborn of the house of Israel. So, according to the law of Moses all firstborn males were dedicated to the Lord in remembrance and thanksgiving. The mother's purification was on the 40th day, so the dedication usually took place at that time.

4. Mikvah: The immersion bath used for ritual cleansing.

Chapter 5: To Egypt
1. A hin equals one gallon plus two pints.

2. Wadi Gaza: Wadi Gaza is a wetland south of Gaza City. Its tributaries are found in the mountains beside Hebron and the upper Negev. They flow into the Mediterranean Sea.

3. The desert temperature could reach 120 degrees. The route from Bethlehem, Judea, to Pelusium, Egypt, along an old caravan route was approximately 200 miles or 323 kilometers. It would take a man on a camel about six days, a family with a baby two weeks, and a family with a baby and an injury much more.

4. Pelusium: This ancient Egyptian city was located on the easternmost mouth of the Nile River. To Egyptians it was also known as Per-Amon (House of Amon). In the Bible the city is called "the stronghold of Egypt" (Ezekiel 30:15).

Chapter 6: By the Nile
1. Cleopatra: There were six Cleopatras before her, but she was the most famous and the last as Rome took over at her capture, so the name became hers alone.

2. As swine, boars are considered unclean and not to be eaten by Jews. See Leviticus 11:24–28.

3. Cleopatra was exiled by her brother. When Julius Caesar came to Alexandria, Cleopatra had herself rolled into a carpet and smuggled into his room. She became his lover, and he helped her regain her throne. Her brother drowned trying to flee Caesar's armies. Cleopatra then married her youngest and last brother, Ptolemy the XIV who was then eleven years. She soon ordered the death of her sister so there was no one left to challenge her. Cleopatra bore Julius Caesar a son who was called Caesarian or Little Caesar. She returned to Rome with Caesar, but it did not go well. His people did not want him to marry a foreigner. Cleopatra remained in Rome until Caesar was assassinated. She became Marc Antony's lover and bore him twins. Antony and Cleopatra and the three children returned to Egypt. The people of Egypt loved Cleopatra. She was the first Egyptian ruler who could speak their language. In fact, she spoke nine languages and could make herself understood anywhere in the world. She traveled extensively gaining support for Egypt. She was ambitious and her life was driven by her desire to keep Egypt independent from Rome. She defeated many male rulers seeking to dethrone her. She did great things for Egypt, including providing medical care to women and setting up business dealing with Herod that allowed Egypt to prosper. She treated her people well and kept them safe under her hand. She instilled great pride in her people, and her subjects believed she and Marc Antony were gods. Cleopatra believed herself to be the incarnation of the goddess Isis.

4. Marc Antony controlled the Eastern Roman Empire, and Octavius Caesar controlled the Western Roman Empire. After the attack, Cleopatra retreated with Marc Antony to a place she had built for her own burial and barricaded them in. Antony died and Cleopatra was trapped under the guard of Octavius.

Chapter 10: Twelve Years

1. Haroset is a mixture of fruit, nuts, and wine and represents mortar for the bricks that the Israelite children made. The bitter herbs represent the bitterness of slavery, and the parsley represents the hyssop used to spread the blood of the lamb on the doorpost so the Angel of Death would pass over that household.

2. At its peak, the Roman road system spanned 53,819 miles. Eventually, the roads were used by Rome's enemies to invade the Empire.

Chapter 11: Favor with the Priests

1. The Temple covered about 35 acres with the Temple plateau being a large square about 1000 by 1000 feet. The Temple stood on a section of high ground called a mount. Herod had enlarged this by filling in the Valley

of the Cheesemakers and reclaiming land from the Kidron Valley. He then brought in huge stones, the largest weighed 626 tons and measured 44.6′ by 11′ to stabilize the Temple mount and support the structure of the Temple.

2. Solomon's Porch has 162 Corinthian columns of white marble.

Chapter 12: Oldest Son

1. A cubit is the length of a man's forearm.

2. Biga currus: A two-horsed chariot.

3. Ketubah: The marriage contract decreed by the great sage Simeon bar Sheta as a way of protecting Jewish women from being divorced and abandoned at the whims of their husbands. The husband committed to provide food, clothing, and marital relations to his wife, and he would pay a specified sum of money if he divorced her. To divorce her, he would give her a "get." Simeon arranged that the husband might use the prescribed marriage gift in his business, but that his entire fortune should be held liable for it. Since a husband of small means could not afford to withdraw a sum of money from his business, Simeon's ruling tended to check hasty divorces. His other important act referred to instruction of the young.

Chapter 13: A Teacher

1. The Romans destroyed the Temple while putting down the Jewish uprising in 70 AD, less than forty years after Jesus was crucified.

Chapter 14: Jerusalem

1. Hatsotsra: Trumpet; only the plural form hatsotsrot appears in the Bible.

2. Mizrak: Bowl to catch the blood.

3. "Shema Yisrael:" "Listen, O Israel," see Deuteronomy 6:4.

4. Yom Ree-Shon: Sunday

5. Hellenism refers to the Greek way of life and culture introduced to the region that included Israel when the Greek leader Alexander the Great conquered all of Persia and then Egypt. He established Greek rule over Palestine in 333 BC. Even though Rome eventually replaced the Greeks as the ruling power in the area, Hellenistic customs and culture continued to shape life and commerce in Jesus' day. Many of these customs and practices were at odds with the laws of Israel's faith.

Chapter 15: Micha

1. The Zealots were a Jewish faction traced back to the revolt of the Maccabees in the second century BC. The name was first recorded by the Jewish historian Josephus as a designation for the Jewish resistance fighters of the war of AD 66–73. This term applied to them because of their dedication to Jewish law and for their opposition to anyone who lacked their strong religious beliefs, including the Romans and fellow Jews who conformed to Roman

ways. The Zealots were organized as a party during the reign (37–4 BC) of Herod the Great, whose idolatrous practices they resisted. Later, when Cyrenius, the Roman governor of Syria, attempted to take a census, the Zealots, under Judas of Galilee and the priest Zadok, arose in revolt against what they considered a plot to subjugate the Jews.

2. Herod Antipas, son of Herod the Great, was married to Phasaelis, the daughter of the Arabian King, Aretas IV who ruled over the land of Nabetea, the land next to Perea which Herod ruled. After a time, Phasaelis, fell from Herod's favor, and he divorced her and married Herodias, the grand-daughter of Herod the Great and the wife of his half-brother Philip, thus making Herodius his niece as well. The Law of Moses did not allow a man to marry his brother's wife, while the brother was still living. That is why John told Herod that marrying his brother's wife was wrong.

Chapter 16: Martha's Story

1. Olive press: A huge stone basin with a smaller round millstone inside

2. Many gravesites were found randomly around the city due to the ordinance of Joshua, which required any dead body found in a field to be buried in the field where it was discovered. Making contact with the dead would have made a person ritually unclean and therefore unable to participate in the festival.

Chapter 17: No Return

1. Gethsemane was a garden located at the foot of the Mount of Olives in the Kidron Valley just east of Jerusalem.

Chapter 20: The Night

1. After Annas was deposed and following a one year office by Ishmael ben-Favis, the office of high priest was returned to the Ananus family. First Eleazar ben-Ananus, son of Annas, then Simon ben-Camithus, son-in-law of Annas, and then Joseph Caiaphas, son-in-law of Annas.

2. Syria was known as Abar Nhara which meant "across the river," referring to the Euphrates River. It was known as Syria, short for Assyria by the Greeks and the Romans, because it had long remained under the rule of the Assyrians during and after the Seleucids were driven out of Mesopotamia in the middle of the 2nd century BC. Under Pompey, several small kingdoms were combined into the province of Syria in 64 BC.

Chapter 21: Outlaw Camp

1. Ilaha Gabal: The Aramaic name of the Syrian god of the sun Elagabal.

2. Reri: Egyptian word for pig.

3. In the line of trades, a perfumer was at the bottom of respectability.

4. Tanner: This trade was also undesirable, due to the odor of dead animals. The tanner's wife was allowed to divorce him if she could not stand the smell.

Chapter 22: Fire Dance

1. The Jewish faith required members to remain clean. They bathed often and wiped the dirt from their feet before entering a home. Food and person must be kept separate from the rest of the world. If there was contact with the unclean, purification was required.

2. Tof: A small drum or tambourine.

Chapter 23: Trial in the Night

1. Pentateuch: The first five books of Hebrew Scripture, Genesis through Deuteronomy.

2. Sanhedrin: This was the supreme court of ancient Israel made up of 71 men, Sadducees and Pharisees. The real meeting place was the Chamber of Hewn Stone near the Temple, but the high priest's house was used at times. The Sanhedrin was led by the high priest and convened every day except during festivals and on the weekly Sabbath.

3. HaKash SheShavar et Gav HaGamal: *The straw that broke the camel's back.*

4. Course: A group or family of priests made up a course with each taking its turn as one of the 24 groups that served the Temple at a given time.

5. Watch: First watch—6:00 p.m., Second watch—9:00 p.m., Third watch—Midnight, Fourth watch—3:00 a.m.

Chapter 24: Caiaphas and Annas

1. Praetorium: Refers here to the palace of Pontius Pilate, the Roman procurator of Judea. A praetorium can also refer to the tent or house of the commander of a guard detail.

Chapter 28: Golgotha

1. Cuirasses: Pieces of armor for protecting the breast and back.

Chapter 30: Woman, Behold Your Son

1. Flagrum: A wooden handle with three leather thongs and two lead balls woven into the end of each leather thong. Jesus would have been hit 40 minus one or given thirteen strikes of the three leather thongs.

2. James: "Jesus in some of his last words on the cross, seeing the disciple whom he loved standing by, says, 'your son . . . your mother,' and from that hour the disciple took her into his own house. The house is clearly none other than the house of James." (Eisenman, Robert, *James the Brother of Jesus,* 1998 Penguin, p. 592)

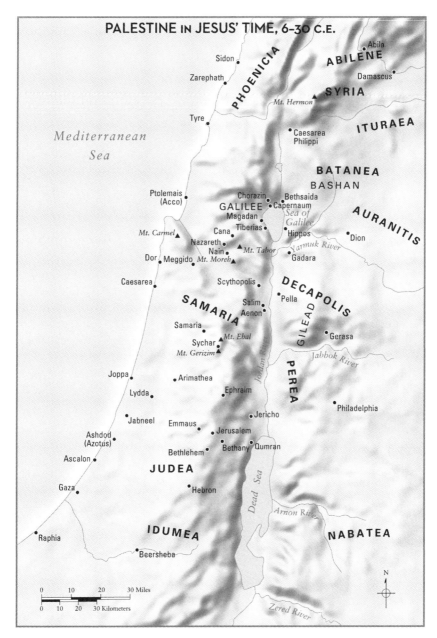

PALESTINE IN JESUS' TIME, 6–30 C.E.

Mediterranean
Sea

PHOENICIA

ABILENE

Abila

Sidon

Zarephath

Damascus

SYRIA

Mt. Hermon

Tyre

Caesarea
Philippi

ITURAEA

BATANEA

BASHAN

Ptolemais
(Acco)

Chorazin

Bethsaida

GALILEE

Capernaum

Magadan

Sea of
Galilee

AURANITIS

Cana

Tiberias

Hippos

Dion

Mt. Carmel

Nazareth

Mt. Tabor

Yarmuk River

Dor

Nain

Mt. Moreh

Gadara

Meggido

Caesarea

Scythopolis

DECAPOLIS

SAMARIA

Salim

Pella

Aenon

GILEAD

Samaria

Gerasa

Sychar

Mt. Ebal

Mt. Gerizim

Jabbok River

Joppa

Arimathea

PEREA

Lydda

Ephraim

Philadelphia

Jabneel

Emmaus

Jericho

Ashdod
(Azotus)

Jerusalem

Bethlehem

Bethany

Qumran

Ascalon

JUDEA

Dead Sea

Gaza

Hebron

Arnon River

Raphia

IDUMEA

NABATEA

Beersheba

0   10   20   30 Miles

0   10   20   30 Kilometers

N

Zered River

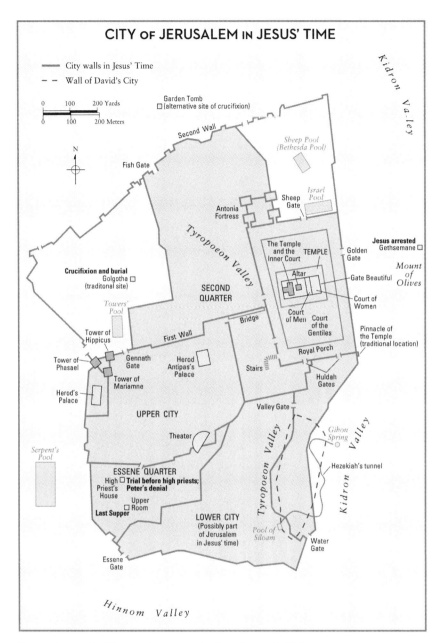

CITY OF JERUSALEM IN JESUS' TIME

—— City walls in Jesus' Time
– – Wall of David's City

0   100   200 Yards
0   100   200 Meters

N

Kidron Valley

Garden Tomb
☐ (alternative site of crucifixion)

Second Wall

Fish Gate

*Sheep Pool
(Bethesda Pool)*

Israel Pool

Antonia
Fortress

Sheep
Gate

Tyropoeon Valley

The Temple
and the
Inner Court   TEMPLE   Golden
Gate

Jesus arrested
Gethsemane ☐

Mount of Olives

Crucifixion and burial
Golgotha ☐
(traditonal site)

SECOND
QUARTER

Altar

Gate Beautiful

Court of
Men   Court
of the
Gentiles

Court of
Women

Towers' Pool

Bridge

Pinnacle of
the Temple
(traditional location)

Tower of
Hippicus

First Wall

Royal Porch

Tower of
Phasael

Gennath
Gate

Herod
Antipas's
Palace

Stairs

Huldah
Gates

Tower of
Mariamne

Herod's
Palace

UPPER CITY

Valley Gate

Tyropoeon Valley

Gihon Spring

Kidron Valley

Theater

Serpent's Pool

ESSENE QUARTER

High ☐ Trial before high priests;
Priest's   Peter's denial
House

Upper
☐ Room

Last Supper

LOWER CITY
(Possibly part
of Jerusalem
in Jesus' time)

Hezekiah's tunnel

Pool of Siloam

Water
Gate

Essene
Gate

Hinnom Valley

About the Authors

Ruth Anderson earned a BA in music from St. Olaf College, North-field, Minnesota, and has done graduate studies in Europe and the Far East. Barbara Swant earned a BA in English and Psychology and an MSE in School Psychology from the University of Wisconsin, Eau Claire.

Mary's Story is their first novel. They have composed and written numerous songs and plays including *Mary's Story,* the play on which this novel was based. They received the Gospel Songwriters of the Year award at the 2006 Nashville Symposium for the music from *Mary's Story.* The music from *Mary's Story* is included in *Donne en Musica Library* in Rome, Italy.

Ruth and Barb live with their families in west central Wisconsin where they enjoy the warm summers, cold winters, and all the activities that the state has to offer. They often speak to church and community groups on topics related to their work.

Mary's Story CD

Composer: Ruth Anderson   Lyricist: Barbara Swant

Join us on another incredible journey!

Experience the passion of Mary's Story as it comes alive as a musical drama. Beautiful songs of Mary's love, Gillaro's anguish, John's anger. Jubilant, inspiring chorus and unforgettable, soaring orchestra.
Stunning, captivating, classical!
Listen . . . You won't forget the music!

ORDER NOW: www.amazon.com
www.cdbaby.com

Mary's Story will Break your Heart . . . Her Songs will Heal It!

Recorded at Minnesota Public Radio Studios by Grammy winning team Steve Barnett and Preston Smith

www.marysstory.com   715-537-3243